LOV...

She sat on the e... ... ...Chester
field and pulled the soothing smoke deep
into her lungs. Ordinary barracks noise
subsided. Women padded towards the
latrine, toiletries bulging from their pockets;
others called to one another, some already
slept, a few read letters whose creases had
frayed from repeated foldings. So many of
them had husbands or boyfriends fighting,
perhaps at this moment, dying. Strange how
sharing their uniform brought women closer
to their men...

PERMISSIONS

LOVE AND GLORY.

Jeane Westin

A STAR BOOK
published by
the Paperback Division of
W. H. ALLEN & Co. Plc

A Star Book
Published in 1987
by the Paperback Division of
W. H. Allen & Co. Plc
44 Hill Street, London W1X 8LB

First published in Great Britain
by W. H. Allen & Co. Plc in 1986

Printed and bound in Great Britain by
Anchor Brendon Ltd, Tiptree, Essex

ISBN 0 352 31988 7

Other than the first OC class, the numerical
designations of WAC units have been invented to
underscore that this is a work of fiction. Any
resemblance to actual persons, living or dead (except
where historical persons appear briefly or are
mentioned in passing), is purely coincidental.

To my dear friends Irma Ruth Walker
and the late Teri Shapiro,
who believed I could, thought I should,
and encouraged until I did write this book.

ACKNOWLEDGEMENTS

In particular I wish to thank Eleanor Fait, member of the First WAAC Officer Candidate Class, and Betty Coyle, member of the Fifth OC Class. Both gave valuable criticism and insight into the early days of women's wartime military service.

Grateful acknowledgement is also made to Colonel Bettie Morden, current WAC historian, and to Mattie E. Treadwell's official history *The Women's Army Corps* for factual information about the Corps during World War II.

BOOK ONE

*1942: From Silk
to Khaki*

PROLOGUE

All that hot July 19th morning the women had come, 440 of them, out of the mainstream of America to the old cavalry post, their bright dresses, spectator pumps and Sunday hats almost garish against a background of khaki uniforms and precise rows of green barracks. They clambered down from canvas-covered six-by-sixes onto the manicured tree-ringed Dewy Parade Ground of Fort Des Moines, Iowa, to begin a new experiment called the Women's Army Auxiliary Corps.

All that summer Sunday morning in 1942 the women had come, the cream of thirty thousand applicants drawn to their country's military services during wartime, not knowing what to expect, or what would be expected of them. One thing they knew: women had no military history; they would have to make their own.

1

US Women Troop to Enlist in Army's First All-Female Force

On May 27, for the first time in history, the US Army began general recruiting of women. The response was terrific. Before the day was ended, 13,208 had applied.

—Life, *May 29, 1942*

Two sergeants, their starched-stiff cotton twill wilting in the humid Iowa heat, stood watching the women as they descended from trucks in front of the reception centre.

'Damned if I don't believe it now,' muttered the one with hash marks to his elbow.

'Believe what?'

'Believe we're gonna lose this war, that's what.' He frowned, deepening the layers of wrinkles on his weather-beaten face, as the last four women were helped to the ground by MPs. 'No sirree, I didn't believe it — not when Corregidor fell, not even when we lost Guam. Now, by God, I do,' he said, finality adding to the rasp in his command-coarsened voice. 'If it don't beat all when they put women in this man's army.'

'You said it, pal.' His younger companion shook his head in disgust. 'Women soldiers? Kee-rist! When I heard they was comin' here, I didn't believe it. What'll the big brass think of next? Hey — ' he ran to catch the other man moving away swiftly along the perimeter of the manicured parade ground ' — hey, Wolford, do ya s'pose they'll put us all in khaki kilts?'

A perspiring young second lieutenant skirted the crowd of milling women exchanging their first shy confidences, and moved towards the last four arrivals, standing uncertainly in a jumble of suitcases. 'Your name, miss?' he asked the first one, resting his clipboard on his hip.

'Page Hannaday, Lieutenant.' Her eyes followed his pencil down the roster.

'Washington, DC?' he asked.

'That's right.'

'Any relation to the General Hannaday on Marshall's staff?'

She hesitated for a moment and dropped her voice. 'Yes, he's my father.'

At that point a group of off-duty soldiers began to chant from across the road that ran along the west side of the parade ground, 'You'll be sorry. You'll be sor-ry.'

Page saw the last woman off the truck, dark-haired and busty, in her late twenties, grin and wave to them. They answered with several loud wolf whistles, and the woman laughed out loud.

The lieutenant motioned them off. '*Your* name, miss,' he asked the woman irritably.

'Call me Bunny.'

'No, miss, your full name.'

'All of them?'

He nodded, a trickle of sweat appearing under his sideburn and sliding slowly towards his neck.

'Okay, Captain, you asked for it. Let's see . . . there's Barbara Eugenia Rose-Marie Patra — that's my maiden name. Then I married Johnny LaMonica, and then I married Johnny Palermo, but — ' she stopped, grinning, as the man flushed red ' — of course, not before I divorced the

10

first Johnny. But then I divorced the second Johnny too. See why you just better call me Bunny?'

Page pressed her lips hard together to keep from smiling. What a clown! Pulling an officer's leg like that during her first hour in the Army. She saw the second lieutenant shift his clipboard uneasily, since the other two women standing close by had overheard the exchange and were smothering snickers.

'Miss,' he said, his voice edged with impatience, 'first, I'm not a captain, I'm a lieutenant, and second, I need to know the name you enlisted under so I can check you present on this roster.'

'Why didn't you *say* so?' the woman called Bunny asked, smiling teasingly up at him.

Then Page saw a tiny woman in a red peplum dress, whom she had first noticed on the truck coming from the troop train, step up boldly and hand the lieutenant her travel orders. 'Jill Hammersmith. My middle name — ' she began and then moved to the officer's side to look at the roster ' — it's Henry,' she said, pointing. 'That's a family name. Anything else you want to know, just ask.'

The lieutenant located her name on the list. 'California?'

'Right. I enlisted in Sacramento, but I live outside — '

'Are you the vet?' He looked down at her, more than a little disbelief in his voice.

'I was studying veterinary medicine, but I'm not a graduate vet,' she offered. 'I just finished my first year last month, and — '

'Excuse me, miss, you can tell all that to the classification people tomorrow.'

Page watched as he stepped in front of a stunningly beautiful blonde standing slightly apart from the others.

'Mrs Marne Pershing Gardner — Elisabeth, that's spelled Elisabeth,' she said, her voice husky and cool despite the heat. 'New York City.'

'Okay, that's it, ladies,' he said, eyeing both his completed roster and Elisabeth Gardner with satisfaction. 'Hannaday, Palermo, Hammersmith, Gardner — you four wait over there' — he pointed to one of the giant elms surrounding the parade ground — 'until I can figure out what company you've been assigned to. We didn't have much time to get ready for you girls — I mean you WAAC officer candidates.'

Now that she was officially checked into the Army, Page eagerly picked up her small valise, containing the one change of clothing she had been told to bring, and carried it into the shade. She did not need a second invitation. Quickly undoing her hatpin, she removed her wide-brimmed straw to catch a stray breeze, fanning herself to move the humid air about her face.

'Hi,' the smiling dark-haired woman said, joining her. 'Is this shade taken or can anybody melt here?'

'It's the Army's shade — everyone's welcome,' Page said and extended her hand in introduction. 'Page Hannaday.'

'Yes, I heard. Mine's — '

Page laughed now. 'Yes, *I* heard — Barbara-Eugenia-Rose-Marie . . . '

Bunny spoke up when Page's memory faltered. 'Patra-LaMonica-Palermo,' and they finished in singsong unison, 'Just-call-me-Bunny.'

The other two women had moved into the shade, and they joined in the laughter, awkwardly, since they'd barely met. Page saw in their three faces that they were evaluating one another, as she was them, but not as total strangers. It was as if being among the first women in the Army they were already linked to one another by the act of enlisting. Their conversation was casual — they could have been four women meeting anywhere — but underneath, Page felt, they all sensed the adventure of this moment.

Bunny broke the mood. 'I thought an army travelled on its stomach. When are they going to feed us?'

Page smiled at her. 'You sound like a regular-army chow-hound already.'

'Is it always this hot?' Elisabeth asked, smoothing the folds of her emerald-green silk dress.

'Probably,' Page said. 'At least a summer I spent at Fort Sill was this hot, or even worse.'

Jill bounced up from her perch on a suitcase. 'It's not so

bad,' she said, looking around. 'I think it's kind of pretty — all those old trees and those white-columned buildings over there beyond the cannon and the flag. It's like one of those covers on *The Saturday Evening Post* — you know, to remind us what we're fighting for.'

Bunny shook her head. 'I'm not sure, kiddo. We may have another war on our hands. Did you see those two grizzled warriors looking like they could bite nails as we got off the truck? If that's the welcoming committee — well, I'll just turn around and get myself back to good ol' Bloomfield, New Jersey.'

Jill shook her head, a determined, even grim set to her mouth. 'Nothing could make me leave.' Then her face lightened. 'Elisabeth, I really love your dress. It's so neat. I couldn't keep mine from wrinkling on the train.'

'Small girls should never wear peplums.'

Page saw that Jill had been hurt, but that Elisabeth had not meant her remark to wound. The pronouncement had been delivered in the matter-of-fact tone of an authority. Jill ducked her head, busying herself with her suitcase lock, and when she looked up again Page could see in the set of her mouth that the hurt had been dismissed. It was obvious Jill was not going to let anything or anyone get in her way. With a wink, Bunny offered Jill a Lucky and then lit it for her.

Page had expected a disparate group, maybe not quite the standard Hollywood film soldier mix, but different backgrounds and certainly different reasons for joining the Army. It was already apparent that Bunny with her wry outlook, delivered in flattened New Jersey vowels, was the group joker; tiny Jill with a giant's optimism written on her gamine face was the gung-ho type; and Elisabeth, with her intriguing elegance and reserve, was the cool one — with a hint of mystery wafting about her like the expensive perfume she wore.

As for herself, she was the army brat. General Dalton C. Hannaday's little girl had been fed to bugle calls and put to bed at the sound of the retreat cannon. But most of her life Page had watched soldiers from reviewing stands. She had never dreamed she'd be part of the parade.

Jill was talking to Bunny. 'What do you mean about the sergeants? You don't think they like us, is that it?'

Bunny shrugged. 'Ask our expert here,' she said, indicating Page.

'I wouldn't call myself an expert.'

'You seem to know your way around this Army better than we do. Come on, give out.'

With everything in her, Page knew that until the Women's Army Auxiliary Corps proved itself to men like the two sergeants they would be invaders in this ancient male bastion, more feared than Japs or Nazis.

She had been in the gallery in early May when the bill to establish the Corps had been argued in the House of Representatives. She had listened in dismay as Hoffman of Michigan had asked from the floor in ringingly righteous tones, 'Take the women into the armed forces, who then will maintain the home fires; who will do the cooking, the washing, the mending, the humble homey tasks to which every woman has devoted herself?' Men around the chamber had nodded in agreement, but it had been New York's Congressman Somers who had voiced the most vehement protest: 'Think of the humiliation! What has become of the manhood of America? The thing is revolting to me.' That the bill passed was due to three forces: the tenacity of its author, Representative Edith Nourse Rogers, General George C. Marshall lobbying behind the scenes, and unexpected support from chivalrous Southern legislators who wanted to humour the ladies.

'Well,' Jill asked Page impatiently, 'do the sergeants like us or not?'

'I can't give you a yes or no. I was a volunteer at WAAC headquarters with Director Hobby —'

Jill jumped in. 'Oveta Culp Hobby — I saw a picture of her last May in *Time* magazine taking the oath.'

'Yes, that's right — and we learned that nearly everybody, Army, government and the public, thought we were a crazy wartime experiment. These next six weeks are crucial for the WAAC. We're all in the spotlight, especially

Director Hobby. As the first women officer candidates, we're going to have to give her something to convince them with or . . . ' She didn't know what might happen.

'You mean,' Jill said, biting her lower lip, 'they could send us home.'

The girl looked so disturbed that Page put a friendly arm around Jill's shoulder. 'Don't worry, I'm betting on us.'

'That's right, kid,' Bunny said, 'we signed up for the duration plus six months, and they'd better get used to it.'

Jill shyly looked up at Elisabeth. 'What do you say?'

'Of course, we can do whatever we must — ' Elisabeth shrugged as she said it ' — how difficult could it be, after all?'

Jill brightened. 'Say, maybe we four could kind of stick together — at least for today.'

The lieutenant who had checked them in reappeared and handed each of them a piece of paper. 'Candidates, this is your meal chit. If you'll form up with the women behind Sergeant Wolford over there — '

Jill asked, 'The one with all the stripes on his sleeve?'

He nodded, frowning ' — he'll take you across the parade ground to your quarters, where you can leave your duffle. Then you'll proceed to the mess hall. After chow, you'll have the rest of the day free to settle in.'

Jill whispered as the lieutenant walked away, 'Did you hear that? He called us candidates.'

The four women joined almost a hundred others straggling across the close-cropped grass, hurrying to keep up with the sergeant's rigid khaki-covered back, and headed towards rose-coloured brick barracks stretching on each side of the white-pillared headquarters building.

'Somehow lunch and a Sunday nap isn't what I expected,' Bunny said. 'A soldier's life might not be so bad, after all.'

Page smiled to herself as she helped Elisabeth, who was struggling with a large Bonwit's hatbox. She remembered the extensive training schedules she had seen at WAAC headquarters. The women were facing weeks of drill and calisthenics, courses in map reading, military courtesy and field sanitation. They would have to master a long list of skills before they could truly call themselves women soldiers.

No one had been more against the idea of women as soldiers than Page's father. At first he had been only amused, until she volunteered to work at the WAAC planning office in Temporary M Building on Constitution Avenue. But his amusement faded when she became engrossed in the work of preparing the Army for its first women recruits.

'Damn it all, Page,' her father would begin his nightly debriefing, 'what do you *do*, anyway? You're spending entirely too much time down there — I won't even dignify that place as a headquarters — with those loonies who think the Army needs women soldiers. And don't remind me that they're there because of an act of Congress. Since when have those dumb civilian bastards on the Hill known how to run an army?'

Page had known he was missing the personal attention that had been his and the knowledge that she was in her place, at home, whenever he took a break in his twelve-hour staff-planning workday. In the ten years since her mother died, she had been the woman of the house, the one who smoothed out the wrinkles of his off-duty life.

'Anyway, what about Randy?' he'd say, playing on her big-sister conscience. 'He'll be coming from the Point for his second-year leave, and his sister won't have the home fires burning for him.'

'Dad, Randy doesn't need me to play housemother. I'd be in his way. Besides, Randy wrote that he thought the WAAC was an exciting new idea as long as I didn't turn into an amazon and beat him on the tennis court.'

At that he had focused his commanding general's eye on her and stiffened to attention. 'You wouldn't be thinking of *joining* this fool adventure, would you?'

'I don't know, Dad,' she had answered, honestly at the time. She had never had the last word with him. He had always appealed to her sense of family duty, rolling over her ideas of independence with as much ease as he had rolled his tank over German trenches in the World War.

'Would it surprise you,' she had asked cautiously, 'if I had inherited the same soldier genes from you that Randy did?'

He had laughed then, and it had hurt her more than his anger could have. 'My dear little girl, surprise me, no, but horrify me — most emphatically, *yes*. I can't imagine a Hannaday woman in uniform any more than I can imagine a Hannaday man out of uniform.' With the assurance of a lifetime of command, he had dismissed any further dialogue. 'Jimmy's death is what all this WAAC business is about' — and then he had dismissed Jimmy — 'but it's been six months since Pearl Harbor. Time to end mourning and get back into circulation.'

Page looked around her at the other women as they passed into the ground floor of Company One barracks. Not exactly the kind of circulation her father had in mind, but then she knew she must stop thinking of her father, and especially of those last horrible days. He had all but disowned her, refusing to acknowledge her enlistment and, finally, not even seeing her off at Union Station. His last words were burned into her consciousness: 'It's a man's duty to serve his country; it's a woman's duty to raise sons to serve. Only traitors deny their duty.'

Bunny unrolled her mattress, let it fall on the bare wire of the grey metal bed, and sat down. Her feet were killing her, and she kicked off her sling-back platforms and rubbed first one instep, then the other. How had her feet ever passed the army physical?

So far the Army seemed to be a succession of lines to stand in: at the train depot, at the reception building, and now one was forming at the bathroom — latrine, as they were already beginning to call it. Across the aisle, Elisabeth and Jill began to unpack. Up and down the room that Sergeant Wolford had called a bay, she saw thirty-five other women of all sizes and ages survey their new home, place their belongings about them in the particular way that was each woman's signature, and wonder aloud how they'd fit everything into such a small space.

Next to her she saw Page placing her clothes neatly in the

wall locker behind her bed, a look of exhilaration on her lovely face. Easy to tell that Page Hannaday had class. She seemed to have an air of surety that came only after long years of knowing and doing and wearing exactly the right thing until poise had become an unconscious part of her. Her thick chestnut hair fell to her shoulders, and her tawny skin, Bunny was willing to bet, looked tanned even in midwinter. Both hair and skin framed intense wide-set green eyes. The woman had the clean long-limbed look that most people thought of as 'all-American girl,' but that was, Bunny knew, quite rare outside magazine covers.

Unpacking her travelling bag and cosmetic case, Bunny remembered the young lieutenant at the reception area. 'I want the name you enlisted under,' he'd said. She'd given him the name then, Barbara Patra LaMonica Palermo; the first one she had been born with, and the second and third she kept to remind her that loving a man was either all-taking or all-giving.

She had grown up in a terraced brick house in Bloomfield, New Jersey, the oldest of four girls, and the only one to go on to Sacred Heart College. Like parents in most second-generation Italian families, her mother had hoped one daughter would find a vocation in the church, and she fixed on Bunny, her oldest, to fulfil this ambition.

But her mother had hardly laid her white confirmation dress away in mothballs when Bunny had changed almost overnight from a skinny carbon copy of every other little girl in the parish into a voluptuous, cocoa-eyed beauty. From that time on, every evening found boys draped over her porch rail, elbowing one another, faking jabs to the midsection and other excesses of hormonal zeal that they hoped would bring them to her notice, all under the unblinking eye of Mama Patra.

During Bunny's senior year at Sacred Heart College, the woman who, for years, had given her an after-school job at La Jeunesse Beauty Parlour decided to retire and offered to sell her the business. With her savings and a loan from her Uncle Sal, Bunny made a down payment and became the owner. It was 1936, she was about to marry Johnny

LaMonica, and life was more exciting than she had ever dreamed it could be.

He was easy to fall in love with; in fact, it was probably inevitable. Their mothers were friends, and the youngsters had grown up in the same parish youth hall. They knew the same people, liked the same food and had the same memories. He had clear skin, a fine job selling Chryslers and had always been in her life. During their courtship, she thought she read in his eyes a thousand well-bred invitations to sex, and at twenty-one she was tremblingly overdue for physical love and dying to go to bed with him. She knew that happy marriages all around her had grown from worse beginnings.

But not this one. It did not take her long to realize that she was number two in his life. His mother had first call on his time and energy and, what was a greater disappointment, filled all his needs, except, of course, the sexual one, for which, she discovered on her honeymoon, he had a low appetite.

All this she could have forgiven him, as women before her had forgiven, but Johnny LaMonica had one overwhelming, teeth-grating trait that drove her wild. Having defined weekend sex as the only kind permissible to a hard-working Chrysler salesman, he answered every hesitant overture testily, 'Not now, Bunny' — and this in an aggrieved tone — 'you know we always read the Sunday funnies on Saturday night!'

In his own way, he had been thoughtful, pampering her, giving her whatever money could buy. But it became increasingly plain and at the end unbearable, that she had nothing he wanted, nothing at all of her specialness that he would take. *Any* woman could have been his wife. Despite her mother's hysterics and innumerable sessions with the priest who had married them, she could not spend her life with a man who compromised her ability to love.

After the divorce she immersed herself in work, hiring and training her three sisters as they grew old enough, on the latest permanent-wave machines. By the summer of 1940 she owned three shops, and marriage was something

19

she thought she'd left far behind her, until she took a short vacation in Atlantic City.

On her first night, she had been drawn from the boardwalk into the Uptown Club by the sound of a drummer who got more out of a snare-drum riff than Gene Krupa.

Johnny Palermo was everything Johnny LaMonica had not been. Having no family ties, he moved restlessly from band to band. He drank too much, but he was intensely sensual. There was never any doubt in Bunny's mind that this Johnny wanted her body. She held him off until, during her last night on the boardwalk, he had flashed a tiny diamond ring at her.

'Baby, let's go to Elkton and get married,' he whispered in her ear. 'I guess I got it bad this time. I'll play your tune and sing your lyrics, if that's what it takes to get you into bed.'

'Maryland?'

'They don't have a waiting period. I'm no good at waiting.'

She hadn't trusted herself to speak; she was afraid she might tell him how close she had come to playing it his way. She was determined to make marriage work this time. Sure, she had her eyes open; Johnny was wild, but he was an antidote to the first Johnny. She would settle him down. She would give him the love that was missing from his life, that had made him run away from a brutal father at fifteen, that had made his life so mean and empty. For a single moment, she felt reason grapple with her reckless passion for him, the overwhelming physical urge to belong to him, to merge into him, that gave him power over her life. But the moment passed and they spun on through the night towards Maryland.

Later in an auto-court cabin next to the office of the justice of the peace who married them, under a blinking sign that said 'We Never Close,' he undressed her and made love to her with the same virtuosity that had brought the patrons of the Uptown Club to their feet. He knew how to light little pyres of pleasure that sent heat racing through her until her skin glowed pink and hot. The relentless rhythm of his mouth devouring hers, of his hands evoking exquisite sensations from her taut body, and finally his body inside hers, released a crescendo of dammed-up passion. Breathless, helpless, she gave herself to each shuddering, rolling convulsion, all her senses melding into a cry of love that had been gathering in her throat for a lifetime, 'Johnny!'

She had taken him home the next morning. 'Mama,' she pleaded, 'try to understand.'

But her mother had cried, wretched as only a mother who dreams for a perfect daughter can cry. 'I understand that you're living in sin, that's what I understand. My baby! My Barbara!'

'What can I do, Mama? You went with me to the monsignor for an annulment. You heard what he said: five years — maybe. Or never.'

'He was a good man, your first Johnny. He worked hard. He didn't drink. He didn't chase other women. What more did you want?'

'He didn't want to be a *husband* to me, Mama.'

'I don't want to hear that kinda talk. What kinda thing is that for a girl to tell her mama? All I know is that now you bring this strange Johnny home, and you can't take communion no more. How can I leave your confirmation picture up here on the mantel next to your sisters'?'

Bunny, hurt and frustrated, left her mother cradling the gold-framed picture to her breast, tears dropping on the green felt backing.

That night Johnny asked her for five hundred dollars. She gave it without question. She would have given him her soul if he'd had a use for it. It wasn't the last time he asked for money, and when, months later, she had no more to give and all three shops were mortgaged, he stole from the till and lied about it. By winter 1941, he was drinking heavily and disappearing for days. One cold Saturday evening in early December after she locked up at La Jeunesse, she found him parked outside in her car with a whore.

Walking through the snow to their apartment, she was numbed, not from cold, but from betrayal; stunned by the realization that all loving was a lie. One man had not wanted her love, another had taken it all and then deliberately tossed it away.

Bunny packed in a frenzy, fearful that Johnny would return to arouse her natural instinct of generous love, the part of her that needed to understand him no matter what he had done. But he had not returned.

She walked out without a backward look, then dropped her suitcase at the head of the stairs. Shouldn't she leave him a message? She went back inside the hollow room, lifted the lid on his Crosley and dropped a record on manual. It would play until he turned it off. Music was the only message Johnny would understand. As she made her way down the wooden stairs, heavy suitcase banging against the railing, Frank Sinatra's voice followed her out the door and into the winter night.

> *'All or nothing at all —*
> *Half a love never appealed to me.*
> *If your heart never could yield to me,*
> *Then I'd rather have nothing at all . . .'*

She had always assumed that feelings were truth; now she found that they were lies, and she couldn't trust feelings anymore.

Her first months without him were full of little terrors. He followed her, telephoned her, gave her no time to retrain her senses to act independent of his touch or his pleasure. Even the divorce hadn't freed her of wanting him, of being afraid that one day, in a moment of remembered passion, she'd run to him. When the call came for women to join the WAAC, she made her youngest sister, Angela, manager of what was left of La Jeunesse, and enlisted. Like some men before her, Bunny saw the Army as a haven from the disappointment of love — her own personal French Foreign Legion.

And now here she was, in the middle of an Iowa heat

wave, a thousand miles from home, surrounded by new faces and the challenge of being one of the first women soldiers in America. What surprised her, since the visible parts of her life had changed so drastically, was how little her desire for Johnny Palermo had faded — as if it fought even harder for existence in alien territory.

2

Once her Mommie made her bed,
Cleaned her clothes and buttered her bread,
And her favourite dress was red
— Oh me, Oh my, that ain't G.I.
   — 'The G.I. Song,' Lieutenant June Morhaman

"'Take All You Want, But Eat All You Take,'" Jill Henry Hammersmith read aloud the sign posted just inside the mess-hall screen door. She had changed into a blue jersey dress and self-consciously tugged at the belt, glancing in Elisabeth's direction. 'Sounds like my mother,' she said, pursing her lips.

Page nodded, smiling. 'The Army *is* your mother. It nurtures you with food and clothing, teaches you how to act properly in a military society, and chastises you if you misbehave.'

'That's Mother, all right.'

'Now I know where I've seen you before,' Bunny said to Page, snapping her fingers. '*Life* magazine — at some swank Washington party with your father. That's it! He's a general or something.'

Before Page could answer, the mess sergeant asked for their chits and pushed his hand-held counter four times. They picked up metal compartmented trays and joined a long line of women making choices from laden steam tables.

'Since your father's a general,' Jill took up the conversation once they'd found seats together at a long trestle table away from the roar of the tall floor fans, 'he must be so proud of you.'

Page looked at Jill and her eyes clouded. 'I hope that someday he will be.'

'You mean he didn't want you to join up?'

Page bent forward. 'No, but we Hannadays have always been regular army since the Revolution.' The intensity of her own response surprised and embarrassed her. She smiled apologetically and added lightly, 'I may have to arrange to fight in a separate war from my father — '

Bunny interrupted. 'That explains what you're doing here, Page. But what about the rest of you?'

'You first, Bunny.' Page looked up, interested.

'It's this way, kiddo. People used to stop me on the street in Bloomfield and ask me, "How's your husband Johnny?" Then I'd have to ask, "Which one?"' They all laughed at her — even Elisabeth Gardner, although Bunny could see that the laugh never quite reached her eyes. Good! She invited their laughter; it was exactly what she wanted. She had learned that a quip was the best way to divert questions that came dangerously close to her emotions. 'Your turn, Jill — although I don't know how a mite like you passed the physical. Don't you have to be at least five foot tall and weigh a hundred pounds to join the WAAC?'

'I am five foot tall,' Jill snapped.

'A hundred pounds?' Bunny teased, eyeing her small frame.

'Well, okay,' Jill admitted reluctantly, 'maybe not all the time. I spent the morning of my physical stuffing myself with bananas and Baby Ruth candy bars. I just *had* to get in. I'd already dropped out of vet school to enlist. You see, I just had to after Neil — he's my fiancé — joined up last January. And besides, this war is going to be the biggest thing that happens to my whole life. I couldn't stay at home and miss a chance to be part of it.'

'Ah ha,' Bunny said, 'we have a gentlewoman adventurer, if a rather small one. When Adolf and Il Duce hear you're coming, they'll just beg us to let them surrender.'

Page said, 'I think Jill will give a good account of herself.'

'Of course,' Bunny said seriously, and placed the palm of her hand against her heart. 'I swear, Jill — no kiddin' now — I didn't mean to get out of line. I've just got a big mouth, that's all. Have I told you about the time that my first husband . . .'

But Jill wasn't really listening. She could see that Bunny was only joking, but still she disliked being teased about her size. She didn't mind not being beautiful in the usual sense. What she minded — hated, even — was always being too small and too young for her brains. Cute, everyone called her. Being cute *and* smart was a tremendous burden that weighed down her small frame and made her try all the harder to measure up to the tallest people she could find — like Page. And she could beat Page at this army game even if she didn't have a general for a father. Worried, Jill looked sidewise at Page listening to Bunny, embarrassed at her unworthy thoughts, and with Page so swell and friendly, not high hat at all.

Sometimes Jill knew she was too competitive, but she hadn't had much choice. Her determination to win had pushed her through high school by age sixteen, and had sustained her through college until she fought her way into veterinary school when everyone had been sure she wasn't strong enough to do large-animal work. It had helped her persuade Neil Martin to postpone marriage when he had been insistent. And now it had brought her to Iowa with the first contingent of women accepted by the Army.

Had it been only a month since the enlistment party — that fateful day? She had relived the scene so often, the smell, the heat, the hurt of those few devastating minutes. Suddenly she was there again in her mind, every detail sharply in focus.

'Please, Jill,' her mother was saying, 'come out of the shade so that I can get some Kodak pictures. I want to send one to your Aunt Celia in Charlottesville.'

Complying reluctantly, Jill had fussed, 'Hurry, Mother, I'm roasting!' She hated cameras. Her curly auburn hair frizzled in the heat or hung limp in the winter, and her brown eyes — the only large thing about her — never seemed to show to advantage.

'Stand still, dear, and pat your hair down. After all, it's not every day a Henry girl enlists in the Army.' Jill remembered how pleased she'd been that her mother seemed to accept her enlistment when just last year she had insisted veterinary medicine was no place for a lady. Her dad said it was the Henry patriotism overwhelming her mother's sense of ladylike propriety.

Poor Dad. An ordinary doughboy with a battlefield commission, he'd married a Virginia belle in 1918 and now found his life defined by her aristocratic ancestors. Well, she'd be damned if hers would be!

Out of the corner of her eye, Jill had seen Mrs Martin rushing into the yard with Mr Martin close behind. She was glad to see them, glad they had been invited to her party, since her mother thought of them as hired hands, not social equals. But wait — there was something strange about Mrs Martin's walk. The top of her body was bent over as if it was more anxious to reach its destination than the bottom half. Her face was swollen and mottled red.

'Congratulations!' The word made no sense, coming as it did from between tightly clenched teeth.

'Well, ah — thank you, Mrs Mar — '

'Now you've got — everything,' the distraught woman interrupted, waving a yellow piece of paper in Jill's face. 'He's wounded. My boy's wounded. Maybe bad. *Now* are you satisfied?'

'Neil — wounded — Oh, God, *no*! Mrs Martin — please believe me, I — '

'You got your way,' Neil's mother sobbed, tears running into her mouth, blurring her words. 'He didn't want to go — to disobey the Lord's Commandment,' she said, appealing, with wild swings of her head, to the crowd of neighbours and friends standing in stunned silence. 'It was her — ' she turned back and pointed to Jill ' — she talked him into it with her fine-sounding ideas, and now — now — the judgement of the Almighty . . . ' She broke into a fresh spasm of sobs.

'Mother, Mother,' Mr Martin said, pulling her backwards out of the yard with both arms, throwing apologetic looks towards the group in the courtyard. 'Please don't mind her none,' he pleaded. 'She's just beside herself since the telegram came from the Navy Department.'

Mrs Martin strained to break out of her husband's arms. 'Don't you tell me to be quiet. It *is* — it's all her fault, just as much as the Jap who pulled the trigger. As God will judge me on the final day, I'll bless no union 'twixt my boy and her. Never as long as I draw breath!'

For some minutes Jill stood scarcely breathing, listening to the sobs retreating through the warm June afternoon.

'Well!' Jill's mother expelled the word. 'What can one expect from such common folk?' Pushing the guests towards the buffet laid out on the patio, she refused to comment further. To May Henry Hammersmith every one of life's crises was a matter of violated tenets of decorum. In her the sense of proper and improper, right and wrong, had descended direct from the old Virginia Henrys and reached its genealogical zenith. She had taught Jill a list of absolutes that were never to be questioned.

Most of these rules had to do with the requirements of being a Virginia lady, requirements so rigid that even Virginia ladies no longer adhered to them, let alone young California girls in the summer of 1942.

From her earliest remembrances, Jill had been caught between her desire to please her mother — no matter how impossible that seemed — and the fury engendered by her own emerging personality yearning to be itself. As adolescence faded into young womanhood, she dated Neil, an 'Okie' boy whose parents worked for her parents and who drove a truck with the legend 'Jesus Saves' painted on the sides. Then she decided to become a veterinarian — an occupation, her mother reminded her in subtle ways every day for months, that was not a fit one for a Henry woman.

Matching her mother will for will, she swore she would be the person *she* wanted to be. But Jill was wrong. She could not as she matured, belie her own inheritance. The result was standards so high she could never quite live up to them. Until now, that is. Today, at Fort Des Moines, she knew she had become a pioneer, one of the first women in the Army, a woman whom others would follow. No one would ever be able to take that away from her. Here in the WAAC she would prove her worth not only to others, but finally to herself.

' . . . and that was the end of that marriage, so be warned, my children,' Bunny was saying through the giggles around her. 'I swear,' she went on in mock bewilderment, 'every word is God's truth.'

'Attention to orders!' The words came from Sergeant Wolford, who was holding the mess-hall door open. Through it marched a tall officer dressed in riding boots and breeches, with a crop tucked under his arm. Jill thought he was the most magnificently handsome soldier she had ever seen.

'Candidates,' he said, and the women fell silent, 'my name is Lieutenant Stratton, officer in charge of Second Platoon, Company One. I will also be responsible for Company One's training in military customs, leadership and close-order drill. But for today I am detailed to assist the reporters and newsreel people who want to interview you and take your pictures. I'm sure all of you realize how important it is to the Army that you cooperate — within reason. Now, I have a request here from the *Herald-American* for New York City girls and one from the *Los Angeles Times* for California girls to meet with the reporters in the Company Two dayroom. Questions?' The lieutenant looked balefully out over the crowded mess hall, and no one dared ask anything. He turned smartly, slapping his riding crop against his shiny boots, and left the mess hall.

'Dismissed!' yelled Wolford.

A voice across the mess hall called after the sergeant,

who was already out of the door, 'Doesn't anybody want to talk to women from the rest of the country?'

An answering voice yelled, 'There *is* no country between New York and Los Angeles,' followed by applause and boos.

'Wow,' Jill said, finishing her dessert. 'Did you see him? What a swell-looking guy.'

'You poor kid,' Bunny said with mock seriousness, 'less than one day in this women's army and already you're khaki-wacky and man-starved.'

'Maybe some of us have not had your generous portion, Bunny.'

'Ouch! Touché, kiddo.'

'Aren't you ever serious, Bunny?' Jill asked.

'Never,' Bunny laughed lightly, but Jill noticed a pensive tightness in her tone. For a moment Jill wondered what it could mean. Then, remembering what the lieutenant had said about the reporters, she started to suggest that she and Elisabeth meet them together, when the other woman jumped up.

'I don't want to talk to them,' Elisabeth said and was pushing her way towards the rear door of the mess hall before Jill could answer.

How strange *she* should be shy, Jill thought. She sighed. If she had Elisabeth's height and looks — well, those haughty cheekbones and that tall, gorgeous figure that clothes looked positively moulded to . . . Jill sighed again at the impossibility and walked towards the barracks with Page and Bunny.

'What got into our glamour puss?' Bunny asked.

Elisabeth Koszivak Gardner hurried into the three-storey brick barracks building and sat down on a grey metal bed halfway down the first-floor bay. She had to admit that, stupidly perhaps, she had not foreseen the possibility that this army post in the middle of the Iowa nowhere would be swarming with press. But she had been in tight spots all her life and got out of them. She would get out of this one too.

Out of habit she opened her purse and snapped open her

compact. She dusted her nose with the puff lightly, added a touch of lipstick and was satisfied. She had the look she had worked hard for over so many years — the soaring cheekbones, heightened by just the right application of darker powder, the narrow Anglo-Saxon nose that had cost her five hundred dollars, and lustrously blonde upswept hair that she vowed not to cut even if General Marshall himself ordered it. The muscles around her lips were drawn into a tight look of self-protection, learned in childhood and deliberately perfected to heighten the dramatic tension in her face. Her blue eyes were remote, like shuttered windows. She liked her look because she alone had made it.

She had not always been Elisabeth. As Mareska Koszivak, she had run away from her home in the Pennsylvania coal country when she was fifteen after one of her father's drunken rages. He had whipped her savagely again, not because she had disobeyed him, but because she was there and she was weak. But the beatings had not been the worst of it. From as early as she could remember, he had crept back to her room after the beating to fondle her, until, lost between hurtful bruises and hate-filled pleasure, she could no longer distinguish between them.

Later she was to learn from her psychology classes at City College that the loss of innocent trust was a far more serious loss to her ego than mere virginity. By then she had learned to live, and live very well, without either.

Elisabeth had discovered easily what impressed people. Scarcely fifteen, a runaway in Depression-ridden New York City, she had rid herself of her nasal western-Pennsylvania twang. After working in ever more exclusive dress shops along Madison Avenue, she had at last acquired the drawling vocal mannerisms of café society.

She knew she could be somebody if she tried. This ambition drove her to finish a high-school correspondence course and enroll in night college. Altogether she packaged her own makeshift finishing school. Leaving Mareska behind to become Elisabeth filled her life so completely that she never made friends, not with co-workers or with fellow students. Being alone was what she wanted; it was the way she knew she was meant to be.

From selling expensive clothes she advanced by the time she was nineteen to modelling them — not in the top fashion houses, but in the second echelon of fashion, the manufacturing houses. Here the boss worked out of his wallet, cheating one supplier to pay another. It was crazy and frenetic, but here Elisabeth learned the reality of her world: she was sent to steal designs and cheat department stores, and she proved adept at it. At Saks or Peck and Peck she would charge an elegant, expensive dress, which she then took back to Marco's Fashions. The dress would be taken apart and a pattern cut from it, and the resewn dress could be returned the next day for credit. At the next market week, a cheap version of the dress would be on its way to stores all over the country and Elisabeth would be fifty dollars richer.

Another kind of reality Elisabeth learned was that during the flurry of market week she was often the sweetener that softened the buyer's bill. All the short, fat out-of-town buyers in hundred-dollar suits were promised a date with a model — and they all wanted a tall, slender blonde to show off in front-row theatre seats at a current Broadway hit. Her ambitions made her a willing partner, ready to entertain in public or in bed, and yet she managed to keep her essential self shrouded and aloof.

After two years of this life, a chance meeting changed her direction.

She had been loaned for a day to model lingerie, when she heard a heavily accented voice straight out of an old vaudeville bedroom farce. Phoney or not the voice was talking about her. '*Incroyable!* Look — zee legs of a colt wiz zee face of a Titian madonna. Tell me, *ma chère*, have you ever thought of working for me?' The speaker was Madame Gabriella, a holy name in fashion, with her black hair pulled strictly back into a bun, those great heavy tortoiseshell glasses perched on her imperious nose, and the ever present pretty boy.

'I have thought of little else, Madame,' she lied. Truthfully, she had fancied herself wearing Gabriella originals purchased for her by an adoring millionaire, but she was not blind to the opportunity Madame presented her.

She left that moment with Madame's entourage, without a word to Marco even though it was a few days before the fall market. She owed him nothing. He had used her and she had used him. They were even.

Men of consequence — with power and money — came into her life then. She made it a practice never to go out with a man who did not buy the gown she was modelling. It was her way of insuring solvency, her very own Dun & Bradstreet rating system. It bothered her not at all that they usually bought the gowns for the women they were with or for some unseen woman. Her turn, she knew, would come. She was momentarily content with the world of long-stemmed roses, jewels from Cartier, Worth perfume and evenings at the Colony Club, Maxie's Bar or 21.

That is, she had been content until First Lieutenant Marne Pershing Gardner had walked into the salon, and into her life. He was simply the biggest man — a Viking of a man — she had ever seen. Redheaded, with sea-green eyes, he stood a head above even the tallest man in the room and weighed more than two hundred pounds. With all his bigness he had an agile figure, thin-hipped and long-legged, which was accented by the perfect cut of his Faber 'pinks'. Marne had been the model of military presence from his erect bearing to his 1940 West Point class ring, and he drew every female eye in the showroom. He reeked of 'old money,' and Elisabeth was on his scent from the first moment she saw him. He was the challenge she had unerringly groomed herself to meet.

Within weeks they were married. She had known he would ask and she had known she would say yes. He had what she wanted, and a lot of it — a respected Boston Brahmin name, money, powerful friends and a future. It did not matter that he planned to make the Army his career; she would change his mind about that quickly enough once the war was over. Like a drowning woman, she could foresee her life with Marne before her eyes: a stately home, social influence, her own lovely designer clothes — security, respect.

Never again would she smell the acrid odour of coal soot or be a prisoner of poverty and ugliness. It was odd that she had been able to tell him about her childhood, not the whole story — she knew too much about men to be sexually honest with him — but enough so that he knew her fears. From the first, she had intuited that her poor-but-honest-girl-from-the-wrong-part-of-town tale was the perfect way to manipulate his latent socialist tendencies. Most of the monied people she met had them, and she knew that raising her from poverty made Marne feel like a saviour, and his money less a guilty burden. She had been right. And to the point, which made everything logical: he was very much in love with her.

After an afternoon City Hall ceremony, they drove up to Newport in his yellow Ford convertible for the four days' leave Marne had wangled before his transfer to the 2nd Armoured Division in Texas, a transfer he had initiated. His decision made without telling her, when she had dreamed of Washington duty for him, with elegant dinner parties and dances for her, had pitched her on her wedding day into a rage which she had barely managed to hide.

'But why, Marne?' she had asked again that night in the huge Newport home lent for the occasion by friends of his family. She could not comprehend his answer that armour was going to win the war, or what that had to do with her.

'We're going to start fighting them back soon — the Nazis and the Japs,' he said patiently, 'and when we do, armour is going to be in the forefront of the fighting. Any first lieutenant is going to come out of this war a major or maybe even a lieutenant colonel. I don't want to spend fifteen years in a company grade the way some of the men did after the last war.'

There was nothing she could do but play the loving wife and bide her time. But it was harder than she'd bargained for.

Marne was an ardent but immensely ordinary lover. That she could have borne, after the succession of Broadway trophy hunters she'd been 'nice' to. What she couldn't bear was his tenderness. He treated her like some fragile porcelain doll, gently stroking, exploring, exposing, without taking her to any heights she had not climbed a dozen times before with other men.

'You're so good for me,' Marne said. 'I want to be so good for you.'

'You are darling — so good,' she automatically repeated the familiar lie.

On the last night of their short honeymoon, he had talked about his father and how he had died in France at only twenty-four. 'He was just my age, Elisabeth. They had only a few days before he left, but Mother told me all my life that Father had left her with me and that he would never be dead to her. I hate to ask you to quit your job with Gabriella, but I want you to think about going up to live with Mother while I'm gone. I know she'd love you to come.'

She had been genuinely alarmed at his obvious purpose. She refused to consider the tiresome possibility of burying herself with an old lady, and having his baby in exchange for a moment of half-satisfied passion. How could she allow Marne's need for immortality to enslave her body? She had no intention of rocking away her youth, knitting booties for a tiny bit of protoplasm he had insisted on implanting in her womb. Fortunately she had taken precautions because he refused to use a condom.

During one climax he cried, his voice romantically prayerful, 'Oh, God, I want to leave you with something of me!'

To herself she said a quite different prayer, *Thank God, these are my safe days*.

She was relieved when he left for Texas, but her relief was short-lived. A few nights later as she stepped from a cab onto the sidewalk, a black Cadillac limousine idled in front of her apartment building.

'Hey ya, Liz. Come 'ere.'

'What do you want?' she said, recognizing Marco's brother, a two-bit mobster named Joe Bonine, at the car window.

34

'Get in. Let's go around the block.'

She hesitated, then took a step back away from the kerb.

'Get in!' There was no mistaking the menace in his voice.

'Well, well,' he said when she was inside, 'I hear you really came up in the fashion world, Liz — and I have to say it couldn'ta happened to a nicer broad.'

'What's this all about, Joe?'

'Now, didn't they teach you no better manners midtown? Don't you remember how friendly you and me used to be?'

The bastard! What did he want? She didn't owe him anything.

'Okay. Okay. I can see you don't wanna talk, so here's the deal. We want you to do a little job for us just like the old days. We want a few little drawings — not even patterns.'

'That's crazy!' she said, suddenly colder than she had ever been. 'Steal Gabriella's fall line? I can't do it, Joe. She's no twenty-five-dollar-a-week salesgirl. She'd know in an instant. No, you can't make me pull a dumb stunt like that.'

She put her hand on the door — would he let her go? And then she caught sight of the photos in his lap and dropped her hand.

'Wanna see some pretty pictures, Liz?' his slimy voice oozed through her. 'Or maybe youse'd rather I showed 'em to that new husband of yours or his high-class family up in Boston — Gardners, ain't they? Wonder how much these'd be worth to them.'

She knew instinctively what was in the photos: documentation of every rotten thing she'd ever done to get where she was. They must have spied on her, taken pictures through peepholes — hell, sold tickets, for all she knew. Marco and Joe had just been waiting for her to have something to protect before they pounced. God, if Marne ever learned of their existence . . .

She had stolen the drawings then, and waited, resigned to being discovered, wondering if Madame would call the police, planning to threaten to spread a bit of nasty business about her latest boy who wore Gabriella's lingerie under his tight suits. The tension was almost unbearable, so the call from Madame's office had come almost as a relief.

Madame's face sagged when she saw her. 'Eleesabet, in this business you can be forgiven a *petit* larceny, but no one in fashion wants a thief who stole a whole collection. You are *finie*. You will never work again as a model in this town. Be assured, I will see to it. Now go!'

At first she was relieved to escape so easily, but then she realized that every door in New York she had pushed open had closed behind her. She didn't know what to do, where to go. Under no circumstances could Marne find out the truth. She couldn't even tell him she was out of a job or he'd insist she go to his mother. Then she'd sit out the war in some Back Bay backwater, growing babies and growing old.

On the second morning after leaving Gabriella's salon, she was walking the Manhattan streets, trying to think of a way out of the trap she was caught in, when she saw a poster in a recruiting-office window: 'RELEASE MEN TO FIGHT! SERVE IN THE WAAC,' and underneath it the legend 'New Faces, New Places, Excitement, Good Pay.' A new start, *that's* what she needed. Then again, maybe she was a bit taken in by Marne's flag waving or perhaps she outsmarted herself in a scheme to get out of trouble and at the same time to impress him and bind him more tightly to her. When you don't love a man, she instinctively knew, you're always afraid of losing him. Whatever jumble of desperate reasons she had, they all came together in front of that poster.

At the last minute before boarding the train for Fort Des Moines, she wrote to him. By that time, Elisabeth had been sworn in and there was nothing either of them could have done to change things.

'There you are, Elisabeth,' Jill called merrily as she and Page and Bunny came into the barracks. 'You didn't miss anything much with those reporters. They just wanted to know what our first impressions of army life were. I told them I thought the Army always ate beans, but we'd had a swell lunch, except for the bologna — and, oh yes, I said the

36

women I'd met so far were great. The reporters kept asking if we'd been issued olive-drab underwear. They made a big thing out of whether the Army was going to supply girdles or not. Pretty goofy stuff.'

'I'm sorry I ran out that way,' Elisabeth said when Jill sat down on the bed next to hers. 'You see, my husband's with the Second Armoured Division training in Texas right now, and there are no reporters down there asking him how he feels about it. I just didn't want any special treatment.'

Elisabeth saw that Jill had admiration in her eyes, and for a moment she half believed her own nobility. A tiny part of her wanted to believe . . .

3

Army's Most Unusual Rookies Are 'Processed' into WAACs

On Monday, the dreary treatment known to the Army as 'processing' began. The recruits were tagged, inoculated, inspected, measured, and given their uniforms. They drew the strangest assortment of equipment that a supply sergeant ever saw. Each issue included: three brassieres, two girdles . . .
— Newsweek, *July 27, 1942*

*U*p, tup, th-rip, four! Company One, First WAAC Officer Candidate Training Regiment, marched towards the quartermaster clothing-supply building to a cadence that only two days earlier had been unintelligible to most of them. Page thrilled to hear the concert of footsteps, the rhythmic, light march step of women stretching to meet a regulation thirty-inch army stride.

The first full day in the Army had been like a summer camp and sorority hall week lumped together. They had been given follow-up physicals, dental checks, the first round of shots — Page felt the aching soreness of both arms as she swung them — and had been taught how to make an army bed with hospital corners, white collars and sheets stretched so tight, according to Sergeant Wolford, they should hum the 'Colonel Bogey March'. The women were barely dismissed from one formation when the call 'Fall In!' echoed down the barracks, and the sound of running feet with an accompanying chorus of groans and gripes began to mark them as real soldiers. Page knew it was a good sign. She had heard her father say it often enough, 'If they don't gripe, they aren't Regular Army.'

For their first thirty-six hours in the WAAC they had retained the vestiges of their civilian identities. They were still newspaperwomen, teachers, lawyers, artists, housewives, secretaries, wearing frilly dresses and open-toed pumps. Page knew that in the next few hours all that would change. Putting on the WAAC uniform would begin the process of turning them into the first women soldiers the country had ever seen.

Page was so busy sorting her first feelings about the Corps that she didn't hear the order to halt and stumbled into the woman at the head of her squad. 'Pardon me,' she said automatically.

'Quiet in ranks,' ordered Sergeant Wolford, glaring at her. 'This ain't no ladies' tea party, *this is the Army*. You women wanted to be soldiers, and soldiers you're gonna be.'

Page felt her face burn red with indignation and bit her lip.

'Don't mind him,' Bunny said moments later after they broke ranks. 'The old boy hasn't got used to an army without horses yet. Now here we women come, and it's just too much for him.'

In a way Page felt sorry for men like Wolford and her father. It must be dreadful to be unchanged in a changed world.

Jill agreed with Bunny, dabbing with her handkerchief at the perspiration on her face. 'I heard that all the cadre are being paid extra to train us.'

'Hazardous duty pay?' Elisabeth asked sarcastically.

'In a way you're right, Elisabeth,' Page said, voicing a feeling that had been strong in her since she arrived at the fort. 'We Waacs are like combat for Sergeant Wolford. He's forced to change his whole idea of what a soldier is — even his idea of himself. I've thought a lot about this,' she told the others, 'and it may sound odd, but, look, men have been putting on armour and going out to meet dragons for thousands of years. Before they'll accept us, we women will have to slay a few dragons of our own.'

'A pretty metaphor,' Elisabeth said. 'But we enlisted to release a man to fight, not to do the fighting.'

'She's right,' Jill said. 'What do you mean?'

'Oh, I don't know,' Page answered. 'It's just a feeling. For now, maybe we just have to outsoldier men where we can — be more spit-and-polish, march better, respond to orders more promptly.'

Bunny squealed. 'You mean I have to use more starch than the sarge? But he positively crackles!'

A solid-looking young woman named Kansas joined them. 'Hey, I don't mind the starch, it's this reveille business. How can I get my eight-hour beauty sleep between eleven PM and five AM?'

A woman in her thirties named Smitty — Page recognized her from the third floor of their barracks — spoke up next. 'We'll have to learn to do what my students used to do — sleep in class.'

Sergeant Wolford came out of the QM building. 'Form a single line,' he yelled, 'and keep it moving.'

The line began to inch slowly up the wooden steps, and they entered the building one by one. A row of men stood behind the counter handing out uniform parts and checking a form that followed each candidate down the line. A barracks bag came first, to hold what followed.

'Six pairs panties, brown,' sang out the second supply clerk.

Bunny whispered behind Page, 'Ahh — the elusive WAAC lingerie. It's a good thing they closed the fort to the press for the next two weeks, or they'd be sneaking pictures through the barracks windows.'

'You said it,' said Kansas testily from behind Bunny. 'I was beginning to feel like a freak. First they stared at me in my hometown when I enlisted, and then they pointed me out on the train, and when I got here some guy was always shoving a camera in my face.'

'Quiet there! Four shirtwaists, tan,' the next clerk said, shoving them towards Page as she walked along.

'One blouse, cotton twill.' A belted jacket plopped into the bulging bag.

'Move to the next area for your fittings,' ordered the supply sergeant at the end of the counter.

Page saw Elisabeth and Jill already standing on boxes being measured by a swarm of fitters from Younkers department store in Des Moines.

'Can't you move this fourth button higher to give a better line to the jacket?' Elisabeth asked.

'We are only authorized to fit the uniform as it is to the figure, miss,' one fitter answered.

Elisabeth's face was set. 'Can't you see that this fourth button will pull the jacket as I sit, giving it a pouched look across the stomach? I'll look pregnant!' Since this was the fate she had gone to some trouble to avoid, she thought the point worth pressing.

'We're not allowed to alter the design.'

'Who made this idiotic design?'

'I believe it was the Quartermaster Corps in Philadelphia. *We* certainly had nothing to do with it,' the fitter answered in a huff of injured professionalism. 'Please don't move while I pin your skirt.'

'Imagine,' Elisabeth said as she and Page sat down to be measured for their shoes, 'that hick seamstress tried to tell *me* how to do a fitting.'

'You obviously know clothes,' Page said. 'Were you in sales or a model?'

'A model,' Elisabeth answered without pursuing the

conversation. She'd said too much already.

How odd she was, Page thought. Sophisticated, cold, and yet she had patriotically joined the WAAC to help her soldier husband. Elisabeth was a contradiction. Her worldliness, even her polished accent, was something she seemed to wear like a borrowed gown; it did not hang comfortably about her like garments she had worn all her life.

'Lights out,' Wolford called through the barracks door that night, setting off a scramble for one last visit to the latrine or a final sentence on the first letters home.

Page, with freshly pressed uniforms hanging in her wall locker, and her foot locker neatly arranged at the foot of her bed, sat cross-legged on top of her blankets, feeling that outer transformation from civilian to soldier was complete. The first clear notes of Taps drifted through windows open to catch a night breeze — the sweet, sad melody that signalled the death of an army day.

'Did you hear that?' Bunny whispered across the six feet that separated their cots, after the last note had faded.

'Yes, I heard it,' Page said softly. 'I've heard it thousands of times, but tonight it's different. Tonight, it's for me.'

'I've been watching you; you're really in love with all this, aren't you?'

Page didn't answer. She didn't know what to say. She was as patriotic as the next woman, but love . . .

'Page,' Jill called drowzily across the aisle.

'Yes, Jill.'

'The dragon you were talking about before — you know, the one we Waacs have to fight. Do you think we'll be able to do it — slay the dragon, I mean?'

'I'm sure of it, Jill. Now get some sleep.'

Page heard Jill say something to Elisabeth and Elisabeth answer, 'Yes, I'm all right, but I can't sleep because those damned shots are throbbing.'

Page rolled over and pushed the brown blankets stencilled with the US Army logo to the bottom of her cot. Something had happened between the four of them in the past two days. Pure chance had placed them in the last truck from the station, in the same barracks and squad, but something more than that had made them care about one another. It was as if each of them knew that the time ahead would try them as no challenge ever had, and that they would need to be friends, a circle, a band of sisters.

Page kicked off the top sheet. It was so humid. She and Bunny and Elisabeth, being Easterners, were used to it, but not the California girls. Poor little Jill was white from near heat exhaustion.

In the cot on the other side of Jill, Elisabeth stared into the dark, slowly rubbing the fevered, swollen lumps in her arms where the needles had penetrated. She had to admit that she had made a horrendous mistake joining the WAAC. She didn't belong here, not like Page and Jill. Even Bunny seemed to adapt to this women's army better than she did. She shifted the thin pillow under her neck. Why had she panicked? Certainly she was clever enough to think of a dozen logical reasons to tell Marne why she had left Madame Gabriella's, and an equal number why she couldn't possibly move to Boston just yet, although, of course, she was dying to. But joining the Army? She must have been temporarily insane. Damn! Damn! She beat her fist silently against the mattress. Whatever the reason, she had been right about one thing: she had to get away from New York City — fast. When the time came, she'd know how to get out of the WAAC too. She turned to a cooler spot on the sheets and fell asleep.

Headline news: Hitler Orders Stalingrad Attack

This is the Army *opens tomorrow, July 27, 1942, on Broadway with an all-soldier cast and a new Irving Berlin song, 'I Left My Heart at the Stage Door Canteen.'*
The individual sugar ration is set at eight ounces per week.

'You've met Director Hobby. What's she like?' Bunny asked Page as they filed into the Fort Des Moines theatre on the fourth morning of training.

'Very determined, a great organizer, but always a Southern lady. You'll see,' Page whispered, since Colonel Faith, the post commandant, had mounted the stage to introduce Oveta Culp Hobby, the Director of the WAAC.

'She'd have to be Scarlett O'Hara to take my mind off my hot, tired feet,' Bunny said. She saw a small, pretty woman with an upswept greying pompadour step to the podium. Her uniform and bearing were impeccably military although she had had no training. All the candidates in the room knew she had begged to be allowed to go through with this first OC group but had been turned down by General Marshall. They had glimpsed her looking on longingly as they practised close-order drill and double-timed between classes. But orders from a four-star general took precedence over desire. As director she wore a colonel's golden eagles on her shoulder, and it was against army policy to train bird colonels with lowly officer candidates.

A riffle of excitement swept along rows of assembled women as the Director's voice reached them. 'You are the first women to serve,' she began. 'Never forget it . . .'

Bunny felt Elisabeth stiffen in the seat beside her and

heard her mutter, 'The hell — I'll forget it first chance I get.'

A woman in the row ahead turned and glared at her.

The Director's soft Texas accent reached to the far end of the now hushed auditorium. 'You have just made the change from peacetime pursuits to wartime tasks — from the individualism of civilian life to the anonymity of mass military life. You have given up comfortable homes, highly paid positions, leisure. You have taken off silk and put on khaki. And all for essentially the same reason — you have a debt and a date. A debt to democracy, a date with destiny.'

No one breathed in the stillness of the theatre while those sentences echoed and re-echoed. Bunny saw that even Elisabeth was paying attention to words no other women had ever heard.

'You do not come into a corps,' the Director went on, 'that has an established tradition. You must make your own. But in making your own, you do have one tradition — the integrity of all the brave American women of all time who have loved their country. You, as you gather here, are living history.'

Suddenly, Bunny realized that for the past few minutes she'd forgotten her sore feet and the heat. The Director's determined voice reached inside her and touched a love of country she had not known was there.

'From now on you are soldiers, defending a free way of life. You are no longer individuals. You wear the uniform of the Army of the United States. Respect that uniform. Respect all that it stands for. Then the world will respect all that the Corps stands for.'

Page felt a thrill of belonging that she had never experienced before. She looked around the room and saw other women, their faces filled with new pride and sense of mission. They shared in that moment what no other American women had ever shared. They were comrades. Now, she knew, that word belonged to women too.

Filing out, Jill whispered with tears in her eyes, 'I was getting a little homesick. I wasn't sure I'd done the right thing by signing up. Now I'm sure.'

As they formed up outside the theatre, Sergeant Wolford yelled with his rising inflection, 'Comp'ny One! Dress right, *dress*! Straighten those lines, people, this is no conga dance.'

Bunny heard a new snap to their execution of his commands. Even Elisabeth seemed to drop her model's glide and step off the cadence smartly.

Officer Candidate Hannaday. Page, keeping the correct distance from the women in front of her, turned this new appellation over in her mind. She had been daughter, friend, sorority sister, fiancée and now she was Candidate Hannaday. All those other selves now seemed like ghosts. As they marched to their next class, Director Hobby's words echoed in her ears: 'You have a date with destiny.'

The next morning Company One was issued gas masks and marched to its first chemical-warfare training class. By the time they broke formation and scrambled into the bleachers, Page was clammy with apprehension.

'What's wrong, Page?' Bunny asked as they took their seats for the lecture. 'You seen a spook — or an old boyfriend?'

'No, it's nothing, really — I mean, yes, there is something. Do you think we'll have to put on these masks?'

'Not only put them on, but yesterday Company Two had to walk in there' — Bunny pointed to a small windowless cinder-block bunker — 'and take them off in front of an open canister of tear gas.'

Page's worst imaginings had been confirmed. Her palms perspired, and the humid air blowing across the open field crept along her neck, leaving behind prickly sensations of damp fear. It wasn't that she was just afraid of suffocating under the mask. Mostly, she was afraid of being afraid, of going out of control and making a fool of herself. No one else could possibly understand how she felt when her face was covered. She didn't understand it herself. Maybe such an unreasonable fear had as harmless a beginning as a childish pillow fight that had got out of hand, or maybe she'd become entangled with her baby blankets in her crib. Whatever it had been, for years now she had awakened shrieking if bed covers had slipped over her face. She'd taken elaborate precautions, pinning blankets low on the mattress . . . But a gas mask, covering, smothering — there was no way out. She tried to slow her breathing, but she was already giddy from gulping air.

A Chemical Corps sergeant, standing on the first bleacher seat below the seated Waacs, held up a gas mask and identified its parts, pointing out the breathing hose attached to purifiers that filtered out small particles of dust, smoke or harmful gases. 'The mask must fit tightly over your head and face,' he said, 'or you could breathe poison fumes. Don't you think you'll be safe because you women won't be in the trenches. Modern gases can reach you by bomber or long-range artillery.'

Next he demonstrated the proper way to don the gas mask. 'Now I want each of you candidates to put on your masks and check the straps of the women on your left and right to see that they are tight. We'll spend about fifteen minutes practising before you get your first exposure to real gas.' He looked at his watch. 'Begin!'

There was a flurry of activity all around her, and soon Page heard the mask-muffled voices of the other candidates. She saw Bunny, looking like a Buck Rogers character, motion for her to put on her own mask, but her hands were frozen at her side.

'Candidate!'

The instructor was calling her.

'Yes, Sergeant.'

'Why isn't your mask on?'

'I — I want to put it on, but . . . there's a problem.'

'What's the problem?'

'I can't breathe with it on.'

'What do you mean? All these women are breathing. You've got five minutes to put it on and prepare for gas drill. What's your name?'

'Hannaday, Sergeant.'

'Well, Candidate Hannaday, this drill is a must. Either you accomplish it or you're a washout. I'm giving you a direct order to *put on your gas mask*.'

'Page!' Jill's blurred voice came through to her. 'Do it — for God's sake . . .'

Bunny shook her arm, eyes wide behind the eyepieces. 'We're all in this together. Come on, don't let us down.'

Page picked up the floppy rubber-and-fabric mask and watched it as it closed in upon her face. Her hands seemed to be responding to something beyond her fear, while the rest of her body tried to shrink away and become invisible. Suddenly, the bitter smell of rubber was in her nose and the sharp taste of it in her mouth, yet she managed to pull the webbing tight on either side. Swallowing compulsively, she pushed down the rising waves of panic and forced herself to breathe slowly so she wouldn't faint. Now her hands dug into the wooden bleacher where she sat. She could feel her fingernails snap off to the quick, but she held on tight to keep from ripping off the mask.

Satisfied, the sergeant nodded at her. 'Form a single line behind me,' he ordered Company One.

They climbed down the rows of seats and marched in a single line towards the cinder-block building. An officer put on his gas mask, opened the door and stepped into the billowing white smoke, shutting the door behind him.

The sergeant spoke, his words terrifying to Page, who experienced an almost continuous sensation of pitching forward. 'One by one you will enter the building. I want you to walk to the officer at the table, take a big breath, remove your mask and give him your name, rank and serial number. Have you got that?' The women nodded, their air hoses wobbling up and down. 'Got that, Hannaday?'

Page nodded, the movement increasing her lightheadedness. She felt Jill's hand steadying her from behind.

'One more thing, Candidates,' the Sergeant said. 'Leave by the door on the other side of the building and *don't* breathe till you're outside. Go!' He opened the door and tapped the first woman on the shoulder.

The line half-stepped forward. First one woman, then the next disappeared inside until it was Bunny's turn. Page saw Bunny give her a cocky thumbs-up before stepping into the tear-gas. Then it was Page's turn.

Jill squeezed her arm. 'We're with you.' The words came to Page as a far-off whisper.

Page was no longer thinking of escape as her fear told her she must. She was acting automatically now, acting out of some ancient military instinct, the same instinct that had made the Light Brigade charge at Balaklava, the Texans remain in a doomed Alamo, the army nurses stick it out on Corregidor. It wasn't just bravery and patriotism. It was an intense feeling that grew with every test they faced together: the knowledge that, as soldiers, they could count on one another. They had to. There was no one else.

Page felt the sergeant's hand push her shoulder hard, and she stumbled inside the bunker. The tear gas was so thick she could scarcely make out the outline of the officer who motioned her forward. He was seated at a small table, his gas mask on. Page knew there was no chance now for a reprieve. She had to come through or admit to her friends, herself and her father that she was unfit to be a woman soldier. Her father . . . She could hear his voice — half amused, half angry. 'Damned if it doesn't sound like you had your date with destiny, Page — and stood him up!'

The officer rose from behind the table and pointed to her gas mask.

Taking a breath so deep it hurt her lungs, Page ripped off her mask. 'Hannaday, Page, Candidate L205720.'

The acrid fumes swirled like a hot fog about her face, creeping into her throat and nostrils, burning, stinging like hundreds of insect bites. Her tear ducts opened, and water cascaded down her cheeks. She flailed at the noxious cloud until she found the door and threw herself near-blind outside, gasping, choking, sucking at the pure air.

Bunny, tears streaming down her own face, grabbed her by the arm and led her away from the blockhouse, from which tear gas escaped every time the door opened. A few feet distant, they stopped, chests heaving, and waited until both Jill and Elisabeth ran out.

Elisabeth looked as wretched as Page felt. 'Are they going to let us go back to the barracks and bathe?' she asked. 'I don't think I can stand to walk around smelling like Chemistry 201 all day. Ugh! My mouth tastes like rotten eggs.'

Jill, wiping her eyes, looked closely at Page. 'Are you all right?'

Taking a lovely, deep breath, Page said, 'Yes, Jill, I'm fine.'

'Well, you sure had me going. I was so scared you were going to goof up.'

'Sorry. I won't ever frighten you like that again.'

That night the foursome nursed Cokes in the PX, too tired to talk or even take off their floppy fatigue hats.

'You ought to have seen them,' they overheard a GI at the next table saying. 'Like a bunch of pigeons in gas masks, flapping around and giggling.' By the time he had finished they knew he was talking about them, and loudly enough so they'd be sure to hear.

Jill, her lower lip thrust out, her cheeks hot with resentment, spoke up for all of them. 'It must be great being a jeep jockey all day. Nothing to do but drive the major's wife to the grocery store.'

Page shushed her. 'Just ignore them.'

'I won't,' Jill said stubbornly. 'If there's one thing I know, it's about bullies like that. You let them think you're scared and they never let up.'

Page's shoulder and neck muscles ached from tensed nerves. She didn't think she could stand another scene.

The GI got up and swept Jill an exaggerated bow. 'Begging my *lady's* pardon,' he said smirking at his friends.

'That's enough, Burt,' one of them, a corporal, said.

Burt looked almost ready to challenge him, but sneered and swaggered away.

'I'm sorry,' their rescuer said. 'He's a show-off.'

Page answered for the still-angry Jill, 'That's all right. Forget it.'

'Can we buy you another Coke — just to apologize?'

When they put it that way, it seemed ungracious to refuse them. 'Okay, guys,' Bunny said.

Returning with the drinks, the corporal turned his chair

49

to face them, as did the two privates he was with. 'We're in finance, not jeeps,' he said, smiling at Jill. 'Payroll division. You'll like us a lot better next month when you get to salute the paymaster for the first time.'

But Jill was only slightly mollified. 'Tell me,' she asked him, 'why don't you guys like us Waacs?'

He seemed astonished more than embarrassed. 'That's not true. Oh, maybe some of the sergeants — the cadre — are pushed out of joint, but we lower ranks don't dislike you. It's — ' he frowned, searching for the right words ' — it's just that we don't understand how you can replace us.'

'Replace you — what do you mean?' Elisabeth asked.

'Well — by the way, my name's Jerry and this is Ben and Leonard — I mean the posters and the slogan. You know — there's a WAAC recruiting poster at headquarters building that shows a buck sergeant with a typewriter chained to his back. It says, "Replace a Man for Combat." I'll tell you, some of us don't want our sisters and our girlfriends to put on a uniform so we can get sent overseas.'

Bunny grinned. 'Well, fellas, *I* don't want to take the typewriter off your back — not even if you gave it to me.'

Ben and Leonard laughed, and even Jerry joined in.

Bless Bunny, Page thought. Always a quip in time.

Soon all seven chairs were crowded around the Waacs' table and they were trading training stories as soldiers do.

'Did you really have to go through the gas bunker today?' Jerry asked.

'That's not Chanel Number Five wafting over the table.' Elisabeth sniffed the air.

'I didn't know they'd make you girls do that,' Ben said.

Leonard, the shy one spoke up. 'Have you had your supply class yet?'

'Not yet,' Page said.

Jerry laughed and slapped the table. 'Boy, are you in for it if you get old Baker, the top S-three noncom. He's a bear on requisition forms.'

Page watched them. We just need to get to know each other, she thought. We have so much in common; it's just the little things that divide us.

50

5

US marines land on Guadalcanal and Tulagi in the Solomon Islands, the opening round of the fight to roll back the Japanese offensive.

Officer Candidate Jill Henry Hammersmith hid in a latrine stall after lights out, her stationery folio on her lap. She chewed the top of her pen, then wrote:

> 7 August, 1942
> WAAC Training Centre
> Fort Des Moines, Iowa

DEAREST, DARLING NEIL,

Tomorrow is our first big command inspection. It's so important that 2nd Platoon do well. I'd just die if I got a gig, but I had my friend Page go over my area and she said even her father (who's a general) would find it strictly GI.

We get our first overnight pass after inspection and we're all heading for a hotel in Des Moines. I'm planning to spend the entire thirty-six hours in a tub.

Do everything the doctors tell you to do, and please write. I understand that you may not be up to it yet, but ask the Red Cross volunteers to write for you. I do need to know how you are.

I know you weren't feeling well when I came to Oak Knoll hospital, but you must believe that I still want to marry you after this war is over. I know you still love me, and you'll see — we can make it work.

She signed the letter, thought about adding a PS, rejected several, then fished in the folds of the folio for a three-cent stamp.

'I thought I'd find you in here, Candidate Hammersmith,' Bunny said, peeking over the stall door.

'What! Is there no time a girl can call her own?'

'Rules are rules, as you're always reminding me. Come on, Mother Bunny will tuck you in bed.'

'*Mother* Bunny?' Jill giggled. 'You're not like any mother I've ever seen.'

'No arguments, kiddo. You work harder than any of us, so hit the sack.'

'Quiet in the latrine,' yelled an irritated voice. '*Some* of us need our sleep.'

Both women put their forefingers to their lips and grinned.

'That's the dean,' Bunny whispered. 'She still thinks we're freshmen in her dormitory.'

Jill made a face, but tiptoed quietly through the darkened barracks. During the past weeks she had learned what a swell gal Bunny was. Sure, she was a kidder, but there was no malice in her. Just the opposite. When their muscles ached after hours of drill and physical-training jumping jacks, and their heads throbbed from classes on morning reports and supply requisitions, she made them laugh in spite of themselves — even when her own poor feet were in the sorest shape of all.

Jill climbed into bed, careful not to step on her shined shoes, their toes aligned in perfect flank formation. All her clothes in the wall locker were on hangers exactly one inch apart, buttons buttoned, all turned one way. At the foot of her bed, her foot locker held rows of neatly rolled bras, hose and panties. She was strictly GI. If only her college roommates could see her now, they wouldn't believe how neat she was.

What would Neil say if *he* could see her? Would he be proud of her or . . . How could she know *what* he was feeling after that horrible day in the hospital?

In late June he had been flown from Hawaii to Oak Knoll in San Francisco. When she visited him on her way to Des Moines — she'd worn that damned red peplum dress because it was his favourite — well, she'd hoped with all her heart that he would understand why she had enlisted, partly for him, partly for herself. But he hadn't seemed to understand anything.

Jill had waited an hour outside the office of the chief of nurses before she was admitted.

'I'm sorry,' the woman in white had said from behind her desk, 'I'm deluged with family requests — who was it you wished to see?'

'Seaman First Neil G. Martin, in Ward Ten.'

'Ward Ten? Are you his wife — sister?'

'His fiancée.'

The nurse consulted a folder and then looked up at Jill, her voice compassionate. 'I don't see your name on the visitors' list. Did Seaman Martin write and ask you to come?'

'Not exactly — no, but, you see, I've joined the WAAC and I'm on my way to the Midwest for training. It might be months before I can get back. He *needs* to see me. I know he does. There is something that I must explain.'

'Miss, er — ' the chief of nurses looked down at the appointment slip Jill had handed her ' — Hammersmith, you should know that Ward Ten is reserved for our most serious cases. You are not prepared for what you will see — and I can't take the chance that you'll make things worse for this sailor.'

'I won't — I promise I won't. I can take whatever there is to take. You must understand — if I don't see him today he might think . . . I . . . I don't know what.'

The woman was obviously sympathetic to Jill's request. 'The regs say no — but wait here and I'll check with the doctor. It may take a few minutes.'

As soon as the office door closed behind the nurse, Jill knew what the doctor's answer would be. What could she do? If she didn't see Neil today . . . It was then that she saw the pad of signed passes on the desk. Recklessly, she tore off the top one and quickly left the room.

Neil's lanky body looked incredibly young huddled under a blanket in the wheelchair at the opposite end of Ward Ten. Walking towards him, Jill thought that he had not aged in combat as men were supposed to do, but gone backwards in time. It was a small-size boy's face he turned towards her — a half-face drawn tight and shrivelled by a cockpit fire as his torpedo plane dived into the sea at Midway — a little blank-faced boy with unfathomably sad, lashless eyes.

Suddenly, she was fighting to keep her own eyes steady, to reject the rising nausea as she came closer and saw that he had no mouth where it once had been. She had never realized how important a mouth was. It's not the eyes that are a beacon for the face, she thought, it's a mouth that gives a face life and humanity.

When she was midway down the ward, he saw her and violently thrust out both bandaged hands to fend her off, as if she were a new fire coming to threaten him. 'Nurse! *Nurse!*' The words were all throat sounds, like shattered gargles.

'Neil, it's me, JILL. Don't — please don't turn away. I love you.' She was faint at the sight of him like this, but she stepped forward, her hand, palm up, held out to him. He screamed and kept on screaming, clawing with his hands against the wheels of his wheelchair, trying to make them roll backwards away from her, until red splotches began to spread on the white gauze wrappings. Never in all her life had she felt so helpless, so frozen in uselessness. Oh, God — why hadn't she listened? From far off, she saw the chief of nurses, followed by a ward nurse, run towards her and felt them take her roughly by an arm. 'You have to leave *now*, miss,' Jill heard them shouting.

Dazed, Jill allowed herself to be propelled rapidly back down the aisle between the rows of white beds where limbless men lay, their eyes full of intolerance at this intrusion into their despair. Later, as she stood outside Oak Knoll looking up at the windows of Ward Ten, she thought she saw Neil watching. Taking a deep, determined breath, she waved and smiled so he would know that nothing had changed, that everything was going to be all right.

A slight Iowa breeze stirred the limp air in Company One's

barrack, as, sleepless, Jill slipped out of bed and padded across the bay to Bunny's area. She whispered, 'Bunny — you awake?'

'Uh-huh.'

Jill sat down quietly on Bunny's foot locker. 'I was writing to Neil — you know, my fiancé.'

'Yes.'

'I — I keep writing, but he doesn't answer.'

'He was badly wounded, wasn't he?'

'Yes, but it's more than that. He hasn't said so, but I think he blames me.' Jill waited, but Bunny was silent. 'You see, he didn't want to go. Oh, he's not a coward or anything, but he was going to register as a conscientious objector. It's his religion, but — well, I told him I'd be ashamed of him, and our children would be, too. Bunny, I forced him, and now he . . . he's terribly scarred — his face . . .'

'Kid, you're not to blame for this war.' Bunny's voice came softly to her in the dark. 'Everything that happens is not your fault. Jill, you've got to learn to trust yourself, to forgive yourself for what you can't change, or the world will eat you up.'

Back on her cot, Jill wondered about what Bunny had said. Maybe it was true, maybe she had never learned how to be a friend to herself. And because she didn't know how, every human mistake she made caused a nagging whisper to rise inside her that said, 'You see, you can't do anything right.'

'Second 'toon!' Wolford yelled. 'Attention to roll call. Adams.'

'Present.'

'Fair.'

'Present.'

'Gardner.'

'Present.'

His voice droned on past Hammersmith, Hannaday and Strayhorn to Thorpe, and then with an about-face he turned to give the all-present-and-accounted-for response to the inspection party. 'Parade *rest!*' Sergeant Wolford projected his voice down the long line of the Company One formation in front of their barracks.

Each woman immediately moved her right foot one step to the right and snapped her arms behind her, hands clasped. Jill was very careful to keep her eyes focused in front, since she knew that this order did not mean she could stand easy. Please, God, don't let them find anything wrong with my work detail, she prayed as the inspecting party passed into the barracks, and knew that all the other women were sending up the same silent plea.

She was sure that her toilet bowls were spotless, all six of them. She had asked Page to check them for her and had stood over them until the last minute to make sure no one used them. Then she had double-checked Page's mop-rack detail for her. The mops were hung on their hooks at attention, bleached white, with the strings cut to uniform length.

What time was it? She strained her eyes to see Elisabeth's watch in the front rank, but couldn't. It must be at least ten o'clock, and she had been on her feet since the reveille cannon went off at 0530. Even though the inspection party had been late arriving, there was no way she could have sat down without putting a crease in her heavy chino skirt.

'I feel like a wooden soldier,' Bunny had said. 'Can't even bend my arms.'

Jill knew Bunny was not really complaining. None of them was. It was just that everyone — the press, Congress, but most of all the Army — was watching the first women soldiers. She only hoped she could stay off the gig sheet, so that Lieutenant Stratton and the others would believe she was mature enough to be an army officer. All her life there had been someone telling her she was too small for this or too young for that. This was her chance to prove them wrong.

'Comp-ny. *Attention!*' Captain Burchette, their CO and an old-time line officer, took the all-present-and-accounted-for report, executed an about-face and gave the same report to Colonel Faith.

This is it, Jill thought, our first training-centre commandant's inspection, and she crossed her fingers quickly for luck.

'Open ranks, march!' ordered Lieutenant Stratton, and the inspection party started down the front rank, the commandant first, then the CO and Stratton, followed by Sergeant Wolford with a little black notebook. She could see them coming along the first rank, Colonel Faith making a left-angle turn in front of each OC. She could see him talking to each in turn, probably asking them their general orders or which poison gas smelled like apple blossoms. Her knees felt wobbly, and she realized she couldn't remember anything she had learned. Not one damn thing!

Straining to hear as the commandant turned into her rank, she heard him ask Page, 'Who is the WAAC training-centre commandant?'

'Colonel Faith, sir.'

And then he was in front of Bunny, next to her.

'Who is the WAAC training centre commandant?' he said.

'Colonel Faith, sir,' Bunny answered.

Jill stiffened into rigid attention: knees straight, hips tucked under, chest out, arms straight — but not stiff — feet at a forty-five degree angle.

He made a left-face — in front of her now. The rest of the inspection party, sun glinting off their brass, trailed behind. 'And what,' he said to Jill, 'is your name?'

'Colonel Faith, sir,' Jill said in her deepest voice before she could stop herself. 'I mean it's Jill — er, I mean, Candidate Hammersmith, J., sir!' She was fairly shouting in his face by the time she got it out. He nodded and moved on. She wished with the fervency of all her twenty-one years that she could simply shrivel up and disappear.

'Jill — it's not the end of the world,' Page argued.

Jill refused to be comforted. 'Didn't you see them? They were laughing at me.'

'No they weren't.' Bunny said, 'They could see how hard you were trying. All except for Stratton. He's so anxious to get out of here, he'd love to see the WAAC fail.'

'Come on,' Page said, 'they're posting the gig sheet.'

Jill's face fell even farther. 'Oh, I know I'll get a personal gig.'

They joined the first-floor squads crowding around the bulletin board. A woman from first platoon let out a wail. '*No!* It can't be. I remember tying all my shoelaces. I distinctly remember . . .'

Jill saw her name with a lovely round zero next to it. 'I can't believe it. No gigs!'

'Damn!' Elisabeth said aloud. After all her hard work, there was one gig next to her name on the detail roster, with the explanation 'Laundry tubs with cleaning powder residue.' 'Damn!' she repeated. 'What do they want? Those tubs are to wash clothes in, not to do brain surgery.'

'Don't worry, Elisabeth,' Page said, eyeing the commendation for her mop rack, 'there were only two gigs in the barracks. That's one short of being restricted to post. We'll all get our passes.'

'I don't know about the rest of you,' Elisabeth said, anger distorting her usually controlled voice, 'but I had no plans to remain in this hell-hole another weekend if we'd got a hundred gigs.'

'You don't mean you'd have gone AWOL,' Jill said, disbelief written on her face.

But Elisabeth, already on her way back to her area, didn't answer.

'Candidate Hammersmith.' Jill saw Sergeant Wolford standing by the screened front door. 'Report to Lieutenant Stratton in the orderly room.'

She felt her knees weaken. 'Oh God, Bunny,' she said, turning to the older woman, 'I knew it! Oh God — they wouldn't wash me out for a dumb mistake, would they?'

'Of course not, kiddo,' Bunny said and gave Jill's arm a reassuring pat. 'Maybe ten lashes with the cat-o'-nine-tails in the PX at high noon.'

Jill, her teeth biting into her lower lip, relaxed somewhat. 'Damn it — be serious?'

'I am, Jill. The best thing you could do for yourself is to let up. You're wound so tight you're going to pop a spring.

Now go see what Lieutenant Riding Crop wants so that we can catch the noon trolley to the big city of Des Moines.'

'Wait for me,' Jill called back just before the screen slammed behind her.

Later, on the trolley crowded with Waacs on their first overnight pass, Jill recalled the kindness in Lieutenant Stratton's voice. 'He's not as bad as he seems,' she told her three friends.

'But what did he want?' Page asked.

'He just told me not to worry. Asked me why I enlisted, how I liked the WAAC so far — personal questions like that.'

Elisabeth stared at the track ahead, a slight smile playing about her lips. Bunny looked at Page, one eyebrow raised.

'I saw that,' Jill spoke rapidly. 'Have you forgotten I'm engaged? Besides, he's not like that.' She was surprised at her own vehemence.

'I'm sure he's not, Jill,' Page said, 'but be careful. You know they can wash out an OC who fraternizes with an officer.'

Bunny rolled her eyes. 'And if he's her own *platoon officer* they stand her against the wall and call the firing squad!'

6

WAAC days, WAAC days,
Dear old break-your-back-days . . .
— *Barracks ditty sung to the tune of* 'School Days'

'Fall out in five minutes!' Sergeant Wolford's command voice filled the barracks. 'Dress for the afternoon is class-A uniform and raincoats.'
Bunny slammed her fist against the foot locker she was

sitting on. 'Damned if I'm going to ruin a starched uniform under that rubber steam bath they call a raincoat, then have to wash and iron all night.' She quickly stripped to her bra and OD panties and slipped into the heavy rubber coat.

Page laughed in spite of herself. 'Bunny, you can't do that.'

'Watch me! I've found the perfect way to stay cool and get out of all that laundry.'

The platoon snapped to under Sergeant Wolford's baleful eye. 'Straighten up those ranks.'

In the midst of their minute shuffling to the right and front, and without warning, the rain that had been falling steadily for an hour suddenly stopped, and the sun came out bright and hot. Stratocirrus clouds of steam swirled about the platoon.

'*Take off raincoats!*' Wolford boomed.

Bunny felt every eye on her and heard some hastily swallowed snickers. Damn!

'Palermo, would you like to join the rest of us?'

'No, Sergeant. I don't think I'd better.'

'Wolford was apoplectic. 'I've had just about enough of your —'

'Sergeant, I'm out of uniform — I mean *really* out.'

The suppressed snickers erupted now from every rank and file.

Wolford's face was red. 'Platoon, *'ten-hut*! Candidate, you've got three minutes to get into Class A.'

Bunny raced to the barracks, threw on her uniform and ran as fast as her sore feet allowed back to the formation. Damn! How was she to know the rain would stop at that very minute?

'Candidate Palermo, you'll walk extra fire patrol for two hours a day in full Class A for the rest of the week. *'toon!* Double time — *march!*'

Sergeant Wolford's command brought an involuntary groan from half of Second Platoon.

'You're at attention in ranks,' his voice grated over them. 'The next time you don't like an order, the whole platoon can spend Sunday afternoon policing the post. Is that all right with you, Hammersmith, if that's still your name?'

Page ground her teeth. The sarge was in a foul mood today. He had pounced on Bunny — but she had pulled a dumb stunt. Still, picking on Jill by reminding her of that silly mistake she'd made during command inspection was just plain mean.

Wolford sang out the fast pace, 'Hut-hut-hut-hut.'

Page settled into the cadence, legs and arms pumping. She knew she had stretched her body beyond any physical endurance level she had ever needed before. How much more could she expect of herself? This morning Second Platoon had completed an hour of close-order drill, an hour of physical training which had left their seersucker PT dresses and fatigue hats limp with perspiration. Jumping jacks, toe touches, knee bends. Now they were being double-timed to class and were expected to be mentally sharp for the next three hours.

Didn't the sarge ever wear out? He seemed to have a body like an iron rod, always straight, always strong.

'Pick 'em up, Palermo,' Wolford ordered.

Out of the corner of her eye, Page saw Bunny skip to get back into step, her face distorted from the pain of pounding her badly swollen feet against the hard-packed earth.

Another brief afternoon shower drenched them as they reached the classroom area, and made everything worse. Humidity. Uniforms. Tempers.

'Got a cigarette, Hannaday?' Henrietta Hawks, a woman from First Platoon, asked, irritation creeping into her tone.

'Sure, Hank.' Page extended the pack. 'Keep it. It's too hot to inhale.'

'When I think I could be sitting in Seattle right now, trying to keep warm . . .'

Page nodded. The heat was everybody's favourite gripe; even mess-hall food ran a poor second.

She heard a man clearing his throat around the corner of the classroom building. 'My God, Sergeant, these women are making better grades in Company Administration than West Point cadets!'

It was Lieutenant Stratton's voice.

'Lieutenant,' Wolford's unmistakable voice spoke next, 'women just naturally take to paperwork, but that don't mean they should be officers, same as men. Come right down to it, sir, they won't cut it in your Principles of Leadership class.'

Page leaned exhausted against the side of the building. She didn't mean to eavesdrop, but she was too tired to move out of range — and now too angry at what she'd overheard.

'I don't know,' the lieutenant was saying good-naturedly. Page had the feeling that he enjoyed the sergeant's ill humour and egged him on.

'Lieutenant,' Wolford said irritably, 'do you want to spend the rest of the war nursemaiding a bunch of women playing soldiers? It's just like when we was kids and our sisters was always pestering to play our games — only this time we can't keep them out.' Page saw Wolford's hand squash a cigarette in the butt can attached to the corner of the building.

'I understand what you're saying, Sergeant, but some of them are kinda cute — that little one from California especially . . .'

''scuse me, Sir.' Wolford blew his whistle. 'Break's over,' he yelled.

Page watched the Waacs field-strip their cigarettes, grind the tobacco into the dirt with their heels and roll the paper into tiny white balls which they tucked into the corners of their shirt pockets. She was curious to hear what the lieutenant would have said about Jill, although Jill ignored any warnings against the handsome officer. Wolford was another matter. She had thought that by excellent work the Waacs would win him over. Instead, the better they marched on the drill field, the higher grades they made in their classes, the sharper their skirt creases, the more he resented them. She wanted to shout at him: we don't want to take anything away from you — we want to add a new dimension to army life. Instead, she wearily took her place in line and marched in to her squad seat next to Jill, Bunny and Elisabeth at one of the front tables.

The windows were open, but not a whisper of fresh air stirred through them. She looked at her friends, all of them hot and tired. She realized that the physical and mental stress of the past three weeks had been the most exhausting period of their lives and that the next three weeks of OC would be even worse. They were cramming three months of training into half that time — up before dawn, working until late at night. The WAAC was on trial, she knew, and Director Hobby needed trained women soldiers to show to the world — and soon. The only thing that made it bearable was the feeling that every woman in Company One and the rest of the OC companies was in the same boat with her.

This military experience with other women was different from any other, she thought, different from boarding school and college, different from civilian friendships. During training the polite barriers of ordinary friendship tumbled and each woman quickly got to know the others' most intimate secrets. It happened to everyone, even Elisabeth. Her cool, aloof manner had not changed much, but since she had shared the same marching, calisthenics and tear-gas drills she had become, not popular in the platoon, but less unpopular than she might have been.

Bunny, with her self-deprecation and the nurturing she disguised as wisecracks, was easily the most popular woman in the barracks.

And Jill? It was just heartbreaking to see how she pushed herself, always demanding so much. She had the rigid determination of the youthful idealist who tries to make wishes become facts through the sheer force of desire. She did not have the self-confidence yet to appear even a little confused. Page hoped with all her heart that Jill would never fall; she might not be able to get up again.

Page looked around the crowded room at the familiar faces of her barrack mates, and outside another WAAC Company passed, their guidon preceding them. All of these women were meeting physical stress — some for the first time in their lives. Girls in America weren't raised to accept sore muscles, fevers from tetanus shots, sprains and bruises, too little sleep, all without quitting. And yet these women were doing just that, and some were doing it while wondering if their men — at Guadalcanal or on the North Atlantic — were still alive. *Oh God, she was proud to be one of them.*

And what about her own evaluation? Everyone assumed for her a worldly competence she knew she did not possess, just because she was an army brat. Nothing substituted for experience, and General Hannaday's little girl had never lived on her own away from her father's plan for her life — to marry a military man and settle into being a professional officer's wife. She had heard so many of the other OCs worry about losing their independence in the women's army, of having to suppress the qualities that gave them their special identity. She almost laughed when she listened to them. These last few weeks had given her the only unobstructed view she had ever had of what Page Hannaday was really like.

She felt like an eyewitness at her own baptism. And she was pleased — thrilled, even — with what she saw. She had learned that she could accept army discipline, that she could march another hour longer than her body told her she could, that she could have a claustrophobic attack and leave her gas mask on anyway — out of loyalty to her comrades, but partly because she gloried in following orders, especially difficult ones. All the superficial things had gone: silly prejudices, the need for personal luxuries — all had melted away, and she discovered that they had really meant nothing to her, less than nothing.

Page recognized the meaning of this new idea of herself. She ought to; she'd heard her father lecture dinner parties, cronies and his son often enough. A soldier's personal pride, he'd called it. He'd never included her in his philosophizing. Women weren't supposed to understand. Would she ever be able to tell him that she understood — no, that *she* had what he admired?

A nudge on her arm erased her father's image and brought her back to the converted barrack classroom. 'Wake up, Page,' Bunny murmured beside her, rubbing her sore feet under the table.

Page whispered back, 'Thanks — but I'm awake.' The classrooms were so hot they took turns keeping each other awake.

Stratton droned on, reading an army manual, which Page had practically memorized the night before. Her mind wandered, and her father returned unbidden to her thoughts. What would he say if he could see his pretty green-eyed daughter with perspiration dripping off the end of her chin, her uniform sodden? She knew better than to wish it. He would not like what he saw. He wasn't opposed to hard work, but he wouldn't understand the self-control she was beginning to exert on her life — a control quite as strong as his own. What a paradox, she thought. Here, in this women's army, she was seemingly totally controlled — marched from one place to another — and yet had more self-control than she had ever had. She had lost her privacy in this mob of women, but she was now more intimately alone with herself than she had ever been in her father's house with a bedroom of her own.

'Candidate Hannaday!'

Page jumped to her feet, realizing by the lieutenant's tone that she must have been called on before but hadn't heard. 'Sir!'

Stratton was striding up and down the front of the classroom as he talked, but the riding crop was no longer part of his outfit. 'Tell us, Candidate Hannaday, what do you think the first duty of a WAAC officer is?'

'To get the job done, sir,' she said, standing to attention. 'To see that the army mission assigned to her and her enlisted women is carried out as swiftly and completely as possible.'

Stratton smiled faintly. 'You can stand easy, Candidate; this isn't a ladies' West Point.' He looked around the room, and his eyes circled back and rested on Jill, although he spoke to Page. 'That sounds like a good book answer, Hannaday, but how does the WAAC officer accomplish this swift, complete mission?'

'Sir, through good leadership. It's easy to give orders,

65

but I don't believe women can be driven, they have to be led. I would treat enlisted Waacs like adult women instead of children, women I expected to do their best. I think people quite often give back just what is expected of them.'

She was surprised at the confidence in her own voice. But she hadn't meant to sound like a know-it-all either. She hadn't known what she believed until he asked her. How much more knowing, she wondered, was there in her that had not been prodded to the surface?

Stratton, his face intent, did not move on to question another candidate. 'Tell me, Candidate Hannaday,' he said, facing her, 'what would you do if you were to find that one of your women disobeyed your orders, but you could not determine which one was guilty?'

'Sir, I would use every means to discover the identity of that individual. Wrongdoing that is not punished is bad for everyone's morale.' *Bless you, Father, for teaching me that*, she thought, gazing steadily at him.

A gravelly cough from the rear of the room reminded her that Sergeant Wolford was an interested onlooker.

'But suppose,' Lieutenant Stratton persisted, 'that you investigate without success. Would you then punish the entire platoon to get to the guilty one?'

'No, sir, I would not.' This time she answered from her own feeling. Her father had often punished whole companies — once a battalion — knowing that the outraged soldiers would take care of the guilty man in their own way. Some instinct told her this would work badly with women. 'I think women rebel at unjust treatment. As a woman, I respond better to positive leadership.'

'Is that right?' the lieutenant answered with a hint of a teacher's sarcasm at being instructed by a student in front of the class. 'And just how would you accomplish this miracle of feminine leadership?'

She could see she had offended him. 'Sir, I'm here to learn. Perhaps I've — '

'No, no, Candidate, please go on and enlighten me — indeed, all of us.'

Page knew there was no retreat possible. She hadn't

wanted to seem like the new girl who wants to change everything, but the lieutenant was not going to let her back down.

'For example, sir,' she plunged ahead, 'I've noticed that when you needle men they become more competitive, but with women — well, the same treatment can frighten them into giving up. I see women responding to firm leadership with lots of praise and encouragement.' From the impatient look on Lieutenant Stratton's face, she knew she was going on too long, but it was as if an idea in the pupal stage had suddenly spread wings, carrying her along with it. 'A leader of women must be a *caring* officer — and show it. That doesn't mean she can't be tough, yes, when the mission demands it, and tough on herself too. But along with toughness a WAAC officer must show compassion and understanding to her troops. I think she must also keep a light touch — humour would help; women tend to see humour as caring, not weakness.'

An hour later, Page was lying on her bed, her heart thumping wearily in her chest. She was sure her out-spokenness had marked her a show-off in Lieutenant Stratton's eyes. God alone knew what Sergeant Wolford thought. She had probably confirmed every one of his Waac-hating views.

'Bravo, Page,' Bunny said, raising herself on one elbow, her feet elevated on her pillow. 'I think you gave our little tin soldier a lesson in leadership today.'

'I didn't mean to do that.'

Bunny shrugged. 'At this point, Page, I think your idea of WAAC leadership is just as good as his. Somebody better tell the lad that women and men are different.' Bunny laughed, her voice just loud enough to tease Jill, who was bent over her foot locker, cleaning her lapel insignia. 'And I know who that someone could be.'

'Say what you want,' Jill said, looking at them from under her lashes, 'I think he's really very nice.' She and Lieutenant Stratton had bumped into each other near the Iowa Hotel last Saturday night, and had met later in an obscure little bar for a drink. She remembered every moment of it, every word he'd said, but most of all she remembered when he had casually covered her small hand with his long fingers. Something had happened then, something physical, warm and wonderful, a feeling she had pulled back from because she knew instinctively that it threatened her plan to devote her life to Neil after the war. Jill felt the remembered warmth return.

'Why, Jill,' Bunny said, 'you're blushing.'

After lights out, Page remembered the look on Jill's face. Surely the girl wasn't falling in love with Stratton. But she'd seen the signs, the unmistakable flush when Jill looked at him, the look of longing instantly suppressed that one woman can read in another woman's face. She met Jill's eyes for a moment, then looked away. The sudden tensing of Jill's cheek muscle made Page feel like an eavesdropper spying on a painful private hurt. How hellish to feel responsible for the crippled shell of one man while falling in love with another — this one quite definitely a whole man.

At least Page had been spared that awful conflict, and then she felt ashamed of the thought. Her feeling for Jimmy Southworth had been more like a passionate friendship than love. When he asked her to marry him at the Annapolis June Week dance, she had said yes without thinking about it too deeply. This was her life, playing itself out as she had always known it must. Her healthy young body responded to his that night. She had halfheartedly tried to twist out of his arms when he took her back to the hotel, but he stepped into her room, held her and kissed her hard, not pulling away until near dawn.

They had announced their engagement and chosen their silver and china patterns. After a month's leave, he had gone off to Pearl Harbor as the newest ensign on the battleship *Arizona*. Then she entered a new and equally predictable phase, months of planning of a June 1942 wedding — the great rite of passage of every woman's life.

When she learned of his death a week after the attack, learned that he would spend eternity sealed inside the hull of the capsized *Arizona*, she had cried for him. She had cried for James Ridgely Southworth III, remembering him, long-legged, suntanned, missing easy tennis forehands because he watched her at courtside instead of the ball. She remembered he loved her in blue; she remembered and cried for the end of a young life.

But she had not cried for Page. In her deepest self, as far inside as she had penetrated in twenty-three years, she knew she felt no deep loss. That inner Page was intact, untouched. Only then had she faced the feeling of relief; she fought it down — but it came back again and again. Something deep inside her hoped that her obligation to fill a role ordained for her at birth had been fulfilled with Jimmy's death. She had done what she had been raised to do, what every young woman of her generation was expected to do. And now why couldn't she be free, free to use her life as she wanted? No answer came to her, so the question remained a question.

7

DIEPPE RAID: On August 19, 1942, some 6,100 British and Canadian commandos with 30 tanks stage a trial invasion of France, but are pinned down on the beaches; 1,179 die, 2,190 are taken prisoner by the Germans.

The following Saturday, after inspection, Elisabeth stood at the registration desk in the Iowa Hotel, oblivious to the stares of the other Waacs and the male officers crowding the counter, hoping to get a room.

'Good afternoon, Mrs Gardner,' the desk clerk said with exaggerated politeness, handing over her key. 'Your room is ready as usual,' he added.

'I hope not, since last weekend the room had not been

properly cleaned.'

'My apologies, Mrs Gardner,' the clerk said, half bowing and muttering something about all the good help quitting to go into war work. 'Today I checked your room myself, and if there is any little thing you need — day or night, mind — please don't hesitate to call on me.'

'Thank you,' she said, ignoring his oily eagerness.

'Oh, Mrs Gardner, don't forget your messages,' he said, stretching over the counter.

She felt his fingertips under the pieces of paper lightly brush across her breast. He was one of those sly, sleazy men who touched women's bodies under the guise of accident. A more naïve woman, seeing his friendly manner, would have felt guilty about her suspicions, but Elisabeth knew such men for what they were, and used their weakness for her own benefit. She smiled slightly. Better to let the clerk win a little and hope to win more. It did her no harm, since she had long ago learned to separate her feelings from her body, and it did wonders for prompt room service.

In her room, she removed her uniform and slipped into a light silk kimono she had purchased locally and kept in the closet, just for the few weekend hours when she could escape from Fort Des Moines. She picked up the phone, ordered ice and took a precious bottle of scotch from her night-table drawer. When the ice arrived, she poured herself a double.

Fluffing the pillows, she propped herself on the bed and took a large, thirsty swallow from the glass, glancing briefly at her messages. All three were calls from Marne in Texas, as she had known they would be. She tossed them on the bed covers. The thought that now consumed her was an idea that had been growing since her first days at Fort Des Moines. Somehow she must find a way to get back to the life she had earned, back to comfort, beautiful clothes and freedom where she belonged, and she had a wild plan that just might get her — well, halfway back. At least it was worth a try.

The phone rang, and she reached for it.

'Hello,' she said.

'Hold the li-on,' intoned the operator. 'That will be one dollar and fifteen cents for the first three minutes, Lieutenant.'

Elisabeth heard the deep bong of the quarters, the clunk of a nickel and the ping-ping of a dime.

'Elisabeth, are you there?'

'Oh, darling, how *wonderful* to hear your voice,' she said. 'I've been waiting here wishing you'd call again.' She did not think of it as lying. She merely gave men what she knew they wanted.

'I can see you now, sweetheart,' Marne said, his voice the musky tenor of some big men, 'and thinking of you drives me crazy. Just a minute,' he said, noise and music temporarily overwhelming his voice. 'Pipe down, you guys,' he yelled.

'Marne, I can't hear you very well.'

'Sorry, honey, just a few of the guys — but how are you? I called your orderly room, and the charge of quarters gave me this number. Said you were signed out for the weekend on a pass.'

'I've taken a hotel room in Des Moines. I know it's horribly expensive — '

'Darling, I've set up a trust fund with my lawyers. You'll be getting a cheque every month — but only if you promise to buy yourself pretty things.'

'I'm so glad you don't mind. I had to get away from all those women, Marne. There's no privacy, no quiet — everything's so public.'

'I know the Army, darling,' he said, and she heard him take a deep breath. 'I still can't understand why you quit Madame Gabriella's and joined the WAAC. Mother is sick over it. She wrote me that she's heartbroken you didn't come to her.'

Elisabeth sighed and expertly punctuated the next sentence with a tremor. 'Please don't be angry with me,' she said. 'I know it was a terrible mistake, but I — I so wanted you to be proud of me. It sounds silly now, but I thought if I was in the WAAC I would be closer to you.'

'It doesn't sound silly, sweetheart. It's exactly what a

71

wonderful woman like you would think.'

Elisabeth held the telephone tightly. 'Please, please, darling, can't you help me get out of here?'

'How, Elisabeth? How could I do that?'

Then she laid out the plan that had taken shape in her mind. 'Marne, your family has connections in Washington,' she began in a rush, afraid he would interrupt. 'I know you wouldn't ask favours for yourself. But ask for *me* — not to get me out of the Army, I know you can't do that, but to get me somewhere I can do what I was meant to do.' She began to sob, and this time the tears were full of real frustration.

His voice faded in a storm of crackling noises as the operator căme back on the line. 'Your three minutes are up. Please signal when through.'

'Don't cry, darling. What do you want me to do?'

'Marne, I'm going to write to the Quartermaster Corps in Washington and outline what I think is wrong with the WAAC uniform and what I could do to help make it right if I was transferred to the QM department. My letter might get lost at headquarters unless someone saw that it got into the right hands.'

'I've got to go, darling.' His voice was clear again.

'Will you do it, Marne?'

'I'll try. Please stop crying, Elisabeth.'

'Darling,' she said, 'I think of you every minute.'

More atmospheric disturbances, and his voice faded in and out. ' . . . hellish field training . . . love you . . . '

Elisabeth replaced the telephone on its cradle, rolled over and immediately fell asleep.

She was aroused by a knock at her door. 'Who's there?'

Jill's voice answered, 'Second Squad, Second Platoon, Company One, First WAAC Officer Candidate Training Regiment.'

Elisabeth unlocked the door, and Jill, Page and Bunny crowded in.

'Wow,' Jill said, looking around curiously, 'a bathroom all to yourself. How do you rate? I have to share one with these two,' she added, plopping onto the bed. 'Do you know that I had to bribe Bunny with my last Baby Ruth to

72

get her out of our tub?'

'And mighty good it was, too,' Bunny grinned. 'There are three wonders of the modern world — bathtubs and chocolate.'

Page laughed. 'That's only two wonders, Bunny.'

'Is it?' Bunny said, looking puzzled. 'Sounds good enough for three.'

'You know, Elisabeth,' Page said, smiling, 'if you listen to her long enough, she begins to make sense.'

Elisabeth offered them a scotch and water, and stepped into the bathroom to wash the glasses. She felt strange — lost — in the midst of their camaraderie. She had lived two separate lives, the first in the dark shadow of her father's needs, the second in a scramble through the lower layers of New York's fashion world. She had never had the kind of confidences she could share with other women without risking their disgust.

'We're going to have dinner and a drink at Babe's,' Page told Elisabeth, 'and maybe take in a movie.'

'Noel Coward's *In Which We Serve* is playing at the Rivoli,' Bunny said.

Elisabeth started to say no.

'Or if you want to forget the war,' Page said, '*The Road to Morocco* is at the theatre across the street, and it's Bank Night too. Come on — go with us if you have no plans.'

'Come on,' Jill said, bouncing on the bed, 'we'll stick together.'

Elisabeth hesitated by the bathroom door. 'It would take me time to get ready . . .'

'We'll wait,' Bunny said with an engaging smile, 'at least as long as your scotch holds out.'

Suddenly Elisabeth wanted very much to go with them.

With the exception of a few bemused civilians, both floors of Babe's restaurant had almost been taken over by contingents of Waacs on weekend pass.

Genuinely puzzled, Elisabeth asked Page, 'Why do they come here? These are the same women they see every weary day — don't they want to get away?'

'I've wondered, too,' Page answered slowly, frowning a

73

bit in an effort to make her words mean what she wanted them to mean. 'I think it's because we all share the same purpose in life. It's a special feeling — more than family, even — but it's a separateness too, a knowing that no one but another Waac can possibly understand what we understand. We're in another world that outsiders can never be a part of. Male soldiers share this intense comradeship, especially in combat, and now I think we women share it.'

'See, Elisabeth,' Bunny said, 'you ask Page a question about the WAAC and you get a whole damned parade.'

Elisabeth laughed aloud. She leaned against the back of the wooden booth and watched the three of them talking, and realized they had drawn a circle of friendship that included her.

8

When I hear that Serenade in Blue,
I'm somewhere in another world alone with you,
Sharing all the joys we used to know
Many moons ago.
Once again your face comes back to me,
Just like the theme of some forgotten melody
In the album of my memory,
Serenade in Blue.
It seems like only yesterday,
A small café, a crowded floor,
And as we dance the night away,
I hear you say 'Forever more';
And then the song became a sigh, forevermore
became goodbye,
But you remained in my heart.
So tell me, darling, is there still a spark,
Or only lonely ashes of the flame we knew;
Should I go on whistling in the dark?
Serenade in Blue.
—'Serenade in Blue,' *Harry Warren and Mack Gordon*

Desmond Stratton waited impatiently across the street from the Iowa Hotel. It was nearly eleven o'clock at night and Jill had not yet shown up. Each time a group of uniformed women approached the door, he looked for a small figure incongruously clothed in belted khaki. He was not exactly sure why he was waiting for this particular Waac, there were dozens of women around, but each time he thought he would not wait any longer he extended the time for another five minutes.

At last he saw her preceded by her three friends. They were the real lookers in second platoon. If he was going to get into trouble with an OC, why not one of them — Gardner was married, but the other two? Oh, to hell with it, Stratton, he chided himself, you were never good at picking the right woman.

Jill saw him as soon as he saw her. 'Wait for me,' she told her friends, and crossed the street. She saluted, and he returned her salute.

'If you were wearing civvies,' he said, 'I'd risk taking you for a nightcap.'

'I have a dress up in the room.' The words were out of her mouth before she could stop them.

'You game?' he asked.

She nodded yes, a kind of stubborn wildness seizing her. Because she was always proving herself, she was particularly vulnerable to dares. 'Wait around the corner,' she told him.

Up in the room Page and Bunny watched her change into civilian clothes.

'Jill,' Page began, 'if you want to go out with him, just wait until you graduate.'

'Listen, kid,' Bunny agreed, 'you know officer country is off limits.'

But Jill closed her ears to what she didn't want to hear. When she was down on the street again, out of sight of the Iowa Hotel, he took her arm and walked her down a side alley to a dimly lit bar decorated in South Sea murals and fake palms.

Finding a small table against the wall, he asked her,

'What'll you have?'

'I had some good scotch earlier,' she answered, as if it were her usual drink, when in fact it had been her first taste of scotch.

'I'll try,' he said, 'but we may have to settle for a blended whisky. There's a war on, you know, and all the good stuff goes to our boys in uniform — and girls.'

Her large dark eyes smiled up at him from under thick lashes, and she pursed her lips self-consciously over a faint overbite into one of the most kissable mouths he had ever seen. Nice going, chum, he thought, she likes you. Now what?

She watched him walk towards the bar, his tall, slim figure trim in summer tropical worsted. He had a boy's narrow hips, but a man's broad shoulders. She could see that other women's eyes followed him approvingly. Why had he asked her for a drink, when he could have asked Bunny, Page or even Elisabeth? She was puzzled by his attention, and maybe — she was reluctant to admit it — a little frightened.

'Here you are,' he said, putting her drink on a cocktail napkin just as the pianist at the other end of the bar began to play and sing 'Serenade in Blue'. 'I wangled some scotch from under the bar.'

'I'm engaged to be married, Lieutenant Stratton,' she announced, unable to completely understand why she was making such an uncalled-for statement, but making it nonetheless.

He was startled for a moment, then threw back his head and laughed. She was absolutely without guile. That must be why he was attracted to her. She was not at all like his ex-wife, Lois — knowing, cold, grasping and, almost incidentally after that, unfaithful.

Jabbing the air with his swizzle stick, he launched into his autobiography. 'I'm divorced, no children, twenty-nine years old, my parents are dead, I have a degree in electrical engineering, I was a reserve officer called up last March, and, oh yes, I like clam chowder — the red, not the white — Humphrey Bogart movies and women, in reverse order.'

Jill was embarrassed at first by her sudden outburst, but by the time he had finished she was angry that he was making fun of her. She might have left him laughing there had he not put out a hand to stop her.

'Truce, Jill,' he said, serious now, 'let's just enjoy a drink together. You needn't worry that I'll carry you off, or try to marry you.' He took his hand away and lit a Camel, inhaling deeply, his mouth twisting sardonically. 'In fact, Jill, if you *don't* want romance, I'm the safest guy in this room — hell, in the whole Army.'

His words, meant to reassure, disappointed her — more than that, made her feel a strange kind of emptiness as if something struggling for life had aborted.

'I wish you happiness with — what's his name?'

'Neil.'

'With Neil, but as for me, I tried love and discovered I was a hell of a lot happier without it. I live for the moment now, not tomorrow, but tonight — ' almost automatically he gave her his standard make-out line and didn't like himself much for it ' — tonight is all you have, too, Jill.'

She felt the sensual power of male sadness, and came to the brink of agreeing before she pulled back.

'I don't think I could live that way, Lieutenant.'

'Call me Des, Jill, short for Desmond — my mother's idea. It's a name only a woman would pick for a man.'

'I like it.'

He took her hand again. 'I'm glad, because I like you — engaged and all.' He smiled across the table. 'Now,' he said, 'it's your turn. Tell me about Jill Hammersmith.'

She told him then about growing up on a peach ranch in California; about her college years and her fight to be accepted in veterinary school.

He shook his head in mock wonderment. 'I couldn't believe it when I read your 201 file. I never met a lady veterinarian. You must love animals.'

Jill waited for a moment, then said in a soft voice, 'I do.' She paused again, aware that her answer was trite but, even more, was incomplete. 'But it's more than loving animals. I — I trust them to love me just as I am.' Again she felt a flush

77

of embarrassment creep into her face. She seemed always to tell this man more than she intended.

Christ, Des thought, why was he trying to seduce such an innocent? He stood up abruptly. 'It's late — finish your drink and I'll take you back to your hotel.'

Jill was wounded. She must have said something to offend him, or he had decided she was too silly and not worth his time. Maybe he was one of those men who couldn't stand the idea of a woman having a profession, even one she hadn't yet qualified for.

They separated a half block from the hotel and appeared to meet by accident in the lobby.

'What floor?' he asked her as they crossed to the elevators.

'Four.'

'Four, please,' he told the elevator operator.

'You don't need to come to the door with me,' she told him stiffly as the elevator opened onto the fourth floor.

'I'll see you safe, then I won't have you on my conscience,' he said, his voice gruff now because he was angry and ashamed of himself. What had he been thinking? She was a child-woman, sweet and uncomplicated, and thus far more dangerous to play around with than an experienced woman. Even an obvious cobra like her friend Elisabeth would have been safer.

'I can take care of myself,' she said for the second time that evening, not understanding his sudden emotional withdrawal.

'Sure you can,' he said, walking fast, forcing her to half-run down the corridor. 'Okay, here you are. Where's your key?'

Her lower lip trembled as she fumbled with her purse, and her vision was suddenly blurred. 'I'm sorry,' she said, looking up at him.

'For what?'

'Whatever I did that made you so mad at me.'

He could take only so much, he thought, and in equal parts of frustration, anger and desire he pulled her to him.

'Des —' His name came in a rush from her mouth, and he

caught the sweet breath of it as he bent to kiss her, his lips trying to match the hardness of his angry heart — trying, but failing. He ached with the taste of her, hungry to learn more, plunge deeper, and for a brief moment he wavered, but finally he thrust her firmly away from him and walked swiftly back towards the safety of the elevator. With each step the distance between them widened and he became more determined never to run the risk of falling in love with her.

'Back so soon, Lieutenant?' the elevator operator snickered, an adolescent leer pulling at his mouth, as the lift started down.

'Yes, I'm back, kid, and I'll give you some free advice.'

'Yeah, I get lots of that.'

'Stay away from the good girls, sonny. They're more trouble than a guy can handle.'

From down the corridor, Jill watched him until the elevator doors shut behind him. She was not sophisticated enough to see his anguish, or to guess at its origin. She only knew that this man's kiss had awakened a need to melt into him, a need that Neil's kiss never had touched and now — oh, his poor scarred face — never could touch. She could only believe that having awakened this need, Des had found it uninviting and rejected it.

Fumbling for the lock, she tiptoed into the room where Bunny and Page were sleeping. She undressed, and burrowed miserably into her pillow.

Bunny heard Jill come in, and guessed at the cause of the muffled sobs. She thought about going to the girl and telling her that no man was worth even one of her tears. But she didn't move.

How could she help the kid? Trying would only stir memories of Johnny P. — all her memories — until she ached and throbbed inside and out with them.

She lay there awake, remembering him, long after the girl in the next bed had ceased her tears and fallen into a restless sleep.

9

*If incendiary bombs fall, play a spray from a garden
hose (never splash or stream) of water on the bomb
. . . A jet splash, stream or bucket of water will
make it explode.*

— Office of Civil Defense Manual

'**M**an in the barracks!'
     Jill heard the cry and grabbed her fatigue
dress to cover her khaki-coloured slip.

'All right, people, *listen up*!' Wolford's gruff croak
echoed down the first-floor squad room.

A collective sigh went up from thirty-five throats. They
had hoped to spend their study hour under cover from the
relentless Midwest sunshine.

'Second Platoon, fall out for an extra drill period in
Class-A uniform. Five minutes!'

The sigh grew to a groan.

Jill knew why. Class-A meant nine layers of soggy
material belted around each waist — heavy jersey panties,
girdle, slip, cotton shirt, double chino skirt waistband,
heavy cotton jacket, double jacket belt.

An inspection was imminent; they were ready for that.
No Waac ever sat on her bed until after retreat call at 17.30
hours. Latrine basins were carefully wiped after daytime
use. But extra drill under the midday sun!

'There's a special place for guys like Wolford —' Bunny
puffed, struggling into a uniform that almost refused to
slide over her damp body and pushing her chronically
swollen feet into dry service shoes — 'but unfortunately it's
not as hot there as Iowa in August.'

'Knock it off, Palermo,' Hank Hawks yelled from the
other end of the barracks. 'He's just doing his job.'

'Damned apple polisher,' Bunny muttered.

'It's the green guidon,' Jill said. 'He wants to win it this
Saturday at the graduation parade.'

'We ought to complain about such treatment,' Elisabeth said, gingerly rubbing her sculptured nose, now tipped a sunburned red.

'And confirm his opinion of us. Never!' Page said, knotting her tie. 'If we do nothing else in the WAAC, let's show Wolford —'

'It won't be easy,' Bunny said, her face pink from exertion.

'Nothing in the Army is easy,' Elisabeth said, wondering how she ever thought it could be. Even Gabriella, a tyrant in her showroom, had been a sweetheart compared to Wolford on the drill field.

Jill smoothed the wrinkles from her skirt just as the whistle blew. The sun was high overhead when she reached the formation. Lights danced in from the side of her vision, and her head spun slowly like a spent top.

Five minutes later, Sergeant Wolford, wearing his usual sour expression, marched them down the broad street past Officers' Row. As the column turned onto the grass of the parade ground, Jill stumbled, then caught herself.

'Pick 'em up and put 'em down,' Wolford roared and glared straight at Jill. 'Hell,' he muttered loud enough for the whole platoon to hear, 'what can you expect of a candidate who doesn't even know her own name?'

Damn him! What did he *want* from her? Jill fixed her eyes on the back of the woman in front of her and tried to count cadence in her mind, but she had trouble concentrating. Her head was whirling faster, and now nausea gripped her.

''Toon, halt!' Wolford yelled. 'Left face! Hammersmith, front and centre!'

Somehow Jill marched to the front of the platoon and faced him.

'What's the matter with you, Candidate Hammersmith?'

'Just a bit dizzy, Sergeant.' Thank God, he had seen she wasn't feeling well. She wouldn't have to fall out on her own and prove to him that she couldn't take it.

'Hammersmith, do you want to go on sick call?' His sceptical tone said more than the words. He didn't believe her!

'No, Sergeant, I don't *want* to go, but — ' she began, hoping he would insist.

'Then get back in ranks, Hammersmith,' he barked, 'and we'll find out if you're any kind of officer material.'

'Yes, Sergeant.'

Somehow she bumbled through the drill and back to the barracks.

'Jill — my God,' Page said, helping her to her bed. 'You're positively green, and shivering. Lie down and I'll make a cold compress. No,' Page ordered as Jill struggled to get up, 'down you go and don't worry about the bed. I'll make it again.'

'What's wrong with Jill?' Elisabeth asked, tossing her hat and gloves onto her bed.

'Heat exhaustion, I think.' Page bathed Jill's face and pressed the cool cloth against her temples.

Elisabeth loosened Jill's tie and jacket belt. 'What was it they said in First Aid class about salt?'

Page checked Jill's clammy skin. 'Have you been taking your salt tablets regularly, Jill?'

'I — I may have forgotten once or twice . . .'

Bunny rushed up. 'Page, what's wrong with the kid?'

'Heat has her down. Bunny, get a glass of salty water for her.'

Jill, fighting the dizziness, tried to focus her eyes. 'Did I show him, Page?'

Page's lips were pressed together in a stubborn line. 'He's not the kind that learns easily, Jill. The sergeant doesn't want us in his Army; I guess we'll never prove to him that women belong here.'

'Page, he has no human sympathy,' Jill whispered, the words an effort. 'Surely, he wouldn't have let one of his men . . .'

'It's obvious he thought you were goldbricking.'

'But, Page,' Jill struggled on, her words mixed with tears, 'I've heard him say that half of us aren't going to make it, that we'll wash out when it gets tough.'

Bunny came back carrying a glass of salt-clouded water. 'Here, drink this.'

Elisabeth came around to the other side of Jill's bed and awkwardly patted her head. 'Don't worry about the sergeant. He's mad because he can't get a reassignment. I saw him almost on his knees to Stratton this morning.'

'I — I don't think I could take washing out with only a week to go.' Jill was scarcely listening to the other women. 'I know that sounds odd, since I took such a stupid chance with Lieutenant Stratton last Saturday, but . . . ' Another Waac had just been discharged by the 'murder board'. Kansas had been the fourth OC to wash out since training began. Jill would never forget how frighteningly empty her bed had looked, mattress rolled slackly to the top, lockers open, clothes gone. Where once had been an OC — someone Jill had spent every minute of training with — there was within the space of a few minutes absolutely nothing left to show that Kansas had ever existed. Why? Nobody knew or was saying. 'That's the awful part, Page — not knowing what they want from us.'

'Ssshh.' Page placed the compress over her eyes. 'You must stop flagellating yourself. You're not going to wash out. Everything's all right now. Save your energy.'

'That's right, kiddo,' Bunny said. 'Just get through the afternoon classes and then you stay flat on that bed tonight — we'll do your detail for you.'

Jill knew that her friends made sense, but she struggled to sit up anyway. 'I can't just *lie* here. I've got my shoes and brass to shine, and — '

'Down on that bed, Candidate Hammersmith — ' Bunny's voice was a perfect imitation of Sergeant Wolford's gravel-flecked growl ' — and that's an order.'

'You two stay with her,' Elisabeth said, a crazy scheme forming in the back of her mind. 'I'll be back.'

'Where are you going?' Bunny asked.

'I've had enough of a certain sergeant.' Elisabeth said, squaring her Hobby hat. 'I'll see you at the mess hall.' She ignored them when they called her back.

Elisabeth was furious as she crunched up the gravel path to the orderly room. She marvelled at how angry she was, not the cool controlled anger she had always used to bend others to her will, but the hot anger of injustice. How dare Wolford treat Jill this way! Of course, she thought, her mouth curving up the tiniest bit, even this sudden concern for fair play had its uses.

She opened the OR door and stopped in front of the company clerk's desk. 'Candidate Gardner requests permission to speak to Sergeant Wolford.'

'Just a minute,' the corporal said, 'and I'll see if the sergeant is in his cubicle.' A minute later he returned. 'Yeah, Candidate — go on in.'

Elisabeth found herself facing a puzzled Sergeant Wolford.

'What is it, Gardner?'

'Lay off Hammersmith, Wolford.' She meant to push him as far as she needed to. *Come on, you bastard, wash me out!* How could she lose? When the word got around, she'd be the heroine, but most of all she'd be out of this women's army.

'What did you say?'

She spoke the words slowly. 'I said lay off Jill Hammersmith or I'll go over your head to Marshall himself if I need to.'

'Candidate, you're insubordinate. When you speak to me you call me Sergeant. I don't give a good goddamn what you think of me, but you will respect these stripes.' He tapped the stripes and hash marks that covered his right sleeve. 'And, another thing, *you* don't give *me* orders. Until you have bars on your shoulders, I give you orders — and you jump.'

'You heard me. If you don't lay off Hammersmith, I'll go to Hobby, Colonel Faith and throw in *Life* magazine. You can kiss your pension goodbye — *Sergeant*,' she added with pointed sarcasm.

He got up slowly from his desk and walked around behind her, but she had played this game of nerves before and remained facing away from him.

Wolford walked back behind his desk and thrust his face towards Elisabeth's. 'Gardner, you're not the smart gal you think you are, even with your high and mighty ways. Do you take me for a sap? I know why you're here. You don't give a small shit about Hammersmith; you want to take a hike through the main gate at high noon.' He smiled, relaxing. Even though he had to admit he might have been riding Hammersmith too hard — tryin' to toughen her up — damned if he didn't enjoy taking the haughty Gardner dame down a peg or two. 'Let me tell you the order of the day. You are *not* gonna wash out for insubordination. You are *not* gonna get another gig, or I'll restrict you to the post till you get your detail right. And don't try to report on sick call too much, 'cause I'll have you recycled, and you can repeat OCs — in my platoon — till the war's over if needs be. Is that clear, Gardner? I'm makin' it my *personal* duty to see you stay in this WAAC for the duration. We didn't want you women, but here you are, and, by God, you're gonna *keep* your oath of enlistment just like the rest of us. Dismissed!'

Elisabeth shrugged, swung on her heel, and left. Her plan had misfired. She'd done no good for herself — or even Jill. How could anyone figure this damned army? None of these dumb jerks played by the rules of probability.

Sergeant Wolford stared at the gorgeous figure in full retreat. Whew! What was a woman like that doin' in this man's army? But the others, now — well, they hadn't whined, and he had been pushing them plenty hard. Maybe they had the makings of good soldiers after all — even that half-pint Hammersmith.

By Wednesday of their last week in OCs, Jill had recovered. And Sergeant Wolford wasn't riding her anymore, thanks to Elisabeth. The story of how she had faced down the sarge for Jill's sake was being retold and embellished in every barrack and dayroom. No matter how many times Elisabeth waved her off, Jill would never forget what a pal she'd been.

Jill felt so much better, she was even alert in the most boring afternoon class of all. She was actually listening intently to Master Sergeant Baker of S-3 drone on about the correct distribution of property accounting forms when he stopped to read a note handed to him.

'Candidate Hammersmith, report to the OC Review Board at headquarters building on the double.'

The shock of it rooted her momentarily to the bench. Page, Bunny and Elisabeth turned apprehensive faces towards her. Jill felt their concern, but she knew they could not help her. This was something she had to face alone. She gripped the table, rose and walked the gauntlet of eyes, some compassionate, some curious, to the rear of the room and out of the building.

The thing she had feared most had happened to her. Washout! She had worked so hard only to have her effort despised in the end. Had Wolford turned her in for heat prostration? Why would he, when it had been his fault? Des, then? She couldn't believe they would kick her out for spending an off-duty hour with Des, no matter what her friends said. The sound of her mother's voice kept time with her hurrying footsteps: 'Jill, you take after the Hammersmiths all right, just can't seem to do anything right.'

She caught sight of herself in a window as she entered the building, shoulders slumped, face contorted. What a sight she was. Unmilitary. Straighten those shoulders, Candidate! She did not know exactly what she faced, but she was certain she would not help her case if she lost her military bearing.

She reported to the counter clerk and was told to sit down and wait. That's the Army, she thought, hurry up and wait. Don't panic, she told herself again; and again, like a silent, tuneless whistle in the cemetery, the words were a litany of comfort. To be on the safe side, she invoked the protection of Pallas Athene, the WAAC symbol borrowed from the Greek goddess of femininity and war. It couldn't hurt, she thought defiantly, as if to silence her Episcopalian forebears.

'This way, Candidate,' the clerk said.

She knocked on the closed door and responded to a muffled 'Enter'.

'Candidate Hammersmith, Jill H., reporting as

requested, sir,' she said smartly, saluting the senior officer and ordering her voice to be firm. They must see her as self-confident and under control.

'Candidate, you don't have to be nervous. The purpose of this hearing is not to hurt you, but to listen to your side in this matter.'

'Yes, sir. I'm eager to answer any questions you might have.' She was pleased with her words and her tone. They showed good military bearing.

'Good.'

He introduced himself as Captain Dawson on Colonel Faith's staff, and then introduced next to him a Lieutenant Giles of Infantry. 'And of course,' he added, 'you know your platoon officer, Lieutenant Stratton.'

Jill felt her head jerk around. She had been so intent on making a good impression she hadn't noticed him at the far end of the table, sitting apart from the others. Relief filled her. They couldn't have been caught or Des wouldn't be here. Whatever this was about, she could count on him. For the first moment in the last hellish half hour she could swallow past the lump in her throat.

The captain, after what seemed an eternity but could not have been more than two minutes passing while he flipped through her 201 personnel file, finally said, 'Candidate, your academic record during officer's training has been outstanding. You deserve congratulations for your intellectual achievements — ' he coughed into his hand '— but there are some questions about your fitness for a commission.' He turned to the lieutenant of infantry and nodded.

'Candidate,' Lieutenant Giles began, 'you're very young. Of course, your age is not your fault, but it does have a bearing on your maturity.' The lieutenant looked at Des.

Des looked up from the papers in front of him, a glint of warning in his eyes, a muscle pulsing in his cheek. He was trying to tell her something, but she didn't know what. 'Candidate — ' his voice thin and flat ' — we have an MP report that you were seen in Des Moines last Saturday night, fraternizing with an unidentified officer.' He looked at her steadily, his eyes flashing messages she could only guess at. 'Are you prepared to name the officer?'

The captain's curt voice interrupted Des. 'It will go easier with you if you do, Candidate.'

Jill's heart beat loud enough for the whole board to hear. Dazed, she wanted to believe that Des wasn't a coward, but she could allow herself no time to think about it. All her energy must be spent in a desperate attempt to save herself from the axe. 'I admit I had a brief social encounter with an officer' — she willed her voice to remain steady — 'but I will not name him. I cannot believe this would bear more on my fitness to command than the record I've made since I've been here.'

A faint note of pride crept into her voice. She had stood up to them. The best thing, her father had always told her, was to meet every problem head on. She couldn't fight their intangible attitudes towards her age and size and maturity, but she would adopt a firm attitude of her own that they could not change. The idea was to be sure about herself. She would have to be stronger in her feelings than they were in theirs.

'Of course, your abilities are not in question.' Des looked directly at her now, his eyes clouded and miserable.

The captain interrupted again, impatiently. 'Lieutenant Stratton, let's not get off target here.' He extracted a sheet from the table and waved it at her. 'Candidate, you are here to answer a specific report, which bears on your ability to accept army discipline. You've already admitted a breach of military custom.'

Jill was enough of a soldier to know that any excuse she offered a superior would go hard on her. No excuse, sir, was the standard military response.

'Sir, I don't question the Army's right to judge me' — all her will went into an effort to keep her voice controlled, knowing that everything depended on the impression she left with them — 'but, Captain, let me say something more for the record.' She forced herself to look them in the eye, one after another. 'I admit my mistake, but I think there's more to judge here today than an off-duty drink with a superior officer. We Waacs need time to learn about the Army, but the Army needs time to learn about us, too — and maybe about the new Army men *and* women must create together. Can the Army really expect its soldiers to deny they are men and women, especially off duty?'

The captain cleared his throat, but Jill plunged ahead. 'Sir, please think about this too: maybe the old ways of evaluating soldiers don't fit women. It's not how tall we are — why, I'm only a little shorter than Napoleon — or how rugged, or whether our voice is deep and loud, that fits us for leadership.'

The captain shifted uncomfortably in his chair. 'Is that all?'

'One more thing, sir.' She felt strong and bold for just a moment, but it was long enough. 'I'll take whatever punishment you order. But I beg you to give me one more chance to make good. When the war's over, and the Allies have won, then, sir, I want you to decide whether I was a good woman soldier, but not now — not before I've shown you what I can do.'

'Wait in the anteroom, Candidate, until we call you.'

'Yes, sir, thank you, sir.' She performed a perfect about-face, her heels coming together with a click after a precise 180-degree turn, which faced her towards the door. As she turned to close it behind her, she saw Des was staring at her.

Outside, the seconds on the twenty-four-hour clock ticked so slowly that they appeared to go backward. No wonder they called the OC Review Board the 'murder board'. This *was* murder. She went over her statements compulsively and thought of a dozen better ways to answer each question. Of course she had told no lies. It was stupid to lie when the truth, told with confidence, was so much more effective. Oh, why were they taking so long? What were they saying about her? What was Des saying? Was he telling the truth?

'Candidate Hammersmith?'. The infantry lieutenant called her from the door. Jill rose and followed him.

'No need to report again,' the captain told her with a grim look.

It was all so obvious. They were going to wash her out. But she wouldn't break down. Damn it — she wouldn't! Resigned, she waited for the axe to fall.

'Candidate Hammersmith,' the captain intoned, sounding for all the world as if he were sentencing her to death and dismemberment, 'it is the judgement of this board that you have answered the questions, put to you in a full and unique, if not necessarily a military, manner and should be given another chance to prove your worth — '

Jill could hardly believe what she heard. 'Thank you, sir!' she said, trying to hold herself at attention when she wanted to jump and shout with relief.

He held up his hand to stop her ' — but the decision is not clear cut. Stratton voted for your dismissal from the service, and — '

Jill swayed, scarcely believing the words she heard, but she forced herself to concentrate as the captain read from the paper in front of him.

' — Lieutenant Giles voted to drop the charges. And I was undecided, so I had to rule in your favour. Therefore, it is my duty to warn you that if there is ever one minor question of fitness to reach your file — even if it is in the last hour of training — I will personally see to it that you are recalled before the board, at which time the results may be quite different. Have I made myself clear?'

Numb she said, 'Yes, sir.'

The axe had fallen, and its blade still rested squarely against her neck. But she knew she would be absolutely perfect for the next four days. No one could keep her from her bars now, not the captain, not Sergeant Wolford — not even Des. Suddenly, she allowed her full fury at his betrayal to emerge. Coward! Traitor! Although he had obviously decided he wasn't interested in her as a woman, somehow she had felt she could trust him. She would never forgive him for not revealing himself, for covering his guilt at her expense. Not that her lack of forgiveness mattered to

90

him. That was obvious now. Repeating the military formalities, she left the room without looking back.

10

In backyards and communal plots, twenty million Victory Gardens produce 40 percent of the vegetables eaten in the United States during the first summer of war.

The final August week of the first WAAC OCs was filled with assignment rumours. On Tuesday, Elisabeth overheard the company clerk say that the whole of Company One would be shipped 'out' somewhere, probably to England. On Wednesday, Bunny saw Jerry again at the PX and he said that Personnel was talking about a big shipment of WAAC officers going to the Pentagon, in Washington, DC, a military complex due to be completed in October.

'Guess what,' announced a breathless Jill, bouncing into the dayroom Thursday night.

'If it's another latrine rumour,' groaned Bunny, who was toughening her feet in a brine soak, 'I don't want to hear it.'

'No, honest. I got this straight from a guy who's cutting the orders.'

'Okay, give.'

'Half of us are going to stay right here as cadre and station complement.'

Elisabeth walked in at the end of Jill's announcement. 'Who's going to stay here?'

'About half of us, according to the latest rumour,' Jill answered her. 'I'm sorry, Elisabeth. I know you're disappointed.' Then she brightened. 'But at least we'll all stay together.'

How did Jill do it? Elisabeth wondered. She'd just had a tremendous scare at her murder board hearing, and here she was as optimistic as a puppy dog. There was something about Jill that reminded her of Marne. Hopeless romantics, the two of them, weaned on Hollywood musicals, happy endings and Horatio Alger platitudes. Those things were illusions. She had none, particularly about the WAAC — although she wouldn't argue about the women's army with Page around. For Elisabeth this was just a period of craziness she had to get beyond. She shrugged. 'We'll all know soon enough, Jill.'

Page had listened intently. 'We really shouldn't be surprised to get orders for troop duty, at least for a few training cycles. Since we're the first class to finish, we're going to have to take over training the OCs and Auxiliaries who come after us, at least until there are enough qualified WAAC cadre to do the job.'

'I think it's a good thing, too,' Jill said. 'At least *we* know what to expect of women.'

The pain of Des's betrayal was subsiding, because she pushed it aside whenever she saw him; she was determined to put him out of her mind. He had tried to talk to her alone twice yesterday, but she had been so militarily formal he had backed off.

Hawks spoke up across the dayroom from behind her inevitable Coke. 'Use your heads, Candidates. This is where all the rank will be made. I bet I make captain before the year's out.'

'You're right, Jill,' Bunny said, lowering her voice and ignoring Hawks, who always seemed to invite herself into every conversation, 'we do know more about women than some of our officers do, but let's be fair. The guys aren't all bad. Wolford is hopeless, but Captain Burchette is a good egg — even Stratton tries after his fashion. That Stratton — can you beat what that guy did? I thought he was a skirt-chaser, but I didn't figure him for —' Bunny looked in Jill's direction, realizing she'd said too much again. At the mention of Stratton's name Jill's face had frozen into a mask of unconcern. Bunny pulled her feet from the basin and dried them. She knew what it was like to be Jill, in love with a man who could only hurt her. 'Sorry, kiddo, you know I shoot off my mouth too much.'

A woman from Company Two drifted over to the piano and picked through the sheet music on top, then sat down and began playing a laboured version of 'Elmer's Tune'. Other Waacs gathered behind her to sing. 'The hurdy gurdy, the birdy, the cop on the beat/ All sing Elmer's tune — yeah . . .'

A tall, slender Waac stopped by Jill's chair. Jill stood up, 'Hi, Eleanor, I've been waiting for you,' she said and, turning to the others, added, 'This is Eleanor Douglas from Third Platoon — used to be a radio announcer. She's going to help me practise my command voice. Anybody else want to come?'

Bunny grinned. 'I'm beyond help.'

'Of course you aren't,' Douglas said, taking her seriously. 'Any woman can project if she knows breathing, and tongue placement.'

Bunny smiled up at her. 'Thanks, but no, thanks. The spirit is willing, but the feet won't move.'

'You need to relax sometime, too, Jill,' Page said.

'I'll relax after I get my bars.'

Page sighed after Jill and Eleanor had left. 'Jill's so hard on herself.'

'I give up. I can't understand this crazy army,' Elisabeth said, leaning back languorously in her wicker chair. 'I've had more gigs than anyone, and there's no question about my graduating, while Jill even irons her shoelaces. It doesn't make sense, does it?'

Page smiled. 'It doesn't have to make sense. Remember what we were told the first day of training: there's the right way, the wrong way and the army way.'

'I have a better theory,' Elisabeth said. 'Jill's so intense, like electricity, she attracts a kind of negative charge.'

'You mean she's so hard on herself that she invites others to join in,' Bunny said.

'Something like that. People with everything to lose seem to bring out the worst in human nature. The trick is

93

never to let anyone know you care about anything.'

Now she tells me, Bunny thought, a half-sad smile twisting her mouth. Changing the subject, she asked, 'Either of you got a nickel for a Coke?'

That night, Elisabeth heard rain tapping insistently on the barracks windows as she prepared for bed. She remembered her nightly routine before joining the WAAC. Had she ever really soaked in a hot tub with expensive bath oils, instead of grabbing a shower on the run? Had she really worn filmy silk gowns and peignoirs instead of blue flannelette pyjamas? Had she once had soft, white skin instead of drying, sunburned skin, and creamed it in a bevelled mirror — one that reflected only *her* face? Now, morning and night, she stood in front of one of twelve washbasins in the Company One latrine with a dozen images reflected. She hated it, hated having nowhere to hide when she needed to hide.

She sat on the edge of her bed, lit a Chesterfield and pulled the soothing smoke deep into her lungs. Ordinary barracks noise subsided. Women padded towards the latrine, toiletries bulging from their pockets; others called to one another, some already slept, a few read letters whose creases had frayed from repeated foldings. So many of them had husbands or boyfriends fighting, perhaps at this moment, dying. Strange how sharing their uniform brought women closer to their men. To her own astonishment, she had thought more often and more tenderly of Marne since she arrived at Fort Des Moines.

For a moment she felt discomfort at the change, frightened by a suspicion of weakness, of an unsuspected need within her. For the first time in her life, other people counted on her, listened to her opinions, even liked her — not because of what they might take from her, but because — She stopped, unable to go further. Her wildest imaginings could not explain a relationship that did not cost her. Elisabeth had no experience in being accepted for herself.

The final day of OC training was a whirl of last-minute

94

testing in each of nine courses to determine that the first women soldiers were ready to be launched into the Army as officers and gentlewomen. OCs were called out of ranks during drill to put their platoons through column rights and left flanking movements, counting cadence with the perfectly imitated nasal tones of their male instructors. Even Jill began to sound more like Sergeant Wolford than the sarge himself. OCs could locate an azimuth on a military map, knew how far to place tents from a slit trench for field sanitation, and that they should send the pink, not the yellow, clothing-requisition copy to S-3 post supply. Every woman had crammed far into the night that last week memorizing military customs, defence against air attack, company administration and mess management, and they had quizzed each other incessantly on field first aid.

The Friday night before the last white-glove inspection and the graduation day parade, barracks details were done until they shone. Though the OCs worked hard, there was an air of manic silliness in the barracks, the natural result of weeks of hard work and tension. After the last rousing chorus of the WAAC marching song, 'Duty' rang through the downstairs bay, Eleanor Douglas hopped atop a foot locker and recited her grammar-school Rudyard Kipling prize-winner to generous applause. Then the clapping had become rhythmic and half the barracks had chanted, 'Robust-and-No-Bust, Robust-and-No-Bust!'

String mops at right shoulder arms, Bunny and Jill broke into a little time step down the bay while onlookers sang 'Through Fort Des Moines, No Mother to Guide Us'.

Laughing and out of breath, they collapsed against the wall near the door. Bunny asked, gasping, 'You really don't mind that silly No-Bust nickname, do you? They wouldn't bother to tease you if they didn't like you.'

'No. I'd rather be No-Bust than Robust.'

'Oh, you would, would you?' Bunny said, thrusting her mop at Jill. '*En garde!*'

'Got any more dandruff shampoo, Bunny?' Elisabeth asked from down on her hands and knees over a bucket and brush.

Bunny passed her a bottle, which Elisabeth up-ended into the bucket. 'This is the last of Mr Fitch's secret weapon. I hope he never finds out what we did with his gift.'

Page, on all fours in her khaki-coloured slip, strands of hair escaping her fatigue cap, looked up from her scrub brush and said, 'I can hear the Fitch Bandwagon ad now.' She began to sing, 'When you go to war, use your head, save the floor, use Fitch Shampoo.'

'Well, what did he expect?' Bunny laughed. 'He sent so many cases of the stuff, we couldn't possibly use it all on our hair. I think I was damned ingenious to think of it. None of the cadre have the faintest idea how we get our floors so clean. Besides, I guarantee this floor will never get dandruff.' She ducked as Page sent a wet scrub cloth flying down the bay. 'Missed me!' she taunted.

'Man in barracks!'

There was a rush for robes, and they scrambled to their feet.

'At ease, Candidates,' Sergeant Wolford said, climbing onto a foot locker at one end of the bay.

'Oh, my achin' GI feet, what now?' Bunny stage-whispered. 'Is he going to drill us by moonlight?'

Wolford cleared his throat and examined some papers he had in his hands. 'Anyone here interested in her assignments?' Fifty women shouted, 'Yes!' 'I'll post it on the bulletin board as I leave.'

He stopped and looked at the papers again, but he didn't get down from his perch. 'Okay, people, listen up, because I'm only gonna say this once,' he began, his voice lacking the familiar gruffness they knew only too well. 'Some of you — ' Wolford stopped again.

Bunny looked at Page, her eyebrows raised, her shoulders lifted in a questioning shrug.

Up and down the First Platoon bay, women turned to their neighbours and whispered about Wolford's uncertainty. Even Elisabeth looked interested.

Finally, with the expression of a man about to dive into icy waters, Wolford said, 'No use beatin' around the bush with you. Guess ya know I never thought this women's-army idea would work. But I'm a man to admit a mistake when I make one — and I *may* have made one. You troops' — and here his voice broke almost imperceptibly — 'have done . . . okay.'

'Well, I'll be damned,' Bunny said aloud.

Wolford ignored her. 'Now go out on the parade ground tomorrow and be the best,' he said, his voice grating again. 'Go out and bring me back the green guidon — or, by God, don't come back without it!'

He stepped down in the hushed barracks, pinned a sheet of paper on the bulletin board and left without a backward glance.

No one spoke as the screen door slammed behind Sergeant Wolford. Then Bunny broke the stunned silence. 'You know, they say if you live long enough you see everything. I think we can all die happy now.'

'Don't you know what it means?' Page said, smiling broadly. 'We won.'

Jill nodded, repeating, 'We won. We won.'

'To hell with Wolford,' Elisabeth said, 'let's look at that assignment sheet.'

'I can't believe it!' Bunny said over her shoulder to Page. 'I'm going to an Auxiliary training company at the Stables. God, why couldn't they give me a nice desk job so I can rest these poor doggies of mine?'

'You'll be a wonderful troop officer,' Page said. 'You know, they're already calling the Auxies at the converted stables "Hobby's horses".'

'That's clever. Just so they don't try to throw a saddle on me.'

A shout went up from several women in Third Platoon. 'Daytona Beach. Wow! That means overseas!'

Page looked for her name and followed it across the page. '"Training Centre Public Information Office,"' she read out loud. 'Oh!' Her shoulders sagged with disappointment. 'I really wanted troop work.'

'But you're a natural for PIO, Page,' Bunny said. 'Who better to give all the visiting brass a first-rate impression of the WAAC?'

Elisabeth called from the back of the crowd, 'Page, I can't see. What's my assignment?'

Page read, '"Gardner, Elisabeth K., Training Centre Quartermaster."'

The crowd thinned and Jill made her way to the assignment sheet. As she read the words beside her name, her eyes widened.

'What is it?' Bunny asked. 'Where are you going?'

'Nowhere.'

'What!'

'Nowhere,' Jill said, a look of pure triumph on her face. 'I'm staying right here. I'm the new Second Platoon officer for Company One.' A look of pure glee swept her face. 'That makes Wolford my noncom.'

'What happens to Stratton?' Page asked her.

'I don't care.'

11

Duty is calling you and me,
We have a date with destiny.
Ready, the Waacs are ready,
Their pulses steady the world to set free.
Service, we're in it heart and soul,
Victory is our only goal,
We love our country's honour
And will defend it against every foe.
—'Duty', unofficial WAAC marching song, sung to
the tune of the 'Colonel Bogey March'; lyrics by
Dorothy Nielsen

At last, August 29, 1942, the first WAAC OC graduation day, dawned — bright, clear and hot. Page glanced quickly down the squad room for one last check just as the inspection party arrived. Every

OC stood straight and still, her starched khaki uniform wrinkle-free. The harsh smells of Brasso, saddle soap and Clorox perfumed the air, now as familiar to her nostrils as Coty and Yardley once had been. She watched out of the corner of her eye as the colonel's glove whisked along a rafter and came away as white as ever. The women soldiers had learned the Army's first lesson well — that dirt was as desecrating to a barracks as a Christian was to Mecca.

They had shined their shoes with two layers of brown and cordovan paste wax heated in a tin over a cigarette lighter and then applied and brushed vigorously. After the polish had thoroughly dried, they had achieved a final glassy finish by buffing each shoe with a precious nylon. The WAAC OCs had become so famous for their shoeshines that half the GIs on the post were begging for their used stockings.

The inspecting officers passed quickly along the bay, looking at the clothing alignment in one woman's wall locker, the rolled underwear in another's foot locker, testing a bed for tightness, pinching a barracks bag for more than one day's laundry or contraband food, and on into the latrine and laundry areas where dirt could hide in far corners. Page knew that the colonel's eye had not missed much, and what he had not seen the captain had.

As the inspection party mounted the stairs to the second floor, Sergeant Wolford called, 'Stand easy.'

'How'd we do?' Jill whispered.

Bunny answered. 'I didn't see Wolford write in his little black book, not even once. You can stop worrying, Jill. It's all over.'

'It's *not* over,' Jill said softly between clenched teeth, 'not until graduation parade, not until those bars are on my shoulders.'

Ten minutes later they heard the inspection party descend the outside fire stairs, and soon Wolford stuck his head in the door. 'Get ready to fall out for parade in five minutes. Hammersmith, report to the orderly room on the double.'

Instinctively, Page moved towards Jill, but not in time to catch her. Bunny grabbed her before she fell, and eased her down on the foot locker.

'It's too cruel,' Jill said weakly, her head spinning. 'The last day — the last minute — they *couldn't* wash me out. Not now, not after all we've been through!'

Page knew that Jill was close to a breakdown. None of them had the strength left to deal with such a blow. 'It's not what you're thinking,' she insisted over and over, not at all sure she believed what she was saying, but knowing that she had to say it. 'Hang on to yourself.'

Wolford was at the door again, shielding his eyes, unable to adjust from the outside glare to the ordinary light of the barracks. 'Hammersmith,' he called down the bay. 'Orderly room!'

'Yes, Sergeant,' she answered him from behind the screen of friends shielding her from his view, her voice quavering imperceptibly.

'On the double, unless you want me to recommend someone else to carry the company guidon at graduation parade. Now *move*!' He slammed the door.

Jill exhaled a long shuddering breath. '*Me* — carry the guidon,' she said, her voice now full of wonder at such an honour.

'See — what did we tell you, kid?' Bunny said, obviously relieved.

'Congratulations, Jill,' said Page. 'You deserve it.'

Elisabeth looked down at the little woman and pushed a lock of Jill's hair up under her Hobby hat, a caring gesture that had come on her so quickly she had not had time to pull it back. 'That means,' she told Jill admiringly, 'you had the highest academic standing of any OC in Company One.'

Jill smiled gratefully at Elisabeth, shook her head to clear it, and felt a surge of energy. 'I'm all right now. I'd better go, but I'll see you right after the ceremony, won't I?' She grabbed her dress gloves from her foot locker and took a deep breath, calling on reserves of energy she hadn't known she possessed. 'Thanks — all of you. I couldn't have done it without you.'

As they watched her run from the barracks, Page knew none of them could have completed OCs without the others. They had been stretched to their physical and emotional limits, and they had learned what few of them could ever have learned outside the Army — that the job, whatever it was, had to be done right; there were no second bests and very few second chances.

Grasping the yellow flag with the big black '1', Jill remembered Sergeant Wolford's admonition. 'Now step out, Candidate,' he had said, shaking his head at her short legs. 'Watch your distance, or the tall girls will climb right up your back.'

From the direction of the Dewy Parade Ground, she could hear the band playing the 'Washington Post March'. The company moved off down the road, while other companies from the OC and Auxiliary training regiments marched before and after them. From each compass point, the first massed units of women soldiers converged on the place where the Army, the press and the public would view the results of their training.

Every cell in Jill's body was keyed to execute all the commands along the line of march as if she had stepped out of the army manual of close-order drill — the perfect soldier. She had failed Neil, and someday she would make up for that failure; but today was special. This was the recognition she had craved all her life. She had shown them, shown them all.

As they approached Dewy, the colour guard stepped off, the first time in history that women had carried the colours in a military review. Right behind them, exactly at 1000 hours, Company One swung onto the close-clipped grass, the OC regiment forming behind. Jill tingled to the sound of hundreds of feet meeting the turf simultaneously, the rasp of chino on chino as arms swung, the concert of heartbeats keeping time to the four-beat cadence sung by drill sergeants on their companies' flanks.

Approaching the tall white reviewing stand, Jill heard Des give the 'Eyes right!' order and snapped the company standard to horizontal salute. The weight of the flag at full extension rested along her right arm. She realized with a happy start that OC training had made her small arms stronger than their size had ever meant them to be.

Page marched behind and to the left of Jill in the third rank. The band was playing her favourite 'Colonel Bogey March', which every Waac now called 'Duty', when she heard an intense whisper sweeping down the ranks behind her: *'Dress and Cover!'* Each woman moved slightly to synchronize exactly with the woman in front and the one on her right. As they passed the stand, flashbulbs popped and the crowd applauded. A sad little shiver shook her. How could any moment in her life ever equal this one? She was a part of the parade at last, a part of the Army, a part of something infinitely greater than anything she had ever experienced.

On the far-left flank, Elisabeth marched, shoulders back, head high. She hadn't expected to feel anything, but the music, the flags flying — all of it must have hypnotized her.

In the middle file, Bunny marched on ravaged feet. She knew this was a moment she would remember for the rest of her life. She may have joined the WAAC to get away from Johnny, but sometime during these past weeks she had begun to believe in what women were doing in the Army.

Company by company, they lined up in front of the reviewing stand. Long trails of packed grass still wet from a morning shower stretched from one end of the parade field to the other, marking their passage.

Colonel Faith's voice carried clearly to the rear ranks. 'You are all a credit to your training cadre and to the Women's Army Auxiliary Corps. Your performance today has set standards for those women who come after you.' After a consultation with other members of the reviewing party, he announced, 'The green guidon for best marching company goes to — OC Company One!'

Jill could hardly believe what she had heard. They had done it! *She* had done it! If only her mother could see her now. And Neil. Even Mrs Martin might forgive . . .

She marched forward alone to the base of the stand, received the green guidon and stepped smartly back to her place in front of the company, her head high.

Colonel Faith commanded, 'Company One, pass in review!'

Once again they wheeled past the reviewing stand, taking their victory turn around the field, the green guidon with the golden-helmeted head of Pallas Athene floating above their heads.

Again they stopped in front of the reviewing stand crammed with general officers, Director Hobby and Congresswoman Edith Nourse Rogers, the tall grey grandmotherly woman who had introduced and fought for the WAAC bill. 'You are soldiers,' she told them, 'and belong to America. Every hour must be your finest hour.'

Page knew that the first WAAC OCs was almost over. The weeks of marching, exercising and studying in almost unbearable heat, under the charge of men who almost dared them to become soldiers, had come to an end — and they had succeeded. *She* had made it on her own, without her father's help or influence. This was one accomplishment even he would have to recognize.

The WAAC band played 'Auld Lang Syne', and the commandant shouted, 'Pin 'em on!'

A shout escaped from 436 throats of the new third officers of the Women's Army Auxiliary Corps. There was a mad scramble of new officers looking for friends and relatives. Page grabbed Jill and hugged her, guidon and all.

'I can't believe it,' Jill said over and over, reluctantly handing the guidon to the Company One clerk. 'We made it. We actually made it.'

Elisabeth and Bunny joined them, holding boxes containing the shiny gold bars that they had all purchased at the PX the night before.

Elisabeth held her two bars out to Page. 'Will you pin mine on?' she asked, her expression shy and haughty at the same time, as if she expected to be refused and intended not to care if she was.

'Of course,' Page said, taking the proffered bars, 'if you'll pin mine.'

'Okay, kid,' Bunny said, grinning at Jill, 'I'll kneel down

and you can — '

Jill pulled back a fist in mock anger.

Bunny raised her hand in the truce sign: 'Okay, okay — no teasing. I forgot you're not the kid anymore, but an officer and a gentlewoman. Hey,' she said as the thought struck her, 'so am I!'

Jill placed one gold bar on each of Bunny's epaulets.

Bunny held out her hand for Jill's bars. 'Now I'll pin yours for you.'

'I'd love that, but I have another plan.'

Bunny watched as Jill walked rigidly erect towards Lieutenant Stratton, saluted and held out the box containing her new golden bars. Bunny saw the lieutenant hesitate, then, without speaking, accept the outstretched box and bend to pin Jill's bars on her shoulder. She saw Jill salute, about-face and walk away without a word.

'Oh God,' Bunny said to Page and Elisabeth, 'would you look at that. Sometimes Jill is an insufferable perfectionist, but you have to say one thing — she has guts. Look at her facing down Stratton — after the guy almost threw her to the wolves. He must feel like two cents right about now.' Too bad, Bunny thought, but didn't say aloud, because it was plain that Jill was trying to compel Stratton's admiration when what she clearly wanted — plain as anything — was his affection. Bunny wondered if Jill would regret this moment she had used for revenge, but there was nothing in Jill's face to indicate regret when she rejoined them, nothing in her face at all.

Page saw Sergeant Wolford then, shouldering through the crowd of excited new WAAC officers. He looked much the same as the first day she had seen him, starched and grim, but with the slightest softening of his uncompromising glare when he looked at them.

'So,' he boomed, facing them, his hands on his hips, 'you're second louies now.'

'Third officers,' Page corrected him with their WAAC ranks.

'Get used to lieutenant, Hannaday. No one can remember those Girl Scout ranks the War Department dreamed up. I still don't think this women's-army idea will work in the field, but shavetails you are, and shavetails I'll call ya'.'

'Not quite yet, Sergeant Wolford,' Page said.

'What?' he boomed.

She smiled at him, no longer awed by his drill-sergeant demeanour. 'It's not official until we receive our first salute and give that person a one-dollar bill.'

He drew himself to magnificent attention and saluted each of them in turn, with all the formality invested in him by a thousand command inspections and his thirty years as a line-company noncom.

Solemnly, they returned the salute as he had taught them to, and each handed him a crisp new dollar bill.

After that, Page knew, no bars had ever rested more firmly on any officer's shoulders. But as the four of them turned towards the barracks and their first weekend pass as WAAC officers, Bunny walked up to Sergeant Wolford and, with a wink, kissed him.

Glancing behind her, Page saw the hand in the hash-marked sleeve reach to touch his cheek, a flush growing under the weathered wrinkles and something close to moisture in the hard gaze that had shrivelled the inside of more than one WAAC OC.

Jill looked back, too, but beyond the sergeant to the place where Des had stood a few minutes ago. He was gone, but it made no difference to her where he went. She wanted never to see him again as long as she lived.

12

By early November, requests for more than 400,000 Waacs lie on Director Hobby's desk. Lieutenant General Eisenhower has requisitioned two WAAC companies to be sent to him overseas, and estimates of 1 million women in uniform by 1946 are being bandied about the Pentagon.

On a cold but clear Sunday, November 8, Page, Jill and Bunny lounged in the Fort Des Moines WAAC officers' club.

Bunny asked, 'Remember Smitty from Company Two? She wrote from Washington that Services of Supply recommended the War Department draft a half-million women next year. Can you believe that?'

Page said, passing a hand over her eyes, which had suddenly blurred, 'That would mean ten new training centres instead of just the new one in Daytona Beach.'

'Page, are you sick?' Jill asked.

'No, just tired.'

'Good. Anyway, as I was saying, we can't train officers any faster than we're doing.' Jill spooned up the last of her hot-fudge sundae.

'Hi.' Elisabeth slid her tailor-made uniform into the booth. 'Jill, how can you eat that goo? Your figure will positively balloon.'

'Gosh, do you think so?' Jill put the spoon down as if it had burned her hand. 'I *am* having trouble keeping my girdle snapped.'

Bunny laughed. 'That's not you kid. It's these damned wartime girdles. You know how they're saving rubber by putting only one supporter on each side. Well, the other day I'm in the middle of Dewy with my Auxie platoon, double-timing to keep them from freezing to death, when both my supporters popped and my hose dropped like a shot. I tripped and went head first into a snowbank.'

They all laughed at the ridiculous picture she painted.

'Oh, that's not all.' Bunny built the suspense. 'Who should come along just then but the new commandant, Colonel Hoag, with some visiting firemen — or rather, I should say clergy — who politely looked the other way while I snapped them back in place and double-timed out of there.'

'Listen everybody,' shouted the bartender, 'we've invaded North Africa!'

He turned up the volume of the radio in the back of the bar, and a sombre voice intoned, advancing and receding with the strength of the transmission, 'Hello, everybody. This is Lowell Thomas in London.' The familiar voice filled the O club. 'Prime Minister Churchill announced this afternoon that a combined US-British force of four hundred thousand men has landed at Casablanca, Oran and Algiers in North Africa. The troops, transported by an armada of five hundred ships convoyed by three hundred and fifty naval vessels, surprised the Vichy French garrisons and overpowered them after brief fighting.'

A spontaneous cheer went up, and someone struck the first chords of 'Over There' on the bandstand piano. Page found herself with Bunny, Jill and Elisabeth shouting a chorus of 'The Waacs are coming, the Waacs are coming . . . ' 'Tomorrow I'm going to walk into the Chief's office and put in for overseas duty.'

'That's easy for you, Page,' Jill said, 'you have a public-relations skill they want. What about me? Have you heard about any requisitions for training officers with one year of vet school? No, you haven't, because there aren't any, and there won't be any.'

'I thought you loved training OCs,' Bunny said.

'I do, but I want to get over there where the war is.' Determination firmed her small mouth. 'What should I do, Page? You must know what skill can get me overseas.'

Without hesitating, Page said, 'Communications. That's what they're going to want from us — telephone operators, radio operators and cryptographers.'

'You mean breaking secret codes? That's for me!

Tomorrow *I'm* going to put in for cryptography school.'

Bunny scooted her chair back. 'This is depressing. Look, the bar's finally open. Anybody want a drink?'

Elisabeth ordered a brandy Alexander. 'And tell them use real cream or forget it.'

'Why depressing?' Jill asked Bunny when she got back with the drinks.

The older woman looked downcast. 'Mother Bunny hoped we'd all stay together, kid, at least for a while longer.'

'If they open several new training centres, you know we'll be scattered,' Page said. 'We're lucky one of us didn't have to go when they opened Daytona Beach.'

'Bunny, why not put in for code school with me?' Jill asked.

'You go to it, kid. You go slay Page's dragon. Not me! I'll stay right here in the dull old US of A hutting my Auxies around Dewy.'

'Elisabeth, have you heard anything about your request for the QM office in the Pentagon?' Page asked.

'Nothing,' Elisabeth said. Almost four months had gone by since she had written to the Quartermaster General detailing the problems Waacs had with the uniform and her suggestion that someone from the field with a model's training — namely Elisabeth Gardner — would be of inestimable help in solving those problems. She knew she should have followed up with a formal request — maybe put more pressure on Marne — but for some reason she had allowed the matter to slide. It wasn't like her to drag her feet about anything. She could hardly put a word to it, but if she must she had to admit that it was out of loyalty to these women. She had grown, in her own reserved way, so close to Page and Jill and Bunny that the thought of leaving them was troubling to her.

'Did I tell you,' Bunny asked between sips of her Tom Collins, 'about this latest crop of Auxies? Some bunch! We've got a concert pianist — she's good, too. Even I can tell that, and I'm boogie, not Bach.'

'What's her name?' Page asked.

'Annaliese Kaplan. She escaped from Nazi Germany in 1939, lost her fiancé, her family, everything, and yet she works as hard as anyone — harder, maybe. There's something very intense about her. She reminds me a bit of you, Page.'

'I can't imagine why,' Page said.

'Now, don't take this wrong, but — gee, how can I put this? — she knows herself too well, like you do, and so she's never surprised. She's like you, but not — or maybe like you could be.'

'Bunny, what *are* you rattling on about? Anyway, I'd like to meet her sometime.'

'Sure, anytime,' Bunny said, relieved that Page wasn't angry at her rantings, and she went immediately into one of her funny monologues about her Auxie platoon. 'We've got this kid, Victoria Hansen, from Parker's Prairie, Minnesota, in this cycle. She makes Jill here sound like Mae West in heat. Talk about innocent! You wouldn't believe the questions Mother Bunny has to answer. The other day she asked me if a girl could have a baby after kissing a boy. Would you believe that — in 1942? I think the kid's a case of arrested development!'

Jill scoffed, miffed because Bunny thought her innocent. 'You're making that up, Bunny!'

''s truth, so help me. But that's not the best of this new lot. We have an ex-Carmelite nun — name's Kathryn Mary O'Conner — and she absolutely refused the captain's direct order to take down a large crucifix she'd hung on the locker behind her bed. Now, aren't you dying to see how the Army deals with *that*?'

Elisabeth smiled and twirled the cherry in her drink. 'That's a classic confrontation all right — army standard operating procedures versus God. If she wins, let me know. I could use someone with her connections to cut through red tape at Supply.'

'Which reminds me,' Bunny said, 'of the uniform shortage. Elisabeth, something's got to be done. I know *you're* concerned with how it fits, but damn it all, recruits are pouring into the Stables and the new Boom Town barracks every week, and there aren't any uniforms for them.' Bunny bent over the table towards Elisabeth. 'Look, I've got some of the Southern and West Coast women marching about in flimsy shoes and lightweight dresses.'

'Didn't the coats help?' Elisabeth asked. She knew that Director Hobby had ordered men's winter overcoats issued until supply caught up with the overwhelming demand for WAAC uniforms.

'You mean those old World War One coats? Yes, they helped, but not enough small sizes are available. I've got some recruits who look like vaudeville comics out on Dewy — empty sleeves flapping and hems dragging to their ankles. Some show for visiting VIPs we make!'

Jill nodded. 'It's not just the Auxies, but the OCs too. The last class had to take all *left* galoshes — you know, the ones they call arctics, with the big buckles. Both feet went sideways. How do you think that looks parade?'

Elisabeth tapped the table impatiently. 'Yes, yes, I know. But it's not my fault. S-Three says it's Hobby's fault — some snafu at WAAC headquarters.'

'That's not fair, Elisabeth,' Page said, coming to the Director's rescue. 'I hear this all the time, from press and parents. You've got to remember that Director Hobby's caught up in the army bureaucracy just as we are. One day she's told the WAAC is authorized a strength of a thousand recruits a week, a few weeks later the figure jumps to five thousand a week, and a month after that the General Staff's talking about drafting hundreds of thousands of women. Can't you guess what happens to supply? Original clothing requisitions go in to the Quartermasters Corps, then they're doubled and redoubled within weeks. Each time, contracts are let and then recalled. It gets to be an awful supply tangle, worse than anything we can imagine. And on top of all this, there are still those people who are just waiting to say we made a mess of our chance.'

'Want another drink?' Bunny asked.

'Not for me,' Page answered. 'I've got letters and laundry.'

Bunny gulped the last of her drink. 'Letters? Gee, sorry, Jill, I almost forgot. This came for you at headquarters, and I picked it up.' She reached into her purse and pulled out a slim airmail letter. Teasing, she held it up to the light. 'Looks like it's another one from your old friend Stratton.'

Jill picked up the letter lying between them on the table and without looking at it tore it in two pieces. Then she placed the two pieces together and tore through them again, repeating the process until she dropped the confetti into the ashtray. 'I've got some duty rosters to make out.' Abruptly, she put on her coat and left.

'Whew,' Bunny said. 'I sure wouldn't want Jill mad at *me*. She's got a stubborn streak that's almost frightening.'

'It's not stubbornness,' Page said thoughtfully. 'She's trapped by her own standards. She can't allow herself a mistake, so she's never learned to forgive other people's.'

Elisabeth raised an eyebrow. 'Nothing wrong with that. You make a mistake in this world and you get eaten alive.'

They walked in silence back to the WAAC BOQ. Page felt the forces of change moving in on them. The Corps was growing rapidly, and they would be obliged to grow with it. Their private lives would have to be put on hold for the duration. For a moment, the thought was comforting, but only for a moment. That's nonsense, she thought. Life doesn't wait, not even for a world war. Even love cannot be denied; not the ache-all-over love that Bunny tried to forget, not the love-hate that Jill rejected, not even the married love that Elisabeth seemed to feel very little. Love. She turned the word over and over again in her mind, examining it. Love was something Lieutenant Page Hannaday could postpone for now. Suddenly Page felt dizzy. She stumbled, and Bunny grabbed her arm.

'Thought you were going to do a good imitation of my girdle dance.' Then Bunny grew serious. 'What is it, Page? Your skin is positively grey.'

'Just tired,' Page mumbled, 'just tired.'

'You better go on sick call tomorrow. Get some of those little all-purpose capsules. You know what Sergeant Wolford says. If APCs won't cure it . . . ' Bunny's voice trailed off as Page turned an anxious, angry face towards her.

'Don't you *dare* say anything about this to anyone,' Page yelled at Bunny, who had never seen her angry before.

13

K rations are packed by Chicago's Wrigley Company and contain compressed graham crackers, canned meat or meat substitute, three tablets of sugar, four cigarettes and a stick of Wrigley's chewing gum. For breakfast a fruit bar and soluble coffee are added; for dinner, bouillon powder and a bar of concentrated chocolate.

By the first anniversary of Pearl Harbor, Page was on orders for an undisclosed overseas destination.

'Lieutenant Hannaday.'

The nurse at the hospital dispensary window was calling her name. 'Report back to Dr Carter in Examining Room Three.'

'Yes, ma'am,' Page answered quietly, longing to ask why she had been asked to wait when all the other officers on overseas orders had been released back to duty.

A major in a white coat with the sewn-on caduceus insignia of the Army Medical Corps, stood by the examining table, another army nurse behind him. 'Remove your blouse and unbutton your shirt, please, Lieutenant.' He patted the table. 'Sit right here.'

He considerately rubbed the stethoscope to warm it and then moved it from between Page's breasts to under her left breast and then around to her back. 'Experienced any dizziness lately?'

She hesitated. 'Just a little,' she answered, not quite

truthfully, 'but I'm sure it's overwork. We've all worked hard, first in officers' training and then getting the training centre going.'

'Tell me,' he said in a quiet, even tone from over her shoulders, 'have you ever had any heart trouble?' Page could feel her heart hammering in her ears.

'Absolutely not, Doctor. I've led an active life — played on my college tennis team — and I've been an A club player since then.'

'Any family history of heart problems?'

'My mother — she died of an aneurysm. They said it was congenital.' She heard the panic rising in her voice. 'What is it? What do you hear?'

'Please don't excite yourself. That's the worst thing you can do. Before I sent you out to the waiting room, I heard an irregular heartbeat — it's called arrhythmia. That's why I asked you to wait. Occasionally, I find that physical examinations are stressful for women, and some men too — that they have elevated blood pressure or unusual heart reactions.' He stopped talking and listened again.

Page stood his silence as long as she could. 'For God's sake, Doctor . . .'

The major shushed her and continued listening. 'It's there all right — a fluttering sound,' he said, removing the stethoscope from his ears and hooking it on his neck. 'I'm sorry, Lieutenant, but I have to mark you unfit for duty.'

'If you do that, I'll be off the overseas shipment.'

'Yes, that's true, and . . .'

Something about his eyes told her that the worst news was yet to come. 'What else?'

'I may have to recommend you for discharge.'

She heard her own dazed voice, thin and frightened, pleading, 'Doctor, isn't there anything — a cure, or some medication?'

He shook his head. 'I'll review your chart, and if hospital rest is indicated, perhaps we'll try that first before I make a recommendation for discharge.'

Page felt abandoned. The Army did not want her, after

113

all. Craziness surfaced in her usually logical mind — maybe the fates had found a Hannaday woman in uniform to be the anathema her father had predicted. She could see his knowing face before her. If she had to go home like this, not good enough for the WAAC, she'd never be able to leave again. He'd see to that, and she wouldn't have the strength to defy him. She felt her world crumbling beneath her. Sitting slumped on the examining table, mourning, she hardly noticed the nurse gently helping her into her uniform.

'Page,' Jill ranted and beat one size-five-and-a-half fist against the other, 'they *can't* do this to you!'

'I'm afraid they can and they did,' Page answered the circle of faces hovering over her hospital bed. 'I'm out of the first overseas shipment. The question is, will they let me stay in the WAAC?'

'Damn and hell!' Bunny said, her dark-lashed eyes blue-ringed after twenty-four hours as training-centre duty officer. 'It's not fair. No,' she said emphatically, 'not you, Page. You're the best — the best.'

'Oh — ' Page realized that tears were gathering and there was no way she could stop them ' — please, just leave now. They're going to try isolation. Complete rest — no visitors, no reading, nothing but sleeping and eating.'

Bunny laughed, a strained laugh. 'Sounds like heaven, you lucky gal.'

Page managed a smile. 'I'll see you in two weeks — one way or the other.'

Elisabeth opened her mouth, and then quickly closed it. She had no words to heal this grief she could not even understand. Page's dedication to the women's army embarrassed her and made her feel an unaccustomed shyness. She knew she would have taken any way out of the WAAC, even this way.

That afternoon Major Carter came to see Page. 'How are you doing, Lieutenant?'

'I'm feeling stronger, Doctor,' she said sitting up, hoping it was true.

He gently pushed her shoulder back to the pillow. 'Well, now, don't expect a miracle in one day. It would be unfair to you to get your hopes up unnecessarily. But I'll tell you one thing, young lady. If your friends have anything to say about it — '

'My friends?'

'Yes, I received an earnest deputation this afternoon at the dispensary, three young women, who tried to persuade me that the WAAC would fall apart if you weren't part of it. Damned near convinced me, too.'

Page could only nod, for once excused of military etiquette; she could not trust the huge lump in her throat to allow the passage of grateful words.

The next two weeks in isolation were the longest Page had ever lived. Cut off from everything — friends, work, war news — she concentrated on ways to help herself. Listening to her heartbeat pounding through the silence, she tried to regulate the echo bounding off the chambers of her heart.

At night she thought of positive, pleasant things. A long-ago memory, a fuzzy image of her mother, gradually formed in her mind. A pretty, dressed-up lady hovered over her bed, saying, 'Think, little love, of fluffy blue clouds, and when they have passed, every tiny one, Mommy will be home again and come in to kiss you good night.'

She could scarcely remember now what her mother looked like outside the family photograph her father had kept in his den: he was holding her, Page, in an ages-ago Panama summer, her long legs dangling down the front of his tropical worsted summer uniform; her mother, young and beautiful, was holding Baby Randy.

But every night that December her mother came to the Fort Des Moines hospital, bending over her bed, repeating the childhood reassurance. Then Page would drop into a deep and even sleep, the blue clouds passing over, one by one.

Page walked slowly down Des Moines' Walnut Street and headed east past Younkers department store. Despite the late-December cold, the night was clear. Iowa's sometime blustery wind was calm, and she was only one of many men and women in uniform celebrating this second Christmas Eve of the war.

The clock in Davidson's window across the street pointed to eight, reminding her that she had eaten little from the lunch tray at the hospital. Not that eating mattered much to her tonight.

She turned into Babe's, walked through the downstairs restaurant full of civilians, who paid no attention to the now familiar uniform, and climbed the stairs to the second-floor banquet room.

Bunny saw her first and waved her to the table. 'You look fantastic, Page,' she said, hugging her.

'Absolutely healthy!' Jill said.

'Well, are you cured?' Elisabeth bluntly asked the question that was on all of their minds.

Page, relief written plainly on her face, nodded happily. 'Dr Carter marked me fit for duty.' Suddenly she stopped. What she had to tell them was happy news for her, but sad too, since it meant she would be separated from them. 'I got word this afternoon that I'm shipping out tomorrow — to the Pentagon. Director Hobby requested me.'

Bunny raised the glass. 'You'll soon get that place organized.' She hid her feelings behind the joke.

Page laughed. 'I can't promise we'll win the war this month — maybe next month.'

Jill picked up her drink and raised it. 'Here's to all of us, Page.'

'What?'

'We're all on orders.'

'Oh — ' she forced herself to be happy for them, even though she knew that an important part of her life had come to an end — 'it had to come, didn't it?'

Bunny said, 'Me to the Air WAAC in Texas — the new CO of a photographic unit. Can you imagine me as a field company commander?'

'And you, Jill?' Page asked.

'Just what I wanted,' Jill answered, her voice happy.

'Cryptography school at Fort Monmouth, New Jersey.'

'And you, Elisabeth?'

Bunny interrupted. 'Where else but — '

Page asked, 'Not to Washington with me?'

Elisabeth shook her head. 'Not the Pentagon, Page, but the big QM depot in Philadelphia. Back to the *fringes* of civilization, at least.'

The jukebox played the 'Warsaw Concerto', its smashing chords a melodramatic underlining to the friendship that had grown into an intimacy stronger than sisterhood. Page wondered if they would ever see one another again after tomorrow.

Bunny ordered a bottle of champagne, but when it came Jill grabbed it before it could be opened. 'Let's all sign the label and leave it at the bar, then when the war is over we can come back here and drink it — and swap war stories. Come on,' she said, excited, 'I saw Gary Cooper do it in a movie once.'

Elisabeth shrugged. 'Jill, that's silly — schoolgirl stuff.'

'No it isn't,' Jill said, determined now. 'It's called the "last survivor" bottle. Let's make a pact to return here — say, the Christmas Eve after the war is over. Whoever shows up gets to drink the bottle in memory of the others.'

Bunny grinned. 'You've got some imagination, kid. We're all coming back.'

But the idea appealed to them after all, and they signed their names and the date, December 24, 1942, on the bottle's label.

'Still seems like a waste of good champagne to me,' Bunny grumbled after they had deposited the bottle with the bartender and watched him put it on a shelf high above the rest of the stock.

'No such thing,' Jill said, pleased with the high drama of it all. 'Tell you what. If I don't come back, Bunny, you can have my share.'

'Praise the lord and pass the ammunition . . . ' the jukebox blared out the big hit song.

But Bunny wasn't listening to the music. A sudden chill

117

— a draft from somewhere — gripped her and she wished she'd never heard of a damned 'last survivor' bottle.

The Des Moines taxi moved through the storm-slowed Christmas Day traffic down Walnut Street.

'I wish we could stop at Babe's one last time,' Jill said, torn between nostalgia for the good times already rapidly receding and excitement over the unknown adventures ahead.

'We will one day,' Bunny said, her voice full of unaccustomed determination. 'We *all* will.'

'Promise, Mother Bunny?' Jill said, laughing.

'Promise.'

Page heard Jill and Bunny's exchange, and saw Elisabeth holding her tightly packed duffle bag, staring out the window, smiling, her blonde hair wreathed in sunlight. The smile was strange, because the rest of them were so close to tears. She never would understand Elisabeth; then, maybe she didn't need to. They had worked together the past five months as no women ever had, suffered identical hardships and forged a bond that would continue even if they never saw one another again.

The taxi pulled up in front of the Rock Island train station, and they gave each other a lift with the heavy bags.

A group of women in civvies huddled under a huge sign on the platform that read: 'WAAC REPORT HERE.' The new recruits stared at the four WAAC officers.

'Remember when we were that green?' Bunny asked. 'A hundred years ago.'

In some way the new Waacs comforted Page. She and her friends had been the first women soldiers, but now that they were moving into the field, others were taking their place — and others after them — assuring a continuity of women soldiers.

They checked the call board for their trains. Jill would be leaving first.

'If any of you ever get up to Monmouth —' she began.

'We'll look you up,' Page said what they were all thinking. 'And if you're ever in Washington —'

118

'I'll look you up,' Jill finished the thought.

'We won't ever lose touch with each other,' Bunny said. 'Promise?' She stuck out her hand.

Like the old children's game of one-potato-two-potato they piled one hand on top of the other until all four of them had promised.

This must be what it's like to have sisters, Page thought, watching Jill's small figure in the olive-drab coat walk away down Track 5.

'Page, I'm really no good at this,' Bunny said, her eyes glistening. 'Now, don't argue, you two — I'm going over to my gate and wait alone.'

'Write when you get to Texas,' Page called after her.

The two of them, Page and Elisabeth, stood there a moment, watching Bunny walk away.

Elisabeth said, 'I must be off myself, Page, but first I'd like to tell you — ' She stopped.

'Tell me what?'

'I haven't made it a secret that I don't like the WAAC, and yet, you were my friend. No — don't say anything. I'm not fishing for compliments. I don't understand it myself, but knowing you and Bunny and Jill has made these the happiest months of my life.' Elisabeth picked up her bag and turned a haunted face towards Page. 'I haven't deserved it, you know,' she said, her usually cultured voice flat with a western-Pennsylvania twang. 'If you knew me, *really* knew me — who I am, where I come from, what I've been — '

Page stopped her. 'I know all I need to know. You're one of us, and if you ever need a friend . . .'

Page watched Elisabeth's tall elegant figure walk towards her gate, hand her ticket to the conductor and turn once again to wave. The smile she had seen on Elisabeth's face in the taxi had returned even more triumphantly. Suddenly and irrevocably Page knew what that smile meant. Elisabeth, at last, had people in her life to care about — and to miss.

Whoo-sh sh-oo. The rush of released air echoed from

brakes all along the length of the sleek *Silver Rocket* as Page swung aboard. The diesel engine whirred, the huge wheels churned, and she took a seat facing forward. The four of them were moving in different directions. She felt regret and the poignant feeling of being alone for the first time since they had all stepped off the truck that hot July Sunday, in what seemed now like another age. But she couldn't quite suppress her anticipation of the adventure that lay ahead of her.

BOOK TWO

*1943: A Date
with Destiny*

14

In 1943, the tide of war begins to turn against the Axis Powers. In the Pacific, Allied forces capture Buna in New Guinea, freeing Australia from the threat of Japanese attack. In North Africa, the US Fifth Army and the British Eighth Army drive forward in Tunisia. On the Russian front, the Germans start a retreat from the Caucasus.

The Waacs are on the move from their Fort Des Moines training centre. Nine full companies have been delivered to commands in the Zone of the Interior, two units are secretly training with anti-aircraft artillery that rings Washington, DC, in case women have to replace men in defending the capital from Nazi planes. Another large unit is on its way to England. It follows in the wake of a torpedoed ship carrying five WAAC officers, who are rescued and delivered to Eisenhower's North Africa GHQ, begrimed and in rags.

O n a blustery Sunday morning, January 3, WAAC Third Officer Elisabeth Gardner arrived at the billet address on her travel orders, a run-down hotel in central Philadelphia, home of one of twenty-seven WAAC Aircraft Warning Service units trained at Fort Des Moines and now spread along the East Coast.

'You're lucky, ma'am,' the first sergeant at the Franklin Hotel WAAC detachment said, consulting her room roster. 'Let's see, now — all the aircraft warning officers are shift workers and you'll be straight day shift, so you've got a single room.'

Lucky! Lucky to be playing soldier in a third-rate hotel? She glanced down the roster and recognized no names from her OC company. Alone again.

'Go on up to Room 301 at the head of the landing, ma'am, and when you've unpacked I'll show you the ropes,' the sergeant was saying. 'You're only attached to us for quarters and rations, but the CO wants you to rotate duty officer with the others. I'll have the new DO duty roster posted this afternoon.'

Elisabeth picked up her duffle bag. 'Is that all, Sergeant?'

'We have no mess here, ma'am, so you'll get a dollar twenty-five a day to eat at any restaurant that accepts government chits. It's not much, but the others can tell you where the good but cheap meals are.'

Two minutes later, Elisabeth opened the door on a room the size of her closet at Madame Gabriella's, dropped her bags and collapsed onto the unmade bed. She stretched her cramped leg muscles, sore after days of travel on a crowded day coach. There had been no roomettes available, not even an upper berth although her ticket called for one. The Pullman conductor had taken a twenty-dollar bribe, then pretended he didn't remember it. The war had ruined men. Or rather, the war had almost ruined her. How could she have been so taken in by Page's noble rhetoric, Jill's heroic determination, even Bunny's good-sport resilience? High ideals were possible in a small enclave of patriotism like the WAAC training centre, but the real world outside hadn't changed. Everybody would cheat you if you didn't cheat him first.

It would have been bad enough if she had just had to sit up in a day coach all the way to Philadelphia, but her coach had been uncoupled somewhere in Indiana and left for an entire night. After that, everything had happened to that damned train. Between Des Moines and Philadelphia it was sidetracked for troop trains, freight trains, probably even milk trains — a half-dozen or more long, frustrating delays. Even a two-day rest at a hotel in Pittsburgh hadn't lightened her mood.

Those days on the train hadn't resembled any travel she'd ever known. As 1942 turned into 1943, everyone in the country seemed to be on the move to somewhere else: older men and boys heading towards war plants and shipyards; young men in uniform trying desperately to get

123

home for the holidays; young wives with screaming babies following husbands some of them hardly knew; even younger girls in Sloppy Joe sweaters and bobby sox trailing anything in khaki pants.

Elisabeth stretched, dismissing those scenes from her mind. She could sleep for a week, but she didn't have a week. Tomorrow she must report to the quartermaster depot. She wondered what job they wanted her to fill. Perhaps it didn't matter. Wasn't this supposedly the culmination of all that marching and those tin-soldier inspections? She was ready to do her bit for victory against the Axis, wasn't she?

Elisabeth smiled ruefully at the ceiling. Some of the gung-ho at Fort Des Moines had infected her for a time — or maybe it had been knowing Page and Bunny and Jill. All through the long train journey, she had examined the past months in her mind. Something wonderful, strangely wonderful, had happened to her, and she would store the memory of it away in a special part of her. With these women who had become her friends, what was honest in her nature had come forth. For a few months, she had thought that the rest of her life might be different, that she might be like them.

She rolled onto her side and stared out at the snow falling past her third-floor window into the alley below, and her smile disappeared. Now that she was alone again, she could see more clearly. She had wanted to be liked by them, but not to be like them. They were nice girls who lived by all the nice-girl rules. Now that she was back in her world, she had to make her own rules to survive. Still, she knew, she would always have three friends who shared a strange new life with her. Nothing could ever take that away.

The next morning she boarded the stubby olive-drab army bus that pulled-up promptly at 0810 in front of the frayed awning of the Franklin's Broad Street entrance. After a twenty-minute ride, she reported to the administration building at the depot.

'You're to see Colonel Nicolson — uhh, Lieutenant,' a young corporal with a GI haircut growing in a half-dozen

124

directions informed her, his voice trailing off into open mouthed awe. She could feel his eyes following her as she walked between the rows of scarred oak desks manned by enlisted men. Several low wolf whistles erupted behind her.

Elisabeth was herself again. All the indecision and self-doubt she had experienced at Fort Des Moines was gone. Again she revelled in what she was, a beautiful, desirable woman, but she was not for the likes of these enlisted men.

She let them know it. The subtle way she moved her body with the conscious grace of a trained model captured their eyes, but she was as untouchable as a crown jewel under glass. And that was the way she had always wanted it and now wanted it again — admiration with no strings.

Nicolson ushered her into his office and held his desk side chair for her. 'Well, well — Lieutenant.' He cleared his throat. 'It's so damned hard to get used to calling a woman by a military title. And I'll never get used to all those made-up WAAC ranks — third officer, second leader and so forth. You understand?'

'Of course, Colonel.' She used her pleasant, deferential tone. 'I'm here to help in any way I can.' Next Elisabeth put on her demure face — the most difficult one for her. 'I have given up my career for the duration, so titles aren't in the least important to me.' She had determined what he wanted to hear and said it.

'Admirable,' the colonel said, pulling a paper from a stack in his in-basket. 'Now, this was quite an impressive letter you wrote the Quartermaster General while you were taking your training. After I saw it, I put in a personal request for you through the OQMG in Washington . . .'

Elisabeth smiled. *Who's he kidding? He got orders to request me.*

'. . . You sounded like you had the kind of specialized knowledge we can use here. We'll carry you on the table of organization as my secretary, but I have something else in mind for you.'

At first she thought he was making a pass. Even though his hair was thin enough to show most of his scalp and his waist had slipped over his web belt, he was a man, after all.

'Lieutenant,' he went on, his mind evidently on business, 'do you know the last Gallup poll revealed that women prospects for recruitment rated the WAAC uniform last after all the women's services? Waves, Spars, Women Marines all scored far higher.'

'No, sir, I didn't know that, but I'm not at all surprised,' she answered bluntly. 'I would have voted the same way.'

'Good! We'll get along. I hoped you'd be as direct as your letter.' He lit a cigarette, after offering Elisabeth one. 'Let me tell you, we've had our problems with allocations from the War Manpower Board — you'll learn about these — but we do want to turn this situation around. Everybody's on my neck about it from your WAAC Director to the General Staff. What I need from you is a detailed report of what a woman of your experience finds wrong with every item of WAAC issue. And *why* — give me the why of it! I'll expect your recommendations in this office by the first week of February, 1943. That's just a month. Can you do it?'

'Yes, sir, this is the chance I've been hoping for.' Jill could not have said it better, she told herself.

The next few weeks Elisabeth found surprisingly interesting. January flew by. Her days were as full as they had ever been at Gabriella's in the busiest season — fuller, perhaps, because she was now much more than a mere mannequin; she was working with cloth, design and the details of procurement. And the wonder of it was, she was good at it. She felt — well, she could only call it excited, as if she had suddenly discovered a lost twin, Elisabeth still but a more perfect Elisabeth.

Although she found that the Quartermaster Corps had legitimate gripes to level at the Requirements Division in the Services of Supply (Requirements seemed completely incapable of approving proposals without lengthy debate over possible cost discrimination *in favour* of women), still the real problem lay, she could plainly see, in the inability of the Army to believe that there were really female bodies in their uniforms, and that female bodies were different from male bodies.

She was shocked to find that a male form had been used

for the WAAC uniform's master pattern. 'This alone would account for many of the complaints I heard at Fort Des Moines,' she told Corporal Danny Barnes, a slightly built young tailor on the uniform specialists' team she had joined. 'Look at this,' she said to him after several days of taking uniforms apart. 'All these jackets have been cut with wide collars and narrow hips as if for men.'

'They've used men's short, regular and long sizing too,' Barnes said. 'The shirts are just as bad. Take a look.'

'This is crazy. They go by neck sizes instead of bust sizes. No wonder I never saw a Waac whose collar wasn't too big or whose shirt wasn't pulling across the bust.'

Barnes was a valuable co-worker. From the first day, he was at her elbow, anticipating her wishes. She soon found he was an indispensable cutter of red tape. He could get her an item she needed when no one else could. It was only slightly inconvenient that he obviously had a crush on her.

At night she returned to the Franklin Hotel, stopping first at a small out-of-the-way family restaurant off Vine Street near the Betsy Ross House. The food was plain but well-prepared, and the papa fussed over her table, giving her extras without charging for them. Best of all, to her mind, she almost never saw other Waacs there, and she took care not to share her discovery with them. Why should she? They talked of nothing but the incessant boredom of their work plotting unidentified planes on the central eastern corridor filter board, of the dreary boyfriends and their equally dreary postwar marriage prospects. Most of all she avoided them because they wanted from her the intimacy they had come to expect from one another at Fort Des Moines, and she had determined she would never succumb to that need again.

Often there were letters from Marne waiting in the orderly room for her, and she methodically answered them letter for letter. He wrote with the same mindless contentment she had observed in people who were sure of their past and of their future and sure, so very sure, of themselves.

The closeness to him that sharing a uniform had first

made her feel had passed.

By late January, Elisabeth was putting the finishing touches on her report for Colonel Nicolson, which included a model uniform incorporating all her changes. The idea had been Elisabeth's but the rest of the team had gone along, especially Barnes, whose talent as a tailor had shown her how to translate her ideas to paper patterns and then into material.

'Let's do one more fitting to make sure we have it perfect,' she said and slipped behind the dressing screen.

Emerging a few minutes later, she smoothed the skirt and well-fitted jacket that no longer flattened her full breasts or bulged over her flat stomach. She looked in the mirror and with her hand smoothed her hair into the elegant wraparound roll that kept it off her collar. Under the overhead lights her hair took on a summer gloss, and her skin, she was pleased to see, was once again ivory with a healthy rose blush. She carefully scrutinized her face with a professional's care, looking routinely for the faint lines and shadows that would mark the end of her youth. Then, satisfied, she became aware that two dark eyes were regarding her with a professionalism of their own.

'Who is that?' she whispered to Barnes, motioning imperceptibly towards a powerfully built man of moderate height who was detached from a group near the colonel's office.

'You don't know Max Stryker? He's Mr Big in clothing manufacture. Besides that, I think he owns half the Philadelphia waterfront.'

He must also own a resort in Florida, she thought, looking at the tanned face, handsome in a leonine way, but too knowing, secretive, full of the old anger of self-invented men. His iron-grey hair still streaked with black swept back from his high forehead. She saw that he knew he'd been observed, but instead of looking away his appraising eyes slowly travelled along her entire body, a faint smile on his wide, sensual mouth.

Elisabeth had been stared at like some prize thoroughbred before and had a standard put-down, but she chose not to turn him away — she could recognize an important man when she saw one. Instead she returned his gaze, her eyes level with his.

She had heard his name around the QM depot. Who hadn't? His critics, and there seemed to be quite a few of them, portrayed him as a rogue Frankenstein's monster who left bloody footprints in the snow. It was common knowledge that he had broken his partner and then bought him out for pennies on the dollar. Yet, far from this making him *persona non grata*, the gossips adored him, reported him squire for half the Philadelphia lovelies, including one Biddle. Altogether a fascinating predator, she decided, excited at the prospect of the old man-woman game she hadn't played for a while.

Max Stryker crossed the open warehouse floor to where Elisabeth stood. 'Lieutenant Gardner,' he said in a baritone but rather breathy voice, 'my friend Nick Nicolson tells me you don't think much of my uniforms. I'd like to hear more, but I haven't time now. Over dinner tonight?'

The question held a hint of a command, and she had it on her tongue to refuse. Experience made her stop. She could scarcely refuse a man who was the colonel's friend. She nodded yes.

'It's settled, then,' he said as if he'd been in no doubt. 'My car will call for you at seven.' He walked away, the sound of his heels falling abruptly on her ears. So that's the awesome Max Stryker. She shrugged, but the amazing vibrance of his person hung in the air about her.

Elisabeth knew men, and she realized she had just been in the presence of raw masculine power — some primitive sexuality that took her unawares and caused the hair at the nape of her neck to tingle its ancient warning. Max Stryker was obviously a man who took what he wanted. She wondered what it was like never to see anyone's needs but one's own, and then, in a flash of insight, she realized that she herself was such a person or would be. Ah, but the difference between them was his money, which he had wrested from lesser men, while she'd been forced to mortgage her body for everything she got.

15

*More than 280,000 jobseekers, most of them young
women, pour into wartime Washington, DC, lured
by high government wages which pay typists $1,600
a year. As many as 35,000 of these workers fill the
newly completed labyrinth across the Potomac
called the Pentagon. People wonder what the War
Department will do with such a huge building after
the war, but President Roosevelt explains that it will
be used to house government records and store
quartermaster supplies.*

A cold drizzle greeted Page's return to Washington.
In the taxi from Union Station to the Pentagon
she made an effort to repair the ravages of a long
train trip, tucking her chestnut hair up under her hat and
putting a touch of Coty powder on the circles under her
tired green eyes before reporting to the Director's office for
duty. She almost wished she had time to stop for some of
the new pancake makeup everybody was talking about.

'Third Officer Hannaday, Page — reporting as ordered,
ma'am.' Page snapped a precision salute, shoulders
straight, eyes front, left hand touching the side seam of her
skirt.

'Welcome back to WAAC headquarters, Hannaday,'
the duty officer said. 'We're on a six-day week now,
sometimes more. A word of advice,' she went on, not
unkindly. 'Carry your rank easily here. You're just in from
the training centre, and — well, you may be a bit too
military for some of the men. Relax a little, and you'll do
well.'

In crowded Washington, Page had the incredible luck to
arrange a three-room apartment sublet, for a very
reasonable fifty-five dollars a month. Its present occupant,
a Finance Corps Waac, had put in for troop duty at the
newly activated training centre of Fort Oglethorpe,

Georgia. Page arrived on the pleasant residential street just as the woman was packing.

'Come on in,' a pleasant voice called when she knocked on the open door, 'but leave the door open, so I can hear the taxi driver.'

'I don't want to barge in before you're out,' Page replied.

'Nonsense.' The voice came from the bathroom. 'Grab some coffee in the kitchen and come help me sit on this bag. I can't even get the darned strap around it.'

'Hi,' Page said, carefully placing her hot coffee cup on a mat on the dresser. 'Want me to hold the lock while you pull?'

'Would you?' the woman said, pushing away the hair falling in front of her eyes, to reveal a mass of freckles. 'I'll die if I miss my train.'

Page steadied the duffle bag while the woman hauled on the webbed strapping. At last the clasp clicked into place around irregular bulges that were obviously not army issue.

'Your name must be Hannaday. First OC, wasn't it? My name's Georgie Morris — and — I was — in the seventh — class,' the woman puffed. 'Got enough candy bars and nylons in here to last a year,' she said, looking at her watch. 'Good! Five minutes left — just time for a quick tour of the palace.'

They walked through the small apartment, Georgie pointing out its idiosyncrasies — a tap knob that came off in her hand, an ancient GE refrigerator that ran better if one leg had a small block under it, throwing it off balance.

'Guess that's it,' Georgie said. 'I better get downstairs. DC taxies won't wait for Eleanor Roosevelt herself.'

'Good luck,' Page said, holding out her hand.

'Thanks,' Georgie said, shaking hands, 'but you better keep your luck, friend, 'cause you're going to need it. Myself, I can't wait to get out of this town.'

'Why?'

'Why? It's a man's town, that's why. The place is jammed full of little frilly things who just *l-o-v-e* a man in uniform. Now, we Waac officers can't wear civvies or have a drink in public, and we work late hours and weekends. We're no

131

guy's idea of a party girl — no matter what you've heard. Let me tell you, this town's a WAAC purgatory. Anyway,' she said, giving Page an appraising look, 'maybe *you'll* do better. Now I really gotta run.' And she rushed, breathless, through the door, her bag bumping behind her down the stairs.

After the first-floor door slammed, Page surveyed her new home. Drab and small though it was, with a splash of colour and a little imagination it wouldn't be half bad, she told herself. She unpacked, pressed her uniforms and placed her cosmetics and toiletries neatly on the dresser and in the tiny bathroom. Actually, this was the first place all her own she had ever had. Why, then, did she feel so glum, so much a visitor, like a small child sent away to school?

She missed Bunny and Jill and Elisabeth, but it was more than that. She missed the staccato bugle notes that signalled the passage of army time, the banging trays in the officers' mess; she even missed the incessant borrowing that was part of life in the WAAC BOQ, the gripe sessions, the rush to the PX when a shipment of scarce items was rumoured — the whole rhythm of a soldier's life. She knew now that she had always longed for it. Even as a child when she had gone away to boarding school, she had missed the ceremony of a military post. She remembered trying to hold fast to those ceremonies, of saluting the school flag on the stroke of five (while her roommates giggled), just as she had with her father at Command Retreat. She had never done it again, but at five every afternoon she had thought herself back to Fort Sam Houston or Fort Sill or to any one of the other posts where her father was serving. Page had always supposed she was missing her father, but now she knew it had been more than homesickness, because that feeling had returned full force to the adult Page now.

Finally settled into her new apartment, without dinner because she couldn't shop until she had been issued ration books, Page fell asleep hungry.

It was dark when a knock at the door awakened her. She turned on the small lamp by her bed and squinted at her alarm. One o'clock! Who could be — ? She heard the faint knock again. Slipping on her robe, she went to the door. 'Who is it?'

'Georgie, it's Paul Burkhardt.'

'I'm not Georgie,' she said.

'Are you a new roommate?' asked the male voice.

'No, I'm Lieutenant Hannaday, but . . . ' she began to explain, then stopped. She couldn't carry on a loud conversation at this time of the night.

Opening the door, she saw a major's gold leaves before she saw his face. 'Major?'

'I'm sorry to disturb you,' he said, peering into the room behind her, 'but is Georgie here?'

'Georgie's been transferred to Oglethorpe. I've sublet the apartment.'

'Oh,' he said, 'I didn't know — then I owe you an apology. You see, I've been at the Farm for over a week, and . . . ' He was obviously embarrassed, and held up the grocery bag he was carrying. 'Food,' he explained. 'When I can get away, Georgie lets me cook home style. But I'm keeping you up,' he added, backing towards the stairs in confusion. 'So sorry.'

'Wait,' she said, wondering for a moment how she could even consider inviting a strange man into her apartment to cook for her. But she wasn't the least frightened of him. He had confident, compelling eyes, dark, yet full of light; not a classically handsome face, but one that was wonderfully self-contained, almost serene. 'As long as you're here, Major Burkhardt,' she said, smiling, 'I must admit I'm famished, if you'd like to practise your culinary art on me.'

'Oh, I couldn't . . . ' he began. 'Are you sure I wouldn't . . . ' he asked, but took off his hat and stepped through the door that Page opened wider.

'I'll dress while you get started,' she said. 'You know your way around the kitchen?' Page put it in the form of a question, but it was obvious that he did. She supposed that all those spices and condiments she had noticed earlier in the cupboard had been his and not Georgie's.

Later, when she came to the kitchen, he had set the small

table and decanted a bottle of red wine, and the smell of sizzling steaks made her ravenous. 'Major, may I do something to help?'

'You can call me Paul,' he said, smiling at her. 'I think cooking for a lady in the small hours qualifies for a suspension of military etiquette.'

'My name's Page Hannaday.'

He nodded. 'Yes, I know. You don't remember, but we've met.'

'Really?'

'At the Army-Navy Club,' he said, flipping the steaks he was frying and handing her a knife, after he pointed towards a large loaf of bread. 'You were there with your father — last April it was — and I delivered a message to him from General Willis. I was on Willis' staff at the time.'

'I'm sorry,' she said honestly, slicing the bread, 'I don't remember, but I promise I won't forget you again — my mouth is absolutely watering.'

'Sit down, then,' he said, putting on his uniform jacket and holding her chair.

He poured her wine and courteously lifted his glass, which she touched with hers, and then they ate in silence, occasionally smiling across the table, not flirtatiously, but comfortably, as if they'd been having late-night suppers like this for years.

'You're really a lifesaver, Paul,' she said, sighing contentedly at her empty plate. 'I won't be able to shop for groceries until tomorrow night. But, tell me, is your farm near here?'

He laughed. 'It's not *my* farm,' he said, 'and it's not that kind of farm.'

She looked at him, puzzled.

'I know it doesn't make sense,' he said, pouring more wine into her glass. 'I can't tell you much, except that I've been working in intelligence since I left Willis' staff. The Farm — with a capital F — is a training station we have over the line in Maryland. I have an arrangement with a mess sergeant who supplies me with the basics for meals such as this one in exchange for my helping him with his German

134

out of class.'

Page knew enough not to probe into why he was teaching German at a place called the Farm. 'I could have guessed you were a teacher,' she told him. 'Even in that uniform you have a professorial air.'

Paul smiled. 'I'm disappointed,' he said, his voice a pleasing baritone. 'I hoped I'd left my tweedy look back at Rutgers.'

'Don't be disappointed. I meant it as a compliment.'

He lit her cigarette and took short puffs on his pipe. 'I should be going. You must be on duty tomorrow.'

'Yes, soon you really must, but finish your pipe first.'

He asked her about her training and her new assignment. She was aware of his controlled interest in her, and in a comfortable way she returned it. Here was a strong man, not in the muscular sense, although he was tall and well built, but in the sense of a man who had claimed his piece of the world and was content. He was like her father in that way, and just for a moment she feared this peculiarly male strength, feared being folded again into a man's life until what was beginning to be Page disappeared again.

'Now I really must go,' Paul was saying. 'Thank you so much for sharing this late supper with me,' he said at the door.

She held out her hand and he took it.

'I hope you'll let me cook for you again,' he said, small lines radiating from the corners of his eyes in a friendly way.

'I'd like that — but just a bit earlier.' She returned his smile.

'Next Saturday — about eight then?'

'Yes, that would be fine,' she said as he stepped onto the landing. 'I'm sorry you missed Georgie,' she called after him softly.

Paul stopped and moved one step back towards her. 'Yes, she was a nice girl — but we were just . . . ' he paused and answered her unasked question, 'dinner partners.'

Waving then, he went quietly down the stairs.

Page undressed and went back to bed. She could sleep three more hours before her alarm went off. Paul. What a sweet man he was, she thought, tucking the covers tight under her mattress. Imagine meeting him before and not remembering. They had probably only spoken briefly to each other, acknowledging an introduction.

Page turned to her side and tucked her knees into her stomach. Most of her life since adolescence she had been her father's hostess, greeting people for him and never really meeting them for herself. She had a feeling that with Paul, this time, it would be different.

'Georgie Morris,' she whispered into her pillow, 'I think Washington is a wonderful town.'

16

All motorists are assigned gasoline ration stickers. Those with A stickers are allowed four gallons a week; with B or C stickers they are entitled to extra gasoline because their driving is essential to the war effort or to public health. Unlimited gasoline supplies go to motorists with X stickers. Pleasure driving is banned, and a 35-mile-per-hour speed limit is enforced.

Promptly at seven on the evening she was to dine at Max Stryker's house, Elisabeth walked through the rococo lobby that served as the detachment day-room. It was filled with Waacs listening to the *Hit Parade* on a Stromberg-Carlson console radio, writing letters and gossiping.

Past the bevelled-glass doors, a black limousine with an X gasoline sticker affixed to the window waited, purring, at the kerb. It was a bright, sharply cold night — no snow — and Elisabeth hugged her WAAC winter-issue coat about her body while the uniformed chauffeur opened the car door for her. After stepping in she could see with some satisfaction that a windowful of Waacs peered out at her with intense curiosity. Elisabeth smiled at the idea that she might be the object of their gossip for the rest of the evening.

She ran her hand over the deep pile upholstery, luxuriating in the space and comfort of the limousine. Tucked in the corner she saw a fur lap robe which she recognized as mink. She spread it across her legs with a shuddering sigh at its sensuous embrace.

'Mr Max say to keep you warm all the way to Drexel Hill, miss,' the driver called through a window he had cranked down. 'Help yourself to some refreshment.'

Elisabeth opened the door of the cabinet located between the two jump seats, to reveal a well-stocked miniature bar, complete with Venetian crystal stemware.

'There's a thermos of coffee, miss, or you can have a brandy.'

She couldn't resist having a cup of coffee with the smallest jigger of brandy in it. It would have been unbearable to have such an opportunity and not take advantage of it. Few of the men she had known in New York had had such a car. She could see she would have to raise her sights.

The tyres crunched up the long, curving drive through a park of old elm trees to the largest Colonial Revival house that Elisabeth had ever seen outside the movies.

A houseman met her at the door, took her coat and ushered her into a large room on the right halfway down the tiled foyer. A wood fire burned in the huge stone fireplace, and Elisabeth thought it was the most consciously masculine room she had ever seen — rubbed wood and soft dark leather permeated with the smell of good Havana cigars; it simply reeked of male virility. She couldn't help but think that in another man she might think it all a pose, but with Max Stryker the room was obviously an unconscious extension of himself.

He left a group about the fireplace and walked quickly towards her, his hand extended. 'Mrs Gardner — it is Mrs, isn't it?' He lifted her ring hand and nodded. 'How nice of you to come. May I tell you how very attractive you look in my uniform.' He smiled, a sardonic but not unpleasant twist to his full mouth.

Elisabeth began to apologize, breaking one of her few rules. 'Oh, I didn't mean your uniform was — '

'Of course you didn't,' he said, holding up his hand to stop her apology, appearing the gracious host. 'Forgive my bad joke. Come. Let me introduce you to my friends.'

Elisabeth was not used to being bullied by a man — indeed, just the opposite — and she did not intend to give him any further chances. She nodded coolly when introduced to Kit Longley, an attractive if no longer young woman in a Trigère gown, prewar no doubt, but timeless in its classic lines.

'My dear, how sweet of you to actually *join* the women's army,' the woman said, placing a proprietary hand on Max Stryker's arm. He bent attentively and kissed the back of the hand.

One of the men, who had been introduced as Clay something or other, brought Elisabeth a martini. 'Isn't it awfully hard on a woman — I mean all the marching and living in tents and all? I'd be in it myself but for a perforated eardrum.'

She was bored with his fatuous questions, but as Max's guest she had to be nice to his friends. 'Yes, it's hard,' she answered. 'No, we don't live in tents. Yes, it's too bad about your eardrum.' She wished they could forget she was in uniform, but apparently she was such an oddity they were going to spend the evening examining her like some Barnum and Bailey freak.

'Well, Max,' Elisabeth overheard Clay say a bit tipsily, 'if all our women soldiers look like Mrs Gardner does in their uniforms, the Army should give you a bonus.'

Max replied loudly enough for everyone to hear, 'Mrs Gardner complements the uniform, Clay. She's a former Gabriella model — one of her best, as I understand it.'

'Beg pardon,' Clay mumbled into his glass. 'Thought she looked too good to be just . . . Max, old boy — ' he raised his glass in a mock toast '— leave it to you to find a diamond in an army uniform.'

At dinner, Kit Longley stared openly and none too happily at Elisabeth from across the table at Max's left. It pleased Elisabeth that she made the other woman nervous. Spoiled rich bitch! Most of all Elisabeth enjoyed the attention of a man like Max. During the months she had played soldier she had forgotten how satisfying it could be. Anyway, this was more like it. For one evening at least she had succeeded in rendering her natural enemy, a patrician woman like Kit Longley, absolutely harmless.

After a dinner of rare roast beef followed by the airiest of chocolate mousses, Max imperiously rushed his guests through their brandy. 'You must excuse us. Mrs Gardner and I have some business to discuss,' he said, signalling the butler to bring his guests' coats.

Kit paused at the door, a full-length sable thrown casually about her shoulders despite the cold. 'I doubt that we'll meet again, Mrs Gardner, but I do hope you'll take care of yourself and not get into any trouble — a young girl in a hungry lion's den, you know.'

'Thank you, Miss Longley, but please don't concern yourself,' Elisabeth replied with matching hauteur. 'I have always enjoyed taming the male animal.' Thrust, parry and touché, Elisabeth thought, not bothering to hide her satisfaction at the riposte. If there was one thing Elisabeth recognized it was a hands-off warning — she had had enough of them delivered in her direction over the years.

'Call me tomorrow, Max,' Kit said, without another glance at Elisabeth. 'I have a darling little Maryland property in mind that I want your advice about — it's so near your own Whiskey Hill.'

When the other guests had left, Elisabeth braced herself — for what, she wasn't precisely sure. Max took her arm and propelled her towards his study. Damn it! She didn't like being treated like a dog on a leash. He had been all solicitous attention while Kit Longley was watching; now he acted as if he owned her. If he thought he could use her to make another woman jealous, he was badly mistaken.

She would never let a man use her again.

'Sit there,' he said, pointing to a sofa in front of the smouldering fire, and without actually meaning to she found herself doing as she was told. She was shocked at how naturally she obeyed his commands. 'Now tell me,' he said as he lit a cigar, 'what's wrong with my uniforms.'

She spared him no detail of the problems she had identified, enjoying her moment in Max's spotlight. He listened attentively, and slowly the anger that had fuelled so much of the evening drained away from her.

'Is this the substance of the report you're going to give Nick — Colonel Nicolson?'

'That's most of it, plus, of course, my recommendation for a new uniform.'

Elisabeth could not tell if he was upset with her. He had hardly stopped moving — pacing up and down in front of her with a relentless energy that was indisputably charming. He moved to the bar enclosed on three sides by glass mirrors, which reflected every angle of his handsome head, and poured two small snifters.

'Here,' he said, 'you've earned part of my last bottle of prewar Courvoisier. It comes from the Charente region; a special white wine grape is grown there and in no other spot on the earth. Do you know France?'

'Madame Gabriella told me a great deal about it,' Elisabeth answered untruthfully, and then said honestly, 'but I haven't been myself — yet.'

'Interesting — since Madame was born and raised in the Bronx and her accent is as phoney as a three-franc note.' He waved his hand abruptly to dismiss the subject. 'Nevertheless, my dear, as soon as this war is over you must go abroad.' He said it as conversationally as if he were suggesting she visit Baltimore. 'Would you like that?'

Yes, she would like that very much. Elisabeth felt the soft sensuousness of the leather sofa gather her body into it as the brandy warmed her blood. It was late. She had only a midnight pass, but she knew she did not want to leave this place or this presence.

He sat down beside her. 'You may be right about some of

140

the problems you cite, but you're incredibly naïve to think they'll remake the entire uniform on your say-so, not with the enormous stockpile they're building. On the other hand, minor pattern alterations are another matter. I'll have something to say about that — don't think I mean to keep my mouth shut and lose a very large contract. I mean to fight you for it — and I mean to win!' He paused, then smiled. 'But I'd so much prefer we work together.'

Elisabeth was off balance. Max Stryker seemed to hold out a mysterious threat and then to change it into a promise. She was aware that he was close to her and that the heat of his body was getting all mixed up with the hot embers in the fireplace and the brandy. Suddenly her head was too heavy to remain erect and she rested it on the back of the sofa; her hair uncoiled from its tightly controlled roll and spread across her shoulders, falling as if she had planned it — and for once she hadn't — next to his hand.

He twisted his fingers in her hair and gently, but relentlessly, pulled her head closer to his. He sought her hand, turned it over and kissed the soft fleshy place under the thumb. His strangely breathy voice excited her.

'Elisabeth, tell me if I'm wrong, but I think you and I would know how to work together.'

For a moment she held her breath. Did he somehow know what she had done at Gabriella's? Was this entire evening a threat? Was he another Joe Bonine, only with fancier tastes?

She reclaimed the hair he had been holding spread between his fingers like the reins to a balky mare. Some primal instinct overtook her, and she stood up abruptly, ready to flee. Slowly, without loosing her hand, Max rose, too, his eyes locked on hers. The fading firelight danced across the angles of his face, now sinister with the power she suddenly knew he exerted over her.

'You see,' he was saying with a disarming smile, pointing towards the wall, 'I do cast a shadow, so I must not be a vampire after all.'

She was hardly aware of his words. All her energy flowed to her legs, telling them to carry her to safe ground.

In a low voice, with just a hint of uncharacteristic sadness, he was saying, 'Don't believe the gossips, Elisabeth. You must have been their target more than once, so you can understand how I've been misunderstood.'

She nodded, drawn now to his steady gaze. Against her will, a will she no longer seemed able to control, she moved an involuntary step closer to him. He was right, of course. She did feel she understood him. The person she didn't understand was herself. Whatever she had been, she knew she had never been a self-deceiver; she had always been on to herself, but here she was ready to fall into this man's arms, to throw herself into his bed. And who was he? A tough amoral bastard who would forget her as soon as the door closed behind her. Besides, it was quite possible, in spite of the passion her practised eye read in his face, that he would use her simply to keep his lucrative uniform contract.

'The next time you come, Elisabeth,' Max was saying, as if she had been a part of his life always, 'I want you to wear one of the gowns I have upstairs. There are several that would suit you well.'

With her last strength she flung a question at him. 'What makes you think there will be a next time?'

He sighed impatiently, his hand tracing the curve of her shoulder. 'Elisabeth, you are the last woman in the world I would expect to play childish games.'

It was no declaration, simply an attitude that made instant sense to her. And then she stepped into his kiss, and was suffused in the glow of his sensuous approval. For the first time in her life she was perfectly honest, not faking her response.

'You're coming with me to my place in Maryland next weekend,' he murmured, his hot breath almost melting her ear.

He walked with her to the portico and stood framed in the double doors as the limousine bore Elisabeth away down the curving drive, a light snowfall glistening in the headlights. She hugged the dark image of him standing there throughout the ride back to the Franklin Hotel, beating back the warnings that every man-knowing cell of her mind screamed out. She willed herself to forget about Marne, about the WAAC, about Page and Jill and Bunny — to forget about anything that might stop her from having Max Stryker. As she climbed the stairs to the orderly room, the shabby carpet suddenly looked as colourful as a just-woven Persian rug.

'Ma'am,' the CO said after she signed in at the pass book, 'your husband called earlier this evening from Texas. He said to tell you he'd be here on leave next weekend.'

17

The Battle of Kasserine Pass in Tunisia pits inexperienced American troops against Rommel's Afrika Korps. Luftwaffe Stuka dive bombers create confusion in the Allied ranks, resulting in ten thousand casualties.

> *AAF Navigation School*
> *Hondo, Texas*
> *Sunday, 14 February, 1943*

HELLO KID,

I know that Mother Bunny has been rotten in the letter writing department, but you should see my schedule. At least, you get Sundays off in code school (Jill, did you get over to see my mama yet? She's expecting you for dinner) but for us poor troop officers there ain't no such thing as a day off. I've written WAAC HQ & they promised me an exec, but they're so busy staffing new training centres, I'm at the bottom of their list.

Sorry — had to stop for an emergency. No heat in one of the barracks. We can't stoke the coal furnace ourselves because we women are too weak (?) so we have to send for two firemen, who have to call for an MP guard before they can enter the WAAC area & on and on. Who dreams up these regs?

I missed Elisabeth's husband last Wednesday. He called to say he was passing through (on leave & on his way to Philly. Overseas?) and asked me to meet him at the O club for a drink. Wouldn't you know that was the afternoon I'd get stuck at the Red Cross because one of my Auxies wasn't writing home — which brought the Post Chaplain & the Grey Ladies roaring to the rescue of American motherhood. By the time I'd called the woman on the carpet, extracted a properly contrite letter, taken it to the Red Cross & dashed to the club, he'd gone. There goes my last chance to see the big guy who talked our glamour queen into marriage. Speaking of E., thanks for the news. Leave it to her to get a cosy set-up like a hotel with civvy chow. Maybe the army does know what it's doing sometimes. I can't imagine *her* here in a Texas sandstorm!

Speaking of husbands (?), I got letters from both of my exs (or is that exes?). I've heard men say that putting on a uniform brings old girlfriends out of the woodwork — Allotment Annies, ya know. Guess there's nothing like a girl in khaki to make a guy straighten up and fly right.

Which reminds me about the latest latrine rumour — next time you hear from me I may be a fly girl on a real air base instead of a school. Talk is they're going to move photo lab tech school to Lowry Field in Colorado.

Take it easy kiddo — AND DON'T TRY TO WIN THE WAR SINGLE-HANDED

MOTHER BUNNY.

Bunny folded the tissue-thin stationery into the matching envelope, licked it thoughtfully and dropped it into the mail clerk's out box. *Damn it!* She missed the kid, and Page too, even Elisabeth — why, she'd give a month's pay just to see that dazzling model's smile of hers, the one she could turn on and off at will.

For a few minutes Bunny allowed herself a reverie back to her OC days when all four of them had been outsiders in the Army, clinging together, overwhelmed by a sense that every day they had to get up and make history.

There was no camaraderie now for Bunny. She was the lone WAAC officer on the post. Another woman in uniform at the officers' club was either Red Cross, USO or a nurse from the post hospital — hardly the same thing at all.

Not that companionship was any problem — especially the male variety. If anything, she felt that she stood at the head of a long line of men, all of them wanting something from her — wanting her to be their lover, their sister, their sweetheart and, at times, their mother. No, the worst part of this duty, she had to admit, wasn't the loneliness. No, the worst part was that Johnny Palermo had begun to write to her (she had her sister Angela to thank for giving him her address), not the kind of letter that Johnny LaMonica and his mother had written, with 'patriotic duty' spelled out all over it, but love letters that interrupted the healing process, a process Bunny knew hadn't progressed as far as it should have. Of course, the simplest solution was to send them back unopened so that he got the idea she was out of his reach. But she hadn't done that.

Outside her office, Bunny heard the orderly room radio blaring reports about a big battle in North Africa. Her head ached — she'd been on duty every day for a month — but she hadn't the heart to tell the first sergeant to turn the news down. The sergeant's son was with the First Infantry Division right in the thick of things.

Bunny opened her desk drawer and saw Johnny's letters lying on top of a pile of requisition forms. For weeks she had read them over and over without answering. What could she say? *Glad you know you made a mistake. Wish you were here.* It was much too late for regrets. It was too late to reinvest the real Johnny with the dreams of perfect physical love she'd had; too late since the night he'd turned on her. How could she ever go back to trusting him? Even if she could trust him — and she knew she would be a fool to try — she was in the Army for the duration.

Bunny sat there in the winter day's half-light. Outside her window she saw the detachment flag tugging against its halyard, as if it was trying to break away.

Her fingers, inside the drawer, traced the stamp on his last letter, circled it compulsively, felt its rough edges and then moved on to outline the letters of his name in the upper left corner — the name he wrote in an awkward boy's script that used no capital letters.

Memories rushed through her fingers. Bunny saw his eyes gleaming darkly up at her from a white pillow as he propelled exciting rhythms from her body. The memory was too vivid. She closed her eyes and, in response to a sudden rush of feeling, pressed her legs together and buried her face in her hands. *Oh, God, all this agony from a few letters!* She'd be crazy to actually see him again.

A knock on her open door caused her to drag her head quickly erect. The mail clerk was eyeing her quizzically. 'Yes, Corporal. What is it?'

'I've got the jeep now, ma'am, so I'm going to run the mail over to the post office,' she said, holding up the contents of her out box. 'Is this it?'

Bunny hesitated for so long the corporal shifted her weight and looked embarrassed.

'No, Corporal. Give me fifteen minutes. There'll be one more letter to go.'

18

President Franklin D. Roosevelt submitted a whopping $109-billion 1943 budget to Congress, $100 billion earmarked for the war effort.

On a snowy Saturday in mid-February, Marne Wilson Gardner burst from the crowd at the main Philadelphia Greyhound depot, his duffle bag slung under his muscular arm, his great green eyes roving the milling crowd of soldiers, sailors and civilians like searchlights at a movie premier.

What if Elisabeth hadn't received his telegram? *Oh Jesus!* There wasn't one precious minute to waste. Maybe she had duty. Seven months was a long time to be away from any wife — but a wife like his! Christ, he'd driven himself half crazy on the bus remembering her body — every inch of it. It was the kind of memory that made a man clench his fists and dig them self-consciously deeper into his pockets so as not to betray their longing. She has *got* to be here, he thought, then stopped his undisciplined searching and began, like any trained combat armour officer, a sector-by-sector survey of the waiting room jammed with uniforms. Suddenly, he saw her coming through the revolving doors from the street outside.

He pushed his way through the crowd to her, oblivious of the men in overalls chewing tobacco, girls in slacks with their hair piled in ringlets on top of their heads and tired women with kids in tow — oblivious of everything until he felt his arms around her, the familiar smell of Worth perfume in his nostrils and her body filling the aching hollows of his own.

'I've never kissed a lieutenant before,' he said after a long embrace, which only intensified his need for her, 'or is that an old joke for a Waac?' He saw that people had stopped in their rush to their own destinations to stare sentimentally at the uniformed man and woman greeting each other. Before she could answer, he rushed on. 'Listen, darling — ' he took charge with an urgency born of empty months ' — let's get out of here.'

He took her straight to the hotel where she had booked a room, passing Independence Hall with scarcely a glance at its perfectly balanced Georgian façade. He held her hand firmly but gently, the words tumbling from him, words he couldn't write in letters or say over the telephone.

Elisabeth's mind, as she sat next to Marne, was engaged with his on a conscious level, acting as a mediator between her husband's need for her and her own deeper needs. That deeper self was thinking of Max, not deliberately, but compulsively, and angrily viewed Marne as an intruder.

He wondered that she was so quiet, almost shy with him. But he could understand. They'd had such a little time together after their wedding. She didn't know him as her husband, but her letters had been so sweet, so loving.

Marne ordered a bottle of champagne sent to their room and tipped the departing bellboy extravagantly.

'Elisabeth, you don't know how many times I've thought of you like this,' he said, drawing her down on the bed beside him, kissing her neck, her eyes, her lips.

She winced and turned her face away from his. 'Your beard, Marne . . . '

What an oaf he was! 'Of course,' he said scrambling to his feet, longing for these next hours to be perfection. 'I'm sorry, Elisabeth. I've been on manoeuvres so long, it's hard to behave like a civilized man.' He rummaged in his bag, extracted his robe and headed for the shower. 'Darling, will you order dinner sent up?' he called over his shoulder. 'I'm not going to share you with a roomful of strangers. Not tonight.'

Elisabeth watched him step into the shower. Less than a year ago, she had been so willing, even eager, to barter her body for the life Marne Gardner offered her. Something in her had changed and she did not understand it. This lack of perception frightened her. She had always been self-knowing, able to trust her own motives, and she had based this trust on her faultlessly realistic outlook.

After he had showered and shaved, they drank

champagne while they waited for dinner. He told her about the months of training and more months of teaching others what he himself had learned. 'I'm up for my captaincy. It's hard to believe — less than three years out of the Point. There's no stopping me now.' He covered her hand with his. 'How would you like to be a general's lady someday?'

'That would be nice,' she agreed with measured enthusiasm.

He reasoned that her coldness to the idea of being a general's wife was due to her hatred for the WAAC.

'I missed seeing your friend Bunny.'

'Didn't you get my letter with the directions?'

'Yes, but she was on duty and couldn't get away. Too bad, I really wanted to meet her because she was your friend.'

'You would have liked her, Marne.' Elisabeth had no doubt about that. The two of them were a type. Bunny carrying that huge torch for her ex-husband, and Marne encasing his wife in marble and imprisoning her on a pedestal.

'Marne darling, do you know where you're going?' she asked, and to him her voice was wonderful even when it questioned him.

'I've a pretty good idea it'll be North Africa. That's where armour is being tested so far in this war.'

'But isn't it almost over in Africa? Rommel will be beaten soon.'

'You can never count the old Desert Fox out. But Rommel's not why we're going to North Africa now. Rumour has it there'll be a second front soon, either through southern France or along the Baltic coast. We've got to be ready to jump off no matter where the Allies decide to go in.'

Dinner arrived, late. Good service was one of the first casualties in wartime, he told her. He didn't mind that the entrée was not steak, but turkey. 'Sorry,' the waiter had said pointedly, 'but we're sending all the steaks to our boys in uniform.' Smart-aleck kid!

Elisabeth had taken off her jacket and tie and loosed her

glorious hair. He was still not used to seeing her in uniform — still a bit stunned, really. He preferred her in one of the fashionable gowns he had first seen her wear, the ones that draped around every curve and hollow of her.

He still could not understand why she had so suddenly left Gabriella's. It was unlike Elisabeth to be impulsive. He decided against bringing up the subject again, since she had written that she was happy with this posting. Still — his Elisabeth with second lieutenant's bars on her shoulders . . .

Marne saw that their windows looked out on a block-square park, two walks crossing in the middle to form an X. A few shipyard workers, from the look of their lunch pails, hurried towards home in the dusk to beat the blackout. One lone lost man stood at the centre where the paths crossed, seeming not to know which to take. A slight shiver shook him, but he shrugged it off. He hated indecision.

Gently, he leaned across the table and covered her smooth hands with his manoeuvre-hardened ones. He could not wait for dessert, or for brandy. He could wait no longer — surely civilized behaviour demanded no more of him than the seven-month sentence he had served. Scooping her into his arms, he carried her to the bed, set her carefully down on the coverlet, threw off his robe, and began fumbling with the buttons on her shirt. Always in his daydreams he was the suave lover, whisking a woman's clothes off without her even being aware they were gone. But when he was with Elisabeth, he was no better at it than he had been the first time he'd got a girl to go all the way in his roommate's Ford run-about.

At last he had her underwear off, her skin shivering under his fingers. He kissed her hard, and his memory of the problems of the past months — of tank tactics, gun trajectories and armoured firepower — was forgotten in the sweet rush of his erection, and the male pride he felt in giving it to her. He determined to keep his eyes upon her face as he took her; he wanted to watch her beautifully curving lips part in an agony of passionate pleading, to see her head arch against the pillow for that uncontrollable moment before she collapsed after climax. He wanted this picture indelibly engraved in his memory, to be called forth at will during the days and nights of combat he knew he would soon face.

Elisabeth lay under the burden of his loving, formless — a mouth, breasts, legs, all unconnected to her feelings. Only one man in her life so far had excited her sexually, and he had shamed her forever in the doing. Since her father, the rest had given her no more than mild exercise. 'I love you, darling,' she told him, more or less automatically.

Later he lay on the rumpled bed, the top sheet pulled across his hard-muscled abdomen, and watched her brush her hair at the dressing table. Something bothered him, something elusive that he tried to grasp but could not. Elisabeth was willing in bed, compliant and yet . . .? 'Tell me darling,' he said and watched her eyes to see if they turned to scorn, 'did you like it?'

'Like what?' she asked, her own eyes foglike as if she were seeing another room altogether.

Ignoring the warning bell that tolled his own contempt for men who begged women for sexual compliments, he repeated, 'Like it? You know — like it when I make love to you?'

She hated it when men behaved like little boys with a crush on the teacher, wheedling compliments after school. 'Of course, darling,' she said and continued brushing her hair.

Her answer wasn't enough for him. Heedlessly he rushed on, knowing he would never trust an answer he had coaxed, but helpless to stop now he'd started. 'Then why do I feel you didn't like it — that something was, well, missing for you?'

She brushed on, but her lips stopped counting the strokes. 'Have I ever said that I didn't like it? Have I ever refused you?'

'It's not that, Elisabeth. *Christ!* It's not anything you've done. It's a feeling I have.'

He saw her eyes lose their private dream and focus on him. 'What makes you think I'm responsible for your feelings, especially when you can't put a name to them?'

151

This was going badly. He had only wanted her to reassure him of her love and desire for him, and now the thin thread that held them together after so many months apart was coming unravelled. He plunged on, knowing it was no longer possible to recall any of their words. 'Did you . . . did you . . . uh, climax?'

She swung about on the dressing-table bench until she faced him, her beautiful features the reality of every dream of woman he had ever had since he was a boy. 'Yes,' she said, her voice plainly bored, which was worse to him than her anger. 'Of course I climaxed. Why do you men always seem to think orgasm is so difficult for women? The truth is, Marne, that there's really not much I can do to stop it if I have a reasonably adequate lover.'

He did not mention their lovemaking to her again. In a way, he almost wished she had lied to him. He would have known it, but somehow the lie would have been better than the truth. At least he could have had something to work towards, to make better. When he made love to her again that night and the next day, it felt stripped of all specialness; and he felt like some cashiered British soldier of old, with buttons and medals ripped off, marching out the fort gate — a man in love still but less than the man he could have been.

During the last of their brief hours together, she was as attentive as he could wish. He began to think that he had pushed her too hard and that her response had been what any normally spirited girl would have made. It had probably been his fault. After all, his wife had been one of New York's top models, not a nun. He'd known that — he was no kid — but he also believed she had a loyal heart. Other men looked at her; the poor bastards almost drooled. But she never gave them any cause. He had watched her covertly since the day they met: she never gave other men a tumble. She was absolutely faithful to him; he was sure of it. For God's sake, she'd even joined the Army to share his life as best she could. He felt rotten. How could he have doubted the best wife a guy ever had?

Finally there was an hour left to catch the bus for the

ninety-mile trip to the New York port of embarkation. 'Darling,' he said and gave his tie one last tug, 'I want to spare you a goodbye at the station. I couldn't bear to leave you standing on the platform alone.'

'But I do want to see you off, Marne,' she said, a soft protest in her tone. 'I don't know when I'll see you again.' Real tears gathered under her lashes and were swept away by the back of her hand in a little-girl gesture that imprinted itself on his memory, wiping away any small lingering doubt.

'Don't worry about me. I'm not a dogface on foot. Remember, I'll be surrounded by two inches of armour plate.' He captured her inside his arms one last time. 'And remember, too, darling, I know what I'm fighting for. I'll have you to come back to and our life together — and the family we'll have. Just knowing you're here, waiting for me . . .' He couldn't go on, the words wouldn't move past the huge lump in his throat.

After one last long look, a look to memorize the tiniest details of her, he closed the door and, taking the steps two at a time, rushed down the stairs, through the lobby and out to the taxi stand near the little park.

Elisabeth saw Marne turn and stare up at the hotel, searching for the window to their room. She sensed the hurt he'd tried to hide, and she was uncomfortable, but she did not accept responsibility for his pain. Whether he knew it or not, she always retained with every man the freedom to leave him emotionally just as she had been left on her own in the emotional limbo of her childhood experience. She pulled back the flowered yellow chintz curtain and waved until he saw her. From the fifth floor she noticed he did not look as tall, his massive shoulders became quite ordinary. She would have to be more careful of his male ego. The bigger they come . . .

More importantly, she would have to rethink her marriage to Marne. It had become terribly clear to her during the last two days that she had made a bargain she no longer wanted to keep.

Idly she ran her fingers down the curtain draw cord as she

153

watched his taxi pull away, and for a moment she resisted the feelings that had been building barriers to rational thought all weekend. Then she swept her mind of all interfering images, walked to the night table and picked up the phone. She dialled Drexel 5-1025. 'Hello, will you please tell Mr Stryker that Mrs Gardner is on the line?'

'Mr Max and his party just comin' in from Maryland now, madam.'

She heard receding footsteps and then the sound of a telephone being picked up.

'Good evening, Elisabeth,' Max Stryker said with no hint of surprise in his voice.

She felt an unfamiliar thrill of excitement that was decidedly physical, more so because these last hours with Marne had been so devoid of real physicality.

Max went right to the point. 'When I didn't hear from you about this weekend, naturally I thought — '

'My husband was here on overseas leave.'

'I see.'

'Max — ' she chose her words deliberately ' — I've been thinking. About my report to Colonel Nicolson, perhaps I've been too hasty.'

19

*Don't sit under the apple tree with anyone else but
me,
Anyone else but me, Anyone else but me,
No, no, no,
Don't sit under the apple tree with anyone else but
me
Till I come marching home.
I just got word from a guy who heard
From the guy next door to me
The girl he met just loves to pet
And it fits you to a 'T'
So don't sit under the apple tree with anyone else but
me
Till I come marching home.*
'Don't Sit Under the Apple Tree', *words and
music by Lew Brown, Charlie Tobias and Sam H.
Stept*

'I t's going to be a thirty-minute wait for West Coast
circuits, Lieutenant Hammersmith,' the woman at
the Red Cross office told her, 'and then there are
three others ahead of you.'

'I'll wait,' Jill said, the balmy early-April Sunday adding
to the natural lethargy of a duty-free afternoon.

For Jill Henry Hammersmith the months at Fort
Monmouth had passed swiftly. The first part of code school
had been devoted to learning the endless details of unclas-
sified communications-centre procedure, Teletype sending
and receiving, message routing and punch-tape reading.
Often she had sent coded traffic on its way, wondering at
the mystery behind the jumbled five-letter groups.

Now at last the waiting was over. Her top-secret
clearance had been approved and tomorrow she would
enter the code room, a guarded windowless vault in the
middle of the comcentre — a place of mystery to the

uninitiated. After three more months of cryptographic training, she would be eligible for an overseas levy. She just *had* to go! If she couldn't get over there where the war was actually happening, all her efforts in the WAAC, her desire to take Neil's place and show him she hadn't asked him to suffer something she wasn't willing to undergo herself — all of it would count for nothing.

Page had agreed that getting overseas was important, last Sunday when Jill called from one of the pay phones at the O club, hoping Page could put in a word for her.

'But, Jill, it's not that easy to get overseas,' Page had said. 'Director Hobby insists that only volunteers go until Congress changes our auxiliary status. I realize you'd gladly volunteer, but that's not the big problem. As long as we're only *with* the Army and not *in* it, a Waac is not legally eligible to be treated in a military hospital if she's wounded, and if she's killed there's no insurance.'

'I know that, Page, but what about the bill Representative Rogers introduced last January to make the WAAC a part of the Army?'

'It hasn't passed yet,' Page answered.

'Where does that leave us?'

Page had been frank. 'I don't know. Anything can happen. Congress is uncertain, as usual. They're arguing now that if women aren't in the front lines they don't deserve soldiers' benefits. We asked them if they would then deny military status to General Eisenhower and his headquarters staff, but who knows whether logic will work with the men on Capitol Hill.'

'Damn it! I don't know why I'm beating my brains out up here at Monmouth.'

'Yes, you do, Jill. Our orders from Marshall here in the Director's office are to forge ahead as if the Women's Army Corps bill will pass. We all have to keep going, especially now that . . .' Page's voice had suddenly grown sad and trailed off.

'Especially now that what?'

At first Page hadn't wanted to tell her, but she had wheedled it out of her.

156

'There's just a lot of gossip about the WAAC, Jill. Bad stuff — organized slander, really. We're all supposed to be pregnant or lesbians, or both — which tells you how crazy the talk is. We've tried to counter with positive stories, but it just keeps coming from everywhere. G-2 thinks it might be Nazi sabotage.'

'Oh, that old stuff,' Jill had said. She had dealt with attitudes like that when she decided to pursue a career in veterinary medicine. When a woman stepped out of the kitchen, the whole world thought something must be wrong with her. The talk had got worse, she remembered, when her paper on chicken pneumonitis had won a national prize. If the gossips are after the WAAC, it must mean we're doing a hell of a job, she thought, and made a mental note to say so the next time she wrote to Page.

'Lieutenant, you're next,' the woman in Red Cross grey told her. In the game room next door, Jill could hear the click of billiard balls and over that the jukebox playing the Andrews Sisters' big hit 'Don't Sit Under the Apple Tree'.

She gave the operator her home number and heard it ring.

'Hello,' a familiar male voice answered.

'Hi Daddy, it's me, Jill.'

'Jewel!' He used his pet name for her. 'How are you?'

'I'm fine, Daddy, just fine. How's everybody there?'

'Everybody's well. Your mother's at the church now — there's a special service tonight for the boys.'

They both fell silent then as people do when they know each other so well they don't need words.

Her father broke the silence. 'You ought to see the trees this year, Jewel — early spring, no late frost. They're all in bloom, especially the ones down by the Martins' house. Looks like a heavy crop of Albertas.'

She had wondered if he would mention Neil first, or if she would have to. 'Daddy, has Mr Martin told you how Neil . . . how he's getting along?'

'Better than that. I saw him two or three days ago.'

'You saw Neil?'

'He's on convalescent leave — between operations, his

157

dad told me.'

'Did you talk to him? Did he ask about me?'

'Well, Jewel, I wouldn't call it a conversation — he a . . . he has a speech problem — but I said hello and he said hello.'

'Are you implying he didn't ask about me?'

'I'm sorry, honey.'

'Oh . . .'

'Give him time.'

'How much time? I've been writing to him for eight months and he hasn't answered once, Daddy — not once. And when I went to see him at Oak Knoll, he . . . I can't describe it, Daddy.'

'Bear's down there with him. Neil seemed to want him to stay, and I couldn't see any harm in it.'

'No — I mean, of course. No harm at all.'

Why not? Bear was her dog, but Neil had loved him since the day her father had rescued the roly-poly albino German-shepherd puppy from a breeder determined to kill it to keep his kennel strain pure. They had named him Polar Bear, soon shortened to Bear, because he looked so much like the cub they'd seen at San Francisco's Fleishacker Zoo on her thirteenth birthday.

Neil and Bear had looked so odd together — like brothers, really: Bear with his thick white coat and pale eyes; Neil, fair and sun-blond, his eyelashes so white they disappeared in the light, leaving his blue eyes unprotected.

Neil had laughed when she mentioned it. 'Maybe in my next life I'll come back as Bear.'

'Jewel?' her father was saying.

'Yes, Daddy, I'm here.'

'I'll go get the dog and bring him home if you want me to.'

'No — leave him for as long as Neil wants him. And Daddy, tell Neil I said so.'

'I will, Jewel. I'll tell him, but . . .'

'But what?'

'He's changed, honey.'

'I know, but they can do marvels of reconstructive surgery —'

158

'No, that's not the kind of change I mean. He's different inside too, Jewel. The Neil you knew is gone — '

'Oh . . .'

'— and I don't think he's coming back.'

Although she didn't tell her father, Jill rejected what he said. If Neil blamed her for his wounds, he'd get over it. He had to. Her mother had taught her that everything in life works out for those who try hard enough and long enough. She'd just have to be patient and keep trying. Maybe Bear could do what her letters couldn't do — remind Neil that she was coming back to him.

For a moment, Des Stratton's face floated unsuppressed to the surface of her mind.

You can't take what you dish out to me, the image said.

It's not the same thing at all, she defended herself. *Neil and I grew up together, while you only pretended to be my friend*.

But her vision of Des wasn't listening to her. He smiled, and said — it was funny how well she remembered his smile — *Answer me, Jill, if you could go back and do it all over again, would you marry Neil?*

But she didn't answer, because she forced him out of her mind, and she didn't have to answer.

Jill paid her telephone bill and started back towards the BOQ. The streets were almost empty. Sunday afternoon was a quiet time on a military post. Dayrooms and service clubs were full of lounging Waacs. In the barracks, laundry and ironing, letters home and gripe sessions spun out the daylight hours until the post theatres opened after chow, which was usually cold cuts.

Jill knew she should get some meat. Tomorrow was a big day — her first inside the code room — and she wanted to be sharp. She really had nothing to worry about. Neil would write soon — Bear would do that for her. As for Des Stratton, she had forced herself not to look at his return address on the last letter she'd torn up, and so now she didn't know where he was.

20

*April 17, 1943: One hundred and fifteen B-17s
bomb the Bremen aircraft plant, shooting down ten
German fighters; sixteen US bombers are lost.*

*A Young & Rubicam advertising campaign
designed to boost sagging WAAC recruiting
changes the unpopular 'Release a Man for Combat'
theme to pretty Waacs saying, 'I joined to serve my
country and am having the time of my life.'*

B unny felt the C-47 bank in a wide arc on its
approach to Bolling Field. Through the forward
window she saw small parks and the Capitol dome
slide past below, followed moments later by the
Washington Monument.

'Fasten your harness, honey,' the co-pilot yelled back
through the open cockpit door.

'Sure thing, Lieutenant.' She shrugged into the webbing
buckled to the metal seats along the plane's bulkhead,
adjusting the straps which had never been meant to accom-
modate a generous female bosom.

They had been five hours out of Daytona's Wright Field,
fighting April head winds all the way. More than once
Bunny had wondered if she had saved herself several days
of furlough travel time only to be turned into a permanent
ice cube. If the crew hadn't shared an enormous thermos of
hot coffee with her, she would have been frozen solid after
the heater had gone out somewhere over Pittsburgh.

The wheels touched down and screeched along the
tarmac; her teeth rattled as the pilot throttled back and
braked to a stop in front of a hangar. The guy must have
raced jalopies as a civilian.

'Thanks for the ride, fellas,' she said, grinning, as they
elbowed each other to help her down the short metal
stairs.

'How about meeting me for a drink tonight, Lieutenant?'

said the co-pilot, who couldn't have been much more than twenty by the sparseness of his moustache. Why did the young ones always seem to go for her? Mother Bunny's fatal charm for children, no doubt.

'I'll take a rain check, guys. See you back at Lowry in ten days.' She didn't want to hurt their feelings — men of any age never could understand a woman wanting to be by herself — but she had a heavy date with a bath tub and room service.

She walked towards the ops hut, put down her flight bag and looked up Page's number at the Pentagon.

'WAAC headquarters. Office of the Director,' a voice answered.

'Second Leader Hannaday, please. Say that Bunny Palermo is on the wire.'

A moment later a familiar voice was calling her name. 'Bunny! Where *are* you?'

'I'm at Bolling — or what's left of me is. Arrgh! The C-47 hasn't been built yet with my anatomy in mind.'

Page laughed. 'Same old Bunny. You never change.' She was glad. The whole world was falling apart, but if Bunny stayed the same . . .

Bunny snorted. 'Of course I've changed. It's been five months, one birthday and two grey hairs since we left Fort Des Moines.' She shifted the telephone to the far end of the counter, making room for a crew studying weather maps. 'Right now, Page, I need a room. Can you tell me a hotel that won't cost me a month's pay?'

'Hotel?' Page repeated. 'There's not a room to be had anywhere in Washington. Besides, I wouldn't hear of it. I have an apartment with the only unrented sofa in town. Have you got a pencil? Take this down. Tell the cabbie to go to 210 Nineteenth Street — that's off Connecticut Avenue near the Mayflower Hotel. When you get there, tell my landlady, Mrs Mallory, that you're a friend of mine and she'll let you in. I'll call ahead so she'll be expecting you. Have you got all that?'

'Sure thing.'

'I'll try to get home as soon after six as I can make it.'

Later, Bunny's taxi crossed the Potomac and was immediately snarled in traffic. She nervously saw the meter edging past the dollar mark. At this rate the money she'd saved for her first leave wouldn't go far.

They passed the Tidal Basin and she drew in her breath sharply at the sight of three thousand Japanese cherry trees in gorgeous blossom.

'Some guys chopped four of them down after Pearl Harbor,' the cabbie told her over his shoulder. 'Shoulda chopped 'em all down.'

Oh no, she thought, they're too beautiful, although she understood his anger. How could a country that sent such a gift, a gift that carpeted Washington with pink-and-white petals every April, drop bombs on a peaceful Sunday morning? It hadn't made any sense on December 7, 1941, and in the spring of 1943 it still didn't.

Three GIs heading for Union Station crowded into the cab on Massachusetts Avenue. As soldiers do, she exchanged names and duty stations with them.

Uniforms jammed the downtown area — olive drab, navy blue, marine green — as they turned into Nineteenth Street.

'Okay, soldier lady, here you are,' the driver said and stopped midway down the block. 'That'll be a dollar eighty-five.'

She took out two one-dollar bills and handed them to him. 'Keep the change.'

'Nothin' doin'.' He handed her a dime and a nickel. 'You keep it. Makes me feel a million bucks just hauling you girls in uniform.'

'Thanks.' She'd heard so many unflattering stories about DC cabbies since the war started. Bad news travelled fast and good news not at all. She made a mental note to relate what the cabbie had done.

Waving goodbye to her fellow passengers, she walked up the wide steps of the white stone building and rang the bell button marked 'Mrs Mallory, Manager.'

'Right this way,' the manager said after Bunny explained who she was. 'Miss Hannaday's rooms are off the second

162

landing, facing the garden in the rear. The garden is lovely this spring. It doesn't know there's a war on. Now, mind that bucket of sand and the shovel in the foyer. Mr Byron, the block warden, is a stickler for all that air raid paraphernalia. But then you army girls know all about that, don't you?'

Mrs Mallory chattered on. She reminded Bunny of her mama, who filled the empty air with words, not to get answers but to occupy space with the familiar and comforting sound of her own voice saying things she could believe. After thanking her for her trouble, Bunny put her bag down in Page's living room. The sun-splashed room full of bulky oak furniture was not up to Page's easy sophistication, but was comfortable and heavenly quiet after hours of thundering airplane engines. The windows looked out over a brick courtyard of clipped privet hedges, blooming ranunculus and anemones. After months of Army Air Forces green and grey, on a base where the only flower beds surrounded the reveille cannon in front of the headquarters building, this patch of colour looked to Bunny like the Garden of Eden. She opened the windows to let in the fresh late-April breeze, took off her shoes and promptly fell sound asleep curled up on the sofa.

'Fall out!'

Bunny's feet hit the floor before she opened her eyes to see a laughing Page standing over her. 'Damn it,' she said in mock anger, 'there ought to be a regulation against barrack jokes when a body's on furlough.'

'I couldn't resist. How are you, Bunny?' Page gave her a welcoming hug.

'They're making one helluva photographer out of me, Page. I wouldn't have believed it, but I'm not bad at it, not half bad.'

Page nodded. 'I knew you must be good when you got out of troop work to train as an instructor. How do you like it?'

'Well enough — no, I'll be honest, I'm crazy about it, especially when I get to go up with the aerial reconnaissance camera.' Then she asked Page the question most on her mind. 'Do you think that means I'll have to go overseas? You know I've never been gung-ho to go — not like Jill.'

'Not much chance overseas, Bunny. Although the requests are flooding in, it looks like only about fifteen percent of the WAAC will get out of the States.'

'I hope you're right. I was never one for camping out. The last time I tried it I was six and I peed in my blanket and ran home crying in the middle of the night.'

Page smiled at the image of a small soggy Bunny dashing through the New Jersey night. 'I'm telling you not to worry. There are plenty of officers who *want* to go,' she said, removing her uniform jacket and undoing her tie. 'More than we can ever use.'

Page bent to pick up a box of groceries. 'Look what I found for us at the corner butcher — lovely thick pork chops, and only seven red points. Mmmm! Come on into the kitchen and keep me company.'

Bunny followed her into the small kitchenette. 'I'm good for more than chitchat. Remember me — Home-and-Hearth Bunny? I come from a big family, and Mama wanted all her girls to be good cooks.' She rolled up her khaki shirtsleeves and set the table, snapped the green beans and blended the orange vegetable colouring into the white margarine. 'It's good to be in a kitchen again, Page. I never knew what a little homebody I was when I was a civilian.'

'The grass is always greener . . . I miss the BOQ and the mess hall. I even miss SOS — mmmh — creamed chipped beef on toast.'

'Shit-on-a-shingle?' Bunny rolled her eyes. 'Next you'll be telling me you miss the coffee?'

'Yes, the coffee too.'

'God, Page, that's carrying nostalgia too far even for you. Have you forgotten how bitter it was?'

Spontaneously they began to sing, lustily, a song from OC days they had often marched to:

> '*The coffee in the Army they say is mighty fine,*
> *It's good for cuts and bruises and tastes like iodine.*
> *Oh, I don't want no more of army life.*
> *Gee Mom, I wanna go, but they won't let me go —*
> *HOME!*'

They laughed uproariously at the memories the song evoked, feeling silly and carefree.

'Bunny, I can't tell you — it's just so *damned* good to see you in this crazy town. Did I ever tell you that you're the sanest person I know?'

As they talked, Bunny was aware that the feeling of specialness she, Page, Jill and Elisabeth had felt for each other was still there. She knew that no matter how often or for how long they were separated, when they came together it was as if they had only stepped apart for five minutes. They had a seventh sense of understanding that neither absence nor distance could erase. 'Wish Jill and Elisabeth were here,' Bunny said. 'Wouldn't it be great if we were all together again — even for an hour?'

Page nodded. 'Elisabeth isn't so far, but her weekends are tied up every time I call her.'

'Uh-oh, sounds like a man.'

'Don't be hard on her, Bunny.'

'No, it's nothing like that. We both know she didn't care a fig about that husband of hers. I've seen her type before, so cool and safe within themselves. But watch out when they fall for some bozo — they take a real nose dive.'

'Hope you're wrong.' Page searched her cupboard for the right condiments, wishing Paul was here to do the cooking. 'There was always something so lost and easy to hurt right under Elisabeth's surface.'

'Page, you always saw more in her than I did, although she *was* absolutely fascinating. Speaking of man trouble — tell me about that new hunk of man you wrote me about. Do you see much of him?'

'Paul? Yes, a great deal.' Page stooped to light the gas under the oven grill, plopping the salted and peppered chops on the tray. 'We'll both be seeing him for dinner

165

tomorrow night. He's so eager to meet you. But I must warn you, I've told him outrageous stories about you.'

'Thanks a lot! A girl can't have any war secrets.'

'He'll adore you, Bunny. I hope you like him. He's the calm, silent professor type — pipe and all.'

'Grab him, Page. Believe me, steady is everything.' Bunny's mouth twisted in a wry grin. 'Well, nearly everything.'

After dinner they settled deep into the living-room chairs, lit cigarettes and sipped V.O. on the rocks.

'Now,' Page said, contentedly exhaling, 'tell me about you. A handsome flyboy in your life?'

'About a dozen at last count.'

'Any special man?' Page probed.

'One who thinks he is, but I'm not falling for his line — you know the one, "Just be patient and I'll divorce my wife."'

Page frowned, suddenly worried. 'Careful Bunny — you're more love's lemming than butterfly.'

Bunny looked up sharply. 'You see that, huh?' She sensed a chance to share a secret part of her life for the first time. 'I don't fool you for a minute, do I?'

'At first, maybe. But gradually I knew that some man must have hurt you badly. It was your last husband, wasn't it? I don't know — something about you changed when you talked about him, even when you joked.'

Bunny shifted in her chair and lifted her glass to study the amber liquid in the glow of a lamp. 'I've never talked about it to anyone before, but I'd like to tell you.' She spoke, haltingly at first, and then in a torrent of words, about the real Johnny Palermo, not the fun-loving satyr she'd made up as a joke to cover the deep scar, but the real Johnny, the one who had squeezed her heart dry and left her empty, unable to trust any man's love, unable even to trust her own sense of love. Finishing, she stared at Page. 'He only wanted my money,' she said bitterly. 'Why did his weakness win out, Page? I thought my love would prop *him* up; I didn't know he'd end up knocking the pins out from under *me*.' Tears threatened to overwhelm her.

Page was silent for a moment and looked down at her hands resting in her lap, trying to give her friend privacy. 'Stop blaming yourself. *You* did nothing wrong.' She was surprised at the words of comfort that tumbled out as if she'd always known them. 'You're not the first woman, and certainly not the last, to confuse physical need with loving some man forever. Bunny, listen, if you blame yourself you'll not be able to recognize the real thing when it comes your way — and it *will*. You don't know what a truly good person you are. Given any chance at all, the right man can and will love you for yourself if you let him.'

Bunny listlessly pulled her hands away from her face. 'I wish it was that simple.'

'It is.'

'No it isn't. He's writing to me.'

'So what?'

'He's asked me to see him when I get home on leave.'

'Are you going to?'

'Page — please don't be disappointed in me . . .'

'Of course not. How could I be?'

'Then yes — yes, I'm going to see him. I have to know, don't you see?'

The next morning was Saturday, and Page asked her section chief for an hour off. 'Bunny, now I've got time to drop you downtown if you want to see some of the sights.'

'Wonderful! Do you know it's been ages since I felt so good? Even my GI achin' feet feel fine.'

'That's good, because you'll have to walk everywhere. The buses are jammed.' She handed Bunny another breakfast dish to dry. 'They've even taken the seats out so they can cram more people in.'

Bunny stacked the dried bowl with the others in the cupboard. 'Now tell me what's going on at WAAC headquarters. There are all kindsa rumours floating around Lowry.'

'What kind of rumours?'

'For instance, that the Corps is going to be dissolved.'

Page bit her lip. 'That's one of many possibilities, Bunny.'

'You can't mean it!' Bunny felt more shocked than upset.

Page nodded, her face grim. 'This spring has been an awful time for all of us at headquarters. Forgive me if I get on my soapbox, but — ' She wiped her hands and took their refilled coffee cups to the table ' — Bunny, it seems that the press of the whole damned country is on our backs. Director Hobby is so distressed by stories that call us "a Corps of whores", enlisted only to service the troops.'

Bunny interrupted, 'I had one mother who called me and told me to send her daughter home. Some of the young kids were afraid even to go home on furlough, because they'd have to face all the dirty stories.'

Page smashed her cigarette in an ashtray. 'We fight them all the time, but they crop up everywhere. One writer in the *Washington Times-Herald* wrote a column about how we Waacs were all going to be secretly issued prophylactics. He thinks we're some kind of New Deal scheme of Mrs Roosevelt's. It's crazy! The press just can't seem to understand that any group of women soldiers might have a serious, patriotic purpose. The WAAC defies their definition of what women are supposed to be — so the only way they can explain us is to make us promiscuous.'

Bunny swiped angrily at the coffee ring her cup had made on the table. 'Is this what we joined the Army for? How can they print that kind of trash?'

'Oh, they're not singling us out — it's happened before. The nurse corps was vilified, and the British military women.' Page's hands unconsciously were fists. 'Bunny, the worst of it doesn't even *get* into print. We've been fighting one slander all spring — you know, the one about Eisenhower expelling a whole shipload of pregnant Waacs from North Africa. The latest wrinkle is that armed guards supposedly had to stand over them to keep them from jumping overboard. If that ridiculous rumour was true, every one of the two hundred Waacs in North Africa would have been shipped back ten times over.'

'Nobody believes that — do they?'

Page clenched her teeth. 'I wish I could say no, but . . . G-Two is busy running every one of these rumours to ground because they're devastating our recruiting campaigns, not to mention morale.'

Page was now so angry her hand shook lighting another cigarette she didn't really want. 'You know what the truth is? We've had exactly one pregnant Waac in North Africa so far — and she was married. But does *that* rumour get around? No! The truth is not nearly so exciting. Do you know that General Eisenhower wants hundreds more of us? He's putting through priority requisitions every week. I won't argue that Waacs are saints — after all, we're mature women, not girls — but our VD and pregnancy rates overseas and stateside are *lower* than the civilian population's.'

Bunny hated to see Page taking it all so personally. 'Page, a lot of it could be Nazi propaganda.'

A haunted look came over Page's face. 'I wish it was. I *really* wish it was.' For a moment she twisted her hands in front of her. 'But most of the rumours G-Two runs down were started by GIs writing from overseas, passing on jokes and stories — and, Bunny, most of *them* never so much as *saw* a Waac. Or by parents of boys sent to the front lines — that damned "Release a Man to Fight" campaign backfired on us. It's gossips in barbers' and beauty shops; it's disgruntled and discharged Waacs trying to justify themselves. No, it's not Nazis, Bunny — it's *us*.'

Bunny frowned. How can we fight everybody? It's hopeless, she thought, but she couldn't bring herself to say so out loud. Instead she asked, 'What's being done?'

'Director Hobby's so distressed by these slanders that she's assigned me full time to counter them with positive publicity about the Corps.'

'That's tough. You can't go around saying, "Hey, look here, we're not pregnant."'

'You're right. It only allows people to hear the slander twice. What I try to do is show who Waacs really are — forty-five-year-old grandmothers, wives and sisters of heroes, J. P. Morgan's granddaughter, farm girls — the diversity of the Corps, the next-door realness of these women.'

'*Now* you're cookin'.' Bunny was quiet for a moment while they finished their coffee. Then she said softly, 'Will this country ever accept a woman in uniform?'

'Maybe after we've slain our dragons.'

For the first time Bunny recognized the true depth of Page's devotion to the Corps. It's like a one-sided love affair, she thought. No wonder Page understands me — she's in love and she's rejected.

With a sigh Page stood up, collected their empty cups and put them into the sink. 'You know, Bunny, there will always be a few who will *want* to believe we're fallen women. I have a nightmare that forty years from now I'll be at a cocktail party and I'll hear these same lies repeated.'

'Stand easy, Lieutenant. You're beginning to sound like Jill, trying to win the war single-handed. Remember you're doing everything you can.'

Page shook her head. 'It's not enough. We're fighting to save the Corps. We must be completely taken into the Army with the same ranks and privileges for women as for men. We can't be an auxiliary any longer — it's not working.'

When Page said that, she seemed even more agitated. Bunny didn't understand. 'But isn't that what you want?'

'Yes, but don't you see the problem? That means every officer and Auxie will have a chance to get out or re-enlist in the new Corps. We're so afraid this slander campaign will cause most of them to take a discharge, and then the Corps will be ruined anyway.'

The idea hit Bunny hard. Johnny's last letter had begged her to try to get out, and suddenly here was an opportunity she'd never have again. But she couldn't bring herself to say so to Page.

An hour later, Bunny was being jostled by off-duty night-shift workers and clerks from the Office of Price Administration who worked around the clock. She wandered from monument to monument and stopped in front of Farragut's statue. 'Damn the torpedoes,' she read on the pedestal,

170

'full steam ahead.' This guy sounded a lot like Page.

She enjoyed a day that did not begin with a bugle call and end with the smell of photographic fixative on her clothes. As much as she loved her work as an Army Air Forces photographer and instructor, this furlough had reminded her that at heart she was a civilian.

By mid-afternoon she was starved, and she found a Rexall drugstore lunch counter where she watched women her age in a marathon search for scarce bobby pins and their favourite soap or shampoo. Everywhere there were lines — lines for cigarettes, for a small shipment of boxed Whitman's candy which was whisked off the shelf in minutes, for a few rare nylon stockings. Bunny saw one woman take her precious new hose, sit down on the kerb and put them on while a couple of sailors ogled her legs.

Ah, Saturday. She had always loved Saturdays for the air of anticipation about it. Anything *could* happen on Saturday night, she remembered telling her first husband. No matter how many Saturday nights she spent when not one thing occurred, like a compulsive gambler she could never escape the feeling that the next time it would. Tonight she knew would be special. Page's major was taking them to dinner at the Shoreham Hotel. Some class! Mama and her sisters would be impressed when she told them she'd dined and danced at the famous Shoreham, rubbing shoulders with congressmen, White House people and military brass from all over the world.

Then she made up her mind. Hang the money! She would have to look special for the occasion. She finished her Coke and rushed out to Garfinckel's for a knock-their-eyes-out dress. She barely heard the headlines being hawked from the corner news-stand. Something about American and British forces in North Africa closing the ring around Rommel's armies at Tunis. She wondered which of the OCs she'd known at Fort Des Moines was in North Africa.

When she left the department store carrying a dress box under her arm, the late-afternoon editions headlined the battle Polish Jews were fighting against the Germans in the Warsaw Ghetto.

21

Nightclub business booms — up 40 per cent over prewar years — despite food, liquor and gas rationing. Long lines form in black-out New York City to see Frank Sinatra at the Waldorf-Astoria's Wedgwood Room, Hildegarde at the Persian Room and Danny Thomas at La Martinique.

Bunny sang as she gave herself a last-minute check in the full-length mirror. It was so strange to see herself in a dress that she looked again to make sure it was really she. The blue shantung with padded shoulders and fitted sleeves clung to her body in just the right places to accentuate the curves that were undeniably there — a few more than she wanted, since she'd lost only three of the ten extra pounds gained at OC. Her breasts pushed against the dress bodice, their fullness accented by a centred sequin clip. Although she felt strange out of uniform, as if she had shed her skin, it was wonderful to feel something next to her body besides wool, barathea cloth and starched cotton poplin.

'Bunny, you're a knockout,' Page said, smiling, from the bathroom doorway.

'Does it really look as good as it feels?'

'Better — and I have some earrings that will complement the clip perfectly.'

The doorbell rang and Page left to answer it. Slipping into wonderfully soft elbow-length gloves and placing a single white gardenia just so above her left ear, Bunny went in to meet Paul, feeling a little nervous. What would she talk about? She'd never been much of a scholar.

'Bunny,' Paul said warmly, taking both her hands. 'Page has told me how your wit saved her many times during your training together.'

Before she could stop herself, she said, 'Only half the time.'

He laughed delightedly at her joke. 'Oh, I would never call you a half-wit.'

She liked him for laughing. Not every man, she'd discovered, felt comfortable when a woman joked. He was the kind of cultivated man she had never known outside the movies. That's it, she thought, he's Ronald Colman with muscles. It was plain to see, from the way his eyes constantly returned to Page, that he cared for her. And it was just as plain to Bunny that Page returned his affection, although in a way Bunny couldn't quite fathom. There was passion all right, but no belonging. Could a woman love and still belong to herself? Bunny knew she herself never could.

On the way to the Shoreham, Paul drove through night-time Washington to show Bunny the sights. The streets were crowded like Times Square on New Year's Eve. There was a festive, even frantic, party atmosphere which seemed not to belong in the same town where soldiers with steel helmets and fixed bayonets patrolled the White House and anti-aircraft guns were camouflaged behind foliage in the parks.

'I must be the most envied man in Washington tonight,' Paul said as they passed into the lobby of the Shoreham. 'I could cause a riot squiring the two most beautiful girls in town.'

Bunny laughed at his obvious gallantry, since everybody knew there were eight girls to every man in Washington. 'I hope I'm not caught out of uniform,' she whispered to Page. 'My arm keeps wanting to salute all this brass. I held on to it so hard back there at the entrance, I thought I'd break it.'

After dinner they were seated at a table in a ballroom jammed with men in uniform on the move, who had just arrived in Washington or were telling their friends goodbye. Bunny had never felt such a concentrated sense of excitement in one room before, a sense of a moment being lived and of its supreme importance over any other moment. There was a palpable vibration between men and women, a sexual hum that pervaded the music, the conversation, the camaraderie.

Paul ordered champagne, apologizing because it was Australian Syspelt. 'That's just one more reason to hate the Nazis.'

'Major,' she heard a voice say from behind her, 'it's absolutely unpatriotic to keep *two* lovely ladies off the dance floor.' A hand seemed to be attached to the voice, and it touched Bunny's shoulder. 'Wanna dance?'

Bunny turned to see a nice-looking young captain smiling down at her. They exchanged names.

'Page, do I dare? It's been ages. Besides, my feet grew two sizes in OC.'

Page laughed. 'They'll give you better balance. Get out there and show them how it's done.'

'Okay, Captain,' Bunny said as he helped her with her chair, 'if you're willing to take a chance.'

The band was playing a hot version of 'I Want to Be Happy,' and other couples were tearing up the dance floor. The eager captain pushed through the crowd and the closely packed tables, half dragging Bunny behind him. In a few minutes they had made their way to a spot on the floor where the crowd was thinner.

'Say, you're a swell dancer,' the captain shouted in her ear, throwing her out and pulling her back. 'Let's show these people how to cut a rug. Where I'm going there won't be any gorgeous gals like you.'

The captain did a hot jitterbug with a little Balboa and Jersey Bounce thrown in. They shagged and trucked-on-down, way down, until Bunny laughed out loud with the delight of moving her body to an upbeat rhythm once again. And he was a sweet young guy even if he did chew a huge wad of Dentyne gum in her ear, and swing her into a back-braking dip at the end of the slow numbers. She was flattered that he would want to have his last stateside dances with her, although she knew that any girl would have served to provide him with the memory he was trying to create for the days and months ahead.

This was going to be a great Saturday night. The band really swung! A great beat! So familiar — she must have heard it on the radio.

'Cutting in, Captain.'

'Nothing doin', Lieutenant,' he said, shrugging off another of the stags hungrily prowling the dance floor.

His grip on her waist showed her he had no intention of sharing his dancing partner with his fellow officers. She was content to alternately gyrate and glide in his arms, the music pulsing through her feet. The misery of her life with Johnny P., the regrets and the self-blame resurrected last night with Page, seemed to fade in the glow of present friendship, and laughter; in this place, her problems seemed small compared to these men going off to war, possibly to die.

Bunny cringed involuntarily as the band began to play the familiar first notes of 'All or Nothing at All', and her partner's arms circled her more tightly. The girl singer stepped to the microphone after a trombone intro. 'This is for Bunny from a friend,' the singer said and started the lyric.

'Hey, there's another Bunny here,' the captain said.

For answer, she grabbed his hand. 'Please, let's go back to the table — right now!'

But she was too late. The hand that tapped the captain on his shoulder was one she knew too well.

'Captain, can a guy get a dance with his ex-wife?'

'Uhh . . . ' the captain said, turning from one to the other, 'is that right, Bunny?'

But she didn't have to answer. Her face gave her away, and the captain reluctantly released her to the darkly handsome man in the white dinner jacket with the Shoreham crest on its breast pocket.

As she'd dreamed for a hundred nights, she was in Johnny's arms again, gliding across the floor to the tune she knew only too well. What was he doing here? She had not expected to have to face him quite so soon.

'So you decided to come,' he said, the voice quieter than she remembered.

She was puzzled. 'Decided to come?' she repeated his statement, making it a question.

'I wrote as soon as I knew I had this gig. Isn't that why *you're* here?'

'I never got your letter. I just came with friends.' Suddenly a feeling flooded her, washing away acquiescence, and that feeling was anger. 'You think that song is a joke, Johnny?' she asked, her right hand clenched inside his hand.

'No. Can't you see what I'm trying to tell you? You were right all along. I see now that it has to be all or nothing with us, babe.' His voice was low next to her ear, sending waves of longing through her body. 'Bunny, I'm trying to tell you I was wrong. And I ain't never said that to a girl in my life.'

She didn't trust the music; she didn't trust herself; she didn't trust him. 'The band — that's why it sounded so familiar,' she said, the truth dawning.

'I saw you when you came in with that army guy and the other girl. In that dress, I coulda picked you out of any crowd.' He drew her tense body into his. 'I may not be as smooth as your new friends, but, Jesus, Bunny, don't you know when a guy is saying he still loves you?'

She heard his voice, his low earnest words, but they were strained as if through a vision, a dream of what might have been. He was from her yesterdays. How could she return there with him? Even if it was possible . . . Her thoughts trailed off as her body responded to his as if it had no connection to her brain. It had been so long . . .

Some survival instinct made her try again to reject her feelings. 'Johnny, there was too much — too much that was bad between us.'

He was as hard to convince as ever. 'It wasn't all bad, Bunny,' he insisted, his mouth moving against her ear. Wave upon sensate wave pulsed through her body. 'Don't you remember our place and how it was when we made love together? All I'm asking is for a chance to show you how much I've changed.'

This was a Johnny she'd never seen before. All the mean cocksureness was gone, leaving only the brilliant smile and the sensual insinuation of his voice into memories that were all at once incredibly fresh. The physical yearning of the past months almost overwhelmed her. But something in her, some sanity, resisted this spell he was weaving. Why — why did he want her after all the past hurt? Did it appeal to his male vanity to regain her lost love? Could the Johnny she had known ever be a straight shooter with any girl? How could she even be here dancing with him after what he had done?

He turned her expertly around the floor. Unlike most professional musicians, Johnny had always been a wonderful dancer.

'I'm on the level, Bunny. We need to go somewhere for a quiet drink and talk. Just for old times' sake, baby — the good times.'

She had to know if she could ever be truly free of him — the old Johnny who had hurt her so terribly, or even this new Johnny, humble and loving with his sex appeal very much intact.

She walked back to the table, where Page and Paul were deep in conversation, their foreheads touching.

'Page — Paul — I'm sorry, but — ' She stopped, not wanting to say too much in front of Paul. 'Johnny P. is here and — I'll catch a cab back to the apartment later. Paul, will you please excuse me? Page will explain.'

Page said, 'Are you sure? Is there anything we can . . . ?'

Reassuring Page that she would be all right, she thanked Paul for the evening and met Johnny at the ballroom door. They walked through the lobby and took the elevator to his room. There was no more pretence of talking. She knew what he wanted, and she had to admit she wanted it, too. Didn't she owe it to herself to find out if there was any chance for a new start?

In the room, an ordinary Washington hotel room with two city-scapes over the bed, Johnny quickly got two glasses, poured two fingers of South African brandy into each, warmed them in his hand and handed one to her. She accepted the drink, but it was the first one in months she hadn't needed. Johnny was here in front of her. She didn't need alcohol to conjure him. While she sipped he moved about the room picking up his possessions, in an effort to make his life tidy for her.

Edging closer to where she sat, he stopped in front of her chair and slid to his knees, burying his head in her lap, like a hurt little boy. 'Baby, I've missed you.' His voice was husky with wanting. 'I've really kicked myself for the way I treated you. I've done a lot of growing up in the past two years. You do believe me, don't you?'

She felt his hands slide up her body and cup her breasts, strong fingers moving over her nipples, while his eyes searched her face for a sign of the old surrender.

Bunny knew that if she had any sense she would leap to her feet and run, fast and far, that she would never stop running. What was it Page had called her? She struggled to remember. A love lemming, that was it, someone who committed emotional suicide.

He stood, pulled her up, turned her around and unzipped her dress.

This is a dream, she thought as she shrugged out of her dress and let it fall to the floor. But she didn't want to wake up. She pulled her slip over her head past his hands, which were now everywhere caressing her. She unfastened her nylons, pulled off her garter belt, stepped out of her panties and lay down on the rumpled bed. These were practised movements, but all done as if in a vision of herself doing them. This was not real. Soon she would wake and know it had all been a dream.

She saw his eyes on her, never leaving her while he threw off his clothes. The room was softly lit and warm as he slipped into the bed and straddled her.

'I'll show you what you've missed, baby,' he said, his voice issuing from between her breasts now shuddering because she was gasping for breath.

She felt his two hands lock tight around her wrists and lift them over her head, pinning her hands to the pillow and simultaneously imprisoning his own. Using his tongue as a third hand, he began to work on the roundness of her breasts, making smaller and smaller circles until his greedy lips covered each nipple in turn. He moved up to her hot, dry mouth and used his tongue to moisten her lips and

178

finally to thrust inside slyly, insinuating a much deeper thrust to come.

Bunny longed for the exquisite moment when she would be filled by him. She no longer cared if there was trust between them. It would grow again. It had to.

He fell upon her then, and to prolong the sweet agony she clamped her legs shut, forcing him to plunge repeatedly between, the friction sending her into a series of rhythmic moans she could hardly recognize as her own music. He released her wrists and with his hands relentlessly parted her legs, which she threw about his back in a total physical embrace. He thrust inside her, steadily, completely, in one deep drive, and with his exquisite sense of drummer's timing he gradually picked up the beat, sending flashes of sensation through her that climaxed in frenzy. He rolled off her, exhausted, while she still throbbed helplessly.

'Baby,' he said, catching his breath, 'there's never been anyone like you for me. See how good we do it together?' He threw one dark leg over her, and the weight of him caused the heat inside to rise again. 'Just tell me what you want, and I'll do it for ya.'

She saw, and felt, and heard. Johnny was not perfect, but he had changed, was still trying to change, was willing to change even more. Maybe they *could* make a fresh beginning. Maybe they could live as if these past months hadn't happened.

Johnny turned her face — warm, with a film of moisture — toward his own. 'Can we try again? I'm gonna get outa the band business — settle down and get a steady job. Maybe you could even teach me to give permanents.' He laughed, his white even teeth flashing in the dim light. He reached over and turned on the radio on the nightstand, and the low, lovely strains of Miller's 'Skylark' filled the room. 'Yeah, baby, permanents — Angela says I'd be good at it.'

'When did you see Angela?'

'I just bumped into her once. I was asking all about you.' He explained that that was how he had got her address in Texas. 'Just ran into her on the street by accident.'

He kissed her, a sweetly questioning kiss that drew every bit of the poison he'd placed there out of her system. She knew he was waiting for her answer, but she hardly knew what that answer would be until she heard it herself. 'I want you, Johnny, and I want us to have a second chance. Give me two or three months and I think I'll be getting out of the Army.'

He pulled her close and she could feel he wanted her again. And oh, how she wanted him, passion overwhelming a final, too late instinct which told her to escape. She had been starving and Johnny was feeding her. Just for a moment she remembered what Page had said about the Corps and felt like a deserter, but then his body recaptured her memory and she thought of nothing but what he was doing to her.

22

Admiral Isoroku Yamamoto, planner of the surprise Pearl Harbor attack, is shot down April 18, 1943 when American fighters intercept his plane over Bougainville Island.

For the third time, Page, thinking she'd heard Bunny knocking, tiptoed down the stairs to the front door, which was locked at this time of night, stared up and down the street, and returned to Paul, seated on her living-room sofa.

'Paul, it's nearly two o'clock. Do you think Bunny will be able to find her way back here?'

'Bunny's a big girl.'

'But that ex-husband of hers is pretty awful.'

'Page,' Paul said, removing his pipe, 'Bunny strikes me as a down-to-earth sort — a realist.'

'She is, but that only makes her more vulnerable to a man like that. Don't you see? Realists think they're so safe they never learn to make good judgements about romance.' She saw that Paul, condescending, smiled at her woman's reasoning. 'Besides,' she went on stubbornly, 'Bunny's realism didn't stop her from falling for the wrong man, a weak, manipulative man. She thought she'd got away from him when she joined the WAAC, but now he's after her again.' Page sighed, and looked at her watch. It was well after 2 AM now. 'Paul, she's given that man so much of her life already. If she starts again, I'm afraid she could be so badly hurt she'd never get over it.'

Paul ran both hands back through his hair. 'Giving and love aren't the same things at all, Page. Giving feels like love, but too much — well, it can stifle a man.'

'You men all stick together, don't you?' It wasn't exactly a question she wanted him to answer. She was really a little angry because she'd expected agreement from Paul and she wasn't getting it.

Paul frowned. 'Page, this is not what I'd planned for tonight, but if we must talk about this, I'll tell you what I think. For most men, love is only part of their experience. They run from women who want to monopolize their lives.' He had said too much and not what he'd meant at all. What he'd meant to say was that he could understand a man who needed his freedom, but as for him, he would like to be monopolized by Page's love. But something in her eyes warned him this was not the time to say so.

Page shrugged. 'I guess I'm just worried that Bunny will get out of the Corps when the changeover comes.'

Paul tapped the ashes from his pipe into an ashtray and, after sucking on the pipe to make certain it was out, dropped it into the ashtray on the end table. 'Page, you know I'm all for the women's army, but if Bunny wants out, then perhaps you shouldn't try to pressure her to stay in. After all, she's older than you are and maybe she should get started on the rest of her life.'

He moved closer to her, and Page saw the antimacassars Mrs Mallory insisted on draping over the dilapidated sofa

181

slipping down behind him as they always did. 'You mean Bunny should think about marriage and a family?'

'Frankly, yes. Isn't that what a woman in her middle to late twenties should be doing?'

Page knew Paul was talking as much about her as he was about Bunny. He was asking *her* to think about marriage, a home and children in a quiet college town after the war — a life so different from her own childhood as an army brat, dragged from post to post and shunted off to lonely schools between times, that she had only a dreamy idea of what it would be like. The stable life he seemed to offer was what a part of Page had always yearned for.

'Page,' Paul's voice insistently responded to her silence, 'as important as the WAAC is now to the war effort, it's only symbolic of the unlimited expansion of wartime. Once the war's over there'll be no need for a *women's* army. In peace-time, women will want to lead their normal lives, to make homes and raise families. There's no place for women in the regular peacetime service. You do see that, don't you, Page?'

'But, Paul, it would be such a shame to throw away everything that women have accomplished in the Army.'

'It wouldn't be throwing it away. You'd always have your niche in history.' He kissed her then and she felt the heat of his hands through her dressing gown. She couldn't think what to answer him when they were together like this. She always felt so much stronger and safer when she put on her uniform.

23

A slip of the lip will sink a ship.
>   *— Espionage warning poster*

Italy faces collapse, but the Italians, bargaining for better than unconditional-surrender terms, delay laying down their arms, allowing the Germans to pour in troops and take up strong defensive positions.

J ill had been sweltering in August humidity close to one hundred all afternoon, but she wouldn't have traded places with an Eskimo. At last the 59th WAC Signal Company was at Camp Shanks outside New York City, waiting to embark for overseas.

'Want a Coke, Lieutenant?'

'Thanks, Sergeant,' Jill said, shoving a nickel across the duty officer's desk.

Until the sergeant had interrupted her, Jill had been immersed in a waking dream of imaginary heroism. In her mind, she stood at the head of her platoon while a crusty French *maréchal* pinned the Croix de Guerre on her blouse and bent, while tears of gratitude welled in his rheumy old eyes, to kiss her on both her desert-tanned cheeks. Flashbulbs popped. Legionnaires in white kepis held back a surging crowd, which included her mother and Neil. 'What has she done?' the crowd asked. '*Mon Dieu*,' the Frenchman said, 'she has broken the German diplomatic code — a numerical double substitution system that has baffled the great cryptoanalytic minds of the entire world!'

Drinking her Coke, Jill let her mind linger on the scene, savouring the triumph. She wondered if she would ever really show them — all those people who had doubted her ability. There was little to do *but* dream. As Sunday-afternoon duty officer in a staging area, she had no detail rosters to make up, no weekly training schedules to prepare. After the rush of shipping the entire company with equipment from Fort Monmouth to Shanks in a few days, she now had empty hours — who knew how many? — to fill. She decided, moving the small electric fan in front of the window, that hurry-up-and-wait was no empty army irony.

She had acquired new skills during her eight months at Monmouth. Learning to type on the clunky electric code machine with its sets of rotating drums marked with numbers and letters, she was now at forty words per minute. Pretty respectable, she thought, for someone who only last year had done all her term papers with two fingers.

At the same time, she had learned to be a field-company troop officer, attending to the welfare and training of Second Platoon, which often meant counselling or meting out discipline to women ten or fifteen years her senior, but more often meant listening to gripes about the mess hall or managing emergencies peculiar to the Army, as she was today.

The great galoshes controversy had erupted three times during the afternoon. The first sergeant had told her that all packing had come to a halt until the women knew whether galoshes were to be worn, or packed in the A bag, which was to be carried on board ship, or in the B bag, which went into the ship's hold. Jill guessed that until final orders came down — to wear or not to wear — the question would ricochet back and forth between barracks and orderly room.

Jill felt she couldn't wait to write Bunny about this one. But she'd have to. No mail could go out now that they were in a total communications blackout.

'Lieutenant Hammersmith,' the CQ announced, standing at the open door. 'PFC Brodzinsky requests permission to speak to you about a personal matter.'

Jill nodded. Here it came again. It seemed to her that every woman in her platoon was in a personal crisis since they had been locked up in Camp Shanks.

'Yes, Private,' she said and returned the salute, 'what can I do for you?'

184

'Lieutenant,' Marie Brodzinsky said, holding out a letter, 'I got this letter from home just before we left Fort Monmouth, telling me that my fiancé will be in New York City on convalescent leave this weekend. I only want to see him for a few hours —' she saw Jill start to refuse ' — just for one hour then.'

'But that's impossible, Brodzinsky. We could be alerted for immediate shipment at any hour of the day or night.'

'I haven't talked to Bill for over a year, Lieutenant,' Brodzinsky said, her eyes filled with tears. 'Just let me call him, then.'

'I can't authorize a telephone call, not even to immediate family — you know that. As far as they're concerned, we're already at sea.'

She got up, came round the desk and put her arm around the woman's shaking shoulders. 'I know how you feel, Brodzinsky, but these orders apply to all of us. One woman's mother died, another's husband filed for divorce, but the blackout has to be complete for the safety of the whole company — even the whole convoy. Try to understand.'

As Private Brodzinsky left, Jill could tell by her stiff gait that her logic hadn't reached the woman. She sighed and thought how different actual field command was from the paper exercises she'd worried over as an OC. Her time was spent between the sadness of such individual appeals and the silliness of the galoshes controversy, once again, apparently, in full swing.

Two standby orders had come down from battalion only minutes apart. Galoshes will be worn! Galoshes won't be worn! She suspected that the women were having a field day railing at the stupidity of the brass, herself included. She knew she had a reputation for going by the book, but she didn't think her platoon held it against her. She had to follow orders like every other Wac. Perhaps the women's obsessive concern these last hours with such piddling details was a good thing after all. At least it kept their minds off the German wolf packs lying in wait for convoys off the East Coast.

The first sergeant was again at the door. 'Lieutenant?'

'Yes, Sergeant Harper?'

'Are the women allowed out of the company area tonight?'

Jill nodded. 'CO says they can sign out for the post theatre or the enlisted service club, but everyone has to sign back in by ten o'clock.'

The women deserved some distraction. They might gripe and grouse as all soldiers did from tedium or tension, but she was immensely proud of them. When the WAAC had become the Women's Army Corps by act of Congress last month, ninety per cent of her platoon had re-enlisted, a Fort Monmouth record.

At seven o'clock, Jill turned her OD armband over to her relief and headed for the O Club before returning to BOQ for a peaceful evening. 'Hi, Kaye, may I join you?' she asked Kaye Young, lieutenant from Third Platoon, sitting at a table alone.

'I wish you would,' Kaye said in a direct manner Jill liked because it reminded her of Bunny. 'I've heard so many hard-luck stories today, I'm beginning to get homesick myself. How about you?'

'I just got off OD.'

'Poor child, you've had your share, then. Want a hamburger? They're not bad today.'

'We'd better have one last one to remember what they taste like wherever it is we're going.' As soon as the steward had taken their order, Jill bent her head close to Kaye's, whispering. 'It has got to be one of two places — England or North Africa. They won't send us into Sicily even though our guys and the Tommies have just taken Messina.'

'It won't be England,' Kaye said, whispering back. 'The First WAC Battalion landed there last month for duty with the Eighth and Ninth Air Forces. They'll wait to see how they work out before sending over any more of us. At least that's the way I've got this man's army doped out.'

Kaye was not really a man-hater — she admired a handsome face like any woman — but she acted as if she was angry at the whole opposite sex. Nobody knew why for

186

sure, except Jill had heard a hot latrine rumour that Kaye had been jilted during OC by a hotshot aviation cadet stationed at Randolph Field. And there were other things — snatches of conversation about her parents' divorce when she'd been in high school. Kaye had good reason not to trust two men, but evidently she'd decided not to give any of them a chance. She usually turned them away with sarcasm. Too bad. Kaye was not pretty — she still had facial scars from adolescent acne — but she was funny and interesting to be with and Jill had seen a lot of guys drawn to her. It was a darned shame. But it was Jill's good luck that Kaye made a perfect friend for her. Since she was engaged to be married, she had to be careful of her reputation around the swarms of young officers she met every day.

'You think it's North Africa, then?' Jill asked her, which set them off on another round of speculation.

The hamburger was thick and juicy, like the ones her father had grilled California style on their patio of a hot summer evening when even the cool adobe had been stifling in the San Joaquin Valley heat. But the memory of her home, her parents, even Neil, was fading like her much-washed khaki shirts. That life and the girl she had been almost belonged in a storybook she had once read, not to the reality she knew now, the one of war and uncertainty and making decisions affecting other women's lives.

' . . . and I can't think why they would show it, can you?' she heard Kaye saying.

'I'm sorry Kaye — show what?'

'*Action in the North Atlantic*,' Kaye repeated. 'That's the movie playing at the post theatre tonight. Whoever chose the film to play at *this* post has a high sense of gallows humour.'

'What's it about?'

'Raymond Massey and Humphrey Bogart have a convoy tanker torpedoed out from under them and they float around on a raft until they're rescued.'

'At least it has a happy ending.'

'Not if half the company has nightmares tonight.'

An enlisted steward approached the table. 'Telephone

call for Lieutenant Hammersmith,' he said. 'You can take it at the bar, Lieutenant.'

She followed the steward and picked up the receiver lying on the bar. 'Lieutenant Hammersmith here.'

'Lieutenant, this is Captain Trueblood.'

Why was the company commander calling her? This must be it. They were shoving off. 'Yes, ma'am.'

'There's been an accident, Lieutenant. I'd like you to come right down to the MP company. Do you know where Kaye Young is?'

'Lieutenant Young is here with me. Is it one of my women, ma'am?'

'I can't talk about it on the telephone, Lieutenant. But I need both of you down here on the double.'

Hurrying back to the table, Jill reported the conversation.

Kaye took one last bite of her hamburger and picked up her purse. 'The MPs are on the main post road — four or five blocks from here.'

'Let's hotfoot it over there,' Jill said. 'The captain made it sound urgent — an accident, she said. Maybe one of the women was hit by a car.'

Kaye frowned. 'They'd take her to the hospital. No, it must be a security violation. Some lovesick idiot tried to get off the post.'

Jill jammed her cap on her head. 'If it's that damned Private Brodzinsky, I'll put her on permanent kitchen police.'

By the time they arrived at the MP company, both a bit winded, they had guessed at a dozen possibilities, none as bad as the one they found.

Jill, with Kaye right behind, was ushered by a sweating corporal into a back office at MP headquarters. Captain Trueblood was there, and next to her a Wac slumped in a swivel chair, uniform torn and dirtied. Jill asked tentatively, 'Private Brodzinsky — Marie?'

The woman's head rose at the sound of her voice, and Jill caught sight of her face — red welts and swollen jaw, making the woman she'd seen a few hours ago almost unrecognizable. Oh, God, she hadn't meant to be so flip about Brodzinsky — she hadn't wanted anything to . . .

'Captain?' Jill questioned, looking up.

'Private Brodzinsky claims she's been raped, Lieutenant. She requested that you be called to hear her story before I file a report.'

'Marie,' Jill said softly and knelt beside the chair. 'What happened?'

'He raped me,' Marie said in an eerie, otherworldly voice that made Jill shiver.

'Did he do this to you, too?' Jill asked, gently touching her face.

'Yes, when I said I was going to turn him in,' the answer came, and then an uncontrollable sob.

Captain Trueblood told them, 'We know that Private Brodzinsky accepted a ride from a station-complement sergeant named Glover, went to the noncoms' club with him, had several drinks and left with him. That much has been confirmed by preliminary MP questioning. According to Brodzinsky, the man took her to a building by the rail terminal and forced her to submit to sexual advances.'

The private, biting her lower lip to stop the sobs, turned to Jill. 'Lieutenant, it *wasn't* that way — not the way it sounds. Three of us were on our way to the service club when this — this sergeant stopped in a jeep and told us to get in. When we got there, he asked us if we'd ever been to the noncoms' club. The other girls got out — but, well, I was mad because you wouldn't let me call Bill in New York, and . . . and I thought I could handle it.' Her sobbing started again, her chest heaving; her arms hugged herself in what looked to Jill like a desperate effort to keep her body from flying apart.

'Private,' the captain said, 'you were off limits, then?'

'Yes, but . . . ' Her voice trailed off at a knock on the door.

Jill opened it.

A major with military-police insignia on his collar leaned inside. 'May I see you, Captain Trueblood? Out here.'

The captain's voice was grim. 'Lieutenant Young, you

stay with her. Hammersmith, you come with me.'

'Captain,' the major said when they were outside, 'let's try to reason this out before you go filing charges.' He sat down on the edge of a desk and picked up a ruler, which he jabbed at the desk blotter, gradually shredding it as he talked. 'Here are the facts as I see them. The girl had too much to drink and went with the sergeant willingly. He swears she submitted, and he's regular army, with a good record.'

'Major,' Captain Trueblood snapped, 'what about her physical condition? She's badly bruised about the face. Did she willingly fall into the bastard's fist, too?'

Jill was amazed at the anger in the captain's voice. The women had nicknamed her 'Captain Blueblood' because she was always such a lady, almost as if she were still teaching philosophy at college. Right now she didn't sound like a lady at all.

The MP major jabbed at the blotter again impatiently. 'I don't think that kind of attitude will help us get to the bottom of this, Captain,' he said and stood up. 'You know that rape in wartime is a capital offence, don't you? The sergeant could be shot. Besides, this could be a black mark against the WAC with the troops. Where there's fire, and all that.'

'I see,' the CO said, her mouth twisting angrily. Then she motioned Jill to follow her and they walked back into the office.

Brodzinsky was no longer crying. Jill saw her staring out the window into the dark that was punctuated by headlights entering the post road. She started up as Jill and the CO re-entered the room, and threw Jill a look of total helplessness.

For a moment Jill wanted to run from so much obvious pain, but she was conscious, as always, that she was being judged on her maturity.

The captain spoke first, her voice weary with what Jill supposed was the agony of a command decision no woman would want to make. 'Private, you've had a terrible experience, but there's something you ought to know before you decide to file charges. You will be kept here and your friends who were with you will be kept here to testify at the sergeant's court-martial. I'll probably be forced to leave Lieutenant Hammersmith behind to represent you.'

Jill started to object, but held her tongue. It was intolerable to think she could be yanked off the levy and forced to spend months in this backwater. After all she'd been through, to miss the war now . . .

The captain was talking. 'If you lose, Private, you could be discharged for false accusation. If you win, the sergeant could get the death penalty. Is that what you want?'

Brodzinsky looked at the captain uncomprehendingly.

Kaye, with a reckless courage Jill had to admire, broke in. 'Marie, that's your *right*. If you want to file charges, go ahead.'

'Lieutenant Young, you're here as an observer,' the captain said. 'I'll explain the private's rights. Do you have anything to add, Lieutenant Hammersmith?'

'No, ma'am.' Jill could see that the captain was upset but under control, governed by the code of what was good for the service. This, then, was what that phrase *really* meant in practice.

'There's another alternative, Private,' the captain went on. 'I could recommend you for discharge — for emotional reasons. Did I hear you say your fiancé was nearby? This might be a good solution for you.'

Brodzinsky stood. She swayed, and Kaye put out an arm to steady her. 'No, thanks, Captain,' she said, her voice sour with betrayal. 'Go to Bill? Now? I can't ever be with him again.' She looked at all of them, and her eyes, naked with rage, stopped at Jill. '*Just one phone call*, Lieutenant, and all this wouldn't have happened.'

The shock of her accusation, the unfairness of it, hit Jill hard later as she returned to the BOQ with Kaye. 'I'm not to blame, Kaye,' she said, and then, 'but why do I feel so terribly guilty?'

'Damn it, Jill, we *should* feel guilty — all of us, including the CO. Do you know what we did to that poor girl? We let her get raped twice! We told her she should forget about the worst thing that can happen to a woman, because the man might be severely punished.'

'But, Kaye, I can understand the captain's problem,' Jill argued. 'She has to worry about getting this company overseas intact, and besides our mission she has to think about what's good for the service.'

'Jill, I like you,' Kaye said, her mouth set in a harsh line, 'but sometimes you're crammed full of horseshit! How can what we just did be for the good of the service? It's bad for Brodzinsky, and it's *bad* for the Corps. Christ! Don't you see that?' Kaye stalked into her room at the BOQ and slammed the door.

What could *she* have done? Jill asked herself. Stand up to the captain, who hadn't liked the whole affair any better than she had, then get left behind, stateside, while the rest of the company sailed. It was a hopeless dilemma. And what about her efficiency report coming up? A good one could mean one step nearer first lieutenancy. Her bars had come too hard to throw them away for a rebellious private who had disobeyed orders. Maybe Brodzinsky *had* asked for it. It came down to being her word against the sergeant's, didn't it? But as she undressed for bed, none of this soothed the sick feeling Jill had or erased the memory of Brodzinsky's battered, pleading face. Page had said once that the only reason the Army needed officers was to take care of their people. One of her people had been in trouble tonight, and she hadn't stood by her.

Where, then, did her first loyalty lie — to her women or to her superior officers? Deep in her conscience, Jill knew she had been loyal to neither. She had been thinking of herself. She wondered what Page would have done, and knew the answer. Page would have spoken, like Kaye, for what was right. Why did she always seem to choose friends who were like moral watchdogs, constantly nudging her conscience in the most painful ways?

But the most troubling aspect of all was the unbidden but persistent memory of Des Stratton. After a year, his face was blurred. Sometimes she could see each individual feature, but she could no longer put them together into a single clear image. But the memory of his voice was certainly sharp enough. *Hey, Jill, how can you call me a traitor because I didn't speak up for you? Didn't you just do the same thing to that poor girl?*

After what seemed like hours of tossing in her bed, she slept fitfully. When her Big Ben alarm sounded the next morning at five, she determined to put the incident behind her. Perhaps it would be better to transfer Brodzinsky to another platoon. The private would be more comfortable with the change of bunkmates, and less embarrassed as the story got around, which it surely would.

After breakfast at the officers' mess, she arrived in the company area at 0700 to find it in turmoil.

Kaye, looking as if she'd got little sleep, rushed past her at the orderly room door. 'Jill, the captain wants us to have all B bags ready for a truck pickup by 0800 hours. I think this is it!'

Making her way through the crowded OR, Jill called on the barracks squawk box, 'Sergeant Harper, assemble the platoon in the downstairs squad room. I'm coming right over.'

The sudden chaos resolved all Jill's questions and confusions of the previous night as she headed for the barracks. This was what she had waited and trained for. As she entered the squad room, the sergeant shouted attention. 'At ease,' Jill said. 'Go ahead and smoke if you want to. Sergeant Harper will read the uniform of the day and the equipment you're to fall out with when the marching order comes down.'

The sergeant stepped to the centre of the bay, and her loud voice droned the list in a staccato singsong. 'You will fall out wearing your helmet, Class-A uniform, utility coat, pistol belt with first-aid packet and canteen. Over your right shoulder you will carry your shoulder bag, gas mask and musette bag. Over your left arm you will carry your winter topcoat. Any questions?'

'What about galoshes?' The same question erupted from all over the room, followed by a burst of laughter.

Smiling, Jill answered, 'Hold them out of your B bags. As soon as we get official word, I'll tell Sergeant Harper.'

She walked down the aisle slowly and talked as she went. 'Any of you who still has civilian clothes must box them to be sent home. The sergeant will march you to the post office at zero eight ten hours. At zero nine hundred, you may visit the PX for last-minute supplies. I'd advise you to take at least a year's supply of cosmetics, and it would be a good idea to have a couple of bars of soap. If you're lucky enough to find some nylons, I don't have to tell you to buy extra pairs. That's it. I know you're tired of waiting, but it won't be long now.'

The sergeant called the platoon to attention as she headed towards the door. 'Harper,' Jill said, 'will you see that the women with pompadours square their helmets when they fall out. I don't want to see any tin pots sitting on the backs of their heads. The men will think we don't know how to wear them.'

24

On September 3, 1943, Allied forces cross from Sicily to Reggio di Calabria on the Italian toe under a nine-hundred gun barrage.

The evening headlines claimed bridgeheads three miles deep into Italian soil as Bunny waited for Johnny to finish his long day shift at Bloomfield, New Jersey's Westinghouse lamp plant. She added up the days since she'd been discharged from the WAAC. It had been one week.

She had decided that April night in Washington to get out of the Army and begin again with Johnny. Maybe she'd been planning it even before, without realizing it, but that night she knew with a certainty that she had to give the two of them another chance or she would forever wonder if it might have worked. What she hadn't planned was the sense of guilt she felt at leaving the Corps. Not just because she knew the Army had spent $10,000 on her training or that Page had been so disappointed — even Elisabeth had written that she'd re-upped — but because she felt so useless out of uniform, as if the world was racing ahead without her.

'Sit still,' Mama told her a dozen times a day while she waited at home for Johnny to finish work.

'I can't. I don't know what to do with myself. It's funny, I prayed to get out of the Army, I wanted it, but now I'm just lost.'

Without looking up from her mending, Mama had said, 'God doesn't give you what you want. He gives you what you need.'

She'd heard that all her life, but it made no more sense to her now than it had when she was a little girl and wanted a pony to materialize in her backyard.

'Go, Bunny — go to the shop,' Mama said, exasperated, when Bunny got too restless.

'I'm taking a little vacation. Besides, Angela doesn't know what to do with me.' But it was more than that. Although Bunny had tried to resume their old habits of affection, Angela was strangely distant, hardly speaking when they were together. The truth, she suspected, was that Angela didn't *want* her at the shop. All the beauticians were new since her two younger sisters had left to go into war work. And most of the customers came now from the Westinghouse plant across the street. She felt like an intruder in her own business.

She'd have to be patient, give her sister some time to get used to the idea before —

'Hi, babe.'

She was swept into Johnny's arms, her face pressed against the rough material of his work clothes. This was a different Johnny from the man in the Palm Beach suit and the wing-tipped shoes she'd met so long ago in Atlantic City. Not just in outward ways; he'd changed on the inside too; she was sure of it. She had to be.

'Let's go,' he said. 'I could eat a mountain of pasta. A sandwich doesn't go far on a twelve-hour shift.'

'I'm so proud of you, Johnny,' she said, motioning towards the plant. 'I know you miss the guys in the band.'

'Sure I do, but they're drafting musicians — hell, Glenn Miller's whole band was inducted and took some Mickey Mouse training in Atlantic City. I knew I had to get into essential war work.'

'Oh, *that's* it.'

'Yeah, little Miss Lieutenant, that's it. Look, one soldier in the family's enough.'

He laughed, heartily for Johnny, and she managed a smile. Sometimes Johnny still said things he didn't mean; he was too wary to show his soft side. But his actions were what was important. He was doing his bit just like everybody — and, most of all, he wanted to make a new start with her.

'Listen,' he said, walking her to the corner, 'give me fifteen minutes, and I'll get to my room, shower and change. Be right back and we'll do the town.'

'I'll be in the shop with Angela.'

'Nah. Wait there — right there. I want to be able to think of you on that spot while I'm gone.'

Bunny saw Angela staring at them through the plate-glass front of La Jeunesse and waved. But Angela turned away without acknowledging it. *Damn!* Bunny knew she'd have to talk with her sister about the shop, but she dreaded family fights. Besides, she could understand how Angela felt. She had put over a year of hard work in La Jeunesse and had begun to feel that it was hers, that Bunny was the usurper. Suddenly it was clear to Bunny what she had to do, and the solution was a relief. She would make Angela her equal partner instead of a paid manager. It was no more than that. Surely Johnny would agree.

But Johnny didn't. 'I want to take care of you this time,' he said as they ate spaghetti in a nearby restaurant.

His tone chilled her.

'Don't you see, that's what broke us up before — you had the money, and I didn't.'

196

She didn't remind him that he had asked for money many times and then used it to betray her. Instead she said, 'It was our money, Johnny.'

He stabbed with his fork at his plate. 'That's just supposed to make me feel good, but I don't buy it. When we're married this time, I don't want you to earn more than I do. Besides, you're going to be too busy being Mrs Johnny P.'

For a long time she had ached to hear him say that, but the ache now seemed more wonderful than the reality. When they had been separated, when she had lain alone on barrack cots, she had cherished all that was young and hurt in him and excused the way it complicated her life. Now she had to face him as he was, and more — the nagging inner voice that told her she had put personal happiness ahead of her country, and her friends.

Impulsively — just the way she liked him — Johnny reached across the table and captured her hands in his, sending shivers of memory along every nerve. Being with him was physically exhilarating, like the aftermath of a hard-fought game; her heart raced, her face flushed, and within the prison of his hands her fingers trembled.

'Well?' he asked.

'What do you want me to do with La Jeunesse? Sell it?'

'Baby, that's your decision.' He looked at his watch. 'Bunny, I'm beat.'

'Oh. I thought we could do something tonight.'

He laughed and winked. 'With two graveyard-shift workers sleeping in the same room?'

'I just meant talk together, make plans . . .'

'We will.' He yawned, his dark eyes drooping under their impossibly thick, curling lashes. 'Tomorrow.'

After he left her to go back to his boarding-house, she walked past the darkened shop. Looking through the front window, she could see the faint shapes of chairs, bowls, dryers, and the passive tentacles of permanent-wave machines. Whatever it had meant to her in the past, that feeling was gone. She would offer to sell it to Angela, then everyone would be happy.

Hurrying home, she found that Angela hadn't yet arrived, and Mama was complaining about the dinner she'd prepared for two ungrateful daughters. 'You off with that Johnny Palermo and Angela callin' at the last minute sayin' she's gonna work late.'

'But . . .' Bunny began and then shut her mouth. If Angela was doing something she didn't want Mama to know about, it was none of her business.

It was after midnight when Bunny wakened from a half-sleep as Angela tiptoed up the stairs. 'Angie, come in here.'

Angela stood at her doorway, a light coat huddled around her to conceal, Bunny surmised, a wrinkled dress. She'd been crying, too.

'What's the matter?'

'Nothin'.'

Then softly Bunny asked, 'Are you having man trouble, Angie?'

'No.' The word was barely audible, and the ones that followed were scarcely more so. 'Why did you have to come back, Bunny?'

There had been a time when Angela had looked up to her adoringly, trying to imitate her older sister, but it was obvious that that time was past.

'Angie, dear, listen — I've decided to sell La Jeunesse to you, if you want it. What do I need with it anymore, huh, kid? Besides, Johnny and I are going to get married again.'

Angela dropped her hand, and her coat fell open. Bunny could see she had guessed right. Angela's dress was creased, hastily put on, not even buttoned.

'Listen, kiddo,' Bunny began as her sister closed her coat quickly around her again, 'are you sure there isn't —'

'Stay out of my business, Bunny. Take a good look — I'm all grown up. I don't need your help.'

'Sorry —'

'Me too. Tired, I guess — but never mind that. What do you want for the shop?'

'I thought about two thousand — land, building fixtures, goodwill, all of it. We can work out the payments so —'

'No payments. I'll pay you cash.'

Bunny couldn't help wondering where Angela could get that much cash, unless it was from . . . Damn! It was more and more obvious she was mixed up with some man. And if she wasn't bringing him home to meet Mama, then she was probably not too proud of him.

Angela's face looked thin and tired in the dim hall light. 'If you'll sign over the deed, I'll have the money for you tomorrow afternoon. Come to the shop around four.'

'Angie, there's no hurry —'

'There is for me.'

Long after Angela had gone to bed, Bunny lay there trying to make sense of her feelings. She had expected Angela to be excited, pleased at least, but the kid hadn't even acted surprised. Bunny shrugged against the pillow. Maybe Mama was right about the ingratitude of the young. Still, she couldn't complain. Everything seemed to be working out for her. She'd wanted out of the Army, and the conversion from auxiliary to army status last month had made that possible. She and Johnny had wanted another chance and they were to be married again. Angela had wanted La Jeunesse and she was getting it. Everyone was getting what they wanted. Then why did she have the feeling something had gone terribly wrong?

The next afternoon she went to a lawyer and had the deed transfer papers drawn up, paid the filing fee and reached La Jeunesse a few minutes after four. A 'Closed' sign hung on the door.

Bunny wondered why Angela would close the shop so early on Saturday. 'Angie,' she called as she knocked.

Angela peeked from behind the window blind on the glass door front and opened the door. 'Hi.'

To Bunny her younger sister looked tense and unhappy. 'I have all the papers here.' Bunny said reassuringly. 'The minute you sign them La Jeunesse is yours.'

'Come on in the back.' Shoulders sagging, Angela led the way towards the small partitioned room that first Bunny and then she had used as an office. Johnny sat behind the desk.

Bunny hadn't expected to see him until he finished his

shift. 'Johnny?' she said, smiling. 'What are you doing here?'

Angela went around behind the desk and stood beside him. 'He's here because I asked him to be here.' Her eyes slid across Bunny's face and then away.

'*You* asked him?' Bunny didn't want to think. What was happening?

'Johnny and I are married.'

'*No!*' The scream surprised her, frightened her, so that she forced herself to repeat Angela's words, as if by the act of repeating she could make them more knowable. 'Johnny and you are married.'

Johnny put his arm around Angela's shoulder, and Bunny saw each of his long fingers dig into the young flesh. 'Clam up, Angie, you're talkin' too much.'

'She's *got* to know. I can't stand this pretence anymore,' Angie said, desperately avoiding Bunny's eyes.

Bunny looked from her sister to Johnny and back again, one question stumbling about in her head: How long had this been going on? She was suddenly aware of the overwhelming aroma of permanent-wave solution and fought down queasiness, but she could do nothing about the dizziness that made her head spin. 'Johnny, can you explain —'

Angela's head jerked up defiantly now, her face red, her eyes flashing. 'Johnny doesn't have to explain anything to you. You walked out on *him*!'

'Angie, you don't know what you're — '

'I *do* know. Johnny told me how you were always lording it over him with your money, making him beg for every penny. I'll never do that. This is all for Johnny. You never loved him — no, let me finish — you never loved him like I do or you wouldn't have left him alone and joined the Army.'

'Angie — how could you — '

'Don't give me that big-sister stuff, Bunny. It's my turn. You always got everything. Mama spent most of the time I was growing up worrying after you. You had the shop, the money — and then you had Johnny. I had nothing, until you turned your back on all of it. Do you think you can walk back in here whenever you want and take everything away from me?'

'Angie, don't you see what he's doing? He doesn't want you. If he did this to me, he'll do it to you.'

But her sister didn't see Johnny's gloating face and, most of all, didn't want to see him as he was. Angie would not know the real Johnny P. until he allowed her to, and by then it would be too late.

Bunny was trembling, but wanted to laugh at herself — at her own stupid self. She had been purposefully blind to what Johnny really was — and, to give him due credit, he'd never really pretended to be a saint. *She* had done all the pretending. Now she saw the real Johnny standing before her, clearly. The liquid black eyes were not sensuous but sly; the hands not loving and artistic but grasping; the unexpected boyishness not vulnerability but a calculated image. Oh, he hadn't lied very expertly at all, he hadn't needed to. *She* had provided the lies for herself.

Bunny closed her eyes, but the scene in front of her refused to disappear. It was like a silent movie where every gesture was exaggerated. And to think she had believed that Angela didn't want to imitate her older sister anymore, while all the time Angela was doing a perfect imitation of her own obsession with Johnny.

She wished her head would stop spinning long enough to be angry, to say to both of them the things she had a right to say. Instead, her voice flat and dry, Bunny asked, 'Angie, why didn't you just write and ask me to sell the shop to you? Why this, and why — ' she directed to Johnny the question her pride compelled her to ask — 'why that night in Washington?'

Her fists clenched, Angela shrieked, 'Go to hell! You can't make me jealous, if *that's* your game. Johnny's already told me how you threw yourself at him when he played the Shoreham.'

At this, Johnny's face broke into a delighted smirk.

The pieces were falling together for Bunny now. Angela's animosity and Johnny's charade almost made sense. 'Answer me, Angie — come on, just satisfy my curiosity,' she said softly, knowing her sister's pain, imagining how much more there would be in store for her. 'Why didn't you just ask me, just write and ask me to sell you the damned shop?'

'Don't tell me you'd have sold it if you knew about Johnny and me.'

Bunny honestly didn't know if she would have. She hardly knew anything anymore. It was as if all the truths of her life were suddenly sliding beyond her grasp. Maybe truth wasn't important now. Her eyes closed and her body swayed. Then she opened her eyes and her purse and placed the deed and the transfer papers on the desk. 'Here — ' and she managed a rueful smile, which she liked herself for even at that moment ' — as soon as you sign it, this place is yours. Now, Angie, you've got everything you want.' Want, yes, Bunny thought, but you can have no idea how much you're going to need, how much he's going to take from you.

Johnny quickly picked up the papers, took a pen from the desk and handed it to Angela. Casually, he fished a roll of bills from his pocket, peeled off twenty $100 bills and pushed them across the desk towards Bunny. 'Count it.'

'Why?' she asked, and some of her anger and bitterness came through. 'You'll pick my pocket before I get out of here.'

He threw back his head and laughed, obviously enjoying himself hugely. 'Baby, your pocket's already been picked.'

'Johnny, don't — ' Angela said.

'Don't hell! The bitch has it coming for what she did to me.' He took the signed transfer papers and put them into his jacket. 'This is our ticket to California.' He patted his pocket. 'We've got an offer to sell this land to Westinghouse for ten times what we just paid you.'

Her head stopped its incessant spinning, and she stared at the two of them, all uncertainty gone. She remembered the child Angela, tagging after her, asking her questions, so eager for her approval; she remembered Johnny on the boardwalk and how blindly she had wanted him to want

202

her. Here were two people she had loved — two people who had ruthlessly killed a part of her. Her heart was empty now, dead.

She left them standing there and walked through the shop. Quickly, she was out of the door, walking faster, the late-afternoon September air, sharp with the smell of smoke from the nearby plants, clearing her head. All her life, it seemed, she had been in search of love, and had recklessly entangled herself with men who could not love her in return. She stopped on the corner where she had waited for Johnny last evening, and rested her aching head for a moment against the cool metal of the signpost. *May God strike me dead if I ever let another man do this to me again!* With those words she thrust away the last flimsy illusions she had nurtured about Johnny P.

'Lady — you all right?'

Bunny looked up to see a middle-aged man in overalls, carrying a dinner pail. 'Yes — yes, I'm all right.'

'Sure, I can see that.' He put his pail down on the sidewalk and stood there looking at her. 'What is it — lose your boyfriend? Why, a great-lookin' girl like you can just whistle up a new one.'

'Something like that, but really — please — I know you're trying to help but — '

'You know what they say' — she wished he would go away and quit talking — 'God sends you what you need. You'll see, it'll all come out in the wash.'

She smiled up at him. 'Thank you,' she whispered. Then she prayed, Thank you for sending me this man, who speaks in everyday platitudes. She had needed to hear old truths and to listen to them just as she needed to see Johnny clearly so that she could know what she really needed.

The next day she caught a train to Washington to re-enlist in the Women's Army Corps. For the first time in a very long time, she liked the way she felt.

203

25

Domestic servants have disappeared into war plants, and the classified ads are full of potent inducements. One desperate Newark, New Jersey, lady offered a potential maid a room, a radio, a good salary and the use of her full-length mink coat on days off.

S tanding naked at the foot of the bed where Elisabet
lay, Max vaguely remembered some Aldington line
about a woman as lovely as gold but far colder. H
stared down at her. 'Do you know the poet Aldington –
Richard Aldington?'

'No.'

'I thought not.'

'Max, don't pull that to-the-manor-born shit on me.'

Max clicked his tongue against the roof of his mouth
'You are a little hellion, aren't you? Maybe you *should* rea
some poetry, my dear. Your veneer of night-school sophis
tication wears very thin at times.'

'That's why I'm so good for you, Max. I remind you c
where you came from. I keep you honest with yourself.'

The bitch was right, damn her! For these past months h
had indeed felt increasingly comfortable with her in hi
wary sort of way. They both understood the way the worl
really was, and therefore he could laugh with her as with n
one else. The Max Strykers of the world, he knew, rarel
belonged anywhere or with anyone, and he'd known th:
for a long time — maybe it was the first truth he'd eve
learned. For that reason alone, Elisabeth could easil
become too important to him.

He had left the world of immigrant needle workers, fifth
floor cold-water flats jammed with three generations ber
over their piecework — left it so long ago he had almos
succeeded in erasing the memory of ever having been pa
of it. In thirty-five years he had recreated his identity to h

own liking: Max Stryker, manufacturing tycoon and sophisticated Maryland country squire. The Philadelphia Mainliners hadn't wanted him, but they had been forced to pay him court — new money could not be ignored especially after 1929. But belonging? No, he didn't *belong* with them, but he had discovered something better, far better. He controlled them just as he controlled this woman on the bed. Not with money alone — lots of men had money; he controlled them with his authority, because he was never in doubt. He always knew what he wanted next and went after it no matter who got in his way. Right now, he wanted this woman again.

He crossed to the empty side of the bed and tossed the wadded satin sheets aside. He must remember to tell Elisabeth to change the bed later; good maids were harder to find than good lovers these days. He stared down at her. 'Now it's your turn to be honest with me. Tell me, did that hero husband of yours ever make you feel like this?' He grabbed her roughly, the welts his hands made on her buttocks thirty minutes before glowing pink on her cool white skin, already tinged with blue.

'How do you feel?' he asked, as he always did. It was part of their love ritual and she challenged him, 'Empty — what are you going to do about it?'

He threw himself on his back beside her and pulled her over on him. Her flesh dominated him — breasts, hips, full lips, all yielding and yet demanding. She lay full length atop him and he could feel her body rubbing up and down, little animal sounds issuing from the back of her throat.

'Max, it's never been like this. Never!'

He grasped her long hair in both hands as the low summer Maryland sun slanting in through the window threw gold tints into its waves, and he twisted it tight, forcing her head cruelly back until her chest arched; then he lowered her slowly until her breasts fell, first one, then the other, into his waiting mouth.

Her hands frantically pushed against his chest; she was trying to slide down on him.

Christ! The woman was insatiable; she relished the

pleasure of pain and love and the sadness that followed. By God, this time he'd give her a ride she'd never forget. Loosing her hair, his right hand groped beside the bed until his fingers closed around the riding crop he had dropped inside his boots early after their morning ride. He raised the crop and flicked it lightly against her heaving buttocks just as she slid down on him and he disappeared into her.

He saw her crouching atop him, the faultless symmetry of her magnificently proportioned body rose and fell like some mad Godiva, her close-to-golden hair a wild torrent about her shoulders, her breasts jutting insolently above him in the midst of his deepest strokes. He flicked the crop again and she laughed, a deep-in-the-throat sound of savage ecstasy.

'Post!' he commanded, slowing her down at will, wanting this moment to last. Oh God! This woman — she could give him — *ahh* — what he needed. 'That's right,' he gasped. 'Now I'll canter for you!' He pushed upward and swung the crop again and again and at last felt the tip deflect and bite into his own leg. The pain referred in a sharp burst of pleasure to his groin and with a surge he cleared the last hurdle, exploding into her. From an incredible distance, he heard a shriek of passion escape her lips. Instantly she tensed, suspended in the air above him, and clamped his thighs tightly with her knees, her whole body shuddering, releasing a cascade of fiery liquid, which enveloped his cock, mingled with his own surge, and dived into a deep, warm pool of delight; then she sprawled forward onto his chest.

He lay under her burden until his breathing slowed, then he slid her limp form off and onto the bed. It was true — goddamn her! She *was* a magnificent thoroughbred. But not for one moment could he lose sight of the danger she represented to him. He needed her on the inside of the quartermaster depot, close to the contract bids, more than he needed her in his bed, and he'd better not forget that fact no matter what a tantalizing piece of ass she was. He had enjoyed stripping away, one layer at a time, the various calculating, worldly, cold images she had shown him, until

206

today he had reached the essential Elisabeth. She was so obvious as to be laughable, and he stretched until his joints cracked, smiling at his own cleverness. Elisabeth simply could never love any man who loved her. Received love was so foreign to her that she was suspicious — contemptuous, even — of men who offered it. That poor fool of a husband had driven her away permanently with his first act of adoration. He smiled again. It wasn't so much that he knew human nature as that he knew human suffering.

'You're smiling, Max,' she said, stirring at his side. 'Are you pleased? With me?'

'With you, Elisabeth?' he asked, answering her question with a question. Indeed he was pleased. She was probably the world's greatest lay, but he had to remember that her body and its pleasures were of passing importance. The important thing, he knew, was to keep her off balance, guessing and wondering how he felt about her.

Lying naked in bed, a total lassitude in her limbs, Elisabeth watched him emerge dripping from his shower. His features — no, it was his compelling expression — forced her to watch him; not that she wanted to turn away. She liked to observe him naked — stark, brutally naked. He was the only unclothed man she had ever seen who did not look less impressive than the clothed man, whose genitals did not dangle like some incongruous anatomical afterthought. Max's cock seemed always sinuous and alert. Looking at him, she felt passion stirring again, and something more, a desire to be with him, like this, forever.

Max's body betrayed to her experienced eyes the lineage of a thousand generations of European peasant toilers. He was thick through his neck and thighs, the muscles rippled across his back when he moved, like tides pounding against boulders; only determined exercise, she knew, kept his stomach muscles taut. A thick mat of black hair covered his chest and trailed in a curling, tantalizing line down to his pelvis. Elisabeth buried her head in the sheets and breathed the primitive love scent of him deep into her, a flash of intuition warning her *not* to tell him how much she wanted him, needed him again — and now. She had learned to repress her insatiable need for him because men, even a powerful man like Max, saw it as a threat. She had been born with such knowledge.

Now, dressed in a Bond Street dark tweed hunting jacket, tartan tie and grey flannel slacks, his face cast in the late-afternoon shadows, Max looked to Elisabeth like a desert sheik transformed into English squire. He bent to kiss her lightly, almost, she fumed, cousinly.

'I've guests, you know,' he murmured. 'They'll be wondering about us.'

'Will they?' she asked, an eyebrow raised.

'Perhaps not.' His voice a deeper match for her irony, he laid the hand she had placed on his during the kiss firmly back upon the bed. 'But they *will* be thirsty, my sweet. We'll have cocktails on the terrace in thirty minutes.' As an afterthought, he added, 'And wear the Mainbocher country-weekend suit. I like you in that, Mrs Gardner,' he said and flipped open the closet door. As he left he called back over her shoulder, 'We're short of help this weekend. Be a sweet girl and strip the bed.'

Before she could tell him to go to hell, he was gone. She swung her long legs out of the bed, wincing at the bruises; applauding, she raised her hands to the door he'd just exited through. Touché. That plantation boss routine was masterful. Max loved the last word.

She crossed to the cheval mirror in the huge bathroom and examined her buttocks with her fingers. Lovingly, she rubbed the welts and the darkening splotches on her white skin, the touch of her fingers bringing a sensation of remembered pleasure and a delayed contraction of the place Max had lately filled so completely.

Max! She rolled his name silently on her tongue and knew that she had fallen in love, totally in love like some Third Avenue shopgirl with her thirty-dollar-a-week office clerk — finally in love, forever. Every man she had ever known she measured against his power, and found them laughable. Even as she examined this new emotion, Elisabeth couldn't help but be onto herself; her feelings for

Max were excessive, she knew it instinctively, but then she had been nurtured by excess — extremes of hate and love were natural to her.

He had introduced her to the world of industry and big money and leisure. She had access to everything she had ever wanted from a man — every man but this one. From Max she wanted more, and, yes, she had to admit it, shivering as she stepped into a tepid bath and shivering even more at the thought, she wanted Max. She wanted to be with him every night, to wake his darkly bearded cheek on her pillow; she wanted him to look at no other woman, to think of nothing and no one but her, to remember no sex, no happiness, no tragedy she hadn't shared with him; she wanted to own his hands, his mouth, his memory and his future.

And why not? She was willing to do anything, to give anything and to dare anything for him. Hadn't she convinced Colonel Nicolson that the existing WAAC uniform could be salvaged with a few changes for which Max got a lucrative contract cost overrun? Hadn't she re-enlisted in the new WAC, when she longed to escape the women's army, because she knew she was valuable to Max inside the QM depot? Oh, he hadn't asked her to stay. He was too clever to place himself in her debt, and she hadn't wanted to rouse his resentment by making him ask. But he had accepted her decision agreeably, and even more agreeably given her a sable cape and this wildly lovely weekend at his Maryland estate, Whiskey Hill. There had been moments during the past two days when she had been certain he would ask her to marry him, and other moments when he treated her no differently from any of his other female house guests.

'Mrs Max Stryker.' She said the words aloud and slipped the Mainbocher jacket on, pulling her near-golden hair from underneath and letting it cascade down her slender neck and over the stylishly padded shoulders. 'Mrs Max Stryker,' she said again softly as she descended the staircase and walked towards the group lounging on the terrace.

26

After refitting the electronic monitoring equipment, 20mm anti-aircraft guns and acoustic torpedoes, German U-boats resume wolf pack operations against Atlantic convoys in September 1943.

Incredulous, Jill turned towards the sound of familiar voices in the crowd on New York's Pier 90, voices she could barely hear above the noise of the band playing a booming chorus of 'Pistol Packin' Mama.'

'Jill Hammersmith!'

'Hey, kiddo!'

She scanned the crowd, and from behind a Red Cross worker with a doughnut tray two women in khaki burst out of the mêlée and hurried towards her.

Suddenly she was the centre of their hugs and laughter. 'Page — Bunny! How did you — what are you — ?'

'Whoa, Lieutenant,' Bunny said, saluting. 'It's simple. I'm a poor enlisted woman waiting in DC for reassignment, and our clever PR friend' — she indicated Page — 'put this bon voyage party together.'

Page nodded with mock importance. 'All very official, too. Permission to photograph Wacs embarking for overseas just came down when I saw your name on the manifest —'

'Sorry, ma'am,' a sergeant interrupted, 'please clear the gangway.'

The three moved aside as a long line of men with backpacks and rifles filed into the hold.

'This is chaos,' Page said, pulling them back against a building, 'but I'm glad we came. I wish Elisabeth could have made it, but . . .'

Jill smiled wistfully. 'Elisabeth wouldn't bother.'

As if on cue, they heard a voice calling, 'Lieutenant Hammersmith!' The crowd parted, and Page saw Elisabeth walk towards them, wearing one of the new overseas caps atop a wonderfully tailored uniform.

'Wow!' Bunny murmured. 'Mama always told me to perfect my whipstitch.'

Shyly, Jill shook Elisabeth's hand. 'How did you — ?'

'It was all Page's doing. She called and talked my colonel into giving me one day of temporary duty to evaluate the condition of WAC clothing at the port of embarkation.'

'One day for me too,' Bunny said, 'but that's all I'll need to photograph you for posterity. Why so surprised, kiddo?' Bunny grinned at Jill. 'Did you think we'd let you go to the ETO without warning you about those suave European men?'

Puzzled, Jill looked at Bunny's uniform. 'But why are you wearing an enlisted woman's uniform?'

'It's a long story, kiddo, I'll write you all about it.' Bunny grabbed a passing GI. 'Take our picture, will you?'

'Sure,' he said, hoisting Bunny's big Graflex four-by-five, 'where do I push?'

They posed smiling together in front of the gangway, three of them in dress uniform and the smallest of them, Jill, green-helmeted, with her musette bag strapped on her back, a blanket roll tied over it. Behind them Jill's platoon marched into the troop transport, all looking like real veterans.

'I better grab some crowd shots,' Bunny said. 'Be right back.'

'I still can't believe you're all here,' Jill said as Bunny left. 'Page, you've got *some* pull with the big brass.' She hoped she hadn't sounded envious, but she was afraid she had because she was, a little, and was ashamed of herself for it.

'No, really, Jill,' Page answered, 'this is a legitimate assignment — though maybe I wouldn't have been in such a hurry if it hadn't been for you.'

'I'm glad you came. I — well I've been too busy today to be lonely, until just this minute. It's just hit me that I'm leaving home, heading for the unknown.'

Page squeezed her arm. 'You'll be fine, Jill. God, how I wish I were going with you.'

Elisabeth snorted. 'You're both bucking for a Section

211

Eight with that kind of talk.'

'Who's crazy?' Jill said, the old closeness of OC returning. 'After all that big talk at Des Moines, you didn't get out of the Army when you had a chance. I think you're more gung-ho than you let on.'

Elisabeth put up a hand in protest, but Jill brushed it aside, refusing to listen to her protests.

Bunny rushed up. 'Did you see it?'

'See what?' Page asked.

'My God! You mean you didn't see what was going on at the other end of the pier?'

'How could we?' Page answered. 'There must be a thousand people milling about. What's up?'

'Kate Smith's down there sending off the troops. She was singing "God Bless America" at the top of her voice when right behind her Rita Rand — you know, the famous stripper — started taking it off, right there in the middle of the song. The guys in the bow of the ship started screaming and stamping, and Kate Smith — she thought they were yelling for her — began to sing louder and louder, really throwing herself into it. Page, I'm not kiddin' you, there's a riot going on down there. I saw one GI try to get out through a porthole and get stuck — somebody said he broke some ribs. A bird colonel told me not to dare take pictures. If the newspapers got hold of them some ladies' church group will start a big stink about our boys' corrupted morals or something.'

Jill grinned, shaking her head in wonder. 'Leave it to you to find the joke in all this.'

The last of Jill's Second Platoon had just passed up the gangplank, their galoshes making a squeaking sound on the metal stairs. Laughing, she told the others about the great galoshes controversy.

Bunny nodded knowingly. 'Situation normal — all fouled up.'

Jill shifted the heavy pack that was digging into her shoulders. 'I wish we had hours, but . . .'

'We know,' Page said. 'We just wanted you to have friendly faces in the crowd.'

Jill held out her hand to Bunny, who took it and then hugged her impulsively. 'There's all kinds of regs against an EW hugging a platoon officer, but . . . ' Bunny sniffed and blinked her eyes quickly. 'Now, don't try to win the war single-handed, kid. Save something for the rest of us to do.'.

'You all right, Bunny?' Jill asked, suspicious, trying to catch Bunny's eye. 'You weren't busted or anything?'

'No, nothing like that. And I'm very all right, kid, maybe I've never been all-righter. Don't worry about me — *you* just take care of yourself.'

Jill blinked. 'So long, Elisabeth. The last batch of uniforms that came through to Monmouth were first class. I knew you'd get everything straightened out down there.'

'I — ' Elisabeth's face flushed, and she bit her lip, 'I'll write more often, Jill.'

Jill set her foot on the first step and felt a loss of contact with home, a severing of roots. She was really leaving. She turned back and took Page's outstretched hand. 'Remember, we've got that bottle of champagne waiting for us at Babe's.'

'I won't forget, Jill.'

The past fifteen months had all been such a dream — Neil's wounds, joining the women's army, getting her bars, meeting and losing Des Stratton — that somehow she had never considered the reality of going into a war zone, of putting her life into jeopardy.

'Come on up, love,' she heard a singsong British accent from above her. 'Don't go getting gangplankitis on us.'

She stiffened and glared into the darkened gangway. She'd heard that sometimes guys simply froze on the gangplank like paratroops at the airplane door. But not Jill. Not *any* Wac in her outfit.

One last time, she turned and highballed a salute at the three women standing on the dock. 'Hey, Page, I'll bring you back the dragon's tail.'

Page gripped the gangplank railing. 'Just bring yourself back,' she called after Jill as she disappeared inside the ship.

'I hate this,' Elisabeth said, her voice low and strained. 'I

213

don't know what I'm doing here.'

Page felt guilty. 'I'm sorry. I forgot — this must remind you of your husband.'

Elisabeth closed her eyes tightly, suppressing her frustration. Why were they all so blind? Couldn't they see she was not like them?

'Come on, you two,' Bunny said, linking her arms in theirs. 'As soon as we launch Jill, we'll just have time for a drink before we catch the *Capitol Limited* at Grand Central. I'll tell you the real inside dope about how my second husband almost became my third. You see . . .'

On board the *Canberra Princess* Jill stowed her gear in the small cabin she was assigned to share with Kaye Young and the company's other platoon officer, Betty O'Neil, and went on deck to watch the pier slide away as the tugs nosed the ship into the river channel. Far below on the dock, she saw her friends, shouldering their way past the bandstand, turn and wave before they passed from sight.

As they picked up speed, she could see up streets running in perfect stone grids right into the heart of Manhattan; then the ship dropped down past the burned-out hulk of the liner *Normandie* lying on her side at her berth and slipped in the late-afternoon light beyond the Statue of Liberty. Jill could not shake the oppressively heavy feeling of farewell, of finality. Of course she was being silly. Page and other Wacs everywhere would give anything to trade places with her, and here she was acting like a child on the first day of school.

That evening after the second sitting, the British ship's captain, Hawkes, invited all Wacs to remain in the dining room. 'Ladies, this ship is the liner, *Canberra Princess*, which before the war plied the Indian Ocean route from Australia to Southampton.' Hawkes was flanked by an officer he introduced as Number One. 'We are a medium-fast vessel and we will convoy during the night off Hampton Roads with other troop transport and cargo ships. Together we will pick up a heavy naval escort by dawn. We have gun emplacements on the upper deck with trained crews. I think it is safe to say that if Jerry has a go at us with his U-

214

boats we'll give a helluva good account of ourselves.'

He looked around the room at the 150 uniformed women. 'By the by,' he said pleasantly, 'in case of emergency come here to the dining room until my officers come from their deck stations to take you to your lifeboats; I don't want you wandering about on deck. Be sure you have your helmets. And you might keep with you a small packet of essentials such as lipstick which you will require in the lifeboats.' He stopped, waiting for the laugh.

'Obey orders,' Captain Hawkes continued, 'keep calm and be good girls.'

'Yes, Daddy!' Kaye whispered fiercely in Jill's ear. 'Some men are such pricks!'

On the first evening out, Jill kept busy checking her women's cabin assignments. Eighteen were packed into the former Queen's Suite all the way forward on the promenade deck. Sergeant Harper had already made a roster for the marble bathtub formerly occupied by cruising society. The women groaned when Jill informed them that there would be only two hours of hot water daily and that they were restricted to one bath every three days. She checked to see that all their musette packs contained emergency supplies. The enlisted women had already begun to call them torpedo bags, and each one had slung hers together with helmet and life preserver at the head of her bunk. Jill gave each EW her lifeboat assignment in time for the first boat drill.

Back in her cabin, she saw that another bunk had been attached to the wall, and on it lounged a woman wearing a WAC uniform with a correspondent's shoulder patch.

Kaye introduced her, 'Jill Hammersmith, this is Dee Gleeson of *Ladies' Home Companion*.'

'Hi, Lieutenant,' said the woman. She was in her late thirties or early forties; her hair in a neat wraparound roll peeked out from under her helmet. She picked up a pencil and a notebook. 'Where are you from?'

Jill told her, and listened while Kaye and Betty recounted every funny army story they could think of. She liked Gleeson almost immediately. It didn't take long to

215

discover that she was the kind of older woman who fitted in with a group of younger ones because she never told them how much she'd learned since she was their age. She was a rare good listener. Jill supposed that was why she was one of the country's top women journalists.

'You're really interested in other people, aren't you, Mrs Gleeson?'

'Call me Dee. And the answer is yes, I'm interested, but mostly in what they do and why they do it. Writers are observers of life, you know — we don't live it, as you gals are doing.'

Jill had never seen a writer in action before. It made her realize that she rarely heard what other people had to say because she was so busy getting ready to defend herself. A banty-rooster complex, some guy in college had once called it. But she'd had to learn to defend herself. Still, she was impressed by Dee's self-assurance mixed with warm caring — so much like Page — and she determined to make these qualities part of her own personality.

Kaye and Betty liked having Gleeson in their cabin for other than her congeniality. As a certified war correspondent she had access to every part of the ship, she knew the latest scuttlebutt almost before it happened, and she even had a shortwave radio she was allowed to keep in the cabin.

At damp first light the next morning, Jill went with Dee up to the section of the promenade deck reserved for WAC use, and they took brisk turns around the deck. The wind that always blows at sea whipped Jill's auburn curls into a tangle.

'You ought to have been on the *Queen Mary* or the *Europe* before the war,' Dee reminisced. 'I often had a seat at the captain's table for meals. There were lounge tea dances in the afternoon and fruit baskets in all the cabins, changed daily when the steward turned down the bed.' She grimaced. 'This voyage will be a bit short on such amenities.'

As far as Jill could see on either side of the ship there were other ships in geometric close order. 'They can't be

216

more than a half-mile apart.'

'They're not, and they'll close up even more at night, although they constantly shift their sailing pattern. That's so if one of Adolf's U-boats is tracking us, it'll have a hard time slipping between us for a shot. See —' she pointed off to starboard ' — there's a destroyer escort darting between those ships now.'

For a civilian, Jill thought, Dee knew a lot about convoy operations and she told her so.

'I don't mean to be such a know-it-all, Jill, but we journalists tend to sound as though we're smarter than we are. We interview so many people and write so many stories that we get to be a little expert in everything without ever really having a great deal of personal experience. That's why I'm with this convoy. I thought it was about time I saw what it was like over there for myself.'

Just then Jill was startled to hear the deafening sound of short, staccato bursts of gunfire from above her on the gun deck and from everywhere around the convoy. Instinctively she flattened herself against the bulkhead, then was ashamed of her momentary panic. What if one of her platoon had seen her? Some example she'd set.

'It's okay, Jill,' Dolores yelled. 'They're just testing the guns. The captain told me last night they . . . ' Her voice was drowned by another burst that sent tracers from the port guns in a trajectory high over the ships.

After that first day's practice, Jill heard no more firing, although the ship's crew were called to battle stations several times a day. It began to look as though that was as close as she would come to the shooting war on the high seas as day melted into September day without one U-boat sighting. She wrote long letters home and to Page, Bunny and Elisabeth, although she knew Elisabeth and Bunny thought she was crazy for volunteering for overseas.

Daily shipboard routine varied little. Each WAC platoon took turns mustering on the promenade deck for exercise and fresh air. Jill tried to ignore the notes that sailed in paper airplane form down from the upper deck, where troops from the ship's hold lined the rail to watch her women go through the familiar cadence of an exercise sequence.

'Where're ya from?' they yelled.

The women yelled back their home states to the inevitable. 'Hey, me too — I'm from right near there.'

Boat drills, chow call twice a day and even some volunteer work in the sick bay and the transport office and regular shifts for radio ops weren't enough to keep the women busy. To fill their time the U-boat rumour mill began to grind at top speed, and Jill and the other WAC officers worried that tension was building to an almost unbearable pitch. Jill did her best to reassure the women in her platoon, but she was on edge herself like everyone else, and she was afraid it showed.

'Lieutenant, how about coming down into men's country with me?' Dee said one day about a week out when she was headed for the hold.

They descended gangways until they were below the waterline. Each compartment in the lower decks had long wooden tables with benches on each side. The place had the stale odour of a gym; it was where the men lived, ate and — in hammocks slung from hooks — slept.

Jill thought Dee had a marvellous way with the men. She knew just how to talk with them to gain their confidence.

'Anybody here from Texas?' she called.

'Yo!'

And again, 'How about Georgia?'

'Me, ma'am.'

'What's your hometown?' she asked, drawing out their stories.

Texas said, looking over his shoulder with a grin at his buddies, 'If y'all promise you won't squeal on us, we'll show you a stowaway.'

And then, passed from one pair of hands to another over the heads of the packed-in men, Jill saw a little furry mutt.

'This here's Princess,' Texas said, holding the pup out to the correspondent. 'We named her after the ship. We all figgered if they could send female soldiers on this ship' —

and here he grinned at Jill — 'well, we could have us a little girl dog.'

After interviewing them, Dee promised to visit again. In the companionway outside, she put her hand on Jill's arm. 'I can see the army regs whirling around in your head, Jill, but I'd appreciate it if the news of the men's dog didn't go any further — as a personal favour to me. We journalists like to think we're as reliable as priests about our sources.'

'Why would you think I'd run to the captain?'

'Look, Jill, I like you, but you've got a reputation with the women as an officer who doesn't know how to . . . '

'How to what?'

'To bend. Sometimes it's more important to care about somebody than to obey the letter of a rule.'

Jill felt the disapproval in her tone. 'Does that come from Private Brodzinsky?' How could she explain to a civilian woman what a tightrope she had to walk between her responsibility for the enlisted women and her duty to superior officers?

Dee shrugged off the question. 'You're a sweet kid, Jill, but you've picked up the idea that rules are more important than people. I hope you don't mind my talking to you like a Dutch aunt, but I hate to see you get hurt — and you will. I know, because I . . . well, once I thought a man should live up to my ideas of perfection.'

'What happened?'

'He left me flat, and I can't blame him.'

Jill searched Dee's face. Did she know about Neil? How could she? 'I won't report the dog, Dee. Okay?'

'Good. The men down there will appreciate it. Anyway, didn't you tell me you had a dog at home? So you know how important a companion animal can be at a time like this.'

'I know. I love animals. I'll be going back to vet school after the war.'

'You've never told me, Jill' — Dee took her arm and they started the climb back topside — 'how you came to join the women's army.'

By the time they got back to their cabin, Jill had told her how she had driven Neil to enlist and how he blamed her now for his wounds. 'You were right, Dee. I forced him to live by my rules, and now . . .'

'Don't blame yourself too much for the tragedy of war.'

Jill nodded, feeling miserable. 'Yes, everybody says so, but oh, Dee, it's not only that. I . . . I met another man during OC training, and I . . . oh, I acted holier-than-thou — refused to listen to him.' She twisted her mouth up at Dee ruefully. 'You know how it is, don't you?'

'You bet I do. But don't let it get you down. Maybe you've wised up in time.'

'No. I tore up his letters and now I don't even know where he is. It's too late. Sounds like a continuing drama of my life, doesn't it?'

Thirteen days out, Jill distributed a pamphlet called 'Guide to North Africa' instructing male troops how to act but not mentioning female troops at all. At least their destination was no longer a secret. But if Jill was excited by the news, she was sobered by the thought that the most dangerous part of their voyage was still ahead.

'The guys in the officers' lounge say the Mediterranean is swarming with U-boats,' Dee told her cabin-mates as they huddled around her shortwave that night. 'The sky may belong to our guys, but the Krauts have submarine pens on the French coast within easy striking distance.'

'But we've got sonar and depth charges,' Jill reminded her.

Betty O'Neil chimed in, 'And torpedo planes will be coming out to meet us from our bases in Morocco.'

'Right you are, you two, and I shouldn't — ' The short wave crackled and an English voice came through strongly. 'It's Lord Haw Haw,' Dee said, shushing them. 'We've got Berlin.'

The cultured traitorous voice opened the broadcast with the familiar 'Germany calling' sign-on and railed at RAF bombers who were killing innocent women and children in the Berlin raids. It gloated over the shooting down of forty-five Allied bombers by German cat's eye night fighters.

'He's not too funny tonight,' Dee said, reaching out to turn the dial.

'Greetings to the lovely ladies of the Fifty-ninth WAC Signal Company now off the Straits of Gibraltar . . .'

'Wait, Dee,' Kaye said. 'That's us. Christ! Someone talked!'

'Hold it, there's more,' warned Dee as the unctuous voice continued:

' . . . Your convoy is taking you into a dangerous area. There is a great naval battle taking place all around you. Do not think that because you are women our U-boat commanders will spare you. You have been tricked by your leaders, who have used you to ensure the safety of the combat troops who cram the hold of the *Canberra Princess*. We do not want you to die and go to a watery grave. Go now to your officers and tell them to turn around and take you back to your mothers and fathers, your sweethearts and husbands, in America.'

'How *dare* he think American women are cowards!' Jill said angrily.

'What scares me,' Kaye said, 'is how much they know — our unit number, the name of our ship . . . I would have sworn we had the tightest information blackout controls ever before we left the States.'

'You probably did,' Dee said. 'They can take little bits of information from everywhere and put them together.'

Theirs wasn't the only shortwave tuned to Berlin frequency. Jill was called the next day to a security lecture, which she passed on to every woman in her platoon. She told them, 'Double black curtains at the doors leading on deck; one has to be closed before another is opened. Keep the portholes closed. If we're hit and the ship listed even a few degrees, open portholes could flood us fast. No flashlights or cigarettes on deck after dark. Don't throw *anything* overboard — no candy wrappers or orange peels. And I don't want any of you women even in the latrine — or anywhere — without your life preserver.'

That night Jill slept in her clothes. She knew half the ship was ready for the sound of a shattering explosion. She was tense and tired the next morning from waiting for it.

The next two nights they zigzagged constantly, but

nothing happened to disturb the sound of the waves washing past the bow and the creaks and groans of a large ship heaving and rolling.

On Monday, September 20, the news that British and American troops had linked up at a place called Eboli in Italy blared from the ship's intercom. Amidst the general celebration between the British crew and their American passengers, Jill helped her platoon trade their dollars for occupation script. 'We'll dock in Algeria in twenty-four hours,' she told them while they cheered.

'We ought to have a gala,' Dee said that night. 'It's a shipboard tradition on the last night before arriving in port. You gals have already got the funny hats,' she laughed, picking up a Hobby hat. 'Jill, why don't you see what you can rustle up at the canteen, and I'll try the male officers' lounge.'

Jill arrived back from the canteen in thirty minutes with four chocolate bars and a pack of Chesterfields. 'This is the best I can do. They're nearly cleaned out.'

Dee showed up ten minutes later with two bottles of Guinness stout under her life preserver. 'Not exactly champagne, gang, but at least it bubbles,' she said. 'Our American officers have no booze at all, so our handsome Captain Hawkes kindly lent me two warm bottles of beer on the condition I pay him back Saturday night at the British officers' club in Algiers.'

Kaye hooted. 'That's swell as long as you don't mind going out with Captain Bligh.'

Jill got glasses for everyone, and Dee carefully poured two ounces into each. 'To warm beer,' Gleeson said, 'stale chocolate, and the best damned gala night ever.'

Jill raised her glass over her head in an exaggerated toast and watched it spin across the cabin and smash against the bulkhead. Only then did she hear the ear-splitting noise of a torpedo exploding.

Kaye and Betty were in a tangle on the floor; blood spattered in bright-red spots on the white sheets of the bunks. Dazed, Jill realized that the blood was pouring from a cut on her hand.

A terrifying claxon went off in the gangway outside the cabin: *WHOOP! WHOOP! WHOOP!* Jill tried to stand, but her whole body seemed to be working in slow motion as if in an escape nightmare where the unknown terror pursuing her got closer and closer while her legs pumped slower and slower.

Dee reached down and pulled her to her feet. 'Let's get out of here!'

Jill grabbed her Mae West and hastily wrapped her washcloth around her bloody hand. 'The torpedo bags — get 'em!' she called over her shoulder and wrenched the cabin door open, feeling the pain in her right hand for the first time. Once outside, she saw that the deck listed in the direction of the stern.

The women in her platoon moved quickly towards the dining room. 'Sergeant Harper!' Jill called in what she hoped was a near-normal voice to the noncom hurrying towards her against the stream of women. 'Check each starboard cabin to make sure all our people are out. I'll check the port side.'

Kaye and Betty rushed past her to see to their own platoons. Dee had already disappeared up the gangway towards the deck. Jill quickly made her way down the passage, opening each stateroom door to see that everyone had gone and that no life preservers remained in the cabins. Satisfied, she rushed breathless to the dining room. Hours seemed to have elapsed, but the big wall clock told her that only four minutes had actually passed.

Captain Trueblood was walking from table to table with first-aid kit, ministering to cuts and sprains. Jill saw one of her women crying, but the woman smiled as Jill approached. 'I feel so silly, Lieutenant — just give me a minute to stop.'

'Take it easy,' Jill said, patting her heaving shoulder. Not one Wac was hysterical, Jill saw with pride, despite the steady sound of exploding depth charges trying to force the submarine to the surface.

'Lieutenant,' Captain Trueblood said, pulling her aside, 'you're hurt.'

'Just a slight cut. Nothing serious.'

'Private Brodzinsky is missing. No one has seen her since we were hit. She must be found.'

A depth-charge explosion closer than the others shook the ship and told Jill they must be on top of the submarine. Gripping the rail, she descended to the promenade deck and again checked all cabin doors until she reached the Queen's Suite. She swung open the big double doors and saw that the room was empty. Damn! Where could Brodzinsky be? It was then she heard the sound of running water from the bathroom. She rattled the door. Good God! It was locked. 'Who's in there?' She could hear the shrill panic in her own voice.

'I knew the captain would send you.'

There was no mistaking Marie Brodzinsky's sarcasm-laden voice.

'Marie — for God's sake, get out of there. We're under attack — unlock this door!'

A moment passed. Jill could hear the incongruously merry sounds of splashing water.

'Ya' know, Lieutenant, every time you want to stop me from doing what I want to do you give me that chummy "Marie this" and "Marie that" line.'

'Private Brodzinsky, you're forcing me to give you a direct order to come out of there — *now!*'

'You see that roster on the door, Lieutenant? Well, this is my first bath in three days and I'm damn sure gonna have it. So call out the MPs. What can you do to me that would make any difference in my life now? I'd just as soon go straight down to hell on this ship.'

'We're not going down.' Jill was not sure she wasn't lying. The deck seemed to be listing even more than a few minutes earlier.

Marie was talking, the bitterness of her words coming clearly through the door. 'I didn't tell you everything back there at Shanks. Bill's letter hadn't just asked me to meet him in New York. He gave me an ultimatum. Said he'd always been against me joining the WAC — said if I didn't meet him we were through for all time.' The bathroom door flew open and Marie, wrapped in a dripping towel, confronted Jill. 'Would it have made any difference if you had known, Lieutenant — tell me, would it?'

'You know it — '

'— wasn't in the rule book.'

Another explosion rocked the ship, threw Jill back against a tier of bunks and sent Marie slamming into the open door. A huge knot raised almost immediately on her forehead.

Jill helped the dazed woman into a utility coat, snatched up her torpedo bag and helmet from under her bunk and, half hauling, half pushing, got her to the dining room.

Captain Trueblood rushed over to them. 'What — '

Jill interrupted. 'Ma'am, she fell — was disoriented.'

'We have a medic here now. He'll check her over. But see if you can find a ship's officer and find out where we're hit. Are we going to abandon ship? Get me some information. These women should know something about what to expect.'

'Yes, ma'am.'

Jill bent over Brodzinsky, who was lying on a stretcher. 'You okay now?'

Brodzinsky opened her eyes, her harsh whisper meant for Jill alone. 'Christ! Am I s'posed to be grateful 'cause you didn't turn me in to the captain? Get this straight! I'll *never* let you forget what you let them do to me.'

Jill ran now from past failure, away from that unforgiving voice, to the sanctuary of the open deck. She edged, in a darkness illuminated by gun flashes from the upper deck, along the bulkhead, careful to stay out of the crew's way, until she saw Dee Gleeson.

'Dee!' she yelled hoarsely.

'You shouldn't be up here. I'm taking a chance they'll forget I'm a woman and think of me as just another correspondent with the run of the ship.'

WHOOP! WHOOP! WHOOP!

A destroyer passed close by at flank speed, depth charges pumping across its stern. A piercing shaft of searchlight on its bridge swept back and forth across the murky water.

Gradually, Jill could see the shape of a conning tower emerge under the light.

The gun crew above cursed at their gun.

'Damn you! Range!'

'One twenty and closing!'

'Fire! Fire! Sink you sonofabitch!'

Jill saw men tumbling like targets in a shooting gallery about the sub's deck as 20mm tracers slammed into them. She saw the destroyer turn and bear down on the U-boat.

'Scratch one Nazi sub,' a sailor yelled in a high voice full of uncontrollable glee.

'They're going to ram it,' Dee shouted above the battle din.

Jill had never witnessed a moment of death before. She stared transfixed as the bow of the bigger ship crunched through the sub just behind the conning tower. In pieces, the sub sank like the stones she used to try to skip on the irrigation ditches back home. Only these stones were full of living men, some tossed over the side, where they struggled in the choppy waves, yelling words she could not hear, but whose meaning she could understand. For a moment she knew their panic. She had felt it before at the embarkation pier, but it had been momentary, not forever. These men were truly stepping off into the unknown before her eyes, and there was nothing she could do about it.

Suddenly, the unfinished business of her life — to beg Neil's forgiveness, to find Des, to grow older and more comfortable with herself — seemed more precious than it ever had. Shivering, she stood there, never more alive, the night air washing over her like the waves closing over the sub.

'Will they pick them up, Dee?'

'No.' Dee's voice was flat and final. 'If they stop dead in the water, they're inviting a torpedo. Probably more than one U-boat out there, you know.'

Jill tried not to think of the alien voices calling through the night in their hated tongue, voices that begged for what she could not give. 'Do you know how bad we're hit, Dee?' she asked, trying to close her mind to the men in the water.

226

'I heard the third officer say that an aft cargo hold had been hit and was flooded. Thank God it wasn't the troop hold.'

They moved to the starboard rail, and Jill, looking over, saw a gaping hole at the waterline, faintly illumined by the bright ribbons of flame from two burning cargo ships. Compulsively, she scanned the flame-lit water for the telltale signs of a torpedo streaking towards them. It was obvious the cargo ships had been hit to create a diversion, pull off the destroyer screen so that the U-boats could get at the troop ships. They weren't yet safe. There might be other prowlers out there in the black night.

'Ladies, what are you doing on deck?'

Jill whirled to see Captain Hawkes in a freshly laundered uniform, followed by Number One. 'Sir, Captain Trueblood sent me to find out if we're going to abandon ship.'

The captain jerked his glance from Jill up to the radar swinging on the mast overhead. 'Number One, have Signal report the first sign of bogeys coming in for the kill.' He returned his focus to Jill and Dee. 'Now, ladies, get below and stay there. Tell your captain that Jerry hasn't finished us. We've slowed to twelve knots, but we'll make headway until we're taken under tow. I'll buy you both a gin in Algiers, Saturday.'

Jill wasn't reassured, but she saluted and left the deck with Dee. They had closed one blackout curtain and were about to step through the second when they heard the watch officer report to Hawkes.

'Sir, that Jerry fish flooded two compartments, we've got rudder problems and gas seepage from the storage tanks. If we're hit again — if there's a fire — '

'Right,' the captain said. 'May God be with us tonight.'

Jill was frozen with one hand on the inner blackout curtain.

Dee nudged her. 'Are you going to tell that to your comrades?'

'No.' Jill made her decision instantly. Right or wrong, she was the only one who could make it. 'If we explode, it'll

227

be over in . . . Why should they spend their last hours in fear?'

Making her way to the dining room, Jill reported, 'The captain says we're going to be taken in tow.'

One Wac pulled out a deck of cards and started dealing a game of acey-deucy. Minutes later a mess attendant served coffee and Spam sandwiches. The scene reminded Jill of one of those scary movies where the guests at the manor-house go on doing ordinary things in the drawing room while the audience knows a mad killer lurks in the closet. But in this case she had chosen to be an audience of one. She had no one to share her fright. That aloneness was the worst part of the long night.

Shortly before six bells she stationed herself in the darkened gangway and watched the sun make the sky salmon pink against the azure sea. She knew now that they would make it. A light easterly breeze was blowing, but she shivered under her Mae West as she watched the Mediter-ranean rolling past the convoy. What an awful way to die — she relived the horror of the sinking sub calling out to life that had already turned away. Suddenly the cut on her hand began to throb, and she made her way to sick bay to get it properly bandaged.

On the second morning after the *Canberra Princess* had been hit, the 59th WAC Signal Company was welcomed to Algiers at a dockside shed by the deputy chief signal officer, Allied Forces Headquarters. Jill stood in the back with a sense of movement which told her she still didn't have her land legs.

'We have a lot of work for you to do,' the colonel said. 'We can use the skills you high-speed radio ops, teletypists and cryptographic people bring us. The only thing I can promise you is long hours and far from ideal conditions — and a chance to kick the Nazi war machine in the backside. Are you up to the task?'

As one woman, the Wacs enthusiastically yelled, '*Yes, sir!*'

'Good!' the colonel said, beaming. 'I'm convinced you

will live up to the Signal Corps motto, which is — ?' he raised his voice in a question.

Back came the strong, proud response: 'We do the impossible and do it well!'

The colonel was pleased. 'And now I'll turn this orientation over to your immediate superior, who will give you your permanent assignments.' The DCSO then motioned towards the door, and Captain Desmond Stratton strode to the centre of the room.

27

To reduce the use of precious cargo space, letters to the troops — called V-Mail — are microfilmed and blown up again after overseas transit.

On a windy late-September evening, Max's chauffeur dropped Elisabeth at the Franklin Hotel after another Maryland weekend with just a few minutes to spare before her weekend pass was up. She was relieved. Of all things, she didn't want to have to answer to Captain Swearingen for late sign-in. She tried to keep a low profile in the company; the less anyone knew about her, the better. She didn't need to belong to any of the company cliques. Sure she'd had friends at OC, but that was different, once in a lifetime, and she didn't want or need to try to duplicate it.

In her box there was a picture postcard from Bunny saying that hello was all she had energy for after fifteen hours on KP, and six V-mail letters from Marne. She picked up the thin envelopes, climbed the single flight to her room and tossed them distractedly onto the small table to one side of her bed. Not now. She couldn't bear the memory of any other man to come between her and the still-warm impression of Max's arms. She relived his kisses, the salt tang of him in her mouth, recreating a deliciously sensual mood.

Finally reality pushed against her. She flipped on her bedside radio and undressed as Frank Sinatra sang 'You'd Be So Nice to Come Home to,' singing along distractedly, ' . . . you'd be all that I would desire . . . ' All her movements seemed unconnected when she had just left Max; she was not grounded, but like a whipping electric wire, full of raw current, landing capriciously here and there. Her sensual memory of him left her with no sense of control over herself, and certainly not over fate.

It was a presentiment of ill-fate that nagged at her, although she chose to think of it as conscience, a new idea altogether in her adult life. She supposed it was left over from saying goodbye to Jill earlier in the month. Somehow it always hurt her to have Page and Jill and Bunny think well of her. And then there was the pressing question of what to do about Marne.

Reaching for the letters, she saw that some were over a month old, while one had been written on September 10, 1943, a little over two weeks earlier. They were all numbered so that she would read them in sequence, and she picked up number one, scrawled in Marne's big-fisted handwriting.

Somewhere in Sicily

Why haven't I heard from you? Only one letter has caught up with me lately — darling, I don't mean to sound angry, believe me I'm not — it's just that I don't think of anyone but you or anything but staying alive. You can bet I don't intend to die, that's not in my plans at all. You're in my plans — only you. I want you and want to tell you how much, but I don't want the censor reading about it.

This is capital H Hell. I slept in a barn last night and worse than the bombs and incoming 88s were the fleas. A whole Panzer column of fleas marched up and down my back until I thought I'd go crazy. And in between I counted eighteen air raid alarms. The Krauts sent in everything they had.

When dawn came there were four Tiger tanks lined up

230

in front of us on the road. One of them had three white rings on its barrel, one for each Sherman he'd knocked out. I radioed the others to go for that sonofabitch, and we put him out of action for good.

Elisabeth picked up and discarded other letters riddled with holes where they had been censored, then Marne's last letter, which seemed to have slipped by the censors intact.

Somewhere in Sicily

Darling Elisabeth, do you know you're famous all over the 2nd Armoured Division? I found a combat artist to paint your picture (from that old *Vogue* layout) on my lead tank the Lucky Liz. I kiss it every morning for luck. Don't laugh, darling. A guy gets superstitious fast in combat.

We've been on the move for days now — heading east —

Elisabeth turned the page over and saw that the next two sentences were blacked out by the censor.

. . . and now we're in a staging area.

If you've heard about that Patton flap — where he slapped the kid with battle fatigue — take it from me it's been exaggerated. He's the best damned armoured commander in the world — that includes Rommel — and we can't win this war without him.

I detoured into a town on my way to Divisional meeting. Since I got my Captain's bars, I'm in on a lot of the staff planning. The place was a smoking mess! The Germans left snipers behind and our dogfaces had to go down each street drawing their fire and flushing them out.

Another thing — if you hear anybody bad-mouthing 'Tommy Atkins,' tell them for me that these British soldiers are some great fighters. We've been bivouacked next to the 'blokes' for the past few days, and they're first rate in my book.

I want you to know I honour my vows to you, and there are plenty of chances for girls here. Death may be all around me, but your love is sacred to me — you are my goddess, the only real thing in my life. I tried to make you feel that in the hotel that last weekend. Did I succeed? Write every day.

She felt an unfamiliar regret that she couldn't be the woman Marne thought she was. Loving Max to distraction had made her more tolerant of Marne's love for her. For a very brief moment, she toyed with the idea of being straight with her husband, of abandoning the charade of faithful, waiting wife — but only for a moment. She couldn't jeopardize a sure thing for Max — not yet.

But she knew vaguely as she went to bed that such a moment of emotional weakness had opened her mind to a fantasy of possibility. She *must* find a way to become a permanent part of Max's life, and then she would let Marne go gladly. Suddenly, she felt a blow of recognition, one she knew came rarely to people before it was too late to take action. What if Max was waiting for *her* to make the first move? What if he needed an unmistakable sign from her that she was his and only his? Elisabeth had known powerful — even brutal — men who placed an impossible emphasis on loyalty in others. She wondered if that could be what bothered Max — he thought she didn't trust him, didn't want him enough to risk everything. It was possible. Look at the way he referred to her as Mrs Gardner when he desired to put distance between them. Could he want her to divorce Marne first to prove herself? In her life she had seen the improbable, even the implausible, come true often enough. *She and Max — together*. There had been things more unattainable in her life and yet by her determination she had made them otherwise. Drifting towards sleep, she wondered what she must do to show Max she belonged to him, only him.

Her chance came almost immediately.

'Elisabeth.' Danny Barnes, thinner to the point of frailty, was waiting for her as she stepped off the Quartermaster-

Depot bus from the Franklin the next morning. 'Colonel Nick wants to see the whole team in his office in thirty minutes.'

'Anything important?'

'Looks like it. He's got three secretaries hopping from one file to the next, digging out every spec sheet and WAC clothing contract. And, by the way,' he said and cast her his shy, intense smile, 'these orders came down for you first thing this morning.'

She held her breath. They couldn't ship her out. *They couldn't!* 'What the hell are they?' she said, half frantic.

Barnes looked downcast. 'Your promotion to first lieutenant came through. The colonel sent his personal recommendation after that job you did on the uniforms. Aren't you pleased?'

Relief filled her. 'A promotion — oh, that.'

'You really don't care?' He looked puzzled then, hurt even, because he'd been part of her success.

She slipped into the safety of her good-soldier role. 'It's not that, Barnes. I just don't want to get shipped out when there's so much work to do here. You understand, don't you?' She needed him on her side. Together they formed half of the WAC uniform specialists' team, and Danny Barnes was the EM who could get things done for her. Master Sergeant Kuban spent most of his afternoons on various 'official' expeditions that ended in nearby bars, while Captain Everson waited for Barnes and Elisabeth to come up with ideas that would guarantee he could sit out the war stateside.

Impulsively, she picked up the telephone on her desk to call Max, then just as quickly put it down. Max hated any hint of female possessiveness. He was a man, and men, no matter what they said, wanted to pursue. Some kind of leftover predator instinct, she supposed, but whatever it was, she wouldn't make the mistake of telephoning Max until she had something of importance to tell him. No matter how she longed to hear his voice, she must remain the assured, cool woman who had attracted him, a pose Elisabeth found it a growing struggle to maintain with him.

'Come on, Lieutenant,' Barnes interrupted her train of thought. 'Colonel Nick doesn't like to be kept waiting.'

'Right behind you.' She took her coffee cup and followed him, taking a seat in front of Nicolson's desk, which looked like a battleground for papers and official memos.

'Okay,' the colonel said, 'let's get to it,' and he sat down on the edge of the desk. 'I don't have to remind you that the substance of this meeting goes no further than my door.' He looked up, waiting for nods of compliance.

Did his eyes linger a fraction longer on her face? She wasn't sure, but the chilling memory of Madame Gabriella's steely gaze shook her for the briefest second before she smiled an innocent agreement.

The colonel shifted to pick up a manilla folder of papers. 'The OQMG has handed us a big job, and as you can guess they sat on it so long they can't give us the time we need. We're directed to develop a WAC off-duty dress, summer and winter, for officer and enlisted. Captain, I'll need material specs from your team on each in two weeks.'

'Very well, sir.'

Barnes asked, 'Colonel, what about the design?'

'I was coming to that. We'll go after the usual women's clothing designers.'

'Sir, may I speak plainly?'

'Yes, Sergeant.'

'Colonel, I think we might be overlooking the talent we have right here at the depot. I mean — ' Barnes paused, looking around at Elisabeth ' — Lieutenant Gardner has made uniform sketches which I think are damned good.'

Kuban interrupted, hung over but looking for a chance to show he was on top of the discussion, 'Colonel, that's one helluva idea. We'd save money and have a great story for the newspapers to boot.'

'Worth exploring, Colonel,' Captain Everson chimed in.

The colonel stared at Elisabeth for a moment. 'I suppose we could include the Lieutenant in the competition. What do you say, Gardner? Want to give it a shot?'

Was he kidding? To actually design a dress — no, four dresses, and see them turned into material, buttons and trim, to see them worn by women. Her designs. 'I can't think of anything I'd like more, Colonel.'

'All right, go to it. But, Elisabeth, I can't promise you more than equal consideration.'

'Certainly, sir, I would want you to be fair to the civilians.' Inwardly she smiled. That was waving the old school tie at a career officer.

Gradually during the meeting she had lost all sense of the danger she had felt earlier. She put it down to a natural tension, because thoughts of Max intruded now into her every thought and act — especially here at the depot.

The colonel continued, 'Everson, I want you to get to work on the production schedule, and have it on my desk by the end of the week. We have to have designs, specs and material allocations ready for contract bids by early November.'

'You'll have 'em, sir.'

Outside the colonel's office Elisabeth threw her arms around Barnes and kissed him while the office Underwoods came to a standstill. 'You're a darling for going to bat for me like that.'

Stumbling, Danny backed away, a look of pure adoration on his face. She observed him more carefully than she usually did. He was infatuated, she could see that, infatuated in a strangely passive way, but Barnes was a man nonetheless and might want more from her than she could give. Christ! She'd have to be careful, she didn't want to encourage or discourage him. Damn! Here was *another* nice guy who wanted to adore and take care of her. It was amusing, after all. She seemed to attract men who needed a goddess to adore. There was just no way to get rid of men like Marne and Barnes, not even in the Army. Irritated, Elisabeth sat down at her drawing board and picked up a piece of charcoal for sketching. She had been nice to Barnes because she could use him, but she couldn't take seriously his response to her, because it was Max she wanted passionately, obsessively and miserably — the one man *she* couldn't fool.

That night she walked down Broad Street to a public

telephone booth and dialled Max's Drexel Hill number.

She waited for him to pick up his extension.

'Elisabeth. What a pleasant surprise,' he said in the breathy baritone that sent pinpricks of remembered pleasure through her body.

His measured politeness established a formal distance from her. She wanted to scream at him, tell him not to talk in that tone with her, but instead she said calmly, 'I've only a moment, Max, but I thought you'd like to hear about an interesting new development at the depot.' She waited. Damn it, she was always waiting.

'Yes,' he said finally.

'The colonel gave my team a new project today — developing WAC uniform dresses for off-duty wear. And, Max, I'm going to submit designs for them — Colonel Nick agreed.'

'I wasn't aware you were interested in designing, Elisabeth,' Max said.

'I didn't know it myself until a few months ago,' she told him, hoping he'd be impressed.

'Why are you telling me this?'

'I thought . . .' She hesitated, knowing she was violating every army reg she could think of, and then began again. 'I thought you'd want to know about a potentially large contract you could bid for.'

She heard his deep breathing through the earphone. 'Aren't you aware,' he said, his voice almost lazy, 'that you could be in serious trouble by giving me advance contract information?'

What kind of game was he playing? She was giving him exactly what she knew he wanted.

Then his voice became intimate, the tone he used when he was aroused. 'Darling, I must go to Washington tomorrow for a hearing at the War Production Board, but I'll be back on Friday. We'll have dinner, then, just the two of us.'

'I'd like that very much, Max,' she said in a voice whose sensuality she could no longer control, suggesting plainly what she'd like much more than dinner.

236

'Until Friday, then.'

She waited for him to hang up the receiver. He didn't. 'Max, are you still there?'

'Yes.'

'Why?'

'No reason, or at least none I want to discuss right now. I'll talk to you about it on Friday.' He hung up then.

What did he want to discuss with her on Friday? Her hand shook as she replaced the receiver and caught her own reflection in the window of the glass booth. Her eyes searched the face to see if it knew something. Was Max going to ask her to marry him? Had her desire to help him get another contract finally convinced him of her love and loyalty? 'Max,' she said aloud, her voice seeming to come from the woman in the window, 'I'll prove it!'

Elisabeth walked swiftly back to the Franklin Hotel and climbed to her third floor room. She had thirty minutes before she had to report for a tour as company duty officer. Pulling from her small writing table one of the tissue-weight V-mail sheets, she looked up the APO number, which she could never seem to remember, and began to write what she knew was a Dear John letter every patriotic American would despise her for:

> *Monday Evening*
> *September 27, 1943*

MARNE,

I have fallen in love with another man and I want a divorce. Sorry, but there is no easier way to say it; the best way is straight out like that.

My mind is made up so please save us both embarrassment and don't ask me to reconsider. However, you should let me know whether you want me to file for the divorce or whether *you* want to.

By this third paragraph you should have begun to hate me for what I'm doing to you. I hope you do hate me. That would be the first wise reaction you've had to me since we met. I was never the woman or wife you thought

I was. Believe me, this is the kindest thing I have ever done for you.

Hastily, she signed and sealed it, carried it downstairs to the orderly room and placed it in the pile of outgoing mail. She was on duty until midnight, but during those hours she wouldn't allow her eyes to stray to the letter box. She wouldn't allow her mind to question or look back. She must strip herself naked of her neatly guaranteed future for Max. It was a risk only Max could appreciate, a move that would convince him she wanted to belong only to him.

Max sat upright behind his great mahogany desk for some time, his right hand resting on the cradled telephone. He had no inkling of why he had suggested that some mysterious message would be given Elisabeth on Friday night. He supposed he was in love with the bitch and his senses had deserted him — a dangerous situation, since she seemed to be taking chances and losing her own well-developed sense of self-interest.

Damn! And Nick had been acting strange, too, lately — standoffish. Did he know about the affair with Elisabeth? What did the colonel suspect? In any event, he'd be a fool to trust her now. When a vain, neurotic, selfish woman falls in love for the first time, she precipitates danger like a loose cannon on a heaving deck. But, damn it, he needed her, just a few more weeks, months at the most. He must find a way to keep her loyalty just long enough, while gradually cooling the situation. When it was safe, he would see that she was transferred to the other end of the country. A word in the right ear would do it.

Anyway, the war would probably end in 1944 and the quartermaster stockpiles would kill the uniform-manufacturing business for years to come. He had already begun to plan his re-entry into the postwar clothing business, when the homecoming GIs would quit making war and start making babies by the millions. Baby clothes, layettes, that sort of thing — *that* was where the smart money would be in the ready-to-wear industry, and for that transition he wouldn't need a has-been fashion model. That was not to say he didn't need a wife, but he needed one who would cover his wartime profits with a patina of respectability.

He rang for his butler.

'Yes, sir.'

'Hinton, I'm driving to the capital tomorrow morning for three or four days. Pack the conservative pinstripes. No evening clothes this trip. I'll be dining at the Army-Navy Club, where tuxedos are considered downright unpatriotic.'

'Very well, sir.'

'Make it the grey pinstripe, Hinton. War profiteers don't wear grey, do they?'

'No, sir, they don't,' the butler said, smiling at Max's little joke.

'And, Hinton, while you're about it, please see if you can get Miss Longley for me.'

A few minutes passed. Max poured a large scotch. The telephone on his desk buzzed.

'Miss Longley on the line, sir.'

'Thank you, Hinton.'

'Kit, darling,' he said.

'Max,' the thin, reedy voice, product of several generations of gentry inbreeding, answered. 'I don't know if I should even *talk* to you. You've been so naughty.'

'A businessman's time is not his own, my dear. Surely you know there's a war on.'

'Don't be tiresome, Max. I've heard you've been fighting on *quite* a different battlefield.'

'Perhaps that is why you should pay special attention to me now that I'm home for good from the wars.'

'*Are* you home, Max — for good?'

'Yes, most definitely, or rather I will be after a run down to Washington. I'm having a little dinner party this Friday. You could see how war-weary I really am, and besides, darling, I've arranged an amusing guest list. Will you come?'

'Yes, I'll come, if only to see this new Max for myself.'

239

28

*In September, German Colonel Otto Skorzeny, in a
daring glider raid, rescues Mussolini, who has been
imprisoned by the new Italian military government
of Marshal Pietro Badoglio. By October, the
dictator, accompanied by his mistress Clara
Petacci, is set up in a German puppet government at
Lake Garda. The Badoglio government is not given
the status of one of the Allied Powers, but is classed
as a 'co-belligerent'.*

By one o'clock on the afternoon of Wednesday,
October 13, Page felt that her stomach had started
a war of its own. All morning she had been unable
to take a break at one of the Pentagon's coffee bars, and she
was well on her way to missing lunch.

The news from the army comcentre that the Badoglio
government had declared Italy to be at war with Germany
had caused a flurry of small celebrations all around the
second floor from A to D ring, but she had not had time to
participate. She had spent the morning polishing press
releases for the all-states WAC recruiting campaign. A
brilliant idea of Page's superior, Major Jesse Rice, the
campaign enlisted women in their own state's training
companies. The drive had given the WAC's public image a
boost and also just about replaced the women who had
chosen discharge during the conversion in July.

There were now 260 WAC companies, stationed in
almost every command in the continental Zone of the
Interior and the overseas theatres. These companies were
doing work vital to the war effort from motor transport,
postal service and parachute rigging to food preparation,
supply and a variety of clerical and administrative work,
but there were never enough companies to satisfy the stock
of requisitions on Colonel Hobby's desk. And no one in the
Director's office believed that the WAC could enlist the

600,000 women General Marshall had asked Colonel Hobby for.

Page wrote '30' on the last press release, marked the routing slip for mimeographing and distribution, and, still concentrating, reached for a cigarette.

'Oh, how soon they forget,' a man's voice said in a familiar tone of mock self-pity.

'Randy!' His voice was deeper, but no older sister could forget a younger brother's teasing tone. Jumping from her chair, she threw her arms about him. 'Let me look at you.' She stepped back, still hanging on to his hands. 'You've changed so — it must be the Clark Gable moustache and the fifty-mission crush to your hat.' She had instantly settled into the habit of easy raillery that was an affectionate shorthand between them. 'I swear, Little Brother, I'd pass you right by on the street. The last time I saw you on leave from the Academy you were but a callow cadet.'

'That was before I towed targets for aerial gunnery practice, Big Sister. Ages a man fast.' He looked quickly at his watch. 'Listen, can you get away for some chow? I've got to be back at Gravelly Point before four o'clock.'

'Let's go.' She jotted an explanatory note and left it propped on her desk.

On the way through the marble corridors, she pointed out some of the Pentagon's landmarks. 'That's Special Services right next door to us. Captain Wayne King, the bandleader, has his office there.'

'Hobnobbing with celebrities must be dangerous work.' He grinned. 'Do you get hazardous-duty pay?'

'Funny boy! As a matter of fact, it has its moments of pure terror. Try coordinating a bond rally with Mrs Winston Churchill, Jeanette MacDonald, and a dozen big brass all trying to stand next to them. I'd have never made it, but I worked with a great officer. You may have heard of him — ' she was teasing again ' — Captain Pat O'Brien?'

'Enough, you shameless name-dropper!' He sighed loudly. 'There goes the hot combat-pilot image I was going to impress you with — shot down.' His hand spiralled down like a falling airplane.

They squeezed into the next elevator. 'And this is the famous concourse,' Page announced guide-fashion when they reached the enormous expanse on the bottom floor. 'The officers' dining room is over here. It's a good thing you came this month. Women officers weren't allowed to dine here until recently.'

'Still leading the charge, Page?'

She grinned. 'Now you sound like my friend Bunny. Little brothers should not be so perceptive.'

'Just so you don't think yours is the only cross being carried in this war, let me tell you my own horror stories. You know the ninety-day wonders hate us West Point guys worse than they hate the Nazis! And the older Point men are unhappy because my class was commissioned in our third year so we could leave our Hudson River paradise to win the war for them. Everybody's somebody's scapegoat — and that's as profound as I'm gonna get this whole war.'

They took their trays to a quiet table against the back wall.

Page had almost forgotten her hunger in the excitement of seeing Randy again. 'Have you heard from Father?' she asked, spooning the split-pea soup she had ordered.

'Not since I went Air Corps over Armoured and disgraced him.'

'No, Randy, that's *my* special niche in his life. But you're wrong not to think he's proud of you. He is — tremendously so.'

'He has one helluva way of showing it, Page. He even reamed me out in a letter which his adjutant signed.'

'It's his way. I don't mean to play Can You Top This, but when I was in the hospital at Fort Des Moines — '

'In the hospital? I didn't know.'

'Oh, it was nothing important, as it turned out. But let me make my point — Dad called the hospital head from London to find out about me. It never occurred to him to ask me directly.'

'Why can't he talk to us, Page?'

'I think he's afraid of loving us too much, and losing us, like he lost Mother.'

242

'They don't teach us Freud at the Academy. I'll have to leave the analysis to you Cliffies.'

Page made a face, then said seriously, 'He always thought you'd take his place, Randy. You know that.'

'Look, he may have written the book of my life, but that doesn't mean I'm going to live it.'

'What are you saying?'

'As soon as I do the duration and six months, I'm resigning my commission.'

'Oh God! Why? I'd give anything —'

'Page, I knew it my first month at the Point. I don't want to spend the rest of my life in uniform, clawing my way up the promotion ladder. He loves it — damned if you don't love it, too — but I hate it.'

'What do you want to do?'

'I don't know. I'm not a very ambitious guy, but I sure know I don't want any part of this life.' He smiled, the wry sideways smile she had always loved. 'Hell, Page, *you* were always a better soldier than I was, even when we were kids. Remember at Fort Sill when I used to make you and your girlfriends be the Indians, and you always won? The general just refused to acknowledge it.'

Page smiled at the memory, but worried that Randy might make some headstrong announcement that would tear apart her family forever. But how much family was there to save? Randy would go his own way after the war; her father had always insisted on his own plan for her. When she thought hard about it, the only real family she had was the Army and her sisters in the Corps. She shook her head to clear it of the thought that had become more and more persistent, one she could not seem to rationalize away permanently — the thought of living a military life even after the war. Again she shook her head. But of course Paul was right. It was ridiculous to think of women soldiers in a peace-time Army.

Randy snapped his fingers. 'Come back, Page, wherever you are.'

'I was just thinking that you certainly have a right to lead your own life, Randy, but you don't have to tell him until

243

after the war. Can't you let it go until then?'

He nodded reluctantly. 'Still the mediating angel between the men in the family. I can't quite believe it yet — that you actually had the guts to defy him and join the Army.'

'I surprised *myself*,' she said, then changed the subject. 'Now tell me all about flight school.'

'Nothing much to tell. I like flying well enough. Bombers, really — B-17 flight school is where I'm headed. I'm not in your hot-stick-jockey, fighter-pilot type. Yeah, flying's fine, I guess. We get the best food and the best girls.' He reached into his inside blouse pocket and dropped a handful of pilot wings on the table, a mischievous grin lighting his face. 'The girls are crazy to get pinned.'

'Randy, that's terrible.' But she laughed in spite of herself.

'Now,' he said, finishing his apple pie and lighting a cigar, which looked impossibly adult against his face still carrying the round-cheeked remnants of boyhood, 'tell me about your Wacs.'

'What do you want to know?'

'You wrote me about the terrible time you were having with the rumour mill.'

'Oh yes, that's always with us, but public acceptance is growing. Our new recruiting campaign involves local communities more, and that's helping people see that Wacs are regular women.' She told him about all the press releases she wrote showing the diversity of women in the Army, ticking off a range of her stories that had been recently picked up by the wire services. 'There's a private whose rheumatic-fever-control experiments at Buckley Field Hospital earned her a commission; the furloughed sergeant who couldn't sleep because the beds at home were too soft. Just yesterday I distributed a report from the Medical Corps giving Wacs with the Fifth Army in Italy a first-class health rating. That's army code for assuring civilians that we aren't pregnant en masse.'

Randy stubbed out his cigar. 'Sounds like pretty tame

stuff to me.'

Though she tried for a lighthearted tone, she couldn't keep the bitterness and frustration out of her words. 'Damn it, Randy,' she said, lowering her voice, 'it's what I *can't* publicize that the public ought to hear. You know that Washington is ringed with anti-aircraft batteries, don't you?'

'Yes. I'd expect the capital city to be protected from air attack.'

'And you think they're fully manned, don't you?'

'Of course, Page, they'd have to be. What is this, *The Sixty-Four-Thousand-Dollar Question*?'

'What if I told you they weren't all manned, that some of them were wo-manned?'

Randy let out a low whistle. 'You're the public-relations expert, but I'd say that's one helluva story.'

'That's what's so frustrating,' she told him, her chin propped on her hand. 'The Army is scared to death of getting a negative reaction from the public, a-little-girl-can't-handle-a-great-big-gun stuff, so I can't mention it, nobody can. Just think, Randy, if flying was woman's work you'd never get the recognition you're due, you'd never be able to brag or pass out wings to every pretty girl you meet.'

'Hey, take it easy, Page. Remember me? I'm just a poor fly-boy on a stopover to see his big sister. I'm not responsible for the Army or the backward ways of the whole country.' He reached for her hand. 'Know what?'

'No. What?' she answered, falling into a silly game they had played as children.

'You always were too serious, reading poetry and all, but now you're positively grim, a Janie-one-note. You've got to get out more. Have some fun. What happened to that Major Whatshisname? Can't he take you away from all this?'

She stopped smiling at the idea that her younger brother was giving her such mature advice, and a memory of Paul's goodbye filled her. 'He's shipped out, Randy. I don't know where. He couldn't tell me, and I haven't heard from him yet.'

'Liked him, did you?'

'Yes — a lot.'

'That's tough, Page. But honest, listen to ol' Randy, now — I'm quite an expert on good times. This WAC thing is really getting to you. You're even beginning to sound like one of those suffragettes, dressed in virginal white, chained to the White House fence. Why don't you try to get a furlough or at least take a couple of days on a pass? Do you good. I'll bet you've been working round the clock.'

She had to admit he was right. In the month since Paul had left she had been working day and night six days a week, sometimes Sundays too. 'I could take a couple of sunny days while Indian Summer holds — maybe even play some tennis at the club. Are you sure you can't stay?'

'I'd love to teach you proper respect for my backhand, but I've got to report to Lockbourne in Columbus, Ohio, tomorrow. Besides,' he said, his grin devilish again, 'there's a girl at the Air Transport Command office out at Gravelly who's just dying for a pair of wings for her cashmere cardigan.'

The short hour they'd had was gone, and they had talked about everything and nothing. The most important question — *Is this the last time I'll ever see you?* — she had never asked.

'Take care of yourself,' she said, 'take exceptional care of yourself, Little Brother.'

He kissed her on the forehead. 'Did I ever tell you you're some swell Big Sister?'

Page went with Randy to the main-floor entrance, and watched him start down the steps to the street below. She wanted to run after him, tell him why he was so precious to her. He was the only other person in the world who shared her blood and her memories exactly. But soldiers didn't run after other soldiers. Instead her eyes followed him until his uniform in the distance was indistinguishable from dozens of others.

29

Yes, I want the war to be over, just as keenly as any soldier in North Africa wants it. This little interlude of passive contentment here on the Mediterranean shore is a mean temptation. It is a beckoning into somnolence. This is the kind of day I think I want my life to be composed of, endlessly. But pretty soon we shall strike our tents and traipse again after the clanking tanks, sleep again to the incessant lullaby of the big rolling guns. It has to be that way.

— Ernie Pyle

'Hammersmith, Second Lieutenant, Jill H., US Army, WAC,' she wrote in the guest book, adding an unaccustomed flourish under her neat signature, not to be outdone by the more elaborate European handwriting style just above hers in the guest book. She placed her Hobby hat on a marble table in the midst of what looked like an internationale of hats — a French general's, two British naval officers', one of them a Wren, and an AAF colonel's overseas cap.

'I have to pinch myself, Kaye,' Jill said to her companion. 'If I had a magic lamp I could never fantasize anything like the Palais d'Été.'

'And those Zouave officers,' Kaye Young said, eyeing the swarthy pantalooned colonials striding about in their boots and tasselled hats, 'all look like Turhan Bey in the Loew's Saturday matinée.'

Jill laughed. 'Come on, Kaye, you can take your pick of dates in Algiers. Besides, you don't even speak French.'

'You know,' Kaye said playfully, 'that's not as much of a problem as you might imagine. I think I'll suggest to Dee that she do an article on nonverbal dating. I've always thought communication highly over-rated — without words you just get down to fundamentals fast. Ugh! Me Kaye, you Tarzan . . .'

Jill giggled. 'Sshhh! What if General Giraud heard you?'

Kaye simulated a shocked tone. 'Sshhh yourself or *you'll* offend him! He's French, isn't he?'

Jill was amazed at the total transformation Kaye had undergone since they arrived in North Africa. While not exactly man-crazy, she certainly wasn't the angry, sarcastic woman she had been. Jill had asked her once about the change. 'It's this way,' Kaye had said. 'I thought it was my fault when Dick wanted out of our engagement, but since I came here I've realized what a bastard he was — after all, forty thousand Frenchmen can't be wrong!' Jill knew there was a basic truth to Kaye's joke. Ten thousand men for every Wac in Algiers can work marvels for a woman's self-confidence. If Kaye had been jilted by one man, the cure seemed to be the droves of attentive Allied officers waiting to shower her with masculine attention in a dozen different languages. The cure, in fact, may have been too complete, because Kaye had taken a romantic's interest in Jill and Captain Desmond Stratton of late.

They moved into General Henri Giraud's receiving line. The commander of the Free French in North Africa was hosting a formal buffet at his headquarters; his spahi honour guard, swords drawn, stood just behind and to either side of him. Only in her wildest daydreams had she seen herself in the company of a famous French general, and now just two short months since the *Canberra Princess* had been towed into Algiers everything was coming true.

She stopped and stood at attention in front of the General. 'Lieutenant Hammersmith, sir, Women's Army Corps, United States Army,' she said. 'Thank you for inviting us.'

He lifted her hand and bent to kiss it. She felt his white moustache scratch her skin. 'General Eisenhower has told me many times that his women soldiers rank with his best troops,' he said in heavily accented English. 'It is always my pleasure to pay homage to good soldiers.'

She was overwhelmed by the warmth of his Old World courtesy. She caught herself almost dipping into a curtsy. Good God, would she never stop responding like a dutiful child? When would she grow up and leave the too self-conscious Jill behind?

'Thank you, General,' she said. She drew herself up to his Croix de Guerre and stepped aside for Kaye.

'Lieutenant Kaye Young, sir.'

'And what is your duty, Lieutenant?'

'I command one shift of the all-nation switchboard, General.'

'Ahh, then it is to you we owe the good telephone service we have here in Algiers.'

'Sir, that credit goes to my operators.'

He nodded. '*Mais certainement!*'

Kaye joined Jill in the main room. 'Not Jean Gabin, but nevertheless a handsome old lion,' she said, relishing her newfound role as expert on the male sex.

'Hello, you two. I hoped I'd find you before I left.'

It was Dee, followed by two army photographers.

Jill shook Dee's hand. 'You're leaving? When? Can you say where you're going?'

'Tomorrow. Flying to London. My magazine wants me to write an article about GI Janes with the Eighth Air Force. Can I send you something from merry old England?'

Kaye laughed, 'How about a nice cool fog?'

Jill frowned at Kaye's levity. 'I wouldn't mind going with you, Dee. It's all over in North Africa. The war has moved on and left us behind.'

Kaye rolled her eyes at Dee. 'Does Rommel know how lucky he was to escape before Jill landed?'

Dee grinned. She was used to the constant ragging of soldiers. Shifting her gaze to the feast laid out for guests, she said, 'Do mine eyes deceive me or are those *eggs* on the buffet table?'

'Eggs! Real ones?' Jill whirled around, scarcely believing it. Eggs were a precious commodity in North Africa — a medium of exchange far more effective in bargaining sessions with native merchants than American occupation scrip. 'I could eat a dozen, but we have to be on our party manners. Besides — ' and she giggled at the idea ' — my mother would find out.'

'I know what you mean,' Kaye said in mock seriousness. 'Even oceans cannot dim the all-seeing maternal eye.' Kaye's own eyes roved the glittering military crowd. 'Look who's here, Jill, your *friend*, Captain Desmond Stratton — and he's heading our way.'

'Where? Never mind, I don't care. Why does he have to show up and spoil things?' Jill asked, her slight overbite giving her mouth a pronounced pout.

She saw Dee glance a warning at her.

'I can't understand these two,' Kaye said to Dee. 'They're like two kids who punch and chase in the schoolyard, when all along the whole thing is about s-e-x.'

'Damn it, Kaye, he'll *hear* you.' Jill knew that the impasse with Stratton wasn't her fault. She'd tried several times during the last six weeks to tell him that she regretted not giving him the chance to explain back at Fort Des Moines, and that she wished now she'd answered his letters. But each time she tried, it hadn't worked; there was still too much anger and hurt between them. Besides, he was her superior officer at the comcentre and — at this thought she frowned to herself — he had obviously learned to keep a proper distance from junior officers. Still, everyone seemed to guess that they had known each other before, and she knew there was a noticeable tension in a group whenever they were together. Kaye certainly hadn't been fooled for a minute.

'Hello, Lieutenant Young,' Stratton said to Kaye, and then with obvious deference, 'and hello to you, Lieutenant Hammersmith.'

'Sir!' Military courtesy demanded that Jill acknowledge his presence.

'Captain Stratton,' Kaye said, glaring at Jill, 'I'd like to introduce Dee Gleeson, the correspondent who was with us when we took the German torpedo.'

'Hello, Captain — Stratton, was it?' Dee's observant eyes were travelling back and forth between Jill and Des.

Jill busied herself with the egg dishes on the laden buffet. A servant bowed each time she pointed to one, and she had to use sign language to keep him from heaping her plate to the point of overflow. Every minute, she was aware that Dee and Kaye and Des were chatting like old friends and that at one point Stratton threw back his head and laughed out loud. His laughter hurt her more than the unresolved problem between them. He had no right to laugh. After what he'd pulled at Fort Des Moines, perpetual hangdog guilt was more appropriate from him. She worked her way to the foot of the long table and examined a bust of Napoleon intently while she tried to eat. Damn Stratton! He'd even spoiled the first nondehydrated eggs she'd had since she left the States.

'Lieutenant?' The voice she welcomed and at the same time dreaded came from behind her, slightly hesitant — not really much like the one he used as chief of the army comcentre in Algiers.

She faced him. 'Yes, Captain Stratton.' She would never let him know how ill at ease he made her.

'You don't have to stand at attention,' he said. 'We're not on duty.'

And to Jill's surprise it was Stratton who seemed uneasy. He looked at her and cleared his throat. 'I see you are admiring the Little Corporal. I studied — ' He saw the instant flash of anger in the way her small shoulders reared back. Damn! He'd forgotten her sensitivity about her size. How could he have made such a pompous blunder?

Jill interrupted just as Des stopped in midsentence. She owed him obedience, but she didn't have to take his condescension. 'Captain, please spare me any wit about short people, Napoleonic or banty-rooster complexes, Lieutenant Half-Pint jokes or . . . ' She finally ran out of breath.

Stratton flushed. 'Now, *wait* a minute, Jill,' he said, using her given name for the first time since Fort Des Moines. 'It was an innocent comment. I was just trying to make polite conversation. Isn't this gathering supposed to promote goodwill among allies? When I saw you here, I hoped it would do as much for the two of us. But I'd probably get better manners from the Germans than from you.'

'Manners! Are *you* complaining about *my* manners?' She

tried to make her voice calm and cosmopolitan, but she felt a furious heat suffuse her face and give her away. 'Why you're nothing but a — a — a coward!'

Instantly, she was sorry. Caution had failed her, and now she had gone too far.

Des felt hurt and disappointed. He knew she was stubborn, but he hadn't suspected she didn't know how to forgive. 'That's ungracious. I wouldn't have thought it of you. Surely I can make no more explanation than I did in my letters.'

'I — I never read them.'

He took a step back, and, afraid he would leave, she put out her hand to stop him. 'Will you tell me now what you wrote?'

He hesitated. 'It's too late for most of it,' he began, only to stop himself before he went further than he intended. 'I explained why I couldn't tell the murder board that I was the one you were with that night at the Palm Bar. You see, Captain Dawson and I had girl trouble. That's not important now — what's important is that he was trying to get at me through you. Don't you see? Dawson thought you'd been with me, but he couldn't prove it. If I'd told him, he'd have thrown the book at the both of us — you know that.'

'But — '

'No, damn it, Jill, this time you're going to hear me out. You can believe it or not, but I didn't care what he did to me — he'd have seen I was transferred to some dead-end desk job. But *you* he'd have washed out of OC school, and I knew that would kill you. Even after the hearing, Dawson was out to get me. Fortunately for me, Algiers was his idea of a backwater.' He had told Jill the truth, at least as much of it as he could, and that was all he could do. He would never tell her how much he'd suffered those last few days before her graduation, or about the months when he had waited for her to answer his letters. Most of all, he'd never tell her that he had wanted her desperately, or for how long, and how many other women it had taken for him to get over the wanting.

Jill saw people staring, especially Dee with a strange, haunted expression on her face, but by now she was almost beyond caring. All the weeks of reporting to Des every afternoon before her shift, of signing for classified material and discussing priority coded traffic in a cool, professional voice; all the weeks of punctilious military courtesy observed, hiding her feelings — feelings she could hardly define herself: all that self-control suddenly collapsed.

She looked up at him, ready to move into his arms. At that moment he looked like the young officer in the mess hall her first day in the Army — the most beautiful man she'd ever seen. His teeth were white against his Mediterranean tan, his deep-grey eyes waited for her to speak.

'Oh, Des — you mean, you really didn't want to let me go through that hearing alone?'

He shook his head almost violently, his teeth clenched. 'It nearly killed me. You looked so frightened. A dozen times I started to speak, but I couldn't take a chance on getting you kicked out. I had to hope you'd understand later. I knew how much getting your bars meant to you. Well, Christ, it was awful! I never saw anybody so brave — the way you stood up to Dawson. I tried to tell you the next day. I *did* tell you in my letters.'

'But I've been here for two months. Oh, why didn't you talk to me about all this before?'

He smiled down at her, with something of the Des Stratton she remembered in his smile. 'Listen, Jill, you've been here all right, but how was I supposed to pierce that armour you wear when you're around me? No, don't tell me now. We'd just argue about it. How about a truce — for the duration, Lieutenant? Or at least while we're both in this outfit. Maybe it's too late to be friends, but at least we don't have to be enemies. Is it a deal?'

It's not too late, she wanted to shout, but her pride nodded yes, and he left. Perhaps it was just as well. How could she be his friend? She had no strategies for casual friendship with Des Stratton. He aroused in her extremes of feeling, more than Neil, more than anyone ever had. He made her happy or miserable; she either hated him or was crazy about him. For the hundredth time, she wished she'd read his letters. Mother had always said her stubborn streak would be her ruination. Why hadn't she listened?

Absentmindedly, she forked some egg from her plate, only to put it down again. Des had hinted that his letters contained more than explanations. What had he written that he couldn't tell her now? As she watched his dark head disappear through the palace entrance, she knew she had forfeited the right to know all that those letters contained. Des had made it quite clear it was too late.

Kaye hurried over as Des made his exit. 'What was *that* all about? The rest of the Palais d'Été couldn't tell whether you two were ready to make love or fisticuffs.'

'Don't be silly, Kaye, and don't see romantic intrigue in every man-woman encounter.' Jill was embarrassed to think that so many people were speculating about her and Des. 'Captain Stratton was taking care of some unfinished business, that's all.'

'Oh, *that's* what it's called these days.'

Ignoring Kaye's sarcasm, Jill looked at her watch. 'Oops, I'm on duty in an hour. Say goodbye to Dee for me. Gotta run.' Leaving Kaye obviously curious and unsatisfied, she did run through the marble foyer, through the double line of ceremonial spahis on white Arabians and out to the square.

Dee sat in front of the fountains in a jeep, the engine idling. 'Hop in, Jill — I'm going your way.'

'I'm not in the mood for a lecture, Dee.' The testy remark was out before Jill could bite her tongue.

'Don't worry, I'm not wearing my Dutch Aunt hat today.'

They drove along the teeming streets in silence. Jill longed for the emotional safety of the picturesque old school building that served as WAC barracks in Algiers.

Finally they drove through the arch into the compound. 'Here you are, Jill. Goodbye — and good luck. You're a great pal. I only hope you learn that someday.'

''Bye, Dee. Sorry I spoke out of turn back there.'

'Forget it. Besides, you already know what I'd advise you

to do, don't you?'

'Yes, I guess I do.'

Dee put the jeep into gear and drove out the compound gate, waving just before she passed from sight.

Jill stood there listening as the distinctive whine of jeep tyres faded into the afternoon. Dee believed in the miracle of romantic love, but Jill knew there would be no such miracle for her. In her life, love must be a duty she owed to Neil. She didn't deserve it for herself.

30

In a patriotic anti-black-market drive, fifteen million housewives sign a pledge that says: 'I pay no more than ceiling prices. I accept no rationed goods without giving up ration stamps.'

P age had no difficulty getting a three-day pass for the last October weekend. The workload at the Office of the Director, WAC, had begun to scale down since the conversion to full Army status. From being the source of all command decisions over women soldiers, Colonel Hobby now had only advisory duties. Files and personnel were being rapidly deployed throughout the Pentagon. Page knew it would be just a matter of days, at most weeks, before she would be reassigned. She didn't look forward to the possibility of sharing the fate of one of her fellow officers: the former WAC historian's invaluable collection of the beginnings of the women's army service had disappeared into Army Service Field files, and she had been relegated to a clerk's job. Damn it! Page knew she had so much more to give. She'd take any way out, other than trade on her father's position, rather than be stalled in a Washington back office for the duration.

For the first two days of her pass Page unwound from the tension of the past months, taking short naps and long walks in the glorious northern-Virginia fall afternoons.

Other than a letter to Bunny, she tried to forget the war, especially now that Paul might be in it somewhere, but the radio and the newspapers wouldn't let her. She'd read somewhere that one third of all broadcasting was war news, and the estimate sometimes seemed low. Everywhere, the dial was full of news about a second B-17 raid over Schweinfurt and the capture of road junctions south of Rome by the British Eighth Army.

Even at the neighbourhood movies, she had a choice between two war films, *This is the Army* and *Mrs Miniver*. She decided against Helmut Dantine's sneering Nazi-pilot portrayal in *Mrs Miniver* and settled for George Murphy's hoofing and Ronald Reagan's haircut — which reminded her so much of Paul's — and found herself enjoying the show although it resembled no army *she* knew.

On the third day, restless and tired of the inactivity, she took a taxi to the St Albans courts, her Wilson racket under her arm. The gut strings were slack and would probably break at the first net volley. She signed the singles match card, and picked up a locker key at the tennis director's office.

The pro on duty was well over fifty. 'Not many women playing today, miss, but I'll do my best to line you up.'

'I'll play the lieutenant,' Page heard a male voice behind her say, 'if she'll promise *not* to take it easy on an old man.'

She faced the voice. 'I'd be happy to play, sir.'

The man wearing a major general's two stars picked up his locker key. 'You don't remember me, do you?'

'Begging your pardon, sir . . .'

'The Philippines. I was Lieutenant Colonel Cecil Willis then — the summer of thirty-six, a dance at Fort Garfield O club. You were home from school and I was attached to MacArthur's staff on Luzon.'

'I've heard my father speak of you, sir, and I know Major Paul Burkhardt, who was on your staff last year. But I'm sorry, General, I don't remember our dance; it was so long ago and there were so many officers.'

'Never mind.' He smiled with a hint of an old sadness in his eyes. 'I remember *you*. I envied Dalt the prettiest daughter at the dance. Mrs Willis and I never had children.'

After changing into whites, they met at the court nearest the pool and began a warmup rally of baseline ground strokes. Page decided she liked him. A general who wanted a pretty daughter to dance with was an image that charmed her. But her own father had been proud of her looks, too; it was her ambition that bothered him. She wondered what General Willis would have thought of a pretty daughter who enlisted in the Army.

Within minutes, she liked the General even more, because he let her know he was trying very hard to beat her and played over his head, taking one of the three sets from her six-four. Maybe here was a man who was blind to her sex and just looked upon her as a worthy opponent. Finally her youth and form triumphed over his male strength and single-minded determination. In the last set she rushed his weak serves and sent one after another down the line to his even poorer backhand.

'Good competition! That's what I like,' he wheezed and plopped down onto the courtside bench beside her. Catching his breath, he asked, 'Where are you assigned, Lieutenant?'

'In the WAC Director's Office at the Pentagon, sir.' Under his questioning, she talked about the breakup of the WAC office, adding that she'd be reassigned before the beginning of 1944.

He wiped down his racket, enclosed it in its leather case and handed it to an aide. 'Have you thought of overseas duty?'

'Almost every Wac wants to go overseas, General.'

'Is that right? I confess I don't know much about the Women's Army Corps, although I will probably have enlisted women in my next command.' He stood to go, and she immediately got to her feet.

He seemed to be evaluating her, taking her measure as she'd seen her father do with new young officers.

'How would you like to go to London as one of my junior staff officers?'

It was her turn to catch her breath.

The General went on, 'It's an intelligence assignment, so you'll need a top-secret clearance. We can work out the details later, but I can tell you that the slot calls for a first lieutenant. Your father's there, isn't he? Well, this would be your chance to see him occasionally.'

'General Willis, you don't have to offer me any inducement beyond the opportunity to serve with you overseas.'

'That's fine — fine, Lieutenant. And if there are any unbombed tennis courts around, I'll see that you do. I hate golf — abominable, boring game — and that's all Ike and the others talk about.'

Page stiffened. 'Sir, I hope I will be judged by my work and not by the quality of my lob.'

The General scowled. 'Lieutenant Hannaday, that's a hair's breadth from insubordination, and I damn well don't need instruction in military ethics from you.' His face suddenly softened. 'But I did phrase the offer badly. I have a pretty good idea what kind of officer Dalt Hannaday's daughter is, so don't get me wrong. I mean to work your butt off twelve hours a day and *then* expect you to play three fast sets. This is no cushy posting I'm offering you. Do I make myself clear?'

'Yes, *sir*!'

Whew! She whistled under her breath as she watched the general head for the showers, with his aide hurrying behind. As barracks talk had it, she'd just been reamed, steamed and dry-cleaned! She wouldn't make *that* mistake again. But her head kept spinning for a different reason. In ten short minutes the rest of the war had been decided for her.

In a way, she hated the thought of leaving Colonel Hobby's office, but it was time for her to move on, to work for promotion and varied assignment experience. Suddenly, she was aware that she was thinking like a career officer. Perhaps Randy had been right; perhaps she had always fitted naturally into military life without realizing it.

Now she definitely needed a swim to cool off. Changing to the one-piece swimsuit she'd tucked in beside her tennis dress, she walked back to the pool and dived in at the deep end, the cold water snatching the air from her lungs. Back and forth she swam, glorying in the way her body smoothly cut the surface of the water. There hadn't been much time for exercise since she'd left Fort Des Moines, and she'd missed the sense of physical power that using her body always gave her.

Exhausted now after forty laps, but refreshed, Page flopped into a deck chair and curled up under her damp towel, allowing the unseasonably warm sun, which was at its zenith, to toast her upturned toes. Drowsy, she thought of Paul that last night before he'd left. She knew she had been shameless, practically coaxing him to her bed. Paul, since the first time he'd cooked for her, had struggled for control, always careful to respect her, but that night she hadn't wanted his respect, she'd wanted him next to her, in her bed. Darling Paul. He'd wanted her, too — she knew it — but he'd insisted on being so protective of her.

'This isn't fair to you, Page. I may not come out of this war alive.'

'You will, I know you will.' Their arms were around each other's waist as they walked to the bedroom, their hungry mouths reaching for each other, their bodies moving swiftly, hips touching as their legs swung in unison. 'But even if the worst should happen at least we'd have this night to remember.'

'Darling, isn't that supposed to be the man's line?' Paul had laughed, she remembered, but his laugh was bittersweet.

Lying there in the dark she'd said, 'I do adore you so, Paul.'

They'd made love to each other then. Vaguely, Page was aware that someone on the first floor was playing Bach — one of the Brandenburgs. And the organdie curtains undulating in a breeze at the window were as sensual to her as watching a log fire. Although she wanted to give her body totally to physical love, her mind was full of these unconnected emotional impressions, almost as if body and mind belonged to two different people.

That night she knew for certain that Paul was in love with

her. He was open, easy to read; his love was writ large for anyone to see. And she knew she loved him, too, but not in the same way, more like fog dipping to touch the ripples of a lake — vaguely. Yet she spent hours dreaming of him and refused to think of life with no Paul in it.

'Page, love me.'

'Oh, Paul, I do, but then . . .' He had covered her lips with his fingers to still the torrent of confused words.

She'd felt his sadness, palpable in the room. 'You don't really know me, do you, Page? I want you — God alone knows how I want you — but I feel like a blind man entering an unfamiliar room. Just when I think I have a firm grip on you, you elude me. You haven't decided what *you* want from life, and you especially haven't decided that you want to share it with me.'

'Paul, give me time.' She didn't want to hurt him. She couldn't bear to see him leave for overseas with things unsettled between them. But there were no choices. He had to go; she needed time.

'Page, I'm not a man who will settle for a crumb when I want the whole loaf.' He'd smiled sardonically in the dim light. 'You'll have to pardon the rotten metaphor, darling. I'm not quite up to verbal brilliance tonight.'

'Professor, you talk too much,' she said, silencing him with her mouth and her body.

Over a month had passed, but she still felt the frustration of that night. Why must Paul not be satisfied with anything less than her total surrender? What was it St Augustine had said? *Love means I want you to be.* Why couldn't Jimmy, and now Paul — or any man — love her like that? Why couldn't they be content to be in her life but not be all of it?

Rousing herself from the poolside chaise longue, Page lazily walked back to the women's locker room and stepped into a shower. She let the cooling water sluice down her body and wash away the painful pulses of desire that Paul's memory evoked, moving next into the outer dressing area, where she towelled herself dry until her skin turned a glowing pink. Voices carried to her from the adjoining lounge.

'My dear, where did you get those hose — they're silk, aren't they?'

'Yes, lovely, lovely silk. I got them' — the voice giggled — 'from *Mr Black*. He can get you anything from tyres to a prime standing rib roast to mayonnaise for only about twice the OPA ceiling price. He doesn't bother with points, either, if you get my drift.'

'Mother says a black-marketeer is as important today as a good bootlegger was in her day.'

Page wasn't shocked. Illicit sales were unpatriotic but common enough, especially when people were making money and had no place to spend it. She suspected that the two women pledged at bond drives, rolled bandages, directed their cooks to save grease and thought they were helping win the war.

'Did you see Page Hannaday playing tennis?'

That's my name, she thought. By now, Miss Silk Stockings' voice sounded vaguely familiar.

The other woman replied, 'Yes, I saw her with General Willis. I knew her only slightly before she joined the women's army.'

'Well, my dear, I knew her. She was at Radcliffe — one class ahead of me. Did you know her mother was one of the Charleston Bidwells? I simply can't imagine *her* associating with all those whores and dykes.'

Idly the second voice said, 'And she seems so feminine, too.'

Page was shaking with fury as she buttoned her uniform blouse and walked deliberately into the lounge.

'I thought I recognized your voice — Lauren Whitaker, isn't it?' She wanted to shout at the woman, but she was bound by a desire to defend, not disgrace, her uniform.

'Why, ah, er — yes,' Lauren Whitaker replied, turning to her companion for help. 'This is Page Hannaday — you remember.' She flushed, floundering.

Page never had more command over her voice, not even during OCs when she had faced the grading pencil of ancient Regular Army drill sergeants on the Dewy parade ground. 'Lauren,' she said, coldly furious, 'I couldn't help overhearing your personal assessment of women serving with our armed forces. Now which is it this week — are we all whores or all lesbians? Of course, you're including the thirty per cent of women who are married or widowed. And don't forget the ones who have sweethearts in Bataan death camps or dead in Sicily . . .'

Page heard her voice begin to quiver and prayed she would keep her composure long enough to say what she had wanted to yell to the world for months. 'On my desk in the Pentagon, there are a dozen photos of a burial being held in North Africa — not startling news in itself these days until you notice that the pallbearers are women soldiers, maybe some of those same whores and dykes you were talking about.'

Her tone was acid, and she ignored the shocked faces of the women she confronted. She knew she was close to breaking down; the frustration of months of combating the slander campaign, and Paul's long silence, had become a mountain of pain to which this nasty chitchat had added the last hurt. 'So, ladies, and that term is so far from describing you it — '

'Now, just a minute!' Lauren interrupted.

Wanting to smash the regained superiority from Lauren's face, Page rushed on, saying aloud the words that had been forbidden her typewriter. 'The next time you're slipping into your black-market silk stockings and passing crude innuendos about women in uniform, maybe you can manage one small thought for an American servicewoman buried under a white cross in the North African sand — a woman who won't ever feel silk against her skin again.' She stopped, almost out of control, close to breaking down. 'You bitches,' she said, and now tears started which she didn't bother to wipe away. 'You malicious bitches!'

Feeling emptied and clean, she heard Lauren sputter behind her, 'Well, I've never heard such . . . such . . .'

The other voice broke in. 'Oh, shut up, Lauren. Just shut up for once in your life!'

31

The Allied forces battle up the boot of Italy, sometimes literally inch by inch. After the Fifth Army captures Naples in October, the Germans fall back, fighting one delaying battle after another. British commander General Sir Henry Maitland Wilson describes it as a 'slow, painful advance through difficult terrain against a determined and resourceful enemy . . .'

In the November days that followed General Giraud's reception, Jill found herself in a limbo as far as Des Stratton was concerned. He was no longer an enemy to be watched and outflanked, but he was no friend to be sure and comfortable with either. Her answer to the dilemma was to be stiffly polite.

Des saw her behaviour as confirmation that she could accept him as her superior officer while on duty, but that her belief that he had played the coward was so ingrained she could neither forget nor forgive. Therefore he was careful to keep their conversations impersonal. They were both still walking on eggshells, he saw, but different eggshells. He didn't know what to do or what he wanted to do. Once, following their encounter at the Palais d'Été, he had a cup of hot coffee waiting for her when she came on duty. She had thanked him, and for a moment the vulnerable look of sweet innocence that had first attracted him appeared fleetingly to cross her face. But he hadn't made a habit of such attentions. It was just as well, since they both had limited time during shift change.

Each afternoon at four, Monday through to Saturday and on alternating Sundays, Jill reported to Des at the comcentre. He was businesslike, although occasionally thoughtful. She sometimes wished there was more time, but he always seemed so busy.

She picked up messages waiting to be encrypted, then

locked herself into the code room with her shift of three EW code clerks and didn't come out until midnight or more often even later. The work was endlessly fascinating. It was her responsibility to take secret words and make them undecipherable by the enemy. After assigning code systems to each message according to its destination and classification, she sometimes thought about this new but hardly more comfortable relationship with Des — she wouldn't call it a truce, since it was more an armed standoff.

As the rotors in the code machines clicked to one of a possible million different combinations for each letter and number in the alphabet, and the sticky-backed tape spiralled out its scrambled five-letter code groups, she caught herself wondering if she would feel today as she had the time he'd taken her in his arms. The memory brought with it both physical weakness and a surge of feeling that — always at this point, she stopped herself angrily. Kaye was putting these silly thoughts into her head with her teasing that Des was sweet on her. Desmond Stratton was her superior officer, and that was the only way she thought of him or wanted to think of him. There might possibly have been something more between them once, but that was all over. He'd said so, hadn't he? They might no longer be enemies but they were far from — anything closer.

Besides, she had promised herself to Neil. They were high-school sweethearts, engaged to be married — despite what Kaye said about a silent fiancé being no fiancé at all. There were lots of perfectly logical reasons why Neil didn't answer her letters. Her father had written about several reconstructive skin-graft operations for his face and hands.

It should be obvious, even to a sceptic like Kaye, that Neil was simply not up to the strain of writing. He did send for Bear whenever he was home on convalescent leave — and Bear was his link to her. After the war everything would be as it had been between them. After the war, she'd forget all about Desmond Stratton. When she was an old lady, rocking the afternoons away on her adobe patio, she'd probably even laugh about him.

These reveries usually lasted no more than a few minutes

before she was interrupted by a rap on the code room door. It was often Des carrying an urgent decrypt just ripped from the Teletype. Once she thought how symbolic it was that there always seemed to be a locked door between them.

On the morning of November 13, 1943, unable to sleep while the Algerian cleaning women banged buckets and mops outside in the hall, Jill sorted through some recent snapshots to enclose in her next letters to Bunny and Elisabeth. Flipping on the radio, she half listened to the news on Armed Forces Radio. Fifth Army troops were engaged in savage fighting between Naples and Rome. Restlessly, she punched her pillow. Italy, not North Africa, was where the real war was. *Damn it!* Was she always to be a bystander?

Someone knocked. 'Are you awake, Lieutenant Hammersmith?' called the company clerk.

'Yes, what is it?'

'Captain wants to see you in the OR as soon as you can make it.'

'Tell Captain Trueblood I'll be there in fifteen minutes.'

'Yes, ma'am.'

Jill needed the time to get into a fresh uniform and try to communicate in high-school French to the women outside her door that they should clean her room while she was gone. '*Maintenant!*' she repeated several times and pointed to her room while making sweeping motions with her arms.

Gingerly she stepped along the wet hall floors in the officers' wing towards the OR. What could Captain Trueblood want at this time of day? Was it Marie again? Damn! Now that the private was back in her platoon, it was always something. Last week it had been late sign-in from an overnight pass, the week before insubordination to a noncom. Marie Brodzinsky delighted in getting into trouble so that Jill would have to reprimand or restrict her to barracks. It was diabolical, that's what it was. The more Jill was forced to punish Marie, the guiltier Jill felt, and that seemed to be exactly what Marie intended.

Descending to the floor that housed the company

administration offices, Jill sighed hopefully. Maybe it wasn't Marie this time. Maybe it was complaints from her nightshift workers about sleeping conditions. There was little she could do about that perennial problem either. It was impossible to monitor every Wac coming off day duty. Sometimes just the volume of well-intentioned *Ssshuush!* in the hallway woke up her code clerks.

She reported smartly, priding herself on punctiliously observing customs of the service. Overseas duty had not made her lax as it had some soldiers.

'Sit down, Jill.'

'Thank you, Captain.'

'How are things at the comcentre?'

It was unlike the captain to encroach on sleeping time for a chitchat. 'Just fine, ma'am.'

'Glad to hear it.' The captain stood up and went to her window and looked out on the courtyard. 'I've got news for you.'

Involuntarily, Jill caught her breath. 'It's not my family? Nobody's . . . ' She couldn't bring herself to say the word 'dead'. She'd heard from others how the CO called you in and tried to break bad news gently.

The captain shook her head and moved to sit on the edge of her desk. 'Nothing like that. No, this is good news for you, at least I think you'll take it as that. I know I'd give anything to be in your shoes.'

'Yes, ma'am?'

Captain Trueblood looked as though she was savouring every word. 'How would you like to be in the first contingent of Wacs to set foot on European soil? Strictly voluntary, now.'

Jill was only partially successful in retaining her military manner. 'Of course. Yes! What do I do? When do I go? Where?'

'I told Captain Stratton you'd feel that way.'

'Captain Stratton. What has he got to do with this?'

'He's commanding a new signal contingent on orders for Italy, and he put in a written request for you. Paid you a high compliment, too. Said you were his best code officer, and the only woman he knew who had the nerve to pull off this assignment.'

'*He* said that?'

'He did. Now let me tell you what you're in for. By the way, Kaye Young will be the other junior officer, with a first lieutenant from Casablanca as CO. Sixty code clerks, telephone ops and postal people will make up the detachment, all of you heading for Fifth Army headquarters in Italy. Conditions will be rough. You may eventually be living in tents right behind the combat troops — subject to bombing and shelling. It'll be dangerous. Are you still game?'

Jill could hardly believe she wasn't dreaming all this — at last she was going to get a chance to be a real soldier. 'I wouldn't miss it for the world, Captain. That's what I joined up for. When do we go?'

'In a few days — by plane to Naples, then ground transport northeast to Caserta. I don't need to tell you there's an information blackout.' The captain stood up and extended her hand. 'Remember Wacs are guinea pigs in this. The Army wants to see if we can measure up when things get tough. If we can't, the Women's Army Corps will not get a second chance.'

'We can, Captain.' Suddenly Jill remembered Page's dragon, and her expression sobered.

'What's the matter — haven't had a change of heart, have you?'

'No, ma'am, nothing like that. I had a friend back at OC in Fort Des Moines who said the WAC would have to slay dragons before we'd be accepted as women soldiers. Maybe our dragons are in Italy.'

'At least the first one is, Lieutenant.'

Jill stood up at attention. 'I'll make the Corps proud, Captain.'

'I'm sure you will. That's why I agreed to *your* going, Jill. You demand a great deal from yourself and set a high standard for the EW. They may not always like it, but they admire you for it. Don't take it amiss when they call you Lieutenant Half-Pint.'

'I did at first, Captain. I've — well, I'm tired of jokes about my size.'

'They're not laughing at you, Jill. It's their way of showing affection, of letting you know they lay claim to you.'

'Thank you for that, ma'am — and your confidence in me. I'd die before I'd let you down.'

32

During the second Schweinfurt raid in October, sixty Eighth Air Force bombers with over six hundred American airmen in them are shot down, wrecking morale and flyers' confidence in the ability of the B-17 to defend itself without fighter cover. Bomber Command in England temporarily abandons deep-penetration daylight raids over Germany.

On Saturday morning, November 13, Page received her promotion to first lieutenant and her reassignment orders to the Chief of Staff, Supreme Allied Commander, in London. General Cecil Creighton Willis, Jr, COSSAC G-2, now with a third star, had also TWXed priority travel orders for her. By early afternoon Transportation had put her on alert for an early-morning flight.

'And, Lieutenant,' the scheduling officer warned her, 'if you haven't got longjohns, better get yourself a pair.'

That probably meant the Greenland route. As excited as she was about going overseas, she wasn't exactly thrilled at the thought of flying the North Atlantic in wintertime.

Page cleared her desk and said goodbye to her co-workers and Colonel Hobby. As she left the Pentagon in the late afternoon, she blushed to remember how she had stammered with the Director, sounding like a gushy schoolgirl with a favourite teacher. How could Page say to the colonel that her words heard so long ago in those first days at Fort Des Moines, '*You have a date with destiny*,' had come to hold a special meaning for her life, even beyond their original intent? She didn't understand this feeling herself, so how could she communicate it?

Through the rear taxi window, she looked back at the huge complex and knew that one door was closing. For eighteen months she had been a part of the idea of a women's army. Now she would become a part of the reality, one woman soldier among many soldiers, both male and female, on the front lines of war. All her life she had been marking time, waiting for an opportunity to find out who Page Hannaday really was and what she could really do.

'WAC Detachment.'

'Will you please call Lieutenant Gardner to the phone. Tell her First Lieutenant Hannaday is calling.'

Page lit a cigarette and surveyed the living room full of half-packed boxes she was readying for storage. From where she sat she could see the open doors of the cupboard in the kitchen with its shelf of cooking spices that evoked a sharp memory of Paul.

'Page! Is that you — and with silver bars?'

'Hi, Elisabeth. It's me, silver and all.'

'Congratulations. Nobody deserves it more, but I thought you said you'd never make first at the Pentagon, that all the rank was going overseas.' Elisabeth paused for a moment. 'Is that why you're calling?'

'You know I can't answer that. I just want to let you know that I'll be . . . out of touch for a while, but I'll write as soon as I can. Is everything all right with you?'

'Why wouldn't it be?'

'No reason — it's just that when we saw Jill off in New York City you looked so tired. No, more than that, and I really don't mean to meddle, Elisabeth — you looked almost haunted.'

Elisabeth laughed, but Page heard a brittle quality, or rather a dry fragility that she would have suspected of anyone but Elisabeth.

'Page, you're becoming as melodramatic as Bunny' —
with finality Elisabeth changed the subject — 'have you
heard from her?'

'I tried to call her earlier, but the CQ said she was signed
out for the weekend. I'll — well, I'll just have to write to
her.'

Almost to herself Elisabeth said, 'Two of us gone and
two of us left. This goddamned war is nothing but one long
goodbye.'

'We can take it.'

'You really believe all that gung-ho propaganda, don't
you? I wish I had your faith.'

'You do, Elisabeth.'

'Oh no — only what passes for faith. But you see, I never
believe in anything, so I'm never disappointed.'

They said goodbye and promised to write and take care
of themselves. As she replaced the phone in its cradle Page
wondered if either of them any longer had control over her
own life. Despite her denials, Page sensed in Elisabeth's
voice a frightening desperation.

Very early the next morning, Page was struggling with
the clasp on her flight bag when her doorbell rang.

'It's unlocked,' she yelled.

'If I'm too early,' a voice said, 'I can wait out here.'

'Heavens, no. Come on in.' A WAVE ensign appeared
at her bedroom door. 'Want to help me get this lock
closed?'

The ensign took her hat off and threw it on the bed.
Together they got both bags locked and pulled to the
landing.

Page said, 'I've left my forwarding address on the kitchen
table. Well, I guess that's it. I'd better be off — DC taxi
drivers, you know.'

'What about all the stuff in the kitchen? There must be a
hundred dollars' worth of spices in there.'

'You keep them. They'll bring you luck.'

'What? I don't understand.'

'Never mind. See you around sometime.'

The Wave, watching her as the driver helped with her bags, gave her a thumbs-up sign as Page turned to wave. 'Keep your powder dry, Lieutenant,' she called after her.

One hour later the door to the storage room at the Bolling Field flight-ops hut flew open suddenly and caught Page literally with her pants down. 'Hey, wait a minute, I'm changing in here.'

'It's okay,' a woman's voice answered.

'Sorry, thought you were one of the ground crew,' Page answered, her words muffled as she tugged on the zipper of her fleece-lined leather flight pants.

'Lieutenant,' the voice said closer now, and Page saw two shoes planted squarely in front of her, 'my name's Joan Wright. Looks like we'll be flying to Prestwick together.'

Page flopped down on a bench. The tall brunette in front of her wore rumpled slacks and a belted blue blouse with pilot's wings over her left breast pocket. 'Hello — Joan, is it?' Page was winded from her struggles. 'Isn't that a WASP uniform?'

'Right — Women's Airforce Service Pilots. I've been detached for a month to inspect British women pilots in the Air Transport Auxiliary. From the look of your gear, you're going for more than a month.'

'Page Hannaday,' Page introduced herself, and shook the other woman's hand. 'I'm going to be stationed in London.'

'Not if you freeze before you get there. First thing on the flight plan is to get you suited up right. Take off your uniform down to your longjohns. Here, let me help you with those ankle zippers. Now put your boots on and zip them up.'

Page stood up and took two steps in the awkward boots. 'I feel like Frankenstein,' she said, awkwardly lifting her arms in front of her.

Joan laughed. 'You'll love them at twenty-five thousand feet. Now let me cross your pant suspenders twice or they'll keep falling off your shoulders and drive you crazy. Okay, now the jacket.' Joan stepped back and surveyed Page.

'You'll pass muster.'

'Thanks to you.'

A few minutes later the two women clomped out into the ops hut. The harassed dispatcher motioned them towards an AAF captain with a clipboard.

'Lieutenant Hannaday? Joan Wright?' the captain asked, checking their names off. 'I'm Captain Willo — Doug Willo. Your gear will be put aboard. Follow me.'

Page walked behind him towards several planes parked on the Bolling Field tarmac. He stopped under the Plexiglas nose of a mammoth B-17G with the name *Flaming Mame* painted along its side along with an artistic rendition of a stripper caught in her act. It was the biggest plane Page had seen since she'd taken the Clipper to Manila years before. So *this* was what Randy wanted to fly.

'Sorry there wasn't room for you gals in one of the regular C-47 flights,' Willo said. 'We've got so much brass hopping over that anybody under colonel gets bumped. You won't find us long on comfort, but we'll do our best.'

Page climbed in through the fuselage hatch and walked forward past the waist gunners and onto the narrow catwalk over the bomb bay, then into the cabin. The captain pointed her towards a pull-down seat against the bulkhead behind the flight engineer.

'Whatcha flying, Joan?'

'Been ferrying PT-19s out of Hagerstown.'

'Ever check out one of these babies? It's quite a thrill.'

'You're telling *me*!'

'After we get up, I'll get the Chief' — Willo nodded towards the flight engineer's jump seat right behind him — 'to let you have his seat for a bit.'

'I'd love that.'

'You had breakfast yet?' It was the young navigator calling up to Page from his plotting table below and forward in the nose.

'No. I didn't have time.'

'When we're airborne and I've got a fix on our heading, I'll send you gals up some breakfast.'

Leaning forward, Page adjusted her seat harness so that

she could watch the co-pilot going over the checklist with Captain Willo.

'Free the controls,' he said. 'Rudder. Ailerons.'

'Roger,' Willo answered.

'Check magnetos on. Ignition left. Right. Both.'

'Number one hydraulic pump switch on,' Willo said.

'Start number one.'

Over on the far left, Page saw the giant blades of the outboard Wright Cyclone engine shudder, cough and start to rotate.

'Pull auxiliary ground power plug,' Willo told the Chief.

With brakes released, the Fortress began to move as Willo used the one engine to swivel the plane onto the runway. There the checkout procedure continued until all four of the engines were roaring, pounding, thundering through the vibrating metal skin under Page's feet. She had never felt the effect of so much raw power surge through her body before. No *wonder* Joan wanted to fly, she thought, to control such a behemoth and ride it through the sky like a modern Valkyrie.

Willo recited, 'Fuel booster pumps on; fuel/air mixture in automatic rich; propellers in full rpm; engine cowl flaps open; wing flaps up . . . '

Page's rubber earphones crackled and she put them on. 'Tower to Baker one three niner. You're cleared for takeoff.'

Willo stood on the brakes, his left hand on the control yoke, right hand advancing all four throttles.

The chief sang out, 'Okay, you have full power.'

Page braced in her seat against the bulkhead wall as the plane surged down the runway, gathering speed until Captain Willo pulled back on the control wheel, and with one last bump they were airborne.

Gradually the tension knot in her stomach disappeared and she was aware of a rarer emotion felt only once before, the day she first arrived at Fort Des Moines — the sense of adventure, of jumping with both feet into the unknown.

'First stop, Gander, Newfoundland,' the navigator announced when they had levelled off at ten thousand feet and reached their 170-miles-per-hour cruising speed. He poured cups of coffee from a thermos and handed out brown bags. 'Breakfast from the Greasy Spoon.'

Joan complained as she opened her bag. 'Oh no! Fried-egg sandwiches. Page, I hope you have a strong stomach. I could swear these eggs have been fried in olive oil *before* the mayonnaise was slathered on the bread.'

'Don't worry, Joan. A stomach that has held SOS can handle anything.'

'You mean Wacs eat ol' shit-on-a-shingle, too?'

'Do we eat it? Army cooks invented it.'

After a few bites Page leaned back in her seat and closed her eyes, listening through her headset to the hum of the navigational beacon they were following. Once it stopped and her eyes flew open. 'Anything wrong?'

'Don't worry,' the radio op told her. 'We're in the cone of silence — directly over the beacon. We're right on the beam, Lieutenant.'

The engine's drone almost drowned out the beacon's sound in her earphones, the two together making a mesmerizing, mind-numbing hum. She couldn't read as she'd planned when she'd zipped an armedforces paperback edition of *The Human Comedy* into one of the flight suit's deep pockets. She couldn't concentrate on plot and character in this din. Instead she drew out Bunny's last letter from between the book's covers.

November 5, 1943
Lowry Field, Colorado

GREETINGS PAGE,

Did I say I wanted to find out what it was like to be an enlisted woman? Ol' Bunny found out all right. I've pulled KP every week since I got back here. KP — take it from one who knows — is an army experience to miss & I mean MISS. Up at 4.30, stumble into my fatigue dress and Li'l Abner boots, trudge to the messhall in the snow and dark. I don't mean to sound like an orphan in the storm, but you get the picture — & that's only the good part. Next, a mess sergeant who looks like she eats

Privates and Corporals for breakfast points at ME and says in impeccable English: 'You girl there — you do grease trap.' Sounds simple enough, but I'd 'rather be in hell with my back broke' as one of my southern bunkmates puts it.

The grease trap in your typical messhall is located in the most inaccessible place in the kitchen — in a concrete bunker under the main sink drain. The only way to get to it is from a kneeling position. It's quite a ritual & goes something like this: down on your knees, drag off the heavy metal lid, dip off the coagulated grease (GOD! HOW IT STINKS!) and place in bucket, carry bucket to GI grease can.

By the time I finish this bit of torture (which the Sarge loves to watch an ex-officer do), I can't eat the chow they pile on my tray & I spend the rest of the day dreaming up incredibly perfect murders which I want — oh so very much — to practise on the mess sergeant.

Other than KP I'm flying high — and as soon as I make sergeant I'll have too much rank for that duty.

You asked why they'd ship me back here as an EW when I'd been here before as brass. PULL, my dear Page — not mine, but my Colonel's, who tells me daily that he'd defy Tooey Spaatz himself for me. Old Harry's not a bad sort plus he's got a great thing going for him in my book — I COULDN'T FALL IN LOVE WITH HIM IF I TRIED. Not that he's not good-looking; and he's a damned fine air recon officer, but I've taken the pledge — for life. You can't imagine how safe that makes me feel — or maybe you can.

Speaking of safe, Harry is keeping me off overseas levies now that I'm working with photo mosaics — the last three noncoms in my job were scooped up within a month of each other. I want to do what I can — you know that, Page, or why would I have re-enlisted? — but I can do it just as well in the good ol' ZI. I'll let Jill carry the flag and you can be the heroine. I'm too old to fight that dragon you're always talking about, even metaphorically.

275

I'm hoping to get a Christmas leave. My mama isn't well, now Angela's gone to California. Poor Mama. Two daughters married to a man she disapproves of — it's been too much for her. I don't hate Angela, you know that, Page. I don't feel anything. I just hope she has the sense to swallow her pride and come home when Johnny dumps her, and he will.

Enough and enough, dear friend. Can you believe it's been almost a year since we left each other at the Fort Des Moines train station? If the four of us have made it this far, 1944 will be a breeze.

Love ya, BUNNY

Page smiled, a wave of affection overtaking her as she refolded the letter and slipped it back inside the book. Here she was in a bomber over the winter Atlantic instead of packing for a skiing trip to Vermont; Jill was in Algiers instead of on a small northern-California ranch; Elisabeth was working in a warehouse in Philadelphia instead of looking out from the glossy pages of *Vogue*; but when all the world was topsy-turvy, Bunny never changed. We need such friends, she thought, for the energy they expend happily pursuing their dreams. And because they keep us from taking ourselves too seriously. No matter what her pain — and Page knew that Bunny had been betrayed as few women had — she kept on meeting life, connecting with it day after day. *God!* She was honest, and so sane, so absolutely steady, and she didn't even know it.

Page's earphones crackled with static interrupted by a voice: 'Gander to Baker one three niner, do you read?'

'Roger, Gander,' the radio op replied.

'Give me your position report.'

Soon they were within sight of the runways, which slashed black lines through the dazzling white of endless snow as far as Page could see.

Joan shouted at her above the noise of the landing gear coming down, 'Storm's coming. The field could be socked in.'

After they were on the ground the approaching storm

was confirmed by the weather officer at flight operations. 'We're going to catch the tail of it. May not get much snow, then again we may get enough to shut us down for two or three days. Hard to say. The billeting officer will take care of you.'

Captain Willo got Page and Joan assigned a room at the visiting officers' quarters and invited them to relax at the O club later. 'Hope you gals play pool.'

Joan grinned. 'I do. My dad taught me.'

Page smiled, but shook her head. 'My game's tennis, Captain. I think I'll just read, but thanks.' She was unexpectedly tired. It's harder to be a passenger, with nothing to do, than a driver who's fully occupied.

'Suit yourself,' Willo replied. 'Come on, Joan, we'll do some hangar flying.'

'Sure. Love it.'

After a quick meal, Page struggled out of her bulky flying suit just as Joan returned to change for the officers' club. 'With that weight off, Joan, I feel light enough to fly by myself.'

'You get used to them.'

'How long have you been flying?'

'Since I was thirteen. My dad was a barnstormer. He buckled me into a special harness when I was a kid. By the time my feet reached the rudders, he couldn't keep my hands off the controls. Natural, I guess. Ever heard of us? Wright and Daughter, Aerobatists — state fairs our specialty.'

'No, I'm afraid not. When did you join the WASP?'

'Last spring.'

'Like it?'

'Yes. Not because I want to blaze trails or anything, I just want to fly the kind of planes I've never had a chance to fly — P-51s and B-17s. Does that sound unpatriotic?'

'No, I think I understand. The country's full of women who want to grab the opportunities of this war. Why not? Men have been doing it for centuries. What's the WASP military status now?'

'We haven't any,' Joan said, frowning. 'Jacqueline

277

Cochran says General Hap Arnold is all for taking us into the Army Air Forces, but he's run into a snag in Congress.'

'I was at WAC HQ in the Pentagon, and I know that Colonel Hobby agreed to WAC commissions for Wasps.'

Joan shook her head. 'No soap. Jackie wants to run the show for her girls, ya know. Well, one way or another, I guess we'll get in. The real problem is at the lower echelon — ' and here Joan twirled an imaginary moustache like the villain in a melodrama ' — "How come a little slip of a girl like you wants to fly that big ol' plane?"' She grinned good-naturedly, and left for her date with Willo.

Outside, heavy snow was falling and a strong swirling wind piled it into instant drifts against the base buildings.

'Looks like we're going to be here for a while,' Joan said hours later when she came in.

Page slammed her book shut. 'Oh, damn! It's so frustrating to be on my way but not, at the same time.'

'I don't blame Willo and the rest if they're not in an all-fired hurry. Pilots over Germany have a three-week life expectancy these days.'

Joan draped her damp clothes over the bedstead. 'Anyway, pilots get used to weather like this. I was delivering planes from the Republic factory last winter and got snowed in at Pittsburgh for three days with nothing on but my flying suit. Just once you should try to explain a woman wearing what looks like rompers with no luggage to a hotel clerk!'

Page laughed. If she had to be snowed in, she couldn't ask for better company.

She had been asleep for some time when she was awakened by a loud knock at the door.

'Lieutenant? Joan?' It was Willo's voice.

'What is it, Captain?' Page called.

'There's a brief break in the weather — a window we can fly through before the main storm hits. We gotta make room for the next flight comin' behind us. Suit up and meet me in the ops building in fifteen minutes.'

Page struggled out from under the warm covers into the icy-cold room, quickly repacking the few articles she'd used the night before.

Joan shivered into her longjohns. 'Brrr. I hate to sound like your mother, but you should visit the ladies' room before we take off and keep your liquid intake down during the flight. It takes twelve hours' flying time, and the only "convenience" on the plane is a bottle with a funnel *definitely* not designed for female anatomy.' Joan giggled. 'A friend of mine nearly froze to death over Oklahoma when she had to drop her entire flight suit to use it.'

By the time Page and Joan hurried to the runway, the bomber was warming up, the snow had stopped and the lights of snowploughs traced narrow yellow paths up and down the runway. The crew chief buckled them in and showed them how to plug in their oxygen masks to the plane's main system. They would be flying most of the way at 25,000 feet, he told them, above the weather and square in the path of the best tail winds.

Captain Willo looked around at Page, his oxygen mask dangling. 'Next stop Prestwick, Scotland, Lieutenant.' He gave her the familiar thumbs-up sign.

Did she look frightened? Probably so, but it certainly wasn't over flying. She was ashamed to admit that the thought of the oxygen mask smothering her face for all the hours ahead brought back the old panic she'd felt in basic. But she'd conquered that fear and taken her place as part of the team; she would conquer it again.

When they'd been airborne an hour, the navigator handed a map up to Page. A long shallow upcurved line skirting south of Greenland and Iceland and ending to the north and west of Glasgow showed their course. It looked to Page as if they were flying across half the globe.

Hours later, she traded seats with the bombardier forward in the nose. They had long before outrun the dark and flown into the rising sun. Cocooned in her flight suit and helmet, surrounded by Plexiglas, Page felt none of the vibration she had in the beginning. The steady drone of the engines were an integral part of her now, like her breathing. She was in an immense quiet bowl, alone in its exact centre, clouds below and ahead of her, and above her the top of the world was painted an incredible deep lavender.

Shortly after noon she took a few quick gulps of hot coffee, happy to replace the oxygen mask after quickly becoming lightheaded in the thin atmosphere. During these hours she thought of the twists and turns her life had taken during the past year. She thought of Paul and couldn't escape the happy feeling that he was coming nearer. Was he in London or on some chancy OSS mission?

It occurred to her for the first time how much of her own life in the past months had been the result of taking chances. Quiet Page, studious Page, obedient Page — all those things she had always been had been replaced by a person who took chances. She'd taken a chance by joining the women's army, by letting a strange major into her apartment in the middle of the night, and finally by joining General Willis' staff overseas. Each one had led her to this moment when she found herself perched in the nose of a Flying Fortress headed towards the maelstrom of war in the ETO. She would most certainly see her father again; but could they learn to be father and daughter in a different way? Could her father ever see her as a person separate from his wishes? And Paul — yes, she would meet Paul too. She could sense it. The two most important men in her life, both different, but both wanting her to be their own version of the perfect woman — they too would be part of this new adventure.

The intercom crackled. 'Say, skipper, there's something wrong with the oxygen back here.'

Willo answered, 'I'll have the Chief check it out. It *is* pretty thin.'

Page looked back and saw the Chief come forward.

Soon Willo's voice rang through the earphones again. 'Goddamnit to hell, Chief. Ground crew at Bolling told us they fixed the *Mame*.'

Page heard Willo ask the crew chief to check the number of oxygen bottles stored in the cabin racks and in the tail section — racks that also held emergency flares and parachutes.

In a minute or two Willo was back on the intercom: 'Pilot to crew. We've got walkaround bottles for an hour — then I'll have to take her down to twelve thousand.'

The bombardier eased in behind Page and pointed up towards the main cabin. She crept past the navigator and regained her old seat. What happened when they descended to twelve thousand feet?

A familiar feeling of panic squeezed Page's chest. She knew it was more than thin air that caused her to hyperventilate; it was the old phobia — the mask was smothering her, claiming her. Minutes passed while she fought down the dizziness and sense of falling that threatened to overwhelm her. She admitted freely to herself the phobia she couldn't seem to be rid of, but gratefully she recognized the greater fear that saved her from cowardice — the fear of proving women were unfit comrades.

'I won't kid you,' Joan told her, 'there's a danger of icing. I heard Willo tell the co-pilot that two planes in the flight ahead of us didn't make it.'

'What happens if there's icing?' Page tried to sound matter-of-fact.

'You either get rid of it or you go in.'

The next hour sped by. Page's mouth grew tender from sucking in pure oxygen. She kept her breathing shallow and minimized movement, but finally her bottle was empty, its comforting hiss stilled.

'Dropping down,' Willo said, pushing forward on the controls. Clouds rushed past the windshield, enveloping them in bluish-white billows.

'Levelling off at twelve thousand,' Willo said on the intercom.

'Outside temperature reads two degrees Fahrenheit, Skipper,' the co-pilot said.

Page tapped Joan's shoulder. 'Where does it ice?'

'Watch the leading edge of the wings.'

At first Page thought it was just eyestrain and worry making ice appear where none truly was, but the longer she watched the more obvious it became that glassy white bulges had formed forward on the wings.

She heard the co-pilot report, 'We're starting to pick up drag.'

'Inflate her damned icebreakers, then!' Willo ordered.

Moments later chunks of ice cracked off the wings and flew past the windows. Relieved, Page leaned back and only then realized she had been straining against the harness, gulping to fill her lungs with precious air. But she had only a few minutes of relief. Almost at once the ice began to rebuild in bigger, even more bulbous chunks.

'It's too heavy, the breakers aren't working this time,' the co-pilot said.

Willo answered, 'I'm losing lift. Gotta try to get under this weather.'

The big plane nosed down through the cloud cover. Page realized that her life was in danger, but her mind could not imagine the world without her in it. That must be what courage really is, she thought, a failure of the imagination.

At one point in the descent they broke through the clouds into dazzling sunlight, which glittered prettily on the ice-packed wings like some macabre joke. Page almost welcomed the fog that erased that picture, although she knew they must have lost more altitude than Willo had intended.

Suddenly in her headset Page heard a low, insistent, comforting hum that made her heart pound with fresh hope.

'Navigator to pilot,' the intercom crackled. 'We've picked up the Prestwick directional beam, Skipper. Give me two minutes and I'll have a revised ETA.'

Page waited with the rest of the crew, watching the rigid arm movements of the captain which told her far more than the calm, professional voice of the navigator.

'Okay, here it is,' the navigator said. 'We've lost our tail winds and we're approximately three hundred miles, or one hundred eight minutes, out. With that ice we'll lose fifty feet every minute, which means we hit the drink nine minutes before ETA. If we lighten load by four thousand pounds, we *might* have the additional lift we need.'

Page saw Willow's shoulders relax almost as if knowing

the worst was a bigger physical relief than blind hope had been. 'Captain to crew. You heard it, guys. If the ice breaks up as we drop down, then we won't have to clean house. If it doesn't, then we'll jettison everything we can just this side of the coast. I don't want to drop a fifty-calibre on a thatched cottage.'

The crew checked in one by one, from the bombardier in the nose to the tail gunner lying on his stomach seventy-five feet to the rear.

Joan reached out to Page and gripped her sleeve. 'It'll be okay,' she said. 'Willo's first rate, and that navigator is a genius coming right in on that radio beacon from dead reckoning.'

Although Page heard reassurance, she also heard the concern in Joan's voice, the experienced pilot in her overcoming the desire to nurture. The minutes seemed to spin away out of her control. Page could see that the ice wasn't increasing, but it wasn't breaking up either, although the co-pilot had tried several times to inflate the rubber-coated icebreakers.

Below, between patches of thick fog, the flat grey ocean gradually broke into ripples that became waves as they dropped lower. Page wondered how long a fifty-thousand pound plane would float or if it could float at all. How could she swim in this bulky flying suit? And if she took it off, how many minutes would it take her to freeze? The crew chief reached over and patted her shoulder. Did her fear show?

'Okay, Chief,' Willo finally called from the cockpit when it looked as though they were within a few hundred feet of the water off the Inner Hebrides, 'let's jettison the waist guns and everything that's not bolted down — ammo boxes, the lot. Jesus,' Page heard Willo mutter then, 'I'll have to sign my ass away on a statement of charges for this gear.'

She pushed against hysteria rising from deep in her abdomen. Oh, God, money — what a crazy, dumb thing to worry about at a time like this.

Then she felt a perceptible lurch. A little bound as if the plane itself wanted to live.

Joan, who was closest to the instrument panel and knew how to read the altimeter, reported regularly. 'The rate of descent is slowing, Page. See the nose — tipping up slightly. I think the ice is melting — not much, but there's more lift. Feel it?'

Yes, she *could* feel it. The fog was thick now, and she couldn't see the entire wing span or the remaining ice, but she knew she felt the plane, which must be skimming the caps of the waves below, push more eagerly towards the Scottish coast. Ahead in the whiteness lay Prestwick.

The radio operator flicked the button on his microphone: 'Prestwick tower, this is Baker one three niner, over.'

Moments passed. 'Roger, Baker one three niner, this is Prestwick tower. We're fogged in here. Visibility zero. What's your position? Over.'

'Prestwick tower, I am about two zero northwest at two hundred contact. ETA in three minutes.'

'Are you in distress?'

'Yes. Heavy icing.'

'Baker one three niner, hold your heading for three minutes. We've got two guys with Very pistols stationed at the north end of runway. Crash truck standing by.'

One minute. Two minutes. Page strained forward, her eyes searching the white blankness ahead for a light. Three minutes.

Willo said, 'Gear down.' The plane lurched. His left hand grasped the yoke of the controls; his right hand gripped the throttle. 'Where are those goddamned flares?' Willo yelled into the microphone.

'Prestwick tower to Baker one three niner. We hear you but we can't see you.'

Another agonizing minute passed while Page braced herself for a crash. She knew that the slightest miscalculation would send them smashing into the ground. They had to be hugging the runway by now, and with a sickening insight she knew that she too might embrace it totally at a blinding instant. Involuntarily her lids closed against the possibility, and almost instantly a sudden flash of light wrenched them open. There to either side of the plane's nose a beautiful red-orange shaft leaped through the fog and formed a brilliant arch over them.

'Full flaps,' Page heard Willo shout as they dived through the arc of light and their wheels at last wedded the earth.

For a moment she clung to the rigid metal of the jump seat and watched as the plane manoeuvred behind a jeep that mounted the sign 'FOLLOW ME'. She knew she had faced death, and discovered the depths of her own courage.

Sixteen hours later, Page stepped from the blacked-out overnight Glasgow-to-London train into Victoria Station. An RAF officer from her compartment deposited her bags on the platform.

'Let me help you with these, Lieutenant, at least as far as the American transport office. Step this way.'

He placed her bags inside the office door, returned her salute and hurried off into the crowds.

'Are you Lieutenant Hannaday?' a staff sergeant asked as she stepped into the office, which had an American flag draped across the window.

'Yes.'

'Right,' he said, picking up her duffle. 'General Hannaday sent his car for you, ma'am.'

'How did he know I was coming?'

'General Willis — '

'Of course.'

'I'm to take you straight to Claridge's.'

'Claridge's Hotel?'

'That's right, Lieutenant.' The sergeant grinned. 'And if you don't mind my saying so, you may want to powder your nose up a bit. The General has a little surprise party cooked up for you. Half the officers at COSSAC will be there to meet you, including one who told me to say, "The professor cooks tonight." Does that mean anything to you?'

Page laughed.

33

In late November, 1943, the Big Three, Roosevelt, Churchill and Stalin, meet in Teheran to plan a second front in Europe. Russia agrees to declare war on Japan after Hitler is defeated.

I n the dark early-morning hours of November 17, Jill arrived in the Allied Forces headquarters at Caserta, bouncing in one of several two-ton trucks which had picked up the detachment of Wacs from the Twelfth Air Force base outside Naples. She was tired, weighed down by a barracks bag and an awkward bedroll, and everywhere she stepped her service shoes went almost ankle deep into chilling, sucking mud. The WAC billets had cold running water, but no hot water and no heat.

'Well, it isn't the Isle of Capri,' she heard one of the EWs say, throwing her gear onto a canvas cot, 'but it's sure better than our guys have it up in the mountains.'

'That's the spirit,' Jill called out to her. 'We're Fifth Army now.' She hoped the women couldn't tell she was whistling in the dark. How were they going to work twelve-hour shifts and live under these conditions?

A few weeks later, writing to Page, she had completely forgotten her doubts.

December 24, 1943

DEAR PAGE,

I was so surprised to hear that you were in England. I can't tell you where I am — the not so sunny Mediterranean will have to do for now and the censor may not even allow me that much, but I can tell you that all the big dreams I dreamed back in OC at Fort Des Moines have come true. I know guys are getting killed and I'm sorry for that, but these are the most important days of my life. I'll never do anything again that will give me quite this feeling of accomplishment.

You'd be proud of these women, Page. Every one of them was given a chance to rotate back to easier duty and not a one wanted to go. These Wacs thrive on hard work and discomfort; the sick call rate is lower than in units stateside.

The other day a Signal Corps major called me from the comcentre to ask me what my women needed, as if he couldn't believe they were happy, or — anyway, what he wanted to know was how the women could display so much esprit after long hours and all.

I told him the only thing I could — that when Wacs are considered to be useful and valuable members of the outfit, and command lets them know it, well, then nothing can shake them. He looked interested but, Page, I could see he didn't really know what I was talking about. Finally, he promised me some beauty parlour equipment just as soon as the generators could handle it. The EWs loved that and so did I. That's the point, isn't it? We can want to get on with the job, but we're still women — the two together and not in conflict.

Wish I could tell you about the Italian people here, but that will have to wait until after the war — at Babe's. Don't forget.

Got to get ready for duty, and I want to write to Elisabeth. Do you think she would send me some long flannel underwear? Oh, and before I forget, I should tell you that S. is my immediate superior here. He's not the man I thought he was. I still don't think I can trust him, not *that* way — you know what I mean — but he's a first class officer and fair.

There goes Armed Forces Radio playing Crosby's 'White Christmas' for the hundredth time today. That's the cruellest song — someone always breaks down. Even I get misty-eyed and I *never* had a white Christmas in my life. Now I really have to double-time to work. Take care, Page. I wonder where we'll be this time next year.

Love, Jill

Taking a quick inventory of the time, she decided she had time to drop a quick line to Elisabeth.

Christmas Eve, 1943
Somewhere in Italy

DEAR ELISABETH:

Sometimes it's uncanny how I seem to get what I wish for. Remember, I'm the gal who didn't want to be my mother's idea of a lady. Well, nothing genteel about me now. I'm sure my crinolined ancestors are absolutely twirling in their graves. I found a tailor who cut down a man's OD wool shirt and trousers for me. Haven't been able to find a pair of combat boots small enough, but I'm hopeful, or someday I'll disappear, worn service shoes and all, into a pothole. All of us dress this way — not Wacs regs, but at least we don't freeze.

Speaking of freezing. Could you send me a pair of flannel longjohns? All I'm allowed is scrip so I'll have my folks send you a cheque.

Afraid you'll have to take me in hand when I get back to the States. What little sense of style I had is long gone now.

Write soon,

LOVE, JILL

As she stepped outside the billets and returned the MP guard's salute, she could see in the northwest sky flashes of light, like summer lightning.

'What's that, Corporal?'

'It's the Long Toms, ma'am, pounding the German defences up in the Mignano gap. Some Christmas present, huh?'

'If we can see them from forty miles away they must be blinding up close.'

'You bet, Lieutenant. I wouldn't want to be one of them poor sonsa — Pardon, ma'am. Talked with one of them sad sacks on a 155mm gun crew — he was pullin' some R and R last week. They stand in a three-foot pit, most times filled with water, wrasslin' those big shells and powder charges as big as fifty-pound sugar sacks. Nope, I wouldn't like that duty.'

'Merry Christmas, Corporal.'

'Same to you, Lieutenant.'

She started down the short block to the communications area. From out of the dark a child's voice called, '*Buona sera, signorina*.' And then the familiar child's plea of '*Caramelle, prego!*'

'*Si, caramelle*.' She reached inside her battle jacket, the smallest made for the US Army and still sizes too big for her, and drew out the chocolate bars and candy orange slices she'd saved from the mess.

'*Mille grazie, signorina*.'

As she walked on, she heard them smack their lips.

There was no street in Caserta where she could walk without seeing the pinched white, hungry faces of Italian children, and the even more pitiful starving animals, pets no family could feed any longer. Their suffering was a reality of her great adventure that she didn't want to face. After all, it wasn't America's fault; if they hadn't followed their Duce . . . She showed her identification at the barbed-wire gate to the comcentre area and hurried over to the command van.

Desmond Stratton was waiting for her. 'Merry Christmas, Captain,' she said, her smile hesitant.

'Merry Christmas, Lieutenant.'

He had tried to overcome their awkwardness with each other, but they were never alone, and the war intruded on every minute. 'Sorry about this one.' He pointed to a thick figure-eight roll of punched, coded Teletype tape. 'This must be the nightly bad news. At least these families won't hear until after Christmas Day. They'll have that much.'

She nodded, took the tape, unlocked the code room and went inside. Within minutes, Christmas 1943 was forgotten as the decoded nightly casualty list unrolled the names of the Fifth Army dead and wounded. At first, she tried to read the names, ranks, serial numbers, looking for one she recognized. What would I do if I found one? she wondered. Cry. Scream. She stopped reading and later mechanically pasted the message, now in the clear, onto paper, stamped it with a big red 'SECRET' stamp and placed it in the locked headquarters pouch for AG Casualty Section.

These men, all these men — had some of them thought, as she had, that the war was the biggest thing in their lives, something they couldn't miss because the chance might not come again? Or were they just drafted, half hero, half scared, trying to stay alive and failing.

Jill heard a knock on the code room door.

'Yes?'

'Lieutenant?' It was Des. 'Can you come out for a break — take a cup of Christmas grog with us?'

As soon as she could break away, she opened the door, stepped out and carefully locked it behind her. 'Where's everybody?'

'You're too late — they've had theirs.' He raised his cup and touched hers. 'Anyway, Merry Christmas and Happy New Year, while we're at it. I'm going forward for a few days, so I'll make my year-end toast now.'

She raised her cup and touched his. 'Happy New Year. And — ' Jill had let it go long enough '— I probably should have said something back in Algiers — you know, about requisitioning me for this duty and all. I mean I want to thank you for choosing me.'

He looked at her, and the softness behind his voice belied his gruff words. 'I get the best man for the job — or woman, if that's the case — and you're the best code officer I've got.'

'Thanks.' She stood there, and though he had put down his cup, he did not move away. Unspoken words seemed to press down on her, his and hers, saying things she didn't want to hear. Embarrassed, finally, she gathered the incoming coded traffic and ducked back into the safety of the code room.

She was confused. Sometimes when she was with him she felt as if any moment she would explode with the tension. Later, she would deliberately avoid deciphering the minutes they'd spent together, because she refused to allow herself to think about him, to dwell on what might have been or could be. Nonetheless, as the sound of someone singing 'Silent Night' came through the locked door something inside her, something embryonic, expanded and stole out of the solitude of her heart.

BOOK THREE

*1944: To the Ends
of the Earth*

34

By early January 1944, eighteen hundred Wacs are assigned in the Mediterranean theatre of operations of the United States Army called MTOUSA for short. Although the bulk of the theatre's women soldiers remain in North Africa, several rear-echelon WAC detachments have arrived on the Italian boot, most of them assigned to headquarters, ordnance, judge-advocate or adjutant-general sections. Some are Air Wacs serving at bases of the Twelfth and Fifteenth Air Forces. By far the most forward Wac unit is a small signal group moving up behind Fifth Army combat troops within sound of the big guns, subject to air raids and perpetual blackout.

Moving up marks a soldier's progress through enemy territory. For Jill and her Signal Wacs, moving up to Presenzano at the base of the Mignano corridor in late January put them only twelve miles behind the front lines, closer to battle than any other women soldiers. Their big truck provided a bone-chilling morning ride even with the canvas end flaps tied down tight. It was their introduction to rugged combat conditions.

'How much longer, driver?' Jill stamped her feet on the floorboards to keep them warm.

'Depends on how long the MPs at the crossroads take to let us through. Believe me, I don't like it any more'n you do. The Krauts just love to strafe convoys before breakfast.'

They had been slowed to a crawl by a snarl of weapons carriers heading towards the front, red-crossed ambulances heading back with the wounded for field hospitals, and even long lines of mules backpacking rations for GIs holed up in the rocky mountain defiles ahead, facing the Germans.

This was the real war. No more O clubs, regular hours or home-away-from-home quarters. The idea excited Jill, and she knew that her women felt the same way. Only two days earlier, on January 22, 1944, as the first news of the Anzio beachhead reached the Caserta Wacs, the detachment had been divided into forward and rear echelons. Stratton had again requested her to head the code operation and move with his command to the forward base.

'You sure, Lieutenant?' he had asked when he called her in. 'Caserta will look like a post resort where we're going. You'll be living in tents with mud for floors, cold rations, the lot.'

'I'll go where I'm most needed, Captain.'

'In that case, I have something *you've* needed for a long time.' He reached under his desk and held up a pair of brand-new size-five combat boots. 'French,' he had explained. 'Not exactly high style, but their supply sergeant's taken a very un-Gallic liking to Spain, so I made a swap.' He thrust them towards her. 'Here, take them.'

She had cradled them like a precious infant in her arms. 'Boots! I can't believe it. At least let me pay you for them.'

'Forget it. I just didn't want to have to report the first case of Wac trench foot.'

Now she looked down at the brown boots planted on the floorboards of the big deuce-and-a-half, caked with mud, but dry inside and sturdy. They were the sweetest thing anyone had ever given her — the man she had hated with such passion had become her benefactor.

Kaye had lifted an eyebrow when Jill showed her the

boots, insisting that Stratton was a virtual fairy godmother, WAC style. 'Mmmm, I wonder, Jill. What else do you suppose he could do with his *magic wand*?' And Kaye bent double laughing at her own joke.

Even though her earthy humour was maddening at times, Jill would miss Kaye. She had a basic good sense and vulnerable sweetness that her bawdy jokes were meant to hide. That was the worst thing about the WAC — not the food or the homesickness or the danger, but the making of close friends that you lived and worked and played with only to leave them behind or be left behind by them, suddenly and forever. First Page, Bunny and Elisabeth, now Kaye. Her bad penny, Marie, was the only Wac she seemed to be stuck with, no matter how many moves she made.

Now the sound of guns pounding up ahead told her she wouldn't have the luxury of time to miss anyone. The barrage grew louder as the truck's driver skidded to a halt on a deeply rutted, frozen road in the middle of a cantonment of pyramidal tents. Before she had a chance to step off the running board, a siren screamed in the frosty morning air.

'Get those women out of the back, Lieutenant,' the driver yelled at her, abandoning the truck in midroad. 'Hit the dugouts!'

Jumping out and dashing to the rear of the truck, the two tugged on the rope to release the flaps, Jill shouting all the while, 'Come on, move, Move, *move!*' She pointed the twenty-two women towards a series of large sandbagged foxholes behind the tent rows as heavy bombers swept in over the north end of the town.

'You, too, Lieutenant!' the driver yelled and dived for the nearest bunker. 'For Christ's sake, move your ass!'

She gulped down terror. 'There's classified material in this truck, and I'm responsible for it.'

A bomb hit in the town. Flames jabbed at the winter-blue sky, followed by a pillar of smoke. In a staggered pattern, the huge bursts marched route step towards the encampment.

A jeep slammed to a stop, slid the last few feet in the frozen ruts, and smashed into the front of the truck.

'Are you crazy?' Stratton called, waving his arm. 'Get outa here now, and that's an order!'

When she didn't move fast enough, he half dragged, half carried her, until they tumbled down under the sandbags of an empty dugout seconds ahead of shrapnel pattering like a spring hail shower behind them.

She was embarrassed and thus furious. 'I could be court-martialled if those code machines are tampered with.'

'A corpse can't be court-martialled,' he yelled back, fury etched on his tired, lined face. 'Don't they teach you Wacs how to take care of yourselves in an air attack, or were you showing off, Lieutenant?' He felt a terrible anger at her. The tension between them for the last four months coupled with his fear for her exploded and demanded an outlet. He grabbed her by the shoulders, shaking her roughly, as they crouched there on their knees in the freezing mud. 'Don't you ever take a dumb chance like that again or I'll send you to the rear! Do you hear me?'

Jill's teeth chattered as much from the damp as from the shaking. Cold and miserable, angry and amazed at his behaviour and terribly aware of his closeness, she began a soundless sobbing, her courage draining away in the tears running silently down her cheeks.

Before he knew what he was doing, his arms had circled her shoulders and pulled her to his chest. Her helmet banged his as his mouth searched her face, tasted her salt tears and at last found her lips.

She heard him calling her name in the semi-darkness, accompanied by the sounds of bombs exploding closer than ever, causing the earth to shake violently under them. He repeated her name as if it was food and he was starving, water and he was thirsty, medicine and he was sick, a map and he was lost, returning to her lips, kissing them tenderly, clutching at her with his hands. Instantly, she realized that none of what he was doing frightened her, or even surprised or shocked her. What did terrify her was the involuntary response of her own body, which pressed insistently, out of

297

control, into his.

'Never — never,' he repeated the words of raw anguish, 'take chances like that, and that's a direct order.'

She nodded, too exhausted to protest, her head resting on his jacket, her nose sunk in the strange odour of it — mud, mildew from the constant damp, and a maleness, or what she thought was a fighting man's scent, the smell of fear and danger and something even more compelling and primitive.

Des shifted and leaned his back against the earthen wall opposite the entrance, pulling her with him. Again, she did not protest his encircling arm. This was no time for coy man-woman games. There was only reality here inside, while a few feet away bombs were exploding and ack-ack guns pumped out shells, adding to the sense of apocalypse. It wasn't even strange to be here in his arms. She could have been parked with Neil in her father's truck on her way home from a college dance, she felt so safe. But this was not Neil, this man who had kissed her and held her out of fear for her safety and, instinctively she knew, out of his own fear — this was quite a different man. More important they had shared the fear of death on the battlefield, and it was a special bond, drawing them closer in a silent pact.

They pressed closer with each fresh burst of ack-ack. Jill clasped his big hand in both of hers, and could feel the steel in his fingers through the wool gloves they were both wearing. But, with all his strength, she felt his human need for reassurance, and she gave it to him with her smile in the half-light.

Minutes later the all clear sounded and they scrambled out of the dugout, Des reaching back a hand for her. She coughed, actually tasting the acrid cordite fumes of gunpowder wafting over the wreckage of the camp. There were many downed tents with piles of smashed cots and gear scattered about, but the comcentre truck was untouched, thank God. She knew she must see to her women, but she was reluctant to leave Des. She wanted to prolong this special connection, but felt equally awkward and embarrassed in the daylight. Did she salute the man who had just kissed her tears away?

Des looked down at her. What kind of hold did this woman have on him? Just like some kid, he got the shakes every time he was near her. 'We've got work to do.' He tried to make his voice matter-of-fact. 'But I'll see you later at the officers' briefing.'

'Of course.' His businesslike tone brought her back to reality. He didn't have to spell it out for her. What had happened had been natural, but had obviously meant nothing to him beyond the need of a man and a woman to comfort each other in the only way they had.

Des saw her face lose its softness, and realized she had misunderstood his meaning — or had he not known what he meant until the words were out? But he knew now. 'Yes, at the briefing, but afterwards too, for a long time afterwards. Look, Jill, there's no reason to keep on with . . . '

'With what?'

'With this pretence that we don't care for each other. It doesn't make any sense, not here, not when the whole damned world is blowing up in our faces.' He took a short step towards her and gripped her arm. 'Jill, darling, let's grab this chance while we can.'

She knew exactly what he was saying. These were words she'd put into his mouth in her reveries, but now that she actually heard them she wished she were a thousand miles away. Her promise to Neil was there between them, like some barrier, bigger even than the war. How stupid she'd been to dream that anything could come of . . . 'Des, I can imagine what you must think — I mean because I was scared and, well, I let you . . . ' She stumbled over the words, which sounded impossibly sophomoric even to her own ears. 'Nothing's changed, nothing *can* change. There's still Neil, and I've promised, I *had* to promise . . . Please understand, it has nothing to do with you.'

He looked at her, and she saw in his deep-grey eyes first hurt, then anger. He saluted her and the salute was an act of proud repudiation of all he'd said. 'That's right, Lieutenant, your private life has nothing to do with me,' knowing his words hurt her, 'but before you get around to choosing your china pattern, perhaps you'd better see to your troops.'

He flung away from her, leaving her standing there alone. Suddenly she was aware that men were running past her and her women were crawling out of the dugouts. She'd have to pull herself together and get busy.

'Lieutenant,' she heard Sergeant Harper's voice yelling to her through the noise and confusion. 'Over here.'

Jill hurried to where Harper, Brodzinsky and others bent over a Wac propped on a pile of sandbags by a bunker. The woman had a bleeding shrapnel wound on her left shoulder. 'Hold still, this won't hurt,' Jill said, ripping open her first-aid kit and pouring sulfa powder directly on the open wound. She applied a pressure bandage, and caught Marie's eye. 'Brodzinsky, get a medic.'

Marie stared at her, eyes wide, pupils dilated, her voice when she spoke rising to the edge of hysteria. 'Two inches lower and she could have lost a breast! How many ways can this war take our womanhood?'

Christ! None of her women had ever had hysterics, and Brodzinsky was not going to ruin their record, especially when it might be just one more way to get even with her. Jill's voice was as cold as the white breath that hung in front of her face. 'Private, you get a medic here on the double or you'll spend the duration wishing you had.'

Instantly, the look of fear was replaced by hatred, an emotion Jill knew her nemesis could cope with very well, and Marie rushed off, returning in minutes with help.

Jill followed the stretcher bearers to the hospital tent, left Harper with the EW after the doctor described the wound as superficial, and ran to the comcentre truck to supervise its camouflage. Work was what she needed, grinding, enervating, numbing work to keep her mind busy so she would not have the time or the energy to wonder what it would have been like if she had said yes to Des — the one word that had tried to push past all the others, the word she had not allowed herself to say. She didn't know at what moment her body had betrayed her by wanting to make love with Desmond Stratton — maybe as long ago as OC training. She only knew she could never allow physical desire to make her fail her duty to Neil.

35

An appearance at New York's Paramount Theatre by Frank Sinatra causes thirty thousand teenage bobby-soxers to riot and takes seven hundred policemen to quell the disorder.

'Hurry, Danny!' Her voice was low and excited. 'I am hurrying, Elisabeth — I'm not exactly an old hand at this.' Danny grunted and motioned for her to move the flashlight to the right.

In spite of a nagging feeling that a thousand eyes watched her in the darkened office, so far everything had gone as they'd planned. Elisabeth was sure no one had seen them enter the administration building. She was surprised at how simple larceny really was. It didn't take grand strategies, just a little nerve. What was nerve but a lot of self-confidence? She checked the lighted clock on the colonel's desk: 0210 hours. They had twenty minutes before the patrol was due to make its rounds.

The tumblers clicked, and Danny swung open the safe door. 'Here are the bids,' he said, 'right where the colonel left them this afternoon.'

'Which one is Stryker's?'

'This one.' He pulled a bound manila packet from the centre of the pile. 'I've to put it back in the same place, just in case Colonel Nick remembers.'

'Why would he, unless . . . ' She left the question of the colonel's suspicions unasked. She must not upset Barnes, who was turning out to be a real nervous Nelly. But most of all, she knew she must not be silly. Why would the colonel

301

be suspicious of his own people? Everybody knew that bid-rigging went on *before* bids were submitted, not after. That's what made this so safe, but, safe or not, this was a stratagem she knew Max would admire, and Max's admiration was what she must have.

Danny twisted around in the harsh glare of the flashlight to look up at Elisabeth. 'Are you dead sure Stryker will give you the photos if we do this?'

'Do you think I'm lying?'

'Of course not, Elisabeth — I'd never . . .'

Elisabeth saw that his hand shook as he handed her the bid packets. She knew she'd have to handle him carefully; there might be a limit to his infatuation. Quickly, she untied the other bids and determined the lowest numbers, then took Max's bid and went to her desk. 'How much time have we got?'

'Ten minutes.'

Danny, using a delicate cleaning solvent that erased ink without leaving a stain, altered Stryker's numbers, and Elisabeth, slipping the forms into her typewriter, replaced the high figures with lower ones. Finished, she folded the contract and put it back inside the packet. 'That's it, then.' They returned to the colonel's office, stopping once to duck out of sight when headlights glared momentarily through the windows.

Danny carefully replaced the bids inside the safe and closed the door, twirling the combination knob anti-clockwise. He turned a white face to her. 'Let's get out of here.'

They left through the offices into the adjoining warehouse and down the rear delivery ramp, stopping suddenly at the sound of voices.

Elisabeth grabbed Danny and pulled him back against the rough plank building into its shadows. Two guards with slung rifles were lighting cigarettes and griping.

'This is the goddamned boringest duty I ever pulled.'

'You want excitement, dummy, why'ncha volunteer for combat. Me, I'm for walkin' these posts 'til the war's over — if I stay so lucky. 'Sides, I got some cute Jailbait on the string and I ain't gonna leave the field to that skinny Four-F crooner Sinatra. Do you know what he's got that the girls go for? Shit — I don't for tryin'.'

'Me neither. Didja try that warehouse door on our last round?' The soldier pointed a finger at the shadows hiding Elisabeth and Danny.

'Hell! What for? Who's gonna break in to *get* a uniform. All the Joes around here want is to get out of OD.'

The guards crunched on through the soot-covered snow between the warehouses until their quarrelsome voices disappeared into the dark. Elisabeth and Danny, holding their breath, moved rapidly along the building until they reached the staff car.

'Danny, we shouldn't be seen together tonight,' she told him. 'Drop me at a cab stand and I'll make my own way to the hotel.'

He nodded. 'We did it. I — I can hardly believe we got away with it.'

'Well, *believe* it. You're a clever guy, Danny — and, oh, you kept that man Stryker from ruining my life. I'll never forget you, darling.'

Even now, weeks later, standing in a public booth, Elisabeth could remember the triumph she'd felt that night. No man, not even Max — perhaps especially Max — could doubt her loyalty after the risks she'd taken for him, first giving up Marne and now ensuring he got a lucrative contract.

Elisabeth Gardner took out her compact and powdered her nose, a professional beauty's reflex before facing anything, in this case even before picking up the telephone to dial Max's Drexel Hill number once again. With one last glance in the tiny mirror, which she rotated in a circle the better to see all her features, she regained the look of assumed hauteur that had been her protective armour for most of her adult life.

The sound of the telephone ringing filled the cramped, dimly lit telephone booth and drowned the noise of passing traffic, of tyres crunching February's refrozen slush.

'Mr Stryker's residence.'

'Hinton, this is Mrs Gardner. I want to speak with Max.'

She felt rather than heard his hesitation, no longer than a single pulse of the vein in her throat.

'I'm sorry, Madam, Mr Stryker is entertaining and cannot be disturbed. May I take a message?'

'You've taken a dozen messages! I want to talk to Max, and I want to talk to him *now*. You tell Max that for me.'

'Just one moment, Mrs Gardner.'

She heard the receiver clatter against the table, and stamped her feet, knocking the snow off her service shoes onto the asphalt floor of the booth, where it melted and puddled while she waited, the telephone cradled against her ear.

'Mrs Gardner?'

'Yes.'

'I'm afraid Mr Stryker cannot speak to you at this time. He wishes me to say he will be in touch in a week or so.' The line went dead.

The bastard! He'd hung up on her.

How strange it was and how frustrating to be here in the same booth she had used to call Max so many times before, times when he had answered her call within seconds and welcomed her in that intimate, enveloping voice of his. How long now since she had heard his voice outside of the terribly formal meeting at the depot? Ten days? Two weeks? When this whole miserable WAC dress contract business had first come up, she had reluctantly agreed that it might be best not to risk being seen together outside the depot, especially since Max was convinced that there had been talk about them and that Colonel Nick had asked probing questions. Max had bluntly told her he couldn't risk a Federal investigation, not even for her. But that had been weeks ago, and after her designs, *her* designs, had been accepted for the new WAC off-duty dresses, and Max had won the contract, there was no longer a need for them to be apart.

She wasn't a naïve shopgirl. She had known when he arranged the cosy little dinner drama last fall with that stick figure socialite Kit Longley that she had a rival — a formidable one. He had told her that being seen on the pages of the Philadelphia *Inquirer* with a banking heiress was good for business, but he didn't really expect her to believe him. It was part of his game, the lion expanding his pride, lazily watching the females manoeuvre for his favour, waiting for one or the other to make a kill to feed his insatiable appetite.

It didn't matter. None of Max's society playthings mattered to her. *She* could give Max something none of them could, understanding that went right to the core of him. She knew his insides as she knew her own, the heightened sensitivity, the protective coldness, the boy's raw survival instinct turned to dangerous manipulation in the man. She understood his need to be powerful, to control, his almost religious desire to dominate everyone around him and yet to avoid any responsibility for those who surrendered their freedom to him. She knew all this, because she saw herself in Max. If she could only be alone with him, he would remember — she would make him remember! Still, a question nagged at her, tugged at her subconscious: was understanding enough for Max?

She dialled Checker Cab, gave the dispatcher her location and the Drexel Hill destination. A half hour later, the taxi was headed towards the northwestern suburbs.

'Mind if I play my radio, miss?' the cabbie asked and held up a leather-covered portable already spouting war news.

'No, but please keep the volume down.'

'I've got it all the way down.'

She needed to think even though the reports of progress from the Anzio beachhead intruded Marne between her thoughts of Max and what she would say to him once she arrived unannounced at his home.

'Boy, our guys are really giving it to them, huh, Lieutenant?' And without waiting for her confirmation he launched into his own analysis of the war news. 'Now if the Fifth Army can just get across that Rapido River and link up with the troops from the beachhead, we'll cut off the Germans' escape towards Rome and then it'd be a sittin' duck, watcha call one of them open cities. We could just walk right in there. What d'ya think, you being in the Army and all?'

'I don't know. My husband may be there.' What a stupid thing for her to say! Now she'd get endless reassurances, and prying questions. But the news from Italy had made her think of Marne, especially since there had been no news from him. Although she had told him not to reply to her letter — okay, she thought with a twinge, her Dear John letter — she had fully expected him to do so. But not one word had come through. She was aware that the driver was talking, talking . . . 'Do you mind?'

'Sorry, lady. Whatever you say.'

Say? Say? The word echoed through her consciousness. As she rode, she had no inkling of what she might say to Max. Maybe it wouldn't be necessary to say anything; perhaps he was even now waiting for her to make a move towards him, one that would assure him of his control over her, while leaving him free of asking her to come. She could play that game, if that's what he wanted; she could even fake losing, if that would really win him.

'Do you want me to wait, lady?' the driver asked her. 'It'll be hard to get a cab out here later. Ya know we gotta save gas — can't come back till a fare's coming this way.'

'No, don't wait.'

Elisabeth pushed the bell button and heard faint chimes through the door. It opened, and Hinton, nonplussed, barred her way, but she brushed past him. 'Tell Max I'm here,' she said, tossing Hinton her winter uniform coat, a move that brooked no refusal.

'Please wait here, madam.' He disappeared in the direction of the study, not bothering to hide his look of disapproval.

While he was gone, she was absorbed by the face in the foyer mirror, the high colour accenting her cheekbones, the blue eyes wary, the nostrils of her expertly modelled nose pinched to narrow slits — the image of a self-satisfied composed beauty, given completely away by the erratic pulse beating in her throat.

306

'Mrs Gardner, you're to go to the study.'

She hadn't heard Hinton return. 'Never mind' — she waved him aside — 'you know *I* can find my own way.'

The double doors to the study were closed. She opened both and stepped inside, hearing them close quietly behind her — of course, Hinton had followed her. Did he think she was going to steal the porcelain figurines?

The familiar furniture shapes, the predatory scent of leather and tobacco and brandy, the scent of Max, enveloped her, the open fireplace drawing the winter cold and hard resolution from her. A faint odour of expensive perfume lingered in the air — ah! the lion's lair had had a recent visitor. Her own senses, even the hair at the nape of her neck, were acutely tuned to the idea that a rival had been here, perhaps only moments earlier, and might still be here. Elisabeth whirled around, searching the room like the fox in a steel-jawed trap ready to bite off its own leg to beat the trapper.

He entered from a side door, stepping towards her deliberately, his eyes seeming to bore into her as if he was determined to avoid the golden package she came in. 'I'm truly glad you've come, Elisabeth,' and his smooth voice enveloped and caressed. He motioned her to the sofa opposite him with elaborate politeness. 'May I get you a drink before we get to business?'

'No, I don't need one, Max, but you go ahead if you do.'

He sighed, but his eyes narrowed, pulling the corners of his mouth up, which was Max's look of admiration. 'That's what I like about you, Elisabeth — right down to it. All right, then, let's not spar. What do you want? Money?'

She looked at him crazily, shakily. 'No.'

'It's the sergeant, then, Whatshisname — Barnes?'

'No, he's never asked for money.'

Max stood up and began to pace, to prowl up and down in front of her. 'I don't know how it was done. I don't even care. Did I ever *tell* you I wanted you to tamper with the contracts? That was *your* idea.'

'Max.' She was weary of this. 'Stop it! Don't play the innocent bystander with me. You knew I intended to get that contract for you any way I could — damn it, don't play this game with me. I'll play your other games, but not this one.'

He stopped pacing and planted his legs apart like a sailor on a heaving deck. 'What's Barnes' payoff?'

'There isn't any payoff. I told Barnes — well, I told him you had some compromising photos of me from New York and that this would buy you off.'

'That's splendid! You tell this sergeant that I'm a two-bit blackmailer, so he risks prison and wants nothing for himself.' In his anger, Max's vowels reclaimed a trace of their guttural heritage. She knew this was yet another betrayal he would unconsciously blame on her.

'Max, don't be so obtuse. He's in *love* with me. He doesn't want anything from me.'

Max sneered now and his eyes lost all trace of admiration. 'You're the blind fool, Elisabeth. Everybody — *everybody* — wants something, including you.'

'I've asked for nothing.'

'I didn't say you weren't clever.'

Without pleading, she asked, 'What do *you* want, Max — from me?'

He shrugged, his face perched on the icy edge of indifference, a look that cut deep into her soul. All her life she had dealt with men's emotions, her father's rage, a customer's desire, a husband's need to devour and own. She could cope with the gamut of male emotion, but not with this indifference of Max's. And she couldn't believe it now, especially from Max, the man she had responded to, felt more with than any other man. But when he spoke, he said nothing of what she wanted to hear. When he spoke, everything in her longed for him to stop.

'At first you amused me.' He knew he had to make this convincing now, or he could be implicated in a government investigation, and everything he'd worked for would be lost. 'My dear, you were — well, you were this marvellous, unexpected find, like a diamond in a coal mine, and, frankly, I thought you might be useful.'

'*Was* I useful, Max,' her voice was a single, flat tone, 'was

308

I useful in your bed?' It was the only place she could strike out at him, the only place he had really given her in his life.

About this he refused to lie; she deserved that much. 'You know you are a magnificent woman, and I confess that I have missed you — no, stay where you are — I've missed your inventiveness is what I meant to say.' He lowered his voice and she knew they were not alone in the house. 'Kit is not your match in bed, no, not even close. But now — and I do regret it, Elisabeth — it is time to say goodbye, to be practical and recognize when something is over.'

He sat down opposite her, crossed one muscular leg over the other. He could have just completed an important business presentation.

Max's civilized veneer and his callous confirmation of another woman in his bed goaded her to sarcasm. 'You're not going to say anything so clichéd as "This is best for both of us", are you?'

'No. I'm just going to ask you to leave, to leave and not come back.' He still wanted her, right now more than he had realized he would, but she was too dangerous and the stakes were too high. He affected a look of boredom because he had to activate her pride before his determination failed him. Boredom with other people was something they had shared together; it was their private joke, something they had laughed about. More than anything, he knew, she would not be able to bear the idea that he could be bored with her.

Elisabeth saw his languorous disinterest, but she could not accept it. She stood up, unfolding her long legs in the one graceful motion her model's training had made second nature. Arousing a man had never been necessary before. Being the pursuer was not her role, and she played it badly. She crossed to the sofa and sat close to him, touching along the length of him, picking up his hands to guide them to his favourite places.

He fought for control. This was so much harder with her here than he had imagined it would be. 'This is unworthy of you, Elisabeth. Why don't you go on back to your husband, and be a good little wife after the war?'

309

How she hated him for an instant! Even the gift of her security he threw back in her face. 'You bastard.' She hoped, nonetheless, to impress him with her loyalty. 'I've already written and asked Marne for a divorce.'

'You told him about me?'

'Yes — oh, not by name, just that I was in love with a man.'

'That's very sweet, my dear, but you see it's impossible.' He rose quickly and moved to a safer distance. 'I'm announcing my engagement to Kit Longley next week.'

'You can't do that!' She hadn't meant to sound so shrill, like a jealous shopgirl.

'Oh, but I can and I will.'

'But don't you see, darling,' and she loathed the pleading weakness she heard in her voice, 'I've given up everything.'

'Elisabeth, I never thought to play such a cheap scene with you, but since you insist . . .' He stationed himself warily in front of the large fireplace. The flames backlighted his hair, outlined his powerful figure, left his face in shadow, and then he pulled the ace he'd been saving from his sleeve. 'Don't give me the "I've sacrificed everything" speech. It's beneath you. Do you really think I don't know you were a common little thief at Gabriella's? Do you believe for a minute that I haven't had you investigated from the first, that I don't know you were Marco's slut, trading your body for every order of twelve-ninety-five dresses? Don't ever insult me by playing the wronged woman. Now, I want you to leave, and I don't want you to return.' He yanked on the tasselled bell pull, and Elisabeth, fascinated, watched it dance up and down like a jolly puppet.

She stood there for a moment, rooted, looking at the man she loved, the great complete love she had not even known she needed or wanted. 'What did I do?' She was startled to hear these oldest and saddest of lovers' words come from her mouth.

'You did nothing,' he said, as close to unhappiness as he was ever likely to let himself come. 'Don't you understand? There was nothing you *could* do — nothing you could ever do.'

It was one thing to lose a man because a new woman had taken your place, but, oh, to hear that your love had never had its chance and all the scheming dreams had been mere self-delusion — *that* hurt most of all. Max, in one short moment, had obliterated a year of her life as if it had never been worth living.

She walked then, a remaining scrap of pride moving her legs like a wind-up doll's, to the study doors, and out into the foyer. Hinton was waiting with her coat.

'The car will take you back, madam,' he said, looking past her, talking to the ghost of a woman who had never really been there.

A sound on the private stairs beyond the formal drawing room caused Elisabeth to raise her head groggily. No one appeared, but the emptiness of the space between was filled with the unmistakable authority of Kit Longley, her presence claimed even the air Elisabeth struggled to breathe. There would be no confrontation scene that Elisabeth could replay later in her mind, no chance to gloat over a telling verbal thrust. There would be nothing at all. The Longley woman belonged to a social class that simply ignored unpleasantness, particularly when it concerned someone outside their circle. To Kit Longley, Elisabeth knew, she no longer existed.

'Your coat, madam,' Hinton's voice said again, slicing through Elisabeth's numbed senses. He opened the door, and a rush of cold February air enveloped her.

Behind her she heard footsteps echo and a door close. Her life as she had envisioned it had stopped abruptly, but the life of this house, of Max, proceeded smoothly with never a ripple to show she had been there. She could see him standing at this moment in front of the fire, vastly pleased with himself. How blind she had been not to really know him before, when now, suddenly, it seemed so obvious. For a man like Max, the greatest aphrodisiac wasn't sex or understanding as she'd thought — God! what puny weapons, she'd had. No, not even money or power drew him like acceptance; the *one* thing she couldn't give him. For acceptance he would sacrifice anyone, even her, perhaps, especially her, because she reminded him of what he had escaped. Oh, she hadn't counted on this, hadn't wanted to think beyond her passion, but there must come a time when men like Max wanted to forget they were ever on the outside. She stumbled getting into the car.

'Careful, madam,' the chauffeur said, catching her by the arm.

Entering the car for Elisabeth was like crossing a mental threshold. Because sanity was so unbearable, her mind began to race into a fantasy faster than the Lincoln rolled down the curving driveway and out onto the street. With each mile, she rejected more of her sudden insight into Max's behaviour, returning again and again to her need to believe that his desire for her would win over any obstacle. How could that dried-up old maid Kit Longley ever think she could satisfy a man like Max? Elisabeth laughed aloud, the high-pitched sound reverberating inside the limousine. She caught the driver's frightened look before she could stop herself from laughing wildly again. For some moments, she maintained a tenuous clutch on reality because what she really wanted was to scream, to crush something, anything, and she wanted most of all to *show* Max, to prove to him what a mistake he had made so that he would beg her to come back to him.

She was almost back at the Franklin before she realized the essential truth of what had happened to her — that she was more in love with Max than ever. Pride, revenge, her own safety, none of it really mattered to her. She loved Max, she ached with it, was sickened by it, exalted by it. These feelings of love had been so hard for her to find that she could not, would not, give them up. He had hurt her. Damn it, he had! But the pain of it had not killed her love. In her life, pain seemed the logical result of love. For Elisabeth pain and pleasure were inextricably mixed.

As the sound of tyres crunching outside on the driveway receded, Max felt a momentary relief that Elisabeth was gone before a heaviness returned to sap the strength from his legs and slow his furious pacing. The bitch! A part of him was filled with rage at the threat she posed to everything he had worked a lifetime for, and a part of him felt utter and absolute emptiness, a part he had not known she filled until she was irretrievably gone. When Kit entered, he wanted to smash that smug expression from her face. Christ! Another woman demanding explanations.

'Darling —' he took her in his arms '— I'm sorry about this tasteless affair tonight. Believe me, I had no idea she would barge in like that.'

'That doesn't worry me, Max, but the look on your face does. The truth, now.' She firmly disengaged his arms and walked to his desk, carefully choosing a cigarette from the silver box. 'Oh, one always sounds like Sam Spade in these matters. Does she have anything on you, as they say?'

'Would it make any difference if she did?'

'None.'

'Then I don't know.'

'Is that your answer?'

'Yes. What I do know is that she's like nitroglycerin. If she's not handled properly, she'll go off and do a great deal of damage.'

'Then buy her off, darling. How much can she want?'

'No, my dear, money is not what she's after.'

'Surely that little nobody didn't really think she could have you. Max, I think you better tell me all of it.' Kit sat on the edge of the sofa Elisabeth had just vacated. 'Sparing me the *amour*, of course.'

Max heard her voice take on a note of ennui, a tone he had always thought she hid behind, but now he wasn't so sure. Maybe her security was so unassailable that nothing really bothered her.

'Max, from the beginning.'

He told her as much as he had to tell, with a growing admiration for the practical toughness he saw just below the surface, a toughness he had once assumed was simply brittle sophistication.

'Max, do you mean,' her tone didn't betray the least inner turmoil, 'she took it upon herself to tamper with

313

sealed bids to your benefit along with this cohort sergeant of hers, with no encouragement from you? Never mind, I don't want to know if it's true or not.'

'Why?'

'Don't you understand, dear Max? It doesn't matter to me *what* you've done. Anyway, what I think is beside the point. Frankly, my darling, not even my Great-Aunt Abigail would believe you, unless . . .'

'Unless what?'

'What is it the generals say — a good offence and so forth?'

He smiled and crossed the few feet that separated them. 'What pretty scheme are you hatching?'

'Nothing at *all* pretty, I assure you, Max darling.' She held up her face to him. 'Kiss me.'

He kissed her thin lips, but they remained lifeless and flaccid. He hid his disappointment expertly. He had discovered during their first night of lovemaking that Kit Longley was frigid. Not frigid in the usual sense of being repelled by the sexual act. That he could have accepted, perhaps even felt some compassion for. No, Kit Longley was fascinated by every kind of love between a man and a woman. She watched him when he mounted her, the way a breeder watches a stud stallion, judging, evaluating, calculating. They had made a mutual exchange of reputations, his as a lover and hers as a woman acceptable to the first families of the country. He had everything but a secure place in the world; she had everything but a sense of her own womanliness. Publicly they gave each other the one thing each lacked, privately they gave each other nothing.

He released her. She rose and moved to the telephone, picked it up and dialled. 'Long distance?' he heard her say. 'I want to place a call to Washington, DC, person to person to Senator Davies Carleton. Tell him Kit Longley is on the line.'

Max crossed quickly to the desk where she stood. 'What are you doing?'

'Trust me and I can get rid of your little lieutenant, my sweet.'

314

Intrigued by her self-assurance, he nodded yes.

'Uncle Carly? . . . Yes, it's so nice to hear *your* voice. You've been neglecting me, and I may not forgive you . . . Yes, of *course* I know there's a war on. Uncle Carly, I need a tiny little favour — well, it just means my whole happiness that's all. My fiancé . . . .' She smiled at Max, who stood next to her. 'Of course you didn't know I was engaged. That's what I'm calling to tell you . . . The favour? Well, Uncle Carly, Max Stryker my fiancé . . . yes, *that* Max Stryker, is being blackmailed by a Wac, of all things, who thinks she's in love with him and . . .'

Max smiled at her. So *this* was what it was like to be on the receiving end of the chain of privilege. How clever Kit was and how absolutely, perfectly old school, closing ranks to protect one's own kind. For the first time in his life, Max felt absolutely safe. Kit was right, of course, the best defence against the threat Elisabeth posed was to light the fuse and let it explode in *her* hand. Why would he expose Elisabeth if he weren't innocent? He was sorry for Elisabeth, sorry there was no other way. His mind wandered as it rarely did. What a fantastic woman Elisabeth had been, her body so golden in the Maryland sun — but that was not important now. With his ass on the line, he'd sacrifice hers without another thought. The world was full of women, wasn't it?

'And you see why this Wac must be stopped from ruining Max's reputation, Uncle Carly. You know all kinds of generals at the War Department, so naturally I turned to you and not to Daddy. It would be just too embarrassing to tell Daddy about my fiancé's former *femme fatale*. You *do* understand. Tell me you do.' Kit paused, listening, satisfaction obvious in her thin face. 'Of course, you have my word that he is absolutely innocent . . . I knew I could count on you.' Adding in a little girl's pleading voice, 'You will come down next week for the wedding. Yes, so soon, of course, so soon. I wouldn't want a marvellous man like Max to slip through my fingers.' Kit paused, listening. 'Absolutely not, I won't reconsider. Max *will* be my husband . . . Of course I'm not angry. Until next week then, darling.'

She hung up.

Here was a new facet of Kit's character, or lack of it. He had thought of her as a dilettante, bored and restless. He knew the type. They loved to circle around the edge of respectability only to dart back to safety if real scandal threatened. But not Kit. From the look on her face, the cat-in-the-cream delight in her eyes, he was forced to view her anew. He could see she was, in her own way, something of a rebel, too. Here she was, nearing middle age, and she'd chosen to marry an outsider, chosen to create a scandal in her society, and was obviously delighted to rub their noses in it. Formidable was the word for her, much more so than he had given her credit for being.

Max bent formally and kissed her hand. 'Kit, I've underestimated you. You're quite a woman. Come upstairs with me now, and I'll show you how much woman you are.' She was the second woman he'd lied to that evening in curiously opposite ways. Telling Kit he desired her was as false as telling Elisabeth he didn't want her. 'By the way, I thought we'd agreed to announce our *engagement* next week. What's this about a wedding?'

'I think it's better that we get married with a minimum of fuss. Big parties are so unpatriotic and all. Anyway, Max dearest, there is really no reason to wait, especially now, is there?' Kit picked up a cigarette and waited expectantly.

Max flicked the crown-shaped table lighter and lit it for her. 'No, no reason to wait — especially now.' He took her arm and they walked slowly to his private staircase. He wondered how long he'd be satisfied with his bargain.

36

In spring 1944, shipment of Wacs to all overseas theatres doubles, but the biggest jump occurs in female troops headed for the Pacific. To process women for overseas duty the Army Service Forces set up a special training battalion at Fort Oglethorpe, Georgia.

'**R**oute step — *march!*'

Two lines of women soldiers in oversize fatigues spread to either side of the road, wet red Georgia gumbo sticking in great globs to their boots. Bunny whispered over her shoulder to the woman behind her. 'Vicki — how far have we come?'

'About five miles.'

'I thought so — my feet hurt all the way to my hips.'

'Hold on, Bunny' — Vicki giggled — 'till we hit the obstacle course.' She giggled again. 'Then you can crawl on your big bazzooms.'

'Ve-ry fun-ny!' Bunny sniffled, wiped her reddened nose gingerly with a Kleenex and plodded ahead, railing silently against the far-off brass who had dreamed up a combat course to toughen women, which meant they trained with inadequate equipment and clothing, resulting in a barracks full of head colds.

'Company — *halt*,' the WAC sergeant yelled. 'Fall out behind the obstacle course. This is your final run-through, so, *people*, give me your best. The CO and the battalion commander are watching from the bleachers.'

The Wacs were lined up behind a long wooden obstacle with boards nailed in diamond-shaped patterns of a scaffold about a foot above the ground. The idea was to navigate it on the run without breaking a leg.

'*Go!*' yelled the sergeant.

Bunny brought her knee up high and jumped into the maze. As long as she had to be here, she wouldn't be last.

Ouch! She could feel the skin scrape from her shin when she got too close to the forward edge. Jump. Concentrate. Jump, jump.

Cadre urged them on. 'Keep moving, women. Down the nets next.'

Her breath was coming in great whooshes from deep in her lungs; she welcomed the respite at the ladder behind the cargo-net scaffold. She jostled Vicki with her hip. 'Now, keep your foot out of my face this time, PFC Victoria Hansen.'

'Keep your face out from under my foot, Sarge.'

Bunny scrambled up the ladder about thirty feet to the top, turned around backward and for a moment jabbed her feet against the cargo roping below, searching for a toehold, then down hand over hand, foot over foot, to the bottom. It was almost too real. With a dozen other women swarming down the netting, it heaved and yawed like the escape net over the side of the sinking ship it was supposed to simulate.

The training cadre stood at the bottom. 'Move out! Move out, people. Gas training ahead.'

Hardly catching her breath, Bunny ran on until she reached the barbed-wire obstacles, then loosened her gas mask from its pack and waited for the command.

'Gas!' somebody yelled, and tear-gas grenades began to plop around her. Coughing, she dropped to the ground, slipped into her mask, pulled the straps tight and winced as rubber met skin raw from exposure. She gave the face piece one last jiggle to make sure it was tightly sealed, and crawled forward. They'd been through this a dozen times. God! She was sick of it. As she scrambled through the white billowing gas clouds, stopping once to disentangle her sleeve from a strand of wire, she wondered whether Page had ever got over her fear of the mask. Damn! If Page Hannaday could take it, scared as she was, Bunny Palermo could stand a little discomfort, and she dug her elbows into the sticky Georgia clay.

Vicki flopped alongside as Bunny wearily reached the far end of the chemical-warfare course and pulled off her mask. 'Gee, you look funny,' the kid said, giggling, 'like one of those African mudmen in an Osa Johnson movie I saw once in school.'

'Oh yeah?' And with her clay-covered fingers Bunny reached over and deliberately painted mud cat whiskers on Vicki's face, which sent the younger girl into another spasm of giggles.

'Bunny!'

'Umm.' Hands were shaking her. 'Can't we win the war after I get some shuteye? I read somewhere Hitler doesn't get up till noon.'

'Bunny, wake up. Killer Crane has called a snap inspection in ten minutes.'

'You're kidding — come on, you're getting even with me for the mud pack yesterday.' Bunny opened her eyes and stared at Vicki Hansen in disbelief 'Not even Captain Crane would pull a surprise inspection on a warm Saturday afternoon with the Georgia sand fleas out for blood.' But the frenzy up and down the barracks marked her words as wishful thinking, and she tumbled out of bed and began to pull on her uniform, thankful she always kept her foot locker ready for inspection, a trick she'd learned as an officer candidate.

'What did I tell you?' Vicki said triumphantly. 'Looks like the Killer's struck again.'

Bunny snapped her sheets tight, then drew her blankets taut and laid out the overseas issue on her bunk: steel helmet, gas mask, bandolier, first-aid kit . . . She winced from the pain in both her upper arms and rubbed them briskly where they had been jabbed full of tetanus, smallpox and cholera vaccines.

Damn Lieutenant Colonel Harry Duquesne, she muttered to herself for the hundredth time. If she ever discovered he had deliberately put her on an overseas levy, she'd strangle him with her own two hands. She sighed loudly and shrugged.

It was too much of a coincidence that she'd been shipped out to Fort Oglethorpe for two months' overseas training in

319

February, the week after he left for the Southwest Pacific. Instinctively she realized he had probably engineered her transfer. He had his good points, more of them than she'd found in any other one man — he was good at his job, with an air of calmness, thoughtful in his way — but Harry was selfish, though not at all in the same way as Johnny P. Harry knew how to take good care of his prize possessions, and his women. Only one thing bothered her. Harry was still married, although he had assured her his marriage was over long before they'd met at Lowry Field. She'd be glad when his divorce was final. She would never do to another woman what Angela had done to her.

She smoothed the wrinkles from her shirt and adjusted the four-in-hand. She had never learned to tie the knot so it didn't tilt crazily within minutes. As she pushed the tie up firmly against the collar stays her mind returned to its familiar hunting ground — Johnny P. She wondered how long she would continue to define her life by what he had done to her. With Johnny she had felt alive every minute, and every day had the potential for novelty, but she had paid a terrible price. With Harry, if she decided to marry him as he'd begged her to do — after his divorce came through — she knew she'd lead a moderately dull life, but she'd be safe. Harry would see she was never exposed to the slightest danger. He wouldn't take her to the brink of anything — passion or hurt — which made him the perfect lover for the kind of life she wanted. Life with Harry looked like a fair trade for love with Johnny. She wanted never again to be the victim of her own need to love a man. Not loving too much was what she wanted, and what she had with Harry, although she *was* fond of him.

And then she saw Captain Crane enter the barracks and float daintily between the bunks. Preceded by choking waves of gardenia perfume, she poked into wall lockers, asking EWs about their training in her high-pitched Alabama-belle accent, for all the world as if Scarlett O'Hara were doing a poor imitation of Captain Bligh. She was called 'Killer' not because she was a tough CO, but for the same reason a fat man is called 'Tiny'. She was not a bad

320

officer, just an earnestly inept one, and because she didn't really know how to command she often did the right thing at the wrong time to prove she had her bars on straight.

'Fall out in front of the barracks!' the first sergeant yelled.

'Oh Lord, now what?' Bunny muttered.

Vicki fell in beside her. 'If she pulls my pass, I'll die. This is my last night to see Hans.'

'Vicki! Are you still meeting that POW on the q.t.? If you're caught . . .'

From out of the corner of her eye Bunny saw the captain sweeping down the barracks fire stairs, holding her skirt with one hand as if she were wearing a dozen silk petticoats. How had she *ever* got troop command?

''toon, ten-*shun!*'

Here it comes, Bunny thought. She didn't care for herself, since she had no plans to go anywhere. But poor Vicki was going to get restricted to barracks her last Saturday night in the States. Bunny knew that when she'd been CO the only reason she'd ever pulled a snap inspection was to shape-up a platoon that had grown sloppy. But with this CO, who could tell?

'Ladeez,' the captain yelled, straining her small voice to be heard to the last rank, 'yoah latrines are lovely. Sergeant, y'may dismiss the women.'

'Dismissed!'

Bunny and Vicki turned and headed for the barracks, running the last few steps, jostling each other to be first. Once inside, they collapsed against the wall, laughing helplessly.

Finally Bunny shook herself. 'Did you ever hear anything like that? Ladeez — ' she began a perfect imitation of the CO ' — yoah latrines are lovely. Ah've never seen such gleamin' beauties in all ma borned days.'

Tears were running from Vicki's eyes. 'Bunny, I can't — really I can't understand the WAC. How they could give her a company when you couldn't get your commission back?'

Wiping her eyes, Bunny shrugged. 'It's my own fault. I

took a discharge, and you know the regs against direct commissions for civilians. I could have gone through OCs again, but I thought I'd see what I was missing with you lowly garbage queens.'

'You don't have to pull KP now that you've made sergeant first class.'

'Listen, kiddo, once you've had KP as many times as I have, it leaves a permanent mark, if not a permanent odour.'

'I don't mind it so much, especially — '

'Especially when you can neck with a handsome Nazi in the storage room.'

'That's not fair. Hans was never a Nazi. He told me he hated it, that he was glad he was captured.'

Vicki had been in Bunny's second basic-training platoon at Fort Des Moines. She'd come a long way from the rookie who wondered if a kiss would make her pregnant, but she was still easily swept into a romance by a pair of soulful blue eyes, or, for that matter, brown, black or green.

'Just don't be foolish, Vic.'

Later that evening when Bunny returned from playing the latest Tommy Dorsey records in the dayroom, she found Vicki sobbing softly into her pillow. 'Come on, kid,' she said, sitting on the edge of the girl's bunk. 'What happened to your big evening?'

'You don't understand.'

'I understand more than you know. When your love is new and you have to leave him, it takes a while to stop thinking about what might have happened if — '

'No, Bunny, that's not it.'

'What is it, then?'

'Hans — he was different tonight when I said I was leaving. He . . . he . . . '

'He what?'

'Oh, Bunny, he said he hoped my ship would *sink*!' At this, Vicki began to cry anew, deeper sobs. 'You were right. He really *was* a Nazi.'

'He didn't mean it, Vic. He cares for you so much he probably just went a little crazy at the thought of losing you,' Bunny lied. She knew she was lying, not only for Vicki's sake but for her own. She had pulled a curtain on her memory and wanted to leave it in the dark. How could she reach through Vicki's childlike vulnerability and tell her that some men who couldn't own a woman wanted no one else to have her, could even want her dead?

Vicki sat up. 'Do you really think so?'

'You bet. Now try to think about the adventure we're heading into. Tomorrow when we get on the train to California, all that crawling around on our stomachs in the dirt, the tear-gas drills, the cargo-net climbs, even when you stepped on my face — it'll *all* make sense. Now get some sleep.'

It was out there, then; loving a man was out there, ready to pounce. She was wary as she undressed and climbed between the sheets. There was a trap she needed to avoid, must avoid, and that was the bittersweet attraction of love. Twice burned, she knew that the pain of betrayal wouldn't last forever, and like the lemming Page had said she was, she was still capable of fighting her way to the sea to drown in some pointless, hopeless, ridiculous love affair. For a moment there was a touch of suffocating panic until she remembered Harry, good ol' safe Harry.

The next day, Bunny and the Wacs at Oglethorpe boarded the train. On the fourth night they marched onto the troop ship *West Point* bound for Australia. The GIs on the dock serenaded them as they sailed from Oakland:

'The Wacs and Waves will win the war.
Parlez-vous?
So what the hell are we fighting for?
Hinky-dinky, *parlez-vous*?'

37

I don't want to walk without you, Baby,
Walk without my arm about you, Baby.
I thought the day I left you behind
I'd take a stroll and get you right off my mind,
but now I find —
That I don't want to walk without the sunshine,
Why'd you have to turn off all that sunshine?
Oh, Baby, please come back or you'll break my
heart for me,
'Cause I don't want to walk without you, No siree.
> —Frank Loesser and Jule Styne

For the next few days after Elisabeth's confrontation with Max, her belief was that Max would send for her; it could only be a matter of time. He could become engaged all he wanted, but he would never be able to get rid of his need for her. Her own physical desires created the logical runway from which she flew every frail fantasy of hope. She had frequent headaches, until she began to fear them and would look for a codeine-APC pill as soon as she felt the pressure start to build in her temples.

'You're taking too many of those things, Elisabeth,' Danny Barnes said from his desk opposite hers, and then asked, 'What's the problem — everything's okay, isn't it?'

'No problem. Everything's fine.' She was annoyed by his interruption, and even more by his proprietary manner.

'Stryker's not bothering you again, is he?'

'No!' she said too loudly, then lowered her voice when those around them stared. 'Don't ask me so many questions. My head is splitting.'

'I'm sorry.' Barnes glanced nervously behind him. 'Have dinner with me after work. I think we'd better talk.'

'Sure.' Why not? What did it matter — what did anything matter without Max?

They drove in one of the olive-drab 1941 Fords assigned